REX

Saskia Walker

REX

CHAPTER ONE

REX CARRUTHERS WATCHED his father's coffin being lowered into the ground and a solid weight lodged in his gut. He told himself he felt nothing. He'd fallen out with his father many years ago.

The vicar's words faded in and out of Rex's consciousness. The Vicar called him "An upstanding member of the community, much respected."

A selfish man too, Rex silently added.

Even now, Rex couldn't forgive.

When indicated, Rex lifted a handful of earth and threw it onto the coffin.

Family friends, staff from Burlington Manor, villagers and local farmers from the surrounding Oxfordshire countryside, followed his lead. Then they stepped forward to offer him solace he didn't crave. They shook his hand and welcomed him home.

Still Rex felt nothing.

These people saw him as the rightful heir to Burlington Manor, he realized. They had expectations. It was in their words and in their eyes. They expected him to take over the estate now his father was gone. Rex wanted none of it.

Then he saw Carmen standing amongst the crowd.

Carmen Shelby – so unobtainable, so elegant. She was the reason he'd walked away from Burlington Manor, away from his heritage. Away from his father.

Finally, he felt something.

Desire.

Carmen met his gaze. The startled look in her eyes accentuated her fragility and her unusual looks. Those dark chocolate eyes of hers were so expressive, and the way her hair was cut, tapered around her jaw before it fell loose to her shoulders, seemed to emphasize that.

Her lips parted.

Rex nodded her way, a silent acknowledgment of their connection.

She glanced away, breaking the contact.

Rex stared at her profile. Time had done nothing to diminish the hunger he felt for her. He glanced at her hand and saw no wedding band. He supposed he would have heard. Mutual friends did like to pass news on, whether it was welcome or not.

The more he studied her, the fiercer the need he felt. His father's death had brought him unwanted responsibilities. It had also brought his stepsister back into his life. The forbidden one.

The old craving he harbored seemed insignificant compared to what was stacking up now.

He had to have her.

The following Monday Carmen awaited her stepbrother's arrival with steely determination. Facing her—and beginning to look rather impatient on the other side of his desk—was Christopher Montague, the Carruthers family solicitor. He gave Carmen an encouraging smile. Nevertheless, he was drumming his fingers on his leather-covered desktop, clearly disapproving of Rex's late arrival for the reading of his father's will. They'd been due to begin half an hour earlier. "I'm terribly sorry about the delay, Carmen."

"Please don't apologize." She gave a quick smile. "My stepbrother always has his own agenda." *That's why I have to keep a clear head.*

Straightening the jacket of her suit, she sat back in her seat. Despite her best effort to remain business like, anticipation ticked in her veins. They hadn't seen each other for ages, not until the funeral the week before. Yet, it was like being thrust back in time, to when she'd stupidly fallen for him, desire swamping her. How was it Rex still affected her this way, after all this time?

Rex. The very sound of his name whispering around her mind made her hot.

She'd been fifteen years old when her mother had married Rex's father. Rex was older than Carmen by four years. He'd been away at university a lot of the time, which was just as well because she'd developed a painful crush on him. Thankfully she'd grown out of it. They'd been thrust together, told to act like brother and sister. An impossible task. Sexual tension swamped her whenever he was around, her stepbrother—the rebel, the gorgeous bad boy.

Then Rex clashed with his father over some matter or other. Rex left Burlington Manor, the stately home that had been in his family for hundreds of years. He'd walked away from his family responsibilities to pursue a start-up career in engine design for the racing car industry. She, on the other hand, had accepted the responsibilities life thrust upon her, taking command at her mother's company after her mother's death.

The door opened, snapping Carmen back to the moment. Rex entered the room. Chris Montague stood up to greet the new arrival.

Carmen took a deep breath and observed as he approached. The dark slash of his eyebrows and the angular bones of his face captured her attention. It was a rugged face, starkly handsome, with unforgettable blue eyes. The stubble on his jaw only made him more attractive. Rex had the kind of intense good looks that meant he could have any woman he wanted, as he so often did. While Carmen stood by, heart-broken.

He shook hands briefly with Chris.

Carmen noticed the fine cut of the clothes. Smart, business-like. Yet the fitted black suit only emphasized the fine male physique it clothed. He was toned, the shape of his shoulders and torso drawing her eye. The open-neck shirt beneath his suit was crisp and charcoal in color. His thick black hair was swept back from his forehead but fell forward as he moved. He pushed it away with one hand as he approached her.

"Carmen, you're more beautiful than ever." Ducking down, he pressed a kiss to her cheek.

The casual brush of his mouth on her skin unnerved her. "Rex, hello."

She crossed her leg at the knee while smoothing her skirt down. Rex stared at her blatantly as he took the seat next to hers, watching her legs as she rearranged her position. The look in his eyes was far too intimate and possessive to be respectable.

Oh, how that used to make her want him—back when she had no sense. Not anymore. She'd grown up since then. She knew what was good for her and the list did not include Rex Carruthers.

He seemed alert and focused, she noticed. The week before, when she'd stood opposite him across his father's grave, he'd been somber and deep in thought, as one might expect. He and his father never made up their differences. Did Rex regret it? He'd barely nodded at the mourners who spoke with him. Only at the end, when he looked her way, had his expression changed—marginally—his eyes hooded and dark with secret thoughts.

Rex avoided the social gathering at the Manor after the funeral, which meant they hadn't had a chance to talk. And now here they were, and he was the personification of suave, the self-assured urbane man. She couldn't let him distract her from her goal, so she pulled her attention away.

She looked at their mediator, who had returned to his seat. "Chris, I have another meeting to attend later today. Can we get on?" Asserting herself was a deliberate move. She had an important deal to discuss. "We're already running late."

Chris didn't have a chance to respond.

Rex reached out and took her hand in his. "Always in a hurry, Carmen. Let's get comfortable before we get down to business."

He flashed his eyes at her.

She arched her brows at him. He always did like to spar, but if he was going to play the bad boy at a time like this she'd find negotiations difficult. "Rex!"

She tried to sound chastising, but her voice came out sounding breathless.

He lifted his hands in apparent surrender. He didn't stop looking at her though. His appraisal was undisguised.

"Besides," she continued, unnerved, directing her comment to Chris. "I'm sure the contents of the will have very little to do with me—"

"I'm sure it has very little to do with me, either," Rex interrupted. "After all, I was disinherited years ago." He stared at her deliberately, making a point.

Carmen frowned. Rex had no siblings, so she'd assumed he would inherit the estate. Despite the rift, Charles Carruthers was deeply traditional at heart. She'd only come to the reading because she was ready to buy Rex out. Rex had never been interested in Burlington Manor, whereas she had a deep connection to the place. She'd been happy there and wanted to recapture those feelings. She looked back at the solicitor. "Chris?"

Chris pushed his glasses up onto the bridge of his nose. "Good. Well, as you're both aware Charles Carruthers and I were old friends. He moved all the family's legal work to me to help me get off the ground when I was starting my own practice here in London, back in the 1980s. There've been several alterations to his will over subsequent years, but I'm familiar with his intentions. There are several bequests for staff. I've arranged to see them later today because you might want the contents of the will to remain confidential for the time being." He paused. "Those that relate specifically to you both, until you decide what to do about it."

Puzzled, Carmen looked at Rex.

He shrugged.

She shook her head to indicate she hadn't a clue what it might be.

His stare lingered on her.

She noticed it too – they were able to communicate silently, as they had done so many years ago. It reminded her of sitting opposite him at the dinner table at Burlington Manor, and how he used to make her smile with the slightest expressive glance.

"Should you have any questions at all," Chris continued, "please just ask."

Carmen forced her attention back. "The staff will be concerned about the estate being sold," she stated, curious he'd opted to deal with the staff separately.

"I daresay they are." Chris gave her a genial smile.

She wanted to state her intention to buy the estate, to own it and keep the staff in their jobs, no matter what. Once they'd heard the contents of the will she could flag it up.

Chris lifted the papers on his desk. "This is the last will and testament of Charles Denton Carruthers."

"His last chance to make us dance to his tune," Rex murmured.

Carmen rolled her eyes.

Thankfully Chris didn't catch the comment and launched into his summary.

Carmen attempted to focus on Chris as he read, but she was constantly aware of Rex at her side. Rex: dark, volatile and unpredictable. He still demanded her attention without doing anything at all. She resisted as best she could.

When she took a quick glance his way she discovered he was staring blatantly at her. Her blood rushed in her ears. Chris's voice faded in and out and she had to struggle to focus on what was being said.

The first part of the document was devoted to Rex's inheritance of various stocks and shares, and a property in the Channel Islands. "To my son, Rex, I leave the marina apartment in Jersey and the mooring rights, in recognition of his attachment to the place during family holidays as a young boy."

Carmen noticed Rex's expression changed on hearing the personal information attached to the request.

Chris summarized some money allocations and provisions for long serving staff, several of them who had retired; the rest still held posts at the manor. "Briefly, the key factor here is the property known as the Lodge House, which is the current residence of Mr. and Mrs. Amery—the caretakers of Burlington Manor—should be granted to them with freehold ownership in recognition of the service they have provided over the years."

Carmen nodded. She was pleased.

Chris glanced up to make sure he had their full attention before he moved on. "Regarding my estate, monies and the ancestral home known as Burlington Manor, it is my wish Carmen Shelby should receive a fifty percent share, the other share going to my only son, Rex."

Carmen blinked. "Excuse me, did I hear right?"

Chris nodded. "Fifty percent ownership each," he clarified.

Carmen's heartbeat faltered. She expected it to go entirely to Rex and she would have to buy the entire property from him. Rex looked surprised by the arrangement, as well. Then he met her stare and his expression changed. His eyes lit.

"Although I have to point out the coffers aren't exactly spilling over," Chris added.

"No surprise there," Rex commented, "the old man was better at spending money than making it."

Chris nodded and continued. "The investment portfolio is reasonably strong, considering, but the property is the main thing we're looking at here – in itself worth several millions."

Carmen stared at Rex in confusion, then looked at Chris. "Are you sure about the share to me?"

He nodded and gestured at the papers, continuing to read. "This is in recognition of it being as much Carmen's home as it was Rex's. I also wish to celebrate the work my wife, Sylvia, did to retrieve the place from long-term neglect, making it an exceptional home for us all, a place I can truly hand on with pride."

Carmen's chest tightened. The references to her mother unbuckled her.

"Carmen?" Chris paused and looked at her with concern.

She'd covered her mouth with her hand. They probably thought she was about to burst out crying. "Please, go on. I'm just so surprised."

That was an understatement. Burlington Manor. Half of it was already hers. The fact her stepfather had considered her in his arrangements touched her deeply. When Chris looked at her she nodded his way.

What did Rex think? She thought he might be annoyed his father had made things rather complicated by sharing it between them, but when she glanced his way he smiled, his eyes narrowed as he watched her. She was sure he had no interest in the house and was ready to buy him out. She'd cashed in numerous investments and her bank had the funds ready for a fast transfer.

Chris was reading on. "In the unlikely event both Carmen Shelby and Rex Carruthers are deceased at the time of the reading of this will, I have named a third party who represents a charity I wish to benefit, Wilmington's Cancer Care."

"He thought of everything," Carmen commented.

"He did indeed," Chris agreed. He studied the papers, but didn't comment further.

"He had a lot of time on his own in the end," Rex commented wryly, "to think on it."

Carmen sighed. "Rex, do you have to?"

He shrugged.

More provocative than ever, Carmen decided.

Chris continued. "Should either Rex or Carmen decide to sell their share, I hope one of them will be able to keep the place going. It's been our family home for centuries." He paused and looked up, taking off his glasses for a moment. "Your father did not make this a condition of the will, however. It was a wish, not an instruction."

Rex spoke then. "I'm sure Carmen and I can come to a mutually satisfying arrangement."

It was time to make her move. "I'm ready to buy you out."

She meshed her fingers together as she stated her intention.

Rex stared down at her hands before he responded. "We can share the playground, can't we?"

Playground? That remark was typical of Rex Carruthers. Her skin prickled. "You've got no interest in the house. You haven't even been back there in years—"

"True," Rex interrupted, with a smile. "There was nothing to draw me back. Not until now…now you're going to be there. Things could get interesting."

Don't let him mess with your head, she told herself.

It was second nature to him, teasing her. Well, she wasn't a gauche teenager any more. She cleared her throat. Luckily she'd been over her proposal and his potential responses several times and the words were in her head. "You've got your business to oversee, why would you want to be in Burlington Manor now?"

He lifted his eyebrows, staring at her pointedly.

Damn him. Flirting with women was a game to him. As teenagers he liked to see her in a state, but then he'd go off with some other girl, leaving her squirming. *How was it he could still do this to her?* She was a grown woman and she'd quelled all her foolish desires for this man long ago.

He appeared to be amused by the set up. "We have to share. Would it be so hard?"

"Not at all," she retorted. "It's a big house. But we both know you don't really want it, this is just a game to you."

Rex gave a faux pained gesture, putting his fist to his chest above his heart. "It hurts you think so poorly of me."

Her cheeks flamed. "That's not what I meant and you know it."

She found herself silently begging for him to be reasonable and to move on, but he kept looking at her as if she was on the menu for dinner and he was considering how to cook and serve her up. Unable to stop herself, she glanced down at her clothing and adjusted the shirt so the line of the buttons was straight.

"I'm not willing to discuss terms right now," Rex said. "We can talk about it when we're at the manor together."

Carmen felt increasingly light-headed when forced to consider what it would be like being alone with him at Burlington Manor. One look at the nonchalant posture of his attractive masculine body had her pulse racing, a nagging ache at her core reminding her she was a woman and she had needs. Dear god in heaven, how was he able to do this to her? *I still want him.* She couldn't trust herself.

She crossed her leg higher on the thigh, attempting to quell the arousal there.

His gaze followed the movement, and his mouth gave a gentle twitch, as if he was restraining an idle remark. When their eyes met, electricity traversed the space between them. His handsome mouth sloped into an insinuating smile.

He wasn't prepared to follow the norms like everybody else. She tore her gaze away. Well, she wasn't going to sit there and let him make fun of her when she knew he had no intention of living in the house. He didn't want it, never had. She should have let her lawyer negotiate with his. Annoyed, she rose to her feet, glancing at her watch. "Chris, do you need me for any other part of this?"

Chris frowned. "I can email you details of the transfer procedures. If you have any questions, get in touch."

"Thank you." She walked out of the office as quickly as she could, out the door and down the steps, heading across the pavement to where her Mini was parked on the street.

Rex was hot on her tail. He was determined.

Opening her bag, she snatched her keys. He reached out and clasped her wrist, drawing her to a sharp halt as she reached the car door.

"Come now," he said, "we haven't even started negotiations."

She huffed a laugh. "Oh, so you're willing to negotiate, now I'm walking away?"

"I didn't want to air all my private thoughts in front of the family solicitor."

He traced his finger along her jaw, setting her nerves tingling. "I'm looking forward to us spending some quality time together, Carmen."

Tease. She shot him a warning glance. Her skin tingled, her senses responding wildly to his proximity. She threw him a querying glance.

"You want Burlington Manor," he continued. "I don't. We can come to a mutually satisfying arrangement." He ran his finger down the length of her neck.

Arousal surged through her. *Don't trust him.* "I have funds available for transfer. My lawyer will be in touch."

Rex ignored that. He lifted her hair free of her cheek. "I like your hair this way," he said, running it through his fingers as he admired it. "It used to be shorter."

The aroma of his cologne hit her. The familiar scent of him took her back. Inside a heartbeat she was seventeen and longed for him to hold her. Instead, he teased her relentlessly—making her horribly aware of her fragile confidence—and then he'd cast her aside and seduced one of her friends. That hurt. If he'd pursued her like this back then, instead of Amanda, it would have been a dream come true. Now it got her back up. He was a playboy, plain and simple He was asserting his power over her because he was a man who assumed he could toy with women for his own entertainment. "Stop playing games, Rex. Name your price."

A slow smile spread across his face, his eyes gleaming as he gazed at her, looking at her lips as if he was about to devour them. "We live together at the house for an agreed term."

It had to be a joke. She stared up at him and his intense blue eyes were so vivid they seemed to burn into her. "Oh for God's sake, just tell me how much you want for your share."

"I don't want money. I want you."

Her lips parted. She was stunned.

"No financial exchange. Just you—" he locked eyes with her "—in my bed, refusing me nothing."

Images flashed through her mind, images of them locked together in fierce passion. Fighting away the rising tide of longing, she shook her head. "You can't be serious."

"I am, entirely so." As if to emphasize his point, he moved one hand inside her jacket, where he cupped her breast and ran his thumb over her nipple.

Carmen couldn't stifle her gasp. His touch knew no bounds, no protocol. It was breathtaking. The only barrier between his skin and hers was her shirt and the sheer lace bra she wore beneath it. Her nipple knotted and tingled. Her emotions were in chaos, and her trust in her body and its responses was fast waning. "You think you can have any woman you want. Well, I'm not for sale, Rex Carruthers."

He shrugged. "I want you, and you want the house. This is the perfect opportunity for us both to get what we want."

What surprised her more—that he claimed he wanted her, or that he knew she wanted the house so much? She wasn't sure, but she despised him for putting her in this position, and even more, she despised herself for considering the idea. Her knees were weak under her. The hard surface of the car was the only thing holding her up.

"Come on, why deny the attraction now?" The lust in his eyes was tempered by humor. "I touched you like this before, my darling little stepling, and you liked it. You liked it a lot."

Stepling. He used to call her that when they got intimate, and it did bad things to her, the forbidden nature of her desire for him making her even hornier.

Shame flooded her. Her eyelids fluttered down, but her attempt to deny the images assailing her was futile. They were scored on her memory, relived many times. He'd flirted with her and out of the blue she found herself in his arms and they were kissing. Their lust unleashed was dangerous, moving like wild fire. In hungry, eager embraces they'd almost gone all the way. Thankfully a noise from elsewhere in the house had broken them up.

"I was young and easily led," she responded, squaring up to him as best she could, "I won't be played with again—and certainly not for your share of the house. The suggestion is outrageous."

His hand on her body felt good, though, and she hadn't pushed him away, hadn't been able to. That old sense of longing was a simmering fire she thought she'd quashed long ago. She forced it back, refusing to let him take charge of her.

"Come to the house this weekend, we'll take it from there."

Perhaps it would kill off all those idiotic teenage fantasies she'd had once and for all. *Or joining him there could be the biggest mistake of my life.* "I'll come to discuss the deal, but you can't force me to sleep with you!"

"I won't force you, I won't have to." The knowing look he gave her right then was infuriating. It was also a massive turn-on. Undeniably masterful, undeniably masculine and controlled, he made her blood pump hard, her pulse wildly erratic.

"Make arrangements to be away from London for the next four weekends. Our time together will begin on Friday evening." He glanced at his watch, stepped away.

"I'll come to the house to negotiate a purchase, that's all." How was it he could push her buttons so easily? He was so self-assured, so knowing, while she clung to the side of the car, filled with torrid imaginings and confused thoughts and needs.

His eyes twinkled with dark humor. "Consider this, my darling stepling, if you don't agree to my offer we'll have to share the house…forever."

Forever?

With that final comment, he inclined his head and strolled back up the steps into Montague's office, leaving her standing there with one hand gripping the car to hold her up—her clothes awry, her body awash with heat, her heart thundering in her chest.

CHAPTER TWO

The train slowed down as it approached Beldover station. Carmen gazed at the wooded chalk hills of the Chiltern hills in the September sunlight. The beauty of the landscape reminded her why she wanted to be here, even while she contemplated the high level of stupidity she was engaging in, entertaining Rex's request to turn up at the time and place he'd suggested.

She supposed she shouldn't have been surprised when he came out with such an immoral suggestion. He probably did it all the time, and some women might love it. What possessed him to think he could treat her that way? She was a mature businesswoman now. And he'd taken it for granted he'd won. Rex was a consummate seducer, an eternal game player and the quintessential bad boy. He was notorious for being a party animal during the Formula One racing circuit social calendar. He also left a string of broken hearts behind him.

Carmen had scarcely stepped off the train onto the platform when Andy Redmond was there by her side, lifting the bag from her hand. Andy ran the local taxi company and she'd organized for him to collect her.

As the taxi turned off the main road from the village and onto the estate, the car passed the old gate house. It was a sizable cottage, a home for Burlington Manor's housekeeper and her husband, the groundsman. The garden was, as ever, beautifully kept and the roses around the doorway were in full bloom. When the car proceeded up the driveway toward Burlington Manor, Carmen's chest tightened with emotion.

"It's good to be taking a fare up this road again," Andy shouted back to her as he drove. "It's been far too quiet up here since you left, Miss Shelby."

"I'm sure it has."

"I used to have a busy schedule ferrying people back and forth when your mother was running her house parties. Can I ask if you'll be staying on?" Andy looked at her in the rearview mirror.

Carmen knew he was asking on behalf of the whole village, because each person who lived in the nearby hamlet of Beldover had a vested interest one way or the other. "I can't say for sure, but I hope I'll be involved in the future of Burlington."

The private road opened out, and there it was.

Set at the end of a sweeping driveway in an elevated position, the placement of the building took advantage of the camber of the countryside, in order to provide stunning views from all the windows in the house. It was an imposing Georgian country home, a crown on the countryside.

"It's a magical house," Sylvia Shelby had told Carmen when she'd first taken her to see the place. Carmen had been fifteen and her mother had recently announced her engagement to Charles Carruthers. Carmen had warmed to him immediately. To her he was a charming, elegant man, and she craved a father figure since her own has lost his battle with cancer when she was four years old. As an only child, the idea of having a big brother in her life was immensely appealing, too, although Rex had turned out to be something very different indeed.

"The history of a house like Burlington Manor has to be preserved," her mother had told her. Sylvia Shelby, an interior designer, had great respect for property steeped in history the way Burlington Manor was. "The current owner of a stately home is like a custodian for the national heritage."

"Like the knight who looks after the Holy Grail until the next keeper arrives?"

Sylvia had laughed at Carmen's correlation. "Will you help me to help Charles be the best custodian he can?"

Her mother had a very romantic view of the British country estate. Carmen shared the view. In days of old, the country estate owner rented out patches of land to tenants and the owners were wealthy as a result. In modern times British estates often open to the public to bring income for maintenance, or they let out part of the property to catering events, weddings and suchlike. The upkeep of an ancient estate in the twenty-first century was no small task.

The driveway passed alongside a large lawned area where Rex used to have impromptu cricket matches with his friends, and Carmen watched. Beyond the house the gardens led on to the riverside, where a man-made lake made a perfect summer hangout. It was a beautiful estate and she felt as if she'd been fed soul food just seeing the place. She looked fondly at the symmetry of the large gray stones, the orderly windows and stone balustrades.

The taxi driver was at the rear of the car, lifting out her weekend bag. The door of the house opened and Mrs. Amery, the housekeeper, appeared there, with a bright smile and a wave.

Carmen turned away and closed the taxi door behind her.

REX

She looked along the forecourt and saw a silver Maserati Gran Turismo parked up at the far end. Rex's, it had to be. Which meant he'd arrived first. Why did he have the upper hand in this situation? Because he was from the family line, he was the natural heir, that's why. The important thing was Rex didn't really want this house. It was all a game for him, a bit of fun for a bored playboy. She was the one who would love the house, just the way her mother had.

"Welcome," Mrs. Amery said, and she looked genuinely moved to greet Carmen. The housekeeper was dressed impeccably in a plain jacket and matching skirt with a round-neck top beneath. Her hair, silvered now and no longer the ash blond it once was, was neatly pinned at the back of her head. Mrs. Amery wasn't the most approachable woman, but Carmen could tell it meant a lot to the staff to welcome them both back to the manor. Rex especially, she had no doubt.

"It's good to be here. Are you well, Mrs. Amery?"

"I am."

"Charles' death has brought a lot of uncertainty for you. Hopefully it'll be at an end soon." Carmen gave her a reassuring smile.

Andy had taken her weekend case into the reception hall, and returned to her side. Carmen opened her purse.

Andy shook his head. "That's not necessary. Mr. Rex has set up an account."

Carmen frowned. So, Rex had installed himself and he'd already made arrangements. She folded several notes into his hand. "Thank you, Andy. I'll be in touch about my return journey. I need to be back in London on Sunday evening."

She walked alongside Mrs. Amery, up the wide stone steps to the front door, an oversize paneled affair with a lion's head knocker. The interior reception hall was one of her favorite places, the sweeping crescent-shaped staircase as impressive as it was welcoming.

Mrs. Amery collected her bag and led the way upstairs. "You'll find your room just as you left it."

It felt like coming home, mounting those stairs. The landing opened out, a huge, elegant space with doorways all around. The family bedrooms were located at this central point. Further rooms were located along the corridors in either direction, in the wings. They'd been closed up for a long time.

Carmen followed the housekeeper into her old room. The sight of it was so familiar she felt as if she were imagining it. "Nothing has changed."

"It was what Mr. Charles wanted. Exactly as your mother had left the place. We could come in and clean, but we were told not to move furniture around or change anything."

"It's like going back in time."

"I expect it is."

The windows overlooked the gardens and lake at the back of the building. The far trees were a little taller. Nothing else had changed.

Carmen's mother had redesigned the room in Bedouin style for Carmen's sixteenth birthday, shortly after they'd moved in. Every sensory detail held a memory, from the dark polished parquet floor underfoot to the scatter rugs in shades of red. The furniture was ebony wood with tiny inlaid stone designs to offset each corner. The comforter on the bed was velvet in harem colors, and the carved ebony struts of the bed frame gave the head and footboards a Moorish look. Sheer red drapes on niches in the wall concealed lamps. When the main lights were off, the room became both mysterious and romantic.

Mrs. Amery watched Carmen taking the view in. "I remembered it was your favorite coverlet so I retrieved it from storage and had it dry cleaned yesterday. I wanted you to feel completely at home."

Carmen rested her hand on the housekeeper's shoulder. "I appreciate that. The room looks lovely."

Mrs. Amery nodded. "Mr. Rex has requested a specific menu and he's asked for dinner service as soon as you're ready." She glanced at her watch. "I could arrange it any time after seven, if it suits you?"

Carmen glanced at her watch. "Seven would be ideal. I'll take a walk down to the lakeside then grab a shower." Carmen sensed the housekeeper's curiosity about the ongoing arrangements for the manor. Had Rex filled her in on the ownership issue? "This situation must be difficult for you. Rest assured you won't lose your job. I won't allow him to sell to a stranger. It's my intention to buy Rex out."

"I appreciate your reassurance, Miss Carmen." Mrs. Amery looked skeptical.

"But?"

"Well, Mr. Rex has been here for the past two days, organizing things for your arrival, and he is settling in nicely. I'd go so far as to suggest he seems glad to be at home."

Mrs. Amery always did have a soft spot for Rex—but then who didn't, the man was charm personified, and he knew it—and the housekeeper was obviously hoping he would change his mind and the Carruthers family would continue to be the custodians of Burlington Manor for another generation.

Carmen offered her a sympathetic smile. "If that's the case, he would've returned before now. I know you'd love to see Rex take responsibility for the place, but I'm afraid it won't last. I will, though."

Mrs. Amery nodded while assessing Carmen thoughtfully.

"Does that help?" Carmen added.

"Perhaps it was his father he fell out with, not the house."

That was something Carmen hadn't considered. If Rex secretly did want the house, then he was toying with her. This could be an even bigger battle than she thought.

"If there's one thing I've learned in all my years in service," Mrs. Amery continued, "it's father and son relationships are difficult enough, without the additional responsibility of a large family estate." She plumped the pillows and cushions on the bed as she spoke. "Rex made a lot of effort after his parents divorced, but in the end he had to forge his own path." She turned back and smiled. "He has other responsibilities now. I'll try to keep an open mind."

Carmen nodded. "As soon as we reach an agreement, you and the other staff will be the first to know."

"Aside from Mr. Amery and myself, we're down to four staff now, three of them part-time."

"How on earth do you manage?"

"They're good people, and Mr. Charles had their loyalty." She nodded at the window wistfully. "The grounds were always the priority. He always cared what people thought of the place, even if he didn't have the funds to do as much as he'd hoped."

Rex could change that. He was exceptionally wealthy in his own right. Once he'd broken with his father he'd used his Oxford University degree to set up a business of his own, a business with high stakes and big payoffs. He raked in investments and the share level rocketed. With an elite team producing designs and parts for racing cars, Rex had paved his own exceptional path. His company was thriving and it gave him access to an enviable lifestyle associated with the racing set. Carmen was wealthy too, but her business wasn't quite so high flying. She had a business degree and could work anywhere, but the company she knew best was the one she'd inherited from her mother. *Objet d'Art* sold interior furnishings—classy, arty, but ultimately functional objects—for the everyday home.

Mrs. Amery tested the bell pull. "I'll leave you to settle in, but do call if there's anything you need."

When Mrs. Amery left her alone she circuited the room. Something had been left on the winged armchair standing in the square bay window. Curious, she stepped closer. It was a box. She lifted the lid. Inside, a sheer black garment was folded in tissue paper. At first glance, it looked beautifully designed. Acting on instinct, she lifted it.

"I believe you'll find it's the right size."

Carmen dropped the sliver of fabric back into its box. Turning on her heel, she stared across the room at Rex. His voice was a trigger on her libido.

He stood in the open doorway, one shoulder resting up against the frame as he watched her. Clad in dark clothing, his pose was casual as he scrutinized her. Rex Carruthers, looking like lord of the manor. His very posture oozed confidence, and ownership.

"You can't be serious." She gave a dismissive laugh. "I don't need you to choose my clothes for me." She shrugged out of her jacket and threw it across the chair, obscuring the offending item completely. Self-awareness flooded her.

"Of course you don't, but I rather enjoyed the task, and this arrangement is about getting what we both want, isn't it?" His voice, resonant and suggestive, drew a physical response inside her.

"Grow up, Rex." She tried to appear nonchalant. His presence in her room, where she'd had so many foolish fantasies about him when she was a young woman, didn't make that easy. Nor did the way he looked. Like a prowling big cat. Worn black jeans outlined the angles and planes of his hips and thighs. A charcoal, long-sleeved T-shirt was snug across his shoulders and chest but fell loosely below, emphasizing his fit physique. "You've already made ridiculous demands on how this will proceed and I gave you my terms. We discuss it this weekend, as adults. I'm a grown woman now, not some dizzy teenager you can push around and play games with."

"I liked that dizzy teenager." He strolled closer to her.

It wasn't what she expected him to say.

His gaze covered her, blatant curiosity in his expression. "And I'm not pushing you around. I admit I did tease you back then, but you loved it."

Forthrightness wasn't a characteristic she remembered in Rex. In fact, he'd often been a mystery to her, oscillating from a chilled, confident young man to a secretive, sullen stranger who stormed out of the house, or arrived back with war wounds from fights he'd got into. It made Rex's father angry in a way they never witnessed at other times.

How did he know she loved his teasing, though? And why did he remember so much? Bristling at the intimacy—at the direct references to the pull between them as teens—Carmen shook her head. "Dictating what I wear isn't pushing me around?"

Rex shrugged. "It's meant as a gift, that's all."

Carmen met his stare as levelly as she could. His expression made her feel as if she was letting him down, a response that baffled her. *I shouldn't care if he's disappointed in me.* How the hell did he do it?

"We came here to thrash out an agreement, didn't we?" Just the way he said it was suggestive.

She felt suddenly light headed, her body strangely wired by the reference to thrashing. "I agreed to come here and discuss it as adults."

"You knew I had certain demands." He lifted his eyebrows slightly. It was an almost imperceptible movement, but it inferred so much. He oozed self-control. He was determined.

"I would prefer a monetary exchange. I stated my case already."

"We'll see." Breaking eye contact, he turned and strolled away.

She watched his broad shoulders as he headed to the door. He was devilishly handsome, even more so than he'd been as a younger man. The intervening years had given him a weathered, sharp look that suited him well. And his physique was breathtaking. The desire to see him naked thrust itself upon her out of nowhere, uninvited and unwelcome, yet fatally arousing.

He turned back at the doorway. "Wear the dress for me, Carmen. Call it a gesture of goodwill."

Before she had a chance to respond he left her, but the instruction held her attention as surely as if he had commanded her.

"Damn you, Rex." She paced to the bedside table and unlatched her watch, flinging it down, wishing she could unburden herself of this age-old desire for him as easily.

She was here as a businesswoman in order to negotiate a monetary exchange for property. She willed herself to focus. It seemed futile, though, what with Rex stalking about as if he owned the place outright—and her included. Then there was the fact she was here in the wildly romantic room where she used to conjure images of him to satisfy her teenage lust.

Returning to the bedside, she plonked herself down on it and gave a resigned sigh. Everything was the same. She turned to look at the wall behind the headboard. Even though she'd dismissed him from her dreams, all through the intervening years she'd been plagued by an image, a remembrance. It was her hand against the wall—her hand, reaching for Rex.

Their bedrooms were only inches apart. Strung out by his presence—so close, so solid, yet so unobtainable—she used to kneel on her bed, closing on the wall, imagining it was him she was touching as she laid her fingers on the surface.

It was more than a wall. It represented an unremitting barrier between her and the stepbrother who filled her thoughts. Yet the surface of the wall received her touches and her kisses, and it witnessed her lying back on her bed with her legs open, touching herself while she thought of him on the other side of the barrier. *Watch me,* her brazen teen self had demanded as she strummed herself to orgasm. *Watch me and want me.*

Carmen didn't want to think that way now. But she still wanted him all the same. "Stupid woman," she whispered to herself.

She glared at the wall, thought of the man whose room was on the other side of it and vowed not to let herself fall under his spell. He was a master of seduction, he could have any woman he wanted. She didn't want to be part of Rex Carruthers's vast casualty list. A trail of broken hearts lay in his wake. She was not going to be one of them.

CHAPTER THREE

Rex looked casual and dishy and seemingly perfectly relaxed as he lounged back in his chair at the head of the table— the captain's seat, the place where his father had always sat. It hadn't taken him long to assume the position. King-like, he surveyed her as she entered the room. His eyes lit, and he nodded approvingly when he saw she'd followed his suggestion and worn the dress.

Self-conscious, Carmen's fingers went to the elegant ruff, a small stand-up collar at the back of her neck. The dress was a beautiful design, a clingy halter neck cinched at the waist. The skirt was scalloped above the knees at the front, and slightly below at the back. It fitted perfectly.

Rex stood. She noticed his smart open-neck black shirt and black trousers as he approached. He pulled out her chair for her, his moves subtly charming. "Beautiful. The dress becomes you."

All of this conspired to make her feel churlish about her initial resistance to the offering.

"Miss Carmen." Mrs. Amery nodded. "Leanne is going to bring dinner in. Her duties are in housekeeping, but she's very eager to meet you."

"That's lovely, thank you." Carmen moved slowly toward the offered seat. Even as she tried to speak normally to the housekeeper, she was aware of Rex's presence and the persuasive touch of his hand on her forearm as she sat down.

When she took the seat, he strode over to an ice bucket set on the side table and lifted up the bottle of champagne chilling there. He strolled about with ease, as if he'd never been away.

"Is that all right with you, Mr. Rex?"

"Mr. Rex?" Rex repeated, with a soft laugh. "Call me Rex, please. I'm not my father and I don't expect the same level of formality he did."

Mrs. Amery looked at him fondly. "I was trained into service when I was sixteen years old. It would be very hard to change now."

"Give it a go, just for me."

Why was he even bothering? Carmen wondered. He wouldn't be here long.

22

"I'll try." Smiling, the housekeeper left the room and returned moments later with a woman in her late teens.

Once she'd put the tray onto the sideboard, Mrs. Amery introduced her colleague.

"Leanne Whitworth," Carmen repeated. "Your dad is the postmaster in Beldover?"

Leanne nodded.

"I remember you helping him out behind the counter when I used to live here. You must have been about twelve at the time?"

"That's right, miss. I've worked here at the manor since I left school."

"How lovely it is to see you again." Carmen was genuinely pleased and studied the girl while she and Mrs. Amery arranged the serving plates on the table.

"Say hello to your dad for me," Carmen added as she finished up.

Leanne beamed. "I will."

As they were about to leave the room, Rex spoke. "Mrs. Amery, you can finish up for the night now."

"Thank you. I'll see you both in the morning. Cook is semi-retired now and only comes when needed, but she'll be here for you tomorrow, bright and early."

When the door closed behind them, Carmen realized the implication. Shortly, they would be totally alone in the house together.

"You've got a better memory than me," Rex commented after the two women had gone.

"I was here more often." When she glanced up at him, his presence filled her consciousness.

"True." He lifted the champagne bottle out of the ice bucket. Once he'd removed the cage, he held the cork and twisted the bottle slowly. His hands were strong, somehow even more solid than she remembered. The intervening years had given just enough muscular bulk to his tall lean frame. The black shirt he wore was open at the neck, and the bare skin of his chest at this collarbone drew her attention. There was no doubt about it, Rex Carruthers had matured well. Was it wrong to want him so? Would it be so awful to give in to his demands? Pride demanded she stay resolute, but desire was swamping her.

He popped the cork and, with consummate grace, filled two flutes. When he returned to her side and offered her a glass, he was close enough that she could smell his cologne.

"Thank you." She sipped from it quickly.

He didn't move away. Instead, he held out his glass to hers. "Here's to the weekend, the first of several we're going to share here at the old homestead."

The look in his eyes was so suggestive she wondered how she could even begin to think of this as a business negotiation. She was right back there, back at the point where he used to come home from university and she was desperate to see him—wildly aroused when he flirted with her, and bitterly disappointed when he walked away.

Carmen gripped her glass tightly. Reluctantly she moved it just enough to clink against his.

When he swallowed, she watched the strong column of his neck. The very look of him stimulated her. That unwelcome reaction made her doubt she could play house for even an hour, let alone several weekends.

Reeling her thoughts in, she attempted to switch into business mode. "It feels strange to be in the old place again."

"It does." He set about serving food for her, which surprised her. "A bit too much like coming home for my liking."

He set a heaped plate in front of her. "I requested beef bourguignon. I seem to recall it was one of your favorites, and Cook confirmed that it was."

Startled, she nodded. She noticed he called Mrs. Summerfield "Cook" the way his dad had.

"She's looking forward to seeing you again, much like the rest of us."

If he continued to be this charming it was going to be hard to maintain a reserved facade. When she looked down at the food, she wondered how she could manage any of it, rattled as she was by his presence and his intentions. Tension racked her, and that wasn't all. Every time he came close to her or even looked at her, she burned up with self-awareness. It was the possessive look in his eyes while she wore the dress he had chosen for her. It hadn't even occurred to her he would look at her as if he owned her, just because she had granted his request and worn the gift. It had been a stupid mistake on her behalf, capitulating.

He served himself, then returned to the captain's seat at the head of the table, opposite her. They were some eight feet apart and yet he managed to make her feel his presence without much effort at all. It stimulated her in every way. Devastatingly attractive and predatory, it was as if he was stalking his next sexual prey. She couldn't help being aware of it and responding to him. She was a woman, after all. Would he laugh if he knew how inexperienced she was with men? Probably.

"Why didn't you come back to the house after your father's funeral?" She was very curious about that.

"People were treating me like the prodigal son returned. I wasn't sure I wanted that." He picked up his fork and began to eat.

"The staff and the villagers are bound to feel that way about you, whether you stay or not."

The frown he wore made her wonder. Did he feel as if he would be letting them down, not keeping the manor in the family?

The beef was succulent and she managed to eat a little, even though the tension she felt made it difficult. The champagne helped, so she concentrated on that.

"It's almost three years since I moved out," she told him. "I left to be with my aunt shortly after Mum's funeral. I came back once a year, on the anniversary of her accident. Your dad met me at the station and we walked up to the graveyard together, catching up on each other's news as we went."

Rex rested back in his chair and listened.

"He'd always take me for lunch in the pub in the village afterward and then put me back on the train. I didn't see the house again until the day of his funeral." She glanced around. "Very little has changed, though."

"Some things don't seem to have changed at all since I was last here." He gazed at her. Was he talking about the fascination they used to have for each other all those years ago?

"I used to love this place," he continued. "When I was a kid, it was great running around the corridors and the grounds. It was home then, but it didn't last. When I was about eight years old, my father told me about the dark side of mortmain, the dreaded responsibility of inheriting an old estate, the curse of the aristocracy. He predicted I'd have it as a young man, and he was right. He told me he'd experienced it and he'd grown out of it."

Carmen froze. Had he grown out of that sense of mortmain now, was he ready to take it on? She concentrated on the food for a moment, cautiously weighing her words. "It's interesting he warned you about it. I suppose he had to. An estate like this is capital intensive and Burlington Manor doesn't generate a whole lot of cash. He was obviously trying to prepare you for what it entails."

"Absolutely," Rex replied, "the manor is a hungry beast, a cash sink."

He pushed his plate aside and rose to his feet. He lifted the cover from the dessert platters and carried the dishes over to her. "Strawberries and cream. Still good?"

It surprised her that he remembered her preferences.

She nodded.

He set the platters down, picked up a plump strawberry from the stack, dipped it into the dish of stiffly peaked cream and brought it to her mouth. He lifted his eyebrows expectantly.

Carmen inhaled sharply. It was too much. She snatched the fruit from his fingers. "Get to the point. You've dragged me up here on a ridiculous scheme because you're bored. Name your price and let's get on with our lives."

"Bored?" He laughed. It was so long since she'd heard the sound, and yet it was so familiar. "No, I'm not bored. Far too busy to be bored, but I've made time for this."

"Why are you doing this, Rex? You don't want the house. You never did."

He returned to his seat. "Perhaps I need to be sure."

So he did want it. Her heart sank. She wasn't about to give up, though. "You've brought me here under false pretences."

"Have I?" The way he smiled, so knowingly, was unbearable.

"You said you were willing to do a deal, to pass ownership. I mean to buy you out." Her face heated when she realized that she'd inadvertently referred to the ludicrous offer he'd made.

There was such deliberation flickering in those eyes of his. "I did mention a deal."

"And I told you I came here to discuss a monetary exchange." She shot the response back quickly, eager to clarify.

"I'm not interested in the monetary exchange. You knew that, and yet you still came." He lounged back in his chair, and ran his fingers along the edge of the table while he observed her.

"I own fifty percent of this property. That's why I came." Her pulse was racing, desire and confusion clouding her reactions.

"And you want to own one hundred percent."

"Exactly."

"My offer remains the same. Four weekends in my bed, during which time I can have you—sexually, any way I choose. That's my deal. Take it or leave it."

The blatant statement shocked her to the core, but it was undeniably arousing. Desire flared at his suggestion, intense and palpable.

Rex cocked his head. "If I'm not mistaken, the idea interests you."

"No, it doesn't."

"I'll give you the property outright at the end of the time."

Carmen fumed silently as she considered her reply. Even while she searched for ways to emphatically deny him, her mind and body launched a wave of erotic scenarios on her, sending her libido wild. Stray, errant questions forced their way into her consciousness. Why not? It was just sex. *Haven't you always wanted him?* No, it would be fatal. She couldn't afford the heartache. "I insist you consider a more rational exchange. I'm not giving in to such an outrageous whim."

"No?" He inclined his head at her. "You already appear to be giving in to my whims...as you call them...by degrees." He nodded at the dress she was wearing.

Carmen bristled, regretting the so-called gesture of goodwill he'd requested.

"It's only a matter of time," he continued. "We both know that. It's always been a matter of time before you and I ended up in bed together."

Carmen gave a dismissive laugh. "Don't flatter yourself. I'm not some bimbo you can toy with and then cast aside."

"On that point we're agreed. You're definitely no bimbo. Alas, that makes you all the more attractive to me."

His dangerous charm had not faded one iota. Instead, his devious talent had magnified and he wielded it with ease and cunning. A master of seduction, he thought he could have any woman he wanted.

"Tell me," he added, "if you don't want to sleep with me, why did you come here?"

Try as she might, Carmen couldn't summon a response—because she wanted him, wanted him so badly she felt as if she'd lost her mind. How could it be even worse than before? Her pride was in danger, but even though she felt it slipping away she couldn't muster the strength to hold on to it.

The sight of him made her weak with lust.

It hadn't gone away, and now it was even worse.

It was completely unmanageable.

CHAPTER FOUR

The brittle tension Carmen gave off failed to dim her beauty. Instead, it drew Rex to her. It made him want her even more. Never had he felt so eager and willing to be here at the house. This situation with the ownership of the estate was, quite simply, the perfect opportunity to pursue her.

She wanted it, too, much as she denied it. She was here, for a start. She could have negotiated through a solicitor, but she'd come, knowing what he wanted. They both knew why. Something had been triggered between them years ago and it had to be burned out in the only way possible—by thrashing it out between the sheets.

The dress she wore looked like a bespoke wrapping on the most desirable of possessions, and he fully intended to be the one to unwrap her. It hadn't occurred to him that she wouldn't be able to wear a bra with it. The dress was backless, though, and he could see her nipples outlined by the clingy, silky material. Rex congratulated himself on a good buy.

He'd bought the dress on impulse, because he'd seen it in a shop front in Milan's design quarter months before and it had instantly made him think of her. Carmen, the forbidden one, his elegant little flyaway bird. He'd kept the dress all this time, not even knowing whether he'd ever have the opportunity to give her the gift, because it felt like a connection with her, the connection that had been absent from his life for so long.

Carmen was the one who'd got away. Not anymore. Circumstances had got in the way, but now the little bird had fluttered back to him, and he was determined to see her relinquish that fiercely held mask of independence she wore and admit the desire that existed between them for so long.

He reached for another strawberry, his eyes on her lips as he feasted on the fruit.

"This is a ludicrous situation." She stood up, throwing the napkin she'd had clutched in her hand down onto the table. As she turned and headed for the door, he rose to his feet, easily halting her in her tracks as she broke for the door.

A warning flashed in her eyes. She trembled visibly.

"Easy," he urged, and drew her in against him.

For a moment she kept her eyes lowered, as if she couldn't bear to look at him, but he could see the pulse at the base of her throat was beating wildly.

Her eyelids flashed up, and she stared at him boldly. "Rex, please don't."

"Why not?"

She shook her head. She didn't try to break free, though, and it felt good to have his hands on her. Her dark eyes were luminescent. So enticing. When her lips parted, he bent his head to kiss her.

At first she stiffened. The resistance was momentary. He felt her soften in his embrace, her lips parting beneath his.

That barrier breached, Rex's hunger for her flared. Too long he'd waited for this, wanting her, and now he had her. He locked one hand on her waist. With the other he cupped the back of her head as he kissed her deeply.

Carmen's hands went to his chest, but they fisted there. Even while she opened her mouth to take his tongue, she pressed hard against him with those fists and moaned her resistance into his mouth.

Her hair was soft and silky in his fingers, while the curve of her waist made his hands ache to rove over her, to outline her every curve. He wanted to explore, touch and taste every part of her.

As the kiss deepened, her body trembled—which only made his grip on her tighten. He wanted to keep his little bird, win her trust and make her sing out with pleasure. First she was warm and supple in relinquishment, and then she was all fire and brimstone in his arms, clutching at his shirt with eager hands and arching her body to his.

He moaned his pleasure aloud.

She froze and drew back, breaking the kiss.

Desire pounded at the base of his spine, his cock semi-hard as his body readied to get closer still.

"I can't. I can't sell myself, least of all to you." She turned her face away.

He shifted, lowering his head to kiss the soft skin exposed beneath her ear when her hair fell back. As his lips made contact with the warm surface, she moaned and shifted in his arms.

"We both want to do this. We wanted it back then, we want it now. That situation's not going to end until we have each other."

She shook her head but he could see the truth in her eyes, the repressed emotion and the obsessive desire that mirrored his own. Carmen had always had the most expressive eyes. It was one of the many things that drew him to her. He felt as if a lifetime of experiences and sensations were offered to him, just by looking into those eyes of hers. His most abiding desire was to be doing that very thing while he brought her to orgasm. Repeatedly.

He continued to soothe her with his hands. "I can't think of a single reason not to."

"I can. Bloody hell, Rex. I have my pride." She tugged free of his grip and stared at him wildly.

The desire he'd harbored for this woman belted through him with a fury in the face of her denial. He had to have her. He ached for the sweetness she possessed. Reckoning with himself, he tried to keep his cool, he didn't want to frighten her. She would relinquish, he knew she would. She was as programmed for this as he was, but the bitter sweetness of her resistance threatened to turn him into a Neanderthal. "What about that time in the conservatory? You wanted me then, didn't you?"

She eyed him disbelievingly.

Tension ratcheted between them.

A red flash flared across her cheekbones. She shook her head, denying him. "We were stoned. You brought that stuff from university and I'd never had anything like it."

He shrugged. "True enough. It got rid of a few inhibitions for sure, but what was left behind, hmm? The honest to God truth of what we were to each other, what we still are."

Her eyes squeezed shut. "No!"

"No? You weren't thinking 'no' when you were on your back and pulling me over you."

She turned her face away and wrapped her arms around herself.

Was it distress, or embarrassment? He had to know. "No, there's no escape from that day, is there?" Obviously she couldn't deny it, so he said it aloud. "Let's see if I can recall...ah, yes. 'I want you, Rex,' that's what you said."

"That was then," she shot back. "I was a stupid teenager with a crush on you." She glared at him as if she hated him for pulling that moment apart. "I've come to my senses since then."

If she'd come to her senses, then what was this about—the trembling, the barely held sexual desire he saw in her? Rex resisted the urge to argue that point some more and got serious instead. "Oh, come now, Carmen, can you honestly say it's gone away?"

He closed on her, cupped her jaw, forcing her to look him in the eye.

She did so, stubbornly, but she didn't say a word.

His hand slid down her throat and, when it did, her eyelids lowered and her head tipped back.

That action—so simple, so telling—triggered something inside him.

With his free hand he captured both her wrists together and locked her hands to his chest. She whimpered and looked at him from under heavy lids.

"You can't deny it, can you?" He laughed softly, his libido sensing victory. "And you like this, being mastered, a touch of kink?" He tightened his grip on her wrists, lifting them easily so that her arms were clearly in his grasp. "That makes it even more tempting for you, doesn't it?"

Her eyes rolled and a low moan emitted from deep in her throat. It sounded earthy, primal, and Rex mirrored those reactions. Gone was the ladylike front, her cool exterior.

"Not tempting," she retorted in a low warning tone, "easier."

He cocked his head, curious.

She flashed her eyes at him. "The way you hold me makes this easier to do."

It was resentful, but it was consent.

Victory.

Easier? Why the hell did I say that?

Rex smiled at her, and it was so filled with wicked intent it made her head spin. Before she had a chance to withdraw her comment he ducked down and scooped her up into his arms, whipping the ground from beneath her feet.

"What the hell are you doing?"

Rolling her in against him, he held her tightly. "Taking you to my bed. Since you've agreed to the terms I see no reason to waste any more time. God knows we've wasted enough already."

Shocked to the core, she realized his intention was to have sex with her, immediately. The fact he'd swept her legs from under her was proof.

As he strode across the hallway toward the stairs, the scent of his body swamped her, enveloping her in his maleness. "Put me down," she demanded, wriggling about.

"Hush now, my sweet, don't get yourself all hot and bothered. You said everything you need to say."

"What does that mean?"

"You gave me consent to take charge of you."

She'd lost touch with what was being said and panic started to rise. "I did not."

"I'm afraid you did." The wicked gleam in his eyes emphasized the point.

Ordering her thoughts didn't come easily. Her body was pounding in response to being in his arms and his blatant statement of intent. He began to climb the stairs, her weight apparently no hindrance as he darted up them with her in his arms. The way he took charge and controlled her physically was breathtaking. Acting on instinct, she locked her hands around the back of his neck.

"Do you want to withdraw your comment about it being easier for you, hmm, playing the sub?"

Carmen stared at him, aghast. *Playing the sub?*

She hadn't said that, but...that's what he'd read into it.

He paused on the landing at the top of the stairs and glanced down at her with a smile. "I thought not."

He crossed the landing fast and kicked the door to his bedroom wide open.

The sight of his bed should have made her squirm. Instead, she just stared at it, her body a rush of longing.

He threw her down onto the surface.

"Rex, please."

"Rest assured I intend to take full advantage of the offer."

"I didn't make an offer." She struggled to her feet. Rex had her caged by the edge of his bed.

He watched her, apparently amused. "Oh, yes, you did. You said me being in charge made it easier."

He had her over a barrel. "It wasn't meant to be an offer, it was merely a comment."

He looked pointedly at what she was wearing. "When I saw the dress, I thought of you."

Another knee-jerk response flew out of her. She couldn't seem to keep on top of the conversation. "Why?"

He lifted one shoulder in a casual shrug. "I saw it and it instantly made me think of you. So I bought it. I carried it with me for months."

Carmen shook her head. "You're just saying that. I'm well aware you've had a very active love life. Why would you buy and keep a gift for another woman while dating some of the most beautiful women in Europe?"

"One of my whims...as you'd call it, perhaps." He gave a wry smile. "It was worth it, though. My expectations have been exceeded. Then again, the prize is so much better than the wrapping."

Don't listen to him, she urged herself. A clever ploy, using his dangerous charm to make her more malleable. "Your other women didn't want it," she said, clutching at anything she might use to defend herself.

"They weren't shown it." His tone was casual and yet there was an undertow there, a weighty inference that defied her to deny him. "The dress was bought for you and you alone."

"That implies you knew we would see each other again."

"Perhaps it does. I always wanted to see you again, but in that sense, it was an impulse buy. It made me think of you, and I wanted it."

Something fluttered inside her. It was the way he looked at her while he said, 'I wanted it.'

"You seem to think I had an ulterior motive. It's simply a gift. And it does suit you, you can't deny that."

Against her better judgment, Carmen was flattered. She glanced down, and instinctively ran her fingertips from the collar along the edge of the fabric where it curved around the outside of her left breast. "It is lovely."

"On that we agree." He was staring at her hand, and the outline of her breast through the sheer fabric. When her hand dropped away, he met her gaze. "Enough stalling."

The comment, so direct and compromising, made her pulse hitch.

Rex strode away across the room and retrieved a chair from beside the wardrobe. Stationing it in front of her—so that she was still trapped between him and the bed—he stood behind it with his hands resting on the back.

Bizarrely, his pose reminded her of a lion tamer.

"What are you wearing under it?"

"As you're well aware, not a lot." The dress was backless so she hadn't been able to wear a bra with it. It scooped low at the back and the fabric rippled across the base of her spine, offering her a sensuous caress every time she moved.

"Show me."

"What?"

He locked her gaze. "Lift your skirt and expose your underwear to me."

A hot rush hit her. She wavered unsteadily. He really intended to do this, to issue her sexual instructions. However, it turned her on so much, it astonished her. What happened to keeping him at arm's length? She'd succumbed, and now he'd well and truly launched his seductive powers on her. She'd walked into his trap.

He sat down on the chair and observed her as she stood there, unable to move without his instruction. Gesturing with one finger, he indicated the scalloped hem of the dress.

It was unbelievable, but some perverse part of her actually wanted to do as he said—she not only wanted to obey, she wanted to reveal herself to him. Good sense had gone. In its place was a visceral physical response to his instructions, as if his command had a magnetic pull on her and she couldn't resist it.

With trembling fingers, Carmen grasped the fabric with one hand and lifted it to reveal her stocking tops. Fixing her attention on him, she watched his response as the silky material swished against her bare skin above the lace-edged black stockings she wore. She paused, her heart thundering.

His eyes darkened. "Higher."

Lifting the fabric with both hands, she revealed her sheer black lace panties. Embarrassment hit her hard, but it was wildly arousing, too, standing there with her skirt pulled up to her hip bones for him.

Rex hummed approvingly. "So beautiful," he murmured.

The pulse in her groin beat wildly, heat gathering fast between her thighs. She squeezed them together.

"So obedient, too," Rex added.

Carmen reacted, dropping the skirt quickly back into place.

Rex laughed. When he made eye contact again, he leaned forward, resting his elbows on his knees. He was a predator, and she was in danger of falling completely under his seductive spell.

"So this really is your kink," he commented. "Well, well, I always wanted to know what made you tick. Now I know. My little stepsister is a secret submissive. It couldn't be more perfect. What fun we're going to have."

Carmen burned up. "This was a mistake. I think I should go."

Rex was on his feet and at her back in a flash, his hands on her shoulders arresting her.

"Let me go." She tensed, her hands fisting by her sides as she resisted him. But his body at her back felt good. Her ability to think straight slipped away.

"You don't mean that." He lowered his head alongside hers, resting a trail of kisses on the sensitive skin of her neck. One hand curved around her hip bone and he eased her back against him. The other was on the opposite shoulder, where he stroked her, soothing and arousing her all at once.

Carmen felt as if she was sinking under his will, but it was too good.

"That's better, isn't it?" He brushed one finger around the curve of her waist.

His touch clung to her, crackling along her nerve endings.

"If I'd known you were like this, well...I would've wanted you even more."

Carmen wavered. "Even more?"

He turned her around and tipped her chin up in order to look deep into her eyes. How easily he controlled her...and how good it felt.

"Even more, yes. I'm going to do something I've always wanted to do, tonight. I intend to watch your face while I make you come."

Carmen's breath caught. Between her thighs, the ache of longing that had built steadily over the course of the evening turned into a demanding need.

"It's been my intention to do so for many years, and now here we are and you're going to do exactly as I tell you, because you want the house. What could be better, we both get what we want?"

It sounded so wrong, as if she was selling herself. She did want the house and she would buy him out, but right at that moment she wanted him to make love to her, whatever the circumstances. It would be fatal to admit that to him, though. His ego was big enough. But he was right; they had to burn this out. There was also the inescapable fact that his magnetic draw defied her to resist him. There was such a seductive invitation in his eyes. "Rex, please don't tease me."

"My intention is entirely more grown-up."

The husky tone of his voice ran over her skin like hot wax, sealing her fate. She swallowed. His eyes narrowed and he closed his hands around her wrists, holding her tightly. She opened her mouth to object, but couldn't. That action was like a key, a trigger. The imprisonment at his hands was a drug to her senses.

Heady arousal sped through her. A muted moan escaped her. The pounding between her thighs had taken her over. Her panties clung to her groove.

"That's better."

There was no point in denying it. She liked his hands on her.

When Rex's mouth covered hers she was all his, a whirlpool of wanting under him. His lips were firm and persuasive and the brush of his stubble sparked her into another level of sensation. Her mouth opened and her body arched to make contact with his. When it did, he moaned approvingly, and his free hand moved against the small of her back, holding her in place. The firm wall of his chest echoed the strength she felt in the hand that clasped her wrists together so easily.

She'd never been kissed the way Rex kissed her—as if the world was about to end, as if he couldn't get enough of her, as if their lives depended on it.

"Oh, yes," he murmured as he drew back and looked down at her with heavily lidded eyes.

Without warning, he freed her wrists, strolled away and sat down again.

Wavering wildly, her pulse tripped.

Get a grip, she told herself, it's so obvious you need him to control you. The fact it was true confused her deeply, but she was locked into it now and he'd walked away.

"The dress, take it off."

Carmen acted immediately. She had to. Unlatching the halter neck, she undid the clothing he'd bought for her. She pulled the loosed fabric up and over her head, dropping it to the floor at her side.

Rex looked at her stocking tops with an appreciative glance. "Take the stockings off. Do it slowly."

Carmen kicked off her high heels and put one foot up against the end of the bed. She rolled the first stocking down. It was hard to do it slowly, so she paused occasionally instead, trying to breathe as she did. Without looking his way she proceeded to do the same with the other one. When it was off she put her hand on her hip and tossed her hair back, trying to level her head. She was completely naked, but for the briefest of lace panties.

"What a memorable sight." He put his hand out. "Bring the stockings to me."

Picking them up, she padded across the thick rug to the place where he sat.

Rex took them from her and tested them, stretching them between his hands. "They'll do nicely. Put your arms out, offer me your wrists."

Dizzy, disbelieving and outrageously aroused, Carmen stared at him.

He arched his eyebrows.

The thought of being so thoroughly helpless while he seduced her was outrageous, but he really meant to tie her up. He actually seemed to think that bondage was something she did, something she was familiar with. It was because she'd melted into submission when he clasped her wrists downstairs. It had felt good, though, as if giving up her sexual self-control in such a way had unlocked a door that hadn't been opened before. Was Rex used to this kind of behavior?

He beckoned with one hand. "Come now." His tone was laden with humor. "Don't forget, it'll make it so much *easier*."

"Don't push your luck," she snapped, but she put her forearms out, palms up, hands clasped into fists.

He shook out one stocking and used it to bind her wrists together. "Carmen Shelby, secretly into bondage and submission. Who'd have thought it?" He seemed to relish the moment, stringing it out. "It's a good job I didn't know. Otherwise, my erotic imaginings would have been even more corrupt than they already were."

"Corrupt? You make it sound…wrong."

Rex inhaled audibly, and Carmen's face grew hot. *What have I said?*

"Well, you don't think it's wrong, obviously." He rose to his feet, grasped the stocking binding her wrists together and used it to raise her arms. Nodding at the enclosures around her wrist, he continued. "You've obviously done this many times before."

Carmen lowered her eyelids.

"Oh, yes, the perfect submissive. You really have perfected the role."

The last thing she wanted him to think was she was still some ingénue. She'd never done…*this*…before. Somehow *this* had just happened. However, she'd had a couple of relationships, ill-fated though they were, so she wasn't going to give him the satisfaction of revealing her inexperience in matters of bondage.

He stepped right up against her, one hand still on her bound wrists, the other at the small of her back pressing her closer to him. "I really didn't need this element thrown into the mix, the dynamic between us was already hot enough."

He whispered the words in her ear, making the world fall away, making the room shrink to the intimate space between them. "But now that you're giving over all your self-control to me, allowing yourself to be plundered while you're helpless in bondage, I find I'm enjoying you even more."

Carmen slammed her eyes shut. What he was saying—the implications—ran through her body like liquid fire. Part of her wanted to run, to break free and forbid him to touch her. Overwhelmingly, she was too aroused to respond. Because deep down she wanted to know what it would be like, and no matter how much she resented him for it, he was right when he said this thing had to be burned out or it would haunt them both forever.

Rex set about using the second stocking to create a leash, tying it between her bound wrists at one end. "Now you're at my mercy. The teasing could go on for hours…if I could bare the wait."

Her nerves strung out.

He picked up the trailing end of the stocking, tugged on it firmly and led her to the bed. As she followed him, allowing him to lead her, myriad emotions assailed her. It was what she'd wanted, long ago, but so much had changed. She wasn't that naive schoolgirl anymore. She couldn't believe she was doing this, allowing him to take control and treat her this way. Yet it was wildly arousing.

Rex nodded down at the bed. "On your back."

The thick quilt was cool beneath her hot skin.

He used the dangling end of the second stocking to secure her wrists to the headboard. He seemed amused, as if it was a kink of hers and he was humoring her.

Damn him. Carmen squirmed, but the tension in her arms was oddly liberating. It was so hard to relinquish control, and yet when Rex took over it made it impossible for her to do anything but submit. It unleashed something unfettered and wild, something that she'd never experienced before.

Then he latched his fingers over the top of her panties, and pulled them the length of her legs and off. Writhing on the bed, she longed for more.

When he pulled his shirt off and abandoned it, her temperature went even higher. His body was hard and fit, so much more muscular than he had been. When she glanced lower and saw the bulge of his erection beneath the zipper on his pants, her eyes flashed closed.

The sound of him opening that zipper ran ragged over her nerve endings. She opened her eyes in time to see his cock bounce free as he shucked off his jockey shorts, long and hard and arced up from his hips.

Her core clenched. "Dear God," she murmured.

He was over her in a flash, crouched on the bed, eyes locked with hers. "What, you can't possibly have changed your mind?"

"Don't bet on it."

He put one hand on her shoulder and then ran it down over her breast. "Whatever comes out of that pretty mouth of yours is only half the story." He ran the palm of his hand briskly over her breast, chafing at the hardened nipple. "Your body is telling me all I need to know, and you're just as ready for this as I am."

Carmen arched up from the surface of the bed. The feeling of his palm over her breast frazzled her. She was so aroused, her body responding to his masterful sense of control. Why did it feel so good to be under him this way, when the last thing she wanted was to relinquish anything to him? "You make it sound like a crime for a woman to be aroused."

He chuckled. "Quite the contrary, my dear. You're the most delicious thing I've ever seen, especially when you're aroused."

He held her gaze and, try as she might, she couldn't look away. What he was saying made the pulse in the pit of her belly pound, her core readying for him in response to his provocative words. "For God's sake, Rex, you're driving me insane."

"It's good to hear you admit you're aroused."

"Stop it, stop torturing me."

"Torture? Is that what you think this is? I want to make this as easy as possible for you. However, should you change your mind, or should I go—" he lifted his brows "—too far...and you feel the need to...take a break, just say the safeword. We can pause and restructure the agreement accordingly." Irony was heavy in his tone.

Heart pounding, imagination running wild, she stared at him. "What safeword?"

He leaned over her, kissed her beneath her earlobe—an action which made her melt into a puddle of lust.

"Oh, I don't know, how about 'boo?'" He whispered the word into her ear, softly.

"You can't be serious." The idea of saying boo while he was doing something outrageous to her was too bizarre.

"Entirely so."

He had her tied up and they were trying to define the terms of what promised to be an extremely compromising sexual situation. His attitude maddened her. "Why do you have to pick such a silly word?"

"Because I don't believe you'll ever want to use a safe word."

"How the hell would you know what I will and won't do?"

"It's written all over you. Always was. You, and your kinky little soul...you won't want to prevent me having my way with you. You want every sordid act imaginable, and then some. I can see it in your eyes."

The brush of his thumbs over her erect nipples made her moan. Infuriated, she flashed her eyes in warning.

"You might resent me, but you still want me to do those things, every bit as much as I want to indulge you."

Carmen arched on the bed, her entire body alive with sensation. The things he said, and the way he was touching her—exploring every inch of her with his fingertips—was a recipe for combustion. "I hate you!"

He laughed. "No, you don't. But I promise you, if you say boo to me, I'll take my hands off you."

The hard length of his erection pressed against her thigh.

Being compromised like this was unbearable, yet the thought of him taking his hands off her right then was more unbearable still. She nodded her agreement.

Rex tweaked her nipples, then teased his fingers along the underside of her breasts while he kissed and licked the sensitive skin behind her earlobe.

A violent physical shiver shot through her.

"Sensitive…" His eyes gleamed, making him look even more wickedly handsome. He stroked her from breast to hip, outlining her curves, then bent to kiss her in the dip of her cleavage.

The way he explored her made her pulse race and the damp heat between her thighs became sweltering. He cupped her pussy in his palm. Direct and demanding, the touch of his hand there triggered a heightened need for release. He stared into her eyes and one corner of his mouth lifted in appreciation. The gentle squeeze he gave her made her gasp aloud.

"Oh, yes, you're ready for this. We both are." He shifted, reached down and lifted one of her feet, running his knuckle under the arch.

He clasped her ankle before he stroked his hands up the surface of her calves, an action which made her nerves leap. With his hands under the backs of her knees, he parted her legs, planting her feet widely on the surface of the bed.

The sound of her blood rushing thundered in her ears.

"Beautiful."

"Oh, God, I can't do this." She closed her legs. "I'm mortified."

"Don't be." He stroked the back of his knuckles over the soft, sensitive skin on her thighs.

Carmen began to pant aloud, her hips rolling from side to side against the bedcovers. Still he stroked her, studying her face all the while. It was torturous—a heady combination of embarrassment and acute arousal making her moan and buck. Her nipples burned with sensation. As she wriggled against the surface of the bed her breasts squeezed together and the nipples jutted out.

Rex smiled down at her. "Don't fight it."

"Easy for you to say." But he was right. She couldn't fight it anymore. The muscles in her thighs began to relax.

He nodded his approval, then lowered his head and closed his mouth over her mound. Carmen jerked against her restraints, then melted.

He dipped his tongue into the damp groove of her pussy. "I've wanted to taste you so badly."

His warm breath over her sensitive folds made her lift and jerk again, but she was weak with lust and it was futile. He pushed his hands under her buttocks, physically lifting her as he went down on her, devouring her.

The rush, the pleasure—Carmen almost passed out, but the lap of his tongue on her clit anchored her. She glanced down and saw the muscles in his shoulders ripple as he worked her. Her clit felt unbearably tight and hot, and so sensitive. Then Rex sucked hard on the hard nub, then thrust a finger inside, and she hit her peak.

The sudden rush of release made her arch and twist. Panting loudly, she squeezed her thighs together as soon as she felt him pull away. The action only made her aware of her own state of wetness.

By the time she surfaced, Rex was kneeling up on the bed with his fist wrapped around the shaft of his erection. He began to ride it up and down. With the other hand, he brandished a condom packet.

"Ready to receive?" His mouth was set in an amused smile, his very posture oozing self-assured confidence.

Carmen bit her lip to stop herself snapping. Despite the fact she'd just come, her body was wired with expectation.

Rex tore open the packet, tossed the wrapper aside and rolled the condom onto his impressive erection.

Carmen watched, mesmerized by the sight of him.

He lifted her legs wider apart and climbed between them. Resting on his elbows, he stared down at her, locking her gaze with his. His cock pressed against her splayed sex, hard and hot.

"Oh!" Her hips rocked, she couldn't help it.

Rex smiled. "Eager. Nice."

"What do you expect?" she snapped, glaring at him. "You've done this!"

"Hey, no need to thank me."

That was the stepbrother she remembered. Cocky. With an exaggerated sigh of frustration, she rolled her head on the pillows and looked away. It didn't help, because when she did she saw them reflected in the mirror beyond. Rex, between her thighs, his muscled physique poised over her, his shoulders and back flexing as he began to roll his hips against hers, his body pistonlike.

Thankfully he reached down and directed his cock inside, stretching her open and filling her. The garbled noise she made in response was a primitive sound, the likes of which she'd never uttered before.

He pushed deeper.

Sheer bliss rolled over her.

Then she wanted more. His thrusts, friction. "Oh, please."

"What? What is it you need?"

Damn him. He was holding back.

When he moved his cock, ever so slightly, teasing her, she moaned aloud. "More," she cried, "more!"

"I thought as much." Pulling back, he rode deep to her core.

Her center throbbed wildly when his crown pressed there, then he drew back and thrust again. Panting for breath, she felt consumed by this act—so longed for, so tangled with implications and ramifications.

He began to thrust faster, massaging her right there in that sweet spot. "Oh, oh!"

"I've got you, my little bird." His tone was tender. "This has been a long time coming."

"Don't…" She couldn't bear to hear him say that. It made something inside her furl and unfurl. Briefly, he stroked her cheek, his thumb moving over her lower lip before he bent to kiss her open mouth.

His tongue thrust in and out each time he worked his cock into her.

The physical echo made her crazy. Arching up to him, she wrapped her legs around his hips while her tongue thrashed with his. It felt like a battle, and neither of them wanted to give in until they had to, until the absolute breaking point was reached.

When her head fell back she saw his eyes flicker, dark and wicked and clearly pleasured by her response. On and on he went, working her. He studied her all the while—just as he'd told her he would. It was so intense and intimate that it felt like a whole other level of penetration.

Her sex spasmed, her body closing on orgasm.

Rex cursed under his breath and thrust ever harder.

His forehead gleamed.

She could hear the slick pull of her sex as he worked his cock into her. Then he rose up on his arms, and the muscles there were taut and visibly pumped. His hips moved fast. The muscles in his neck and shoulders were tight.

"Rex," she managed to whisper when she began to flood again.

He nodded. "Oh, yes, I can feel you."

He paused, as if to savor what her body was doing. He shook his head, then thrust again. Pressed fully against her, he kept his cock right there, grinding his hips against hers as she came.

The release was so great, she hung limp in her tethers, but the hard rod of his cock inside her and the pressure of his body against her clit kept her there. A second wave washed over her, her thighs shuddering against his hips as her every nerve ending was strung out with the raw pleasure of another heady orgasm.

"Rex," she whispered again, and this time it was with gratitude.

His cock jerked and his head lifted, his eyelids lowering as he jerked again, his body taut and arched as he pumped himself into her.

Even while she shuddered and battled to control her breathing, he pulled free, stretched up and undid her binds. When it was done, he went to his bathroom.

Carmen could scarcely muster the strength to pull off the loosed stockings. By the time she did so, Rex returned.

He rolled her onto her side as he climbed back into the bed, pulling the covers over her. He kissed the side of her face as he moved in alongside her.

"I can't sleep in your bed with you." Panic hit her. She had to be alone, to regroup her faculties. "Let me go, I refuse to—"

He locked his arm around her, leaned over her and silenced her with a kiss—a gentle kiss, the brush of his lips over hers, so fleeting and yet somehow so deeply meaningful that she lost the power of speech.

"Yes, you can. We'll sleep in the same bed. Tonight and every other night we're here together, even if I have to keep you tied up all day long in order to fuck you all night long."

"You wouldn't dare."

"You'd probably enjoy it far too much. And just think, you could blame me for enjoying yourself, even though I made it so much easier for you."

Was there no end to this embarrassment? "You're enjoying this."

"Of course I am. Why wouldn't I?"

"I opened myself up to you. Stop trying to embarrass me about it."

"Me, embarrass you? Man, you're one screwed-up, kinky woman."

He was deliberately trying to wind her up, even now, and she resented that. "Shut up!"

"No way. You can't take charge of the situation now, not since you've given in to me so spectacularly." He kissed her shoulder, and snuggled closer.

Carmen pressed her lips together hard, fighting the urge to reach back and thump him. It was true, though. Somehow, he'd assumed leadership and it was so overwhelming, she lost her fiercely protected self-control. She'd become malleable under his exploration, relinquishing all sexual power to him.

"And to think you said you hated me." He stroked his hand along her side, his fingertips trailing over her skin as if he still wanted to explore her, even now.

Carmen closed her eyes tight. It only made things worse. She felt as if she were sinking under his will, but his arm around her made it impossible to do anything but drown in the pleasure.

CHAPTER FIVE

Rex worked his body hard, using the early-morning air and the physical exercise to focus his thoughts on Carmen. Jogging across the grounds didn't need his full concentration anyway, because he was on a familiar path. He'd run here many times as a teenager. It gave him time to think, and to clear his head. Not that he wanted to forget what had happened the night before, no way. What he wanted to do was try to understand the intensity of what had passed between them.

Being with Carmen was everything he thought it would be in terms of hot sex, but there was a mind shock there he hadn't anticipated. He had no idea Carmen was a submissive. Smiling to himself, he relived the memory of waking up at dawn to find her splayed on his bed, sleeping soundly after a seriously good session between the sheets. That was a sight he'd wanted to enjoy for years, and the sense of victory it gave fuelled his early-morning run.

He changed direction, heading through the trees toward the lake beyond. After the path forked, he glanced back over his shoulder at the house, acknowledging it was good to see the old place again.

At first the house had seemed strangely empty without his father's presence. When he'd wandered the halls and rooms he found everything so familiar, so unchanged, he was forced to admit he had grudging affection for the old place. That positive feeling intensified once Carmen arrived. Burlington Manor was greatly enhanced with the mysterious, ethereal beauty of Carmen Shelby present inside its walls once again. He hadn't doubted it would, not for a moment.

The early-morning air under the trees sharpened his concentration.

When the path opened up at the lake, he slowed the pace. In the past, this would be the part of his morning run where his father's hounds would break free of him and run on ahead. The dogs had long since passed on, and, for whatever reason, his father hadn't brought new pups to the house. Much as he hadn't replaced any of them when they'd left his side. It was a lonely end for the old man.

It occurred to Rex that the route and speed of his morning run was the same as it'd always been, as if he was programmed to undertake his jog in exactly the same way. The connection to the past didn't sit well. To break the habit, he stopped running and put his hands on his hips as he surveyed the lake.

Maintenance work was needed on the banks of the lake. It had been built into the landscape gardens over a hundred and forty years earlier, a man-made lake fed by the local river. The water was fresh and it was safe to swim there. The sloping bank of the lake side was covered in thick, lush grass, and had been a picnic ground throughout many generations of the family. On the far side, the edge of the lake was overgrown and lacked order. The lily pads that floated there had grown too thick and unruly. They were meant to be an embellishment, not a mask. But with a skeleton staff at the house nowadays the jobs had to be prioritized. They seemed to be managing fairly well given they were so shorthanded.

He circuited the banks at a walking pace, and when he glanced back at the trees flanking the path to the house, he almost saw his young self idling there, watching Carmen. On one of his visits home he arrived in the late afternoon on a hot sunny day, and one of the staff told him Carmen was down by the lake. As he approached, he caught sight of her swimming there. The sun glinted on her wet hair as she made her way back and forth across the small lake. He'd been about to strip off his T-shirt, run down there and join her, when she emerged and stood by the edge of lake squeezing out her hair.

That's when he'd become transfixed by the sight of her. He'd stayed under cover of the trees so he could admire her before he made his presence known. She'd been wearing a red swimsuit and the damp fabric clung to her outline. He'd ached for her then, and it was with a fierceness so strong it took root in him.

"Good morning to you, sir."

The sound of the voice behind him drew Rex's attention.

"Bill, it's good to see you." He strode over to where Bill Amery stood, glad to see the familiar face. Bill, who was married to the housekeeper, was the head groundsman and had worked at Burlington Manor all his life. Apart from a few more white hairs in his beard, Bill looked the same, and he wore his trademark overalls covered over by a waterproof jacket. His flat cap was possibly a new model, but it was exactly the same as the previous ones he'd worn. As a young lad, Rex had been a complete nuisance to this man while he went about his duties on the estate, but Bill was patient and Rex knew he and his wife had brought a lot of stability to him in what was otherwise a wreckage of a family life during his early years.

He shook Bill's hand and nodded. "You're doing a good job."

"Not as good as I'd like. Your father had to pare down the number of staff. What was it, six of us here on grounds duty, when you were a lad?"

Rex nodded.

"Now I've only got Gary, who does three days a week on the shrubs and terraces, and Jason here, who works mornings on general duties alongside me. Both are good workers, and Jason makes a worthy home brew ale, which he generously shares with us." Bill grinned back at the lean young man who stood beyond him. "I could do with him being full-time."

It was unlike Bill to make demands, but these people were effectively in a state of limbo between official owners. They didn't know if their jobs were safe or who they would be working for if they were even kept on after the property was sold. Bill was stating his needs up front, most likely because of his uncertainties.

"Leave it with me. I'll do what I can." Rex nodded over at the man who stood beyond Bill, listening. "Good to meet you, Jason."

"Likewise, Mr. Carruthers."

Rex put out his hand and Jason hesitated, then shook it. "How long have you been working here at the manor?"

"Just a few weeks, but I like the place. Better than being cooped up packing boxes in a factory."

"Being outside certainly has its advantages," Rex agreed, nodding. He was enjoying the countryside more than he thought he would.

Rex estimated the newcomer was in his mid-twenties. He stared at Rex strangely, glancing away and then back as if shy. He was lean and there was a wiry quality to his build. Bill, on the other hand, was somewhere in his mid-sixties and probably should've retired already. Rex wouldn't want to part with either him or his wife, but they were the ones who should be part-time, as supervisors.

His train of thought stalled. *Why am I thinking about this?*

Because, temporarily, he was part-owner. Assuring himself it was only that and no greater sense of responsibility, he attempted to shrug off the odd notion. It didn't go away. He cared about these people. They'd been part of his childhood. Rex hadn't realized he'd be pulled into everyday details, but there was no denying that responsibility was playing its part in how he felt.

He shoved his hands in his pockets and looked back at the house while Bill talked about some of the adjustments they'd made in the land maintenance in order to make it manageable. He listened, and engaged, but his moment of self-scrutiny lingered.

He did want to sort out the best long-term plan as possible for the manor, even if that meant selling to a stranger. Right at that moment he wasn't sure buying the house was right for Carmen. The thought of her living up here alone was too weird. Time would tell.

However, what surprised him most of all was the fact that he wasn't averse to the feeling of responsibility building in him. He'd assumed it would happen but it would feel like a burden, the old issue of mortmain. He'd assumed he'd want to get the hell out once he'd spent some time with the lovely Carmen—the woman who'd haunted his thoughts and dreams for all those years in between. But it seemed the connection he had to the old place wasn't tainted with mortmain, after all.

The house was his leverage to get to Carmen, he reminded himself. It was Carmen he wanted. Carmen he wanted to make happy.

The house would be hers.

Carmen inhaled deeply, snuggled deeper into the pillows and then remembered where she was. Sitting up with a jolt, she peered around Rex's room. He was nowhere to be seen. Waking up in Rex's bed was disorienting enough without waking up there alone.

Carmen took a moment to run through what had happened, to assure herself it wasn't some weird, lurid dream. It was surreal, though.

Sex, with Rex? *I really did it, after all this time.*

Slumping back on the pillows she tried to take stock, walking through what had happened in her mind. Her body was quick to reassure her it had really happened, her libido stirring.

Somehow, she'd given in to his deal. It hadn't been something she intended to do, nor had she envisioned it panning out the way it had. Even though she'd given in to that age-old desire, she'd assumed it would be a wham-bam-thank-you-ma'am shag, an event that would put an end to her stupid crush. However, she'd been shocked by Rex—his intense masculine persona and his powers of seduction. Christ, he was good. His dominance had triggered a wild streak in her, and it had taken her completely by surprise. *Did I really do those things?*

She had. She'd lifted her skirt, she'd stripped at his command, she'd handed over her stockings so he could tie her up with them, making her his—no matter what.

Fevered by the truth, the actualization of such a long-held fantasy, she rolled facedown on his pillows, inhaling his scent. Her body rocked against the surface of the bed. *Rex, oh, Rex.*

A sound from beyond the room broke her reverie. She shifted and sat bolt upright on the edge of the bed. Glancing at the clock on the dresser, she saw it'd just gone seven. It could be Mrs. Summerfield, the cook, arriving. It could also be Rex returning from wherever he'd disappeared off to. The last thing she wanted was him returning to find her there, languishing on his sheets while she retraced memories of the night before. That would be too compromising. Rising quickly from the bed, she pulled her clothes on and escaped the room without being seen.

Back in her own room, she showered and dressed. Then she ruffled her bedding because it occurred to her that if she didn't the staff would know they'd slept together. She wasn't sure she wanted anyone to know. It'd be over soon. The last thing she wanted was speculation in the meantime. That's when the reality of the situation rushed back in. Doubts quickly began to gather.

What the hell am I doing? As much as she wanted the manor, she didn't want to sell herself to own the house.

She would pay him. However, if she insisted on paying him now, he could walk away. Even though she knew it was dangerous and that she ran the risk of getting too involved, she wanted her four weekends with Rex. The night before was like nothing she'd ever experienced. To carry on with it was dangerous, an arrangement fraught with pitfalls, but she wanted more of him.

The fact was she'd given in to his demands now, but she'd enjoyed it. When their agreement came to an end she would pay him, then she wouldn't feel sullied. She couldn't live with herself if she accepted fifty percent of the manor for a few bouts of hot sex. It was the only way to handle it, but she had to keep it to herself. Let him believe he was in charge and getting what he wanted. She'd get what she wanted, too, and in a professional manner she would be able to live with after the event.

Somewhat more at ease with herself, she plugged in her hair dryer and set about preparing herself for a day at the manor. There was a lot she wanted to check, and plans to be made. Then she saw Rex, and those plans drifted away. Standing in the bay window, deep in thought, she caught sight of him jogging around the lakeside path.

Carmen lowered the hair dryer, and stared.

It was little wonder she'd given in to him so quickly. The man was more handsome than ever, his maturity adding a new level of attraction to an already gorgeous-looking male specimen. And as he'd said, the seed had been planted a long time ago. Because of that, he was able to instigate this curious deal where she exchanged herself for rights to his share of the property. There was no denying it had been satisfying, but the days and weekends ahead were now filled with uncertainty. Could she even trust him to stick to his own terms? What exactly did he expect?

Everything and anything, he'd said.

She switched off the hair dryer. When she went to unplug it, her hand shook. Taking a deep breath, she told herself to shape up. She absolutely had to make him stick to the terms. And she had to push him to make it legal as quickly as possible, at which point she'd pay him. She wanted it on a contract—it was the only way to herd him into it—and she would get his signature even if she had to write it with her own blood.

At the dresser, she rooted about in her makeup bag and applied a little lipstick and minimal foundation, nothing fancy. Then she left the safety of her room and made her way downstairs.

The staircase was one of her favorite features, curving as it did in a huge crescent into the center of the hallway. She trailed her fingers down the polished banister, and at the bottom paused before she left the plush carpeting of the staircase and walked across the marble tiles in the entrance hall. Turning back on herself, she headed into the kitchen.

"Mrs. Summerfield." Carmen was delighted when she saw the familiar figure of the cook standing by the sink filling the kettle.

The woman turned and put down the kettle, stepping over quickly to meet Carmen halfway across the kitchen. They embraced. Carmen had always got on well with Mrs. Amery, but it was the cook who she was closest to. They'd exchanged cards and gifts by post each Christmas since Carmen had moved away, and seeing her brought a badly needed sense of contentment to Carmen's troubled spirit.

"You look lovelier than ever," the older woman commented as she looked Carmen over. "If a bit too thin," she added, gently squeezing Carmen's upper arm.

Carmen chuckled. Mrs. Summerfield had always used that line on her. "So you say, but according to the guidelines I could do with losing a few pounds."

"Guidelines, what nonsense. Now, would you like to have breakfast in the dining room?"

"No, I'll take breakfast in here, as usual."

Mrs. Summerfield smiled again. "I thought as much. I'll be making a full breakfast for Rex. What would you like?"

"Tea and toast is enough for me." At the mention of Rex's name, Carmen moved to the large scrubbed pine kitchen table. The thought of sitting here eating breakfast with him after what had passed between them the night before made her nervous.

Mrs. Summerfield had already set out two places with cups and saucers and cutlery. They were close together at one end of the table. Carmen shifted one setting a bit farther away and moved the chair before sitting down.

Thankfully she was in place when the door to the outside lobby sprung open and Rex joined them. "Something smells good," he commented as he entered the room.

"Crispy bacon in the oven," Mrs. Summerfield informed him, "just how you said you like it these days, nice and lean. I'm cooking eggs now. There's tea brewing."

Rex listened while he looked across at Carmen.

Carmen reached for the teapot. *It really should be illegal for a man to look that good,* she thought to herself as she glanced at him from under her lashes. He'd been out jogging, which apparently made him all the more attractive. The white T-shirt he wore clung to the heat of his body. The loose jogging pants only seemed to emphasize his hard male physique. He looked wired, energetic and vital. The essential woman in her responded, her core tingling, her skin pricking with expectation. Out of nowhere, Carmen felt a rush of pity for her poor teenage self. It was no wonder she'd been such a tortured soul, nursing romantic dreams and lusty fantasies about her stepbrother. Having to share space with a man like Rex Carruthers wouldn't be easy for any woman, let alone an inexperienced teenager.

Now, though, now I should be able to handle him.

Mrs. Summerfield nodded at the table. "What else would you like? Some juice, perhaps?"

"A glass of skimmed milk, if we have it."

"Lean protein breakfast on the weekend," Carmen commented. "Things have changed."

Rex stared across at her, his mouth curling. "Haven't they just."

It was there all the time, the subtle reference to the lust between them. Even now, after it had been dealt with. He obviously intended to keep that particular attitude on the go. To her mortification, he approached.

"You're looking particularly radiant today." He ducked down and kissed her cheek.

Say something, she urged herself as he hovered expectantly. "Thank you," she managed.

Apparently satisfied, he took a seat.

"So, have you seen how high-tech we are here now?" He nodded at the wall behind and above her head.

Carmen turned around and looked up, above her seat. There, fixed to a bracket on the wall, she saw a CCTV screen showing a picture of the front driveway. A moment later it altered to the delivery entrance, and then back again. "That's new."

"About time, too. For decades the staff here have been expected to miraculously know when people are arriving. I'm glad to see the old man finally gave in and got with the times, primitive though it is." Rex's tone was largely disapproving.

Mrs. Summerfield chuckled at his comments as she went about her business.

"There's a screen in the hallway, too," he added.

Mrs. Summerfield brought a basket of hot toast over, then served Rex's cooked breakfast. Carmen buttered her toast while Rex listed some of the changes he'd spotted. Why was he taking such an interest?

"I notice you haven't been the face of *Objet d'Art* the way Sylvia was," he stated while he peppered his eggs. "Why is that?"

Startled and wary, Carmen put down her toast and reached for her teacup. Anonymity suited her, that's why. "Did it do her any good, being the public face?"

His mouth twitched at one corner. If he was amused by her grief she'd never forgive him. Carmen gripped the armrests on her chair tightly, in order not to push the chair back and leave. Suffering his warped sense of humor was not part of the deal.

"I believe it did, because it did the company good and that's what she wanted, for you as much as her." He paused deliberately. "She was proud of what she'd created, and she gave the company a human face."

His comment surprised her deeply, because it never occurred to her that he'd taken any interest in *Objet d'Art*. Carmen struggled to find an answer, mostly because she didn't know how to respond without snapping at him. She didn't want to do that in front of Mrs. Summerfield. She also didn't want to talk about things that were close to her, because if they shared too much it would no longer be a business arrangement. Or was it too late for that already?

Guarded, wary and confused, she couldn't help offering a defensive response. "That sounds like a criticism of me."

"Not at all. I'm aware that you'll have good reasons, and you clearly run the company every bit as well as your mother did. I'm just curious as to why you run that angle differently."

All she could do was state the truth. "It was her thing. Mum loved leading the PR for *Objet d'Art*. She pulled a terrific team together to run the place so she could concentrate on the public image of the company. It was lucky for me she worked that way. When she died in the car crash, I'd completed my business studies degree but I was just starting my Masters in Business Admin. I had to drop out and move into position much earlier than planned."

"That must have been tough for you," Rex commented, "especially under those circumstances."

"I had a lot of support. Besides, it helped keep my mind off what happened to Mum, which has never been easy."

She paused. Rex nodded. He knew they'd been close.

She hurried on so that she didn't get upset. "I had to learn fast, and from the bottom up. The board ran things so I could do that. It took time and we hired a new PR person to cover what my mother used to do. I'm okay with most aspects of the company now, but I've still got heaps to learn. I'm content our PR officer continues to do what she does so well, better than I ever could."

Mrs. Summerfield had finished up what she was doing and disappeared off into the adjacent storerooms with her notepad and pen.

Carmen took the opportunity to lay some ground rules. "Look, Rex. I'm not here to discuss my business with you. We should discuss the future of this property."

"We've got three more weekends ahead, plenty of time for that. I want to know all about you. This is our time to catch up on each other and I intend to make the most of every moment." He picked up his teacup and stared at her across the rim, his sharp blue eyes commanding her attention. "So, when did you get into the kinky sex thing?"

Bloody hell. Carmen pursed her lips and concentrated on buttering a second piece of toast. Continuing the previous line of discussion suddenly seemed preferable. Why in God's name did he have to throw that out there?

What on earth could she say? The truth of the matter was she'd never done anything remotely kinky before. Something about him had made her click into a different level of sexual mood and experience. Then again, kinky sex hadn't ever been on offer before, as far as she knew. She'd only had two lovers, and nothing like the night before had ever occurred. Was being restrained a deep part of her psyche? If it was, it hadn't been revealed before.

But she'd never been held by a man with the presence that Rex Carruthers owned, the determination, the virile masculinity and strength. It had affected her and he, it seemed, knew exactly how to respond. She wasn't going to tell him that, though. Neither was she going to make up some fictional dominant lover to fulfill his curiosity. Instead, she ignored his comment and ate her toast. It had made it easier, though.

It means I can blame him.

And it was outrageously hot.

Why? Why the hell did I enjoy submitting to him that way?

As she stared across at him the answer hovered, but she pushed it away, unwilling to acknowledge she still wanted him so very badly after all these years.

He lounged there in his chair, sipping his tea while he watched her over the rim of his cup. It was a crime for a man to be so blatant, so forthright and suggestive, surely?

"I can't help being curious," he added. "The woman I knew before was a sensual kitten, but now…" He gestured at her and his mouth moved in a suggestive smile.

A sensual kitten? Was I ever that? Carmen supposed she must've been, or at least he saw her that way. She had flirted with him, a hell of a lot. She didn't do that anymore, not on a regular basis. With the other men she'd been involved with it hadn't been like this. Then again, no one had ever spoken to about her sexuality, not like he did. Was that part of his charm, the dark side—the provocative, confrontational Rex who could so easily command a woman's attention?

"You're a dangerous temptation now, Carmen Shelby." He smiled, as if he approved.

"You do so love being provocative, don't you?"

Mrs. Summerfield emerged from the cold storage area with a stack of supplies on a tray. Carmen nodded her way, but Rex already seemed to be aware of her presence.

"I understand you're semi-retired these days, Mrs. Summerfield," he said before he looked in the cook's direction.

She put the tray down on the work surface before turning to respond. "That's right. It's not necessary to be up here all the time for one or two, so I come and go. It's a pleasure to do so when required. I thought some nice chargrilled salmon with sides would do well for you tonight, if that suits you both?"

"It sounds good to me." Rex turned her way and rested his elbow on the back of his chair.

The muscles in his upper arm flexed and Carmen noticed the dark hair on his forearm. Rex had always been muscular, but he'd been leaner before. There was no denying his physique turned her on.

"Did my father leave anything in the cellar for visitors?"

Carmen thought Mrs. Summerfield might be offended, but she chuckled. "A case or two survived. Would you like me to chill a bottle of white for dinner?"

"No, that's okay. I'll check it out later."

"We can fend for ourselves for lunch," Carmen added. She wasn't used to being waited on anymore, not for a long time.

"If you're sure?"

Carmen nodded.

"Right." Rex took a sidelong glance at her as he rose to his feet. "I suggest we take a walk around the grounds together."

Carmen froze. "Why?"

"I want to hear your ideas for the place, your long-term plans."

She broke into a smile, relieved. It seemed that he did intend to stick to his side of the bargain.

He held the door open for her. As she passed he rested his hand briefly between her shoulder blades. It was the gentlest of touches, yet there was intimacy there. Carmen was wary of it. It didn't feel wrong, though, not after what happened between them the night before. They'd had sex and they'd slept alongside each other all night. However, that brief touch alerted her to his proximity, and his intentions. It wasn't exactly possessive, but she did feel he could put his hands on her and she'd know what he wanted. It was exactly what he'd done the day before, and even when they met for the reading of the will he'd claimed rights in some way. This was different. This was even more intense, because they'd slept together now.

It was a glorious morning outside, mid-September showing no signs of giving up on the summer. The trees were still laden with greenery.

The flagstones outside the lobby adjacent to the kitchens ran onto a gravel path, and it crunched beneath their feet as they walked. It was a familiar sound. The path forked, and Carmen paused.

"Lead the way," Rex suggested, gesturing at the path that went around the front of the property toward the cricket pitch.

"Thank you," Carmen said, then turned on her heel and went in the opposite direction.

When he raced alongside her, she glanced away so he wouldn't see her smile. Instead, she looked up at the exterior of the building as they went, using the opportunity to gauge the state of repair. "I want the place to come alive, to be full of visitors and parties again."

"It obviously hasn't witnessed any of that, not since you left."

"I don't suppose it has." It was sad to think of Charles Carruthers here alone, but he'd assured her he was happy whenever she'd been in touch. "My first priority will be to secure the place. I see a lot of things that need immediate attention." She gestured at a stone carved pot on top of a podium. The podium was cracked.

Rex nodded. "Dad obviously let the place go. The staff have done their best, but the resources just aren't there."

Was it her imagination, or did he look dissatisfied, ashamed even? Even a slight indication of his bond with the place made her wary.

"I intend to take up where my mother left off," she stated as an opening gambit, claiming rights from the off. "I've managed her business interests well enough. I think she'd be happy with my efforts there. Now it's time to look at the other love of her life."

She glanced back at him. He was observing her closely.

Rex nodded. "She invested a lot of her time and funds in the manor."

"Indeed, and many people have commented on it over the years."

"What do you mean?" His eyebrows drew together.

"I'm often told your dad didn't have the funds to restore the place. Marrying my mother changed that."

"Ah. Well, people will talk, but we knew how happy they were."

"Exactly. People do like to put the knife in, don't they?" Carmen observed him from the corner of her eye. Interesting he'd experienced the hearsay, too. Of course, she supposed he would've had the full set of accusations and suggestions she'd suffered over the years, maybe even more so. Some of the comments had really hurt, especially close to the time of her mother's fatal car crash—remarks about her mother's death being conveniently timed, speculation about whether Charles Carruthers would marry again. He didn't. It came with the territory, though. Any family who had a name, lineage or a prestige property were talked about, their lives dissected like public property.

"Aren't you worried people will say the same thing about you," Rex asked, "you're investing your personal income from the company in a crumbling British estate?" There was a mischievous look in his eyes.

Carmen was getting used to it again, though, and she felt able to manage when it was about this particular subject. When it was about sexuality that was different. "Ah, well, I do intend to make it a personal investment, the project, a continuation of my mother's work. I don't have a personal cause, or hobby, so Burlington Manor will be that. But it'll also be a home. I plan to spend all my weekends here. I might even work from home part of the time."

"Alone? Or is there a partner you plan to feather your nest with?"

Amused, Carmen gave him a quizzical glance. "Isn't it a bit late to be asking whether I have a partner or not?"

"Not really. What I meant was…you might have someone in mind. I knew you weren't attached when I propositioned you. I asked around. We have mutual friends. It wasn't difficult to be sure."

For some reason the notion of him researching her relationship status before coming up with this ludicrous deal amused her.

"Besides, I know you're an honorable sort of woman and you wouldn't have got yourself into this arrangement had you not been in a position to do so."

He really had done his groundwork. "Quite so. And you, have you left some poor woman at a loose end in London while you entertain yourself up here?"

Rex's mouth curled. "You seem to have a very low opinion of me. I assure you I've never been unfaithful to a woman."

He eyed her steadily.

Carmen felt an objection rise inside her—an objection that formed because of an old memory of him bedding a friend of hers at a time when she felt sure they were destined to be lovers. But he hadn't been unfaithful. Much as she liked to think they were an item back then, they weren't. Foolish fantasy on her part.

Rex seemed more grounded these days. His actions and comments were more measured. The mature Rex could still be provocative and play free and easy with people's emotions, but there was an underlying sense of honor she hadn't been aware of as a teenager.

"I should go into the village," she said, desperate to change the subject matter.

"I'll drive you."

"No. I can walk."

He looked at her with curiosity. "Sorry, I'm not ready to drive around Beldover because of my mother's car crash. I can still picture it, you see." The sight of her mother being sealed in a body bag on the side of the country road was always with her, the car flipped on one side where she'd veered off and hit a tree.

"I'm so sorry I wasn't here at the time." He squeezed her upper arms with strong, reassuring hands.

"It was awful, but we got through it. Your dad was devastated."

"Did they ever find out what caused the accident?"

"No." Her thoughts slipped back to the moment, to the sight of Charles Carruthers when he came to tell her the news. Remembering the pain in his eyes, her chest tightened.

"Carmen," Rex whispered, and moved closer, looking at her with sympathy.

She tried to buckle herself up, emotionally. "Sorry. It's just…even now I can't shake the suspicion it wasn't an accident."

"The investigation, was it thorough, did Dad make sure?"

"Yes, of course. There was no evidence." She had no grounds, but she remained convinced someone had caused her mother's death. It wasn't an easy thing to live with. "Sorry." She mustered a smile. "Grief talking, I suppose." It's what people told her, because there was no other explanation.

"This place holds many secrets and mysteries." Rex stared back at the house as he spoke. "I wonder if we'll ever uncover them all."

We?

Feeling awkward, she stared at the surrounding landscape, to the fringes of the estate and beyond. Setting off again, she cleared her throat. "The estate needs to earn money. It's only right and just for an estate like this to do so in the modern age. It's contingency for the future, as well. If my business fails to be lucrative, I have to be sure Burlington Manor can bring in funds for its own maintenance, going forward."

"An admirable plan. Tell me more." He looked genuinely intrigued.

Relieved they'd moved on, she breathed easier. "Oh, I don't know whether I should. What if I share my development ideas and you change your mind and refuse to sell?" She smiled to soften the accusation a bit. "It wouldn't be sensible business practice, would it?"

"Probably not. However, I assure you I have quite enough to do developing my company. A shame, perhaps." He paused and looked at her deliberately. "My business isn't established the way yours is. It's fledgling, and it would be hard for me to devote the amount of time this place needs, even if I did feel loyalty or obligation to do so, which I don't."

They'd skirted the side of the building, and they'd reached the corner where the grounds had previously run down to open meadowland. Most of it had been sold to local farmers, but not all of it. There was some older property on the estate she was particularly interested in. She left the gravel path, and pointed in the direction of the outbuildings.

"The old cottages." She gestured at the run-down stone buildings. Originally built to house servants in a bygone age, they hadn't been used for decades and were scarcely more than empty shells. The traditional York stone walls and interior beams were solid, though, and in her mind's eye she could picture the cottages renovated and functioning.

"I used to play down here as a child," Rex commented.

The sun lit the gray slate roofs, which meant if she squinted her eyes, Carmen could almost imagine them brought back to life, made pretty and habitable. "They haven't been used in decades. I thought it would be an interesting project to restore them."

"You think there's potential there?"

Carmen paused on the brow of the hill and took the countryside in, reveling in it. "Holiday rentals, perhaps?"

Rex nodded.

"I'm considering a similar plan for the stables." She gestured to the left where the old stables were located. "There are also three disused barns on the property, of varying sizes. They've been abandoned for many years, but the shells are sturdy and they'd make terrific barn conversions. Maybe to sell, or they could be rented out to cover the renovation costs and ultimately feed income back into the estate."

"You've given it a lot of thought."

"I don't go into things without thinking through the implications."

She'd meant it in a business sense, but as soon as she said it and saw his response, she realized what he was thinking about. Sex. His eyebrows lifted. It was almost imperceptible, but so suggestive, and his eyes simmered as he looked at her.

Carmen started walking again and thankfully a breeze lifted, cooling her. At her side, his presence didn't let the silent exchange end. As they skirted the lake together, Carmen felt his attention intensify.

"One of the things I'd like to look into is developing some sort of scheme with the fishing rights. The owner of the manor has fishing rights to a stretch of the river. It's about three-quarters of a mile in length."

"I remember my father mentioning it, but I guess he never did anything about it."

"No, he didn't. It was your grandfather who set about making it official, but apart from the groundsmen and the occasional poacher nobody uses it. It's a beautiful stretch of the river and the estate could offer a scheme with the bed-and-breakfast in the village and the pub, too. A lot of visitors come to enjoy the surrounding countryside. We could offer day passes for fishing and hire equipment. The bed-and-breakfast would run it. At this end it would only need the groundsmen to monitor the situation. They already keep an eye out for poachers, anyway, so it wouldn't be an awful lot more work for them, and it'll engage the estate with the local hospitality businesses."

She rattled on in an attempt to ignore Rex's insistent presence, his brooding glances. She couldn't look at him when he was focused on her, so she directed his attention elsewhere. Then she noticed when she pointed things out, he looked at the place fondly.

A shiver ran down her spine. *Never trust Rex Carruthers*. It'd been her motto, and now here she was giving him a blueprint on how to improve the property. What if he refused to sell? What if he used his sexual hold over her to force her to capitulate, then stole her ideas for the place? When the doubts took hold, she drew to a halt. "Why do you even care what I plan to do with the place?"

"Stop worrying." He actually grew serious for a moment. "I enjoy watching you, and your enthusiasm is impressive. You deserve to be mistress of this place, you'll make it work. You're much more committed to it than I possibly could be." He glanced back toward the manor itself, his gaze shifting over it. "It's a grand old house, it really is, but my relationship with the place was brought up short twice. First when my parents split, then my father and I couldn't see eye-to-eye, so it was never going to work." His gaze returned to her and he was silent a moment as he considered her.

"If you truly believe that, then you'd arrange for the transfer papers to be prepared instead of holding me over a barrel with this silly arrangement of yours."

"A silly arrangement, is it?" He lifted his eyebrows and his mouth twitched in amusement as he looked at her.

So much for being serious. It hadn't lasted long, but then again she'd rather stupidly referred to the arrangement, which had automatically taken the subject back to sex. She could have slapped herself for being so stupid. "It's just because you can have any and every woman you want, that's why you've done this, to prove it to me."

"I told you why I did this. We had to. Too much wanting."

His tone was intimate, his voice lowered, and she felt herself melting under his persuasive reasoning. Part of her remained guarded, and that part of her rose up and told her to beware. "But I see how you look at the place—you do have a connection, you'll change your mind."

He laughed softly, reaching out to cup her cheek. "My dear Carmen," he murmured. "You're so prickly."

She gave a dismissive laugh. "You may think you know me, but you don't."

It was a knee-jerk reaction. He was right about her being prickly. She found it difficult to trust people. Especially when it came to him.

His expression changed. "Let me in, then. That's what this is about, these weekends together. We're both getting what we want. You get the house, I get to know you. Intimately. I always wanted to know you better."

She huffed in disbelief. "You have a weird way of showing it."

"Weird? Direct, maybe. I can't think of a better way of kicking aside a few barriers than making an agreement that involves us getting naked whenever we want."

Carmen steeled herself. "Playing games, it's what you do."

"Perhaps. But you seem to think I don't learn anything about you while we're…'playing games' as you call it." He stepped closer, and put his hand under her jaw, his thumb beneath her chin, lifting it so she was forced to meet his gaze. "I've already learned so much about you."

There was a suggestive accusation there in his expression and it triggered an electric response in her. Carmen struggled to find a retort, her emotions spinning.

"Think about it. Every time I touch you, pleasure you, you show me some facet of yourself you can never hide again. Within moments I can take us both back to that place, to revisit. That's how close we're getting." His hands moved, stroking down the sides of her waist and lower, around her hips. He backed her toward a nearby tree.

When she came into contact with it and felt the rough bark behind her, she let out a startled cry.

Rex responded by moving one hand over the fly on her jeans, before dipping down between her thighs. "You see, we're right back there, with you letting yourself go before my very eyes."

He was right, damn him, they were right back there. She looked away. She wasn't going to give in to his reasoning.

Did he really want to know her? The question made her ache with longing. Deep inside, in some long-hidden part of her, she wanted to trust him. Memories of the night before—when he had mastered her so thoroughly—shot through her mind.

His fingers stroked her through the fabric of her jeans. She whimpered under his exploration, but met his gaze. The look in his eyes grew hotter and more demanding, his lust tangible, as if he, too, was remembering.

The sound of her zipper opening was too real. "Stop it," she begged, "please."

"You don't mean that. I can see what you really want in your eyes."

"Don't tell me what I want." She squirmed in his grasp. However, the rough surface of the tree at her back stimulated her wildly, as if it was colluding with him to undermine her.

His knee was between hers, pinning her there while he moved his fingers inside her underwear. She gasped aloud when he cupped her mons. All the while, he stared at her from under hooded eyes, his lips pressed together as he explored her. It was too much. Thumping him with her fisted hands, she twisted in his grasp and attempted to break free, but her pussy was throbbing with arousal from the steady, rhythmic invasion of his fingers, making her fume. She turned her face away but he forced it back with one hand, then kissed her demandingly.

Her hand splayed against his chest, meaning to push him away, but the feeling of his hard chest beneath his T-shirt triggered another memory, one of him over her, naked, thrusting between her thighs. The situation echoed the same from the night before, but not fiercely enough. How could her body do this to her? Even while she squirmed, her mouth opened, taking his tongue, and before she knew it she was returning the kiss just as demandingly. Her hands roved over his shoulders and chest, clutching at him instead of pushing him away. Her hips rolled into his hand, enabling him easier access to her.

Murmuring encouragement, Rex stroked his finger over her swollen clit. "Relax," he whispered, "let it happen."

His voice, his actions—so persuasive. Carried away, she wrapped her arms around his neck when he kissed her mouth again. It was hard, hungry, insistent, and he was bruising her lips, but she wanted it. She lifted one knee against his thigh. He clasped it to his hip, holding her steady while he stroked her to orgasm.

She was close. Her head rolled against the bark of the tree.

A moan escaped her.

When he drew back, his expression was victorious. "I always knew you'd be like this."

Furious, she locked eyes with him, but it was too late to deny it, because her clit thrummed, her core spasmed and she came—suddenly, and violently, in his hand. Panting for breath, she closed her eyes and rested her head back on the tree.

"You look so good when you come. I have no idea why you fight it so."

"Because you're the most arrogant man I've ever met."

"What can I say? You bring out the worst in me."

Listening to his voice while her eyes were shut and her body was drifting on the release, she felt strangely dreamlike.

"And you make me hard."

The comment brought her sharply out of her dreamlike state.

When she opened her eyes, he had his hands flat to the tree on either side of her head, and he was studying her intently.

His eyes glittered. "Back to the house. Now."

That brought about a fresh wave of annoyance.

He studied her in silence, yet she knew what he wanted. Not just because he'd said it once already. He wasn't about to repeat it. He didn't have to. She could feel it, the silent demand, both a weighty instruction and an insistent tug, as if he held her on an invisible leash. Did he? The thought should have shamed her, should have made her balk. Instead, it turned her on, immensely.

He lowered one hand to her wrist, locked his fingers around it.

There was no doubt he meant to take this further. Immediately.

Carmen grappled with her fly, tugging it up, and shook her head.

"I don't think you're in any position to deny me," he said, and drew his free hand to his lips, where he licked his fingers clean.

Astonished at his blatant display, her cheeks flamed.

Then he tightened his grip on her wrist, and led her off at a pace.

CHAPTER SIX

"The trouble with this arrangement," Rex commented as he walked across Carmen's bedroom, minutes later, "is that I'm enjoying it rather too much."

He turned around to see her reaction.

Carmen stopped dead, standing on the patterned rug in the middle of the room, as if refusing to follow him any farther. "What are you saying?"

Rex sat down in the winged armchair in the square bay window of her room. It was the very spot where he'd left the dress for her the day before. He gestured at her. "Well, for a month you do everything I want, every weekend, absolutely anything and everything." He paused, allowing his message to sink in. "And in return for that you get my half of the property."

"I told you I'll pay you."

Those eyes of hers, such defiance. How delicious it was to see her fire.

"Oh, that won't be necessary. You'll have earned every tiny part of the property by the time I hand it over. Don't worry about the money."

She knotted her fingers together. "You're trying to embarrass me, Rex. That wasn't part of the bargain."

"I don't agree. Mostly because I don't seem to have to try very hard before you get embarrassed. I think you're embarrassment trigger and your arousal trigger are very close together." He lifted his shoulders in a shrug. "I can't help that, and neither can you."

She pressed her lips together. She was clearly annoyed, and yet he could also see she was acutely aroused. The hands-on treatment he'd given her out in the grounds had her poised for action. She was taut and watchful, barely waiting to be instructed. Rex took a deep breath and savored the heady atmosphere of sexual anticipation.

When she noticed, she hissed as if in objection.

Rex lifted an eyebrow. She lowered her eyelids, but watched him from beneath her lashes. Rex laughed. Had Carmen Shelby always had these withheld submissive desires? It hadn't been obvious before, of that he was certain. And the constant battle she was having with her needs—was that part of the package? Or was this dilemma of hers because she'd revealed her trigger to him, perhaps inadvertently? Whatever the reason, neither of them could put it back in the box now. No way. Now that he knew her little kinks and foibles he intended to play them out to their full extent.

"So what's the problem?" she demanded after he left her standing there in silence while he admired her.

"A month might not be enough."

She glared at him.

"It's day two and I'm loving every moment," he continued. "Seems such a shame to put an end date on it."

"You're winding me up."

"I'm being honest." He was. This was too good.

"In which case you lied to me. If you don't intend to stand up to your end of the deal, I'm walking out of here right now, and if I have to do that I promise you I'll only deal with you through a solicitor!"

Angry Carmen was hellishly hot.

"Is this the ballsy businesswoman speaking now, or are you saying you can't handle more than a month of this?"

Her eyes blazed.

"Seriously, aren't you enjoying our time together?"

"You know I am, in some weird fucked-up way." Her voice was low and barley audible, and she folded her arms across her chest. "But I want a limit on it, for the sake of my sanity."

Sanity? What did that really mean? He'd find out, all in good time. He knew he'd pushed her on the terms. "Fair enough. I suppose I'll have to stick to my word."

"It's only sex," she blurted, as if it was an afterthought.

"It is…and I must say I'm liking these kinky sex games of yours."

"Mine?"

"Yes. Yours. Okay, let's begin."

She rolled her eyes.

"I'd like you to prove to me how much you want the house and how hard you'd work to get it."

"Now you really *are* trying to humiliate me."

"Not at all. You said it made it easier for you when I took charge. Although I do think there's a part of you that likes the humiliation."

Oh, how her cheeks flamed.

Rex smiled. "Strip for me."

Instantly she began. Even though she looked at him resentfully, it was as if she didn't have the ability to refuse him. Rex allowed himself to get high on that concept. Carmen Shelby, his. The woman who was down to her underwear and looked like a captured nymph—dark eyes wide and expressive, her body outlined like a classical sculpture. Sprawling in the armchair, he watched as the sunlight from behind him dappled her skin with warmth during the slow reveal.

Her torso arched when she moved her hands behind her back and she undid her bra, peeling it away. Her breasts were tilted up, the nipples betraying her state of arousal. No matter what she said, she responded to being dominated. *Who had introduced her to this line of erotic behavior?* Rex wondered on it as he watched her roll her panties down her hips, revealing the soft curve of her pussy.

It wasn't a striptease. It was a woman getting undressed.

It was simple, and yet so much hotter than any striptease he'd ever witnessed. And he'd seen a few. She was under instruction to do so—that was the key. Her head was lowered, deferring to him. Yet still he felt her fire, her resistance. What a curiosity she was. It was her willingness to do as he instructed sexually that hit him so hard. Perhaps willingness wasn't exactly the right turn of phrase. She went with it, but there was underlying resentment in her eyes. It was obvious she did want to do these things, so why the black looks, the palpable tension?

She was an enigma, even more so than she ever had been.

Naked, she stepped forward, looking at him from under her lids. Her lashes were thick and dark, and sometimes they hid her thoughts and mood too well. Nevertheless, she was aroused, her body told him. Her nipples were dark as claret and knotted. Her arms didn't hang by her sides. One hand was against the front of her thigh, the other on the opposite hip. There was tension in her; she was ready to act. Was she anticipating his next instruction?

Rex liked the idea.

It was so tempting to continually take her to this place where she lowered her head and her eyes became dark with arousal and her breasts peaked. Effortless, and yet so hot. Still it nagged at Rex, her history. Had she lived with the man who'd played the Dom to her sub? How long had it gone on for? Had she loved the guy, whoever he was?

Rex rose to his feet and went for his belt, but when he began to undo it, Carmen lifted her head and looked at him directly, boldly even. Her lips were parted and she wore a hungry gaze.

"Ah, so you're willing to demonstrate?"

She nodded.

It flitted through his mind that it was a good job he hadn't known she would be like this. He always knew she was a sensual woman. But that mask—the independent facade she'd developed over the intervening years—had worried him at first. Not anymore. Not now he knew what lay behind it. His desire to test her, to push her, only grew. "Despite your apparent resistance, you look hellishly horny to me."

She pursed her lips.

"Are you horny?" He waited. "Carmen?"

"Yes." She stared at him. "It's just sex, isn't it?"

She was underlining the point. He took note and ran his hand over the bulk of his erection. "Just sex. So this is what you want, is it?"

She muttered under her breath.

Rex didn't catch what she said, but it amused him.

A sidelong glance captured his attention. It was a momentary gleam in her eyes, but he caught it, and it was the hottest thing he ever could've imagined. Her hunger, her raw desire. Power plumed in him. Especially when he nodded, and she quickly closed the space between them and dropped to her knees before him.

Her hands were on his belt. Her eyes glinted. It was fire he saw there, like she had something to prove. "Permission to demonstrate?"

"Permission granted."

Hastily she unbuttoned his fly, stroked her hand against the front of his jockey shorts, then latched her fingers over the waistband. There, she paused. When he met her upturned gaze, he nodded.

Carmen held the waistband tightly and then pulled his jockeys lower, to the tops of his thighs. When his cock stood out, she leaned in and stroked her cheek against its length from base to tip where she rested a kiss. The sigh she gave sounded like relief.

Rex rolled his head back.

A moment later her hands cupped his balls and squeezed.

His cock jerked up in her grasp. With her free hand, she embraced and stroked it again, then ran her tongue over the swollen crown.

"May I suck you?"

His balls tightened. "You think you can handle it?"

He rocked on his heels and his hands closed on her head, holding her gently as she sucked him into the warm cavern of her mouth.

Her tongue worked at the underside of his cock while she held the shaft and moved it in and out of her mouth, sucking him off.

REX

The question drummed at his temples—who taught you to be such a good sub? With effort, he pushed it back. Staring down at her, Rex felt her eagerness, her agility and talent pushing him dangerously close, and fast. Then she took him deeper, and the hand stroking his shaft moved. Instead, she gripped his hip, her other hand still massaging his balls.

"Need to stop," he rasped, "need to fuck you."

Carmen whimpered, and her nails drove into his buttock.

"I'm warning you." He stroked her head, afraid to overwhelm her.

She encouraged him on, and she was showing him so clearly what she wanted Rex couldn't hold back. A fierce orgasm racked him, his cock pumping into her mouth, just as she'd insisted.

Carmen rested back on her haunches and looked up at him—which looked sexy as hell, given her naked state, and his erection was going nowhere—and with an elegant maneuver, wiped a spilled drop from her mouth.

"You do realize I'll have to punish you for not stopping when I requested you do so." His pants and shorts had fallen around his ankles and he stepped out of them and kicked them away.

He wrapped his hand around the base of his cock, jerking it. She might have made him come, but it wasn't enough. Especially not with her squatting there, naked, with such a look in her eyes—the one that said: *You wouldn't dare.*

Her gaze drifted down to his cock, and while she watched him working it, a flush formed on her collarbone. The tight buds of her nipples grew more erect still.

"Get on your hands and knees immediately."

She did as instructed.

Rex paced around her, slowly massaging his erection as he absorbed the sight of her from all angles. She arched her back, displaying her beautiful derriere, and yet she hung her head. The way her breasts swayed made him want to cup them while he banged into her from behind.

He stepped behind her and put one foot between her legs. "Wider."

Carmen moaned. Resistance poured out of her, and yet she did as she was asked, placing her knees wide, opening up her delicious cunt for him to see. Her pussy lips were pink and swollen. She glistened there, clearly aroused.

Rex grabbed a condom from the dresser drawer.

Once the condom was on, he dropped to his knees. For a moment longer, he studied her glistening slit while he stroked the rubber down the length of his erection, then he had to be inside. With a thumb on either side of the dark hollow of her beautiful cunt, he opened her up, and eased the swollen head of his crown inside.

Carmen cried out, her head lifting and tossing.

His chest felt tight, as if the pleasure of her holding his cockhead snaked around his entire body. Her cunt was so hot and inviting.

He pushed deeper.

"Oh, God, Rex."

Her body writhed, but he locked his hands on her hips, holding her steady. Then he pushed her knees together with his own, so that he was totally in charge of her movements. When he pushed deeper still, she was tight and slick, and her body sucked him in.

"Easy." With his thumbs pressed deep against her buttocks, he forbade her to move.

"Rex?" Her head hung down, and he could feel her cunt palpating, squeezing around his erection rhythmically.

"So needy."

"Bloody hell," she shot back. "You've been driving me crazy. What the hell state do you expect me to be in after the past hour?"

"Nothing less than this."

That quieted her.

"We're in agreement, then. You're desperate for this." He eased out, and then thrust back in, deeper still, which caused her to cry out again. "And I'm more than ready to give it to you. Have I got that right?"

"Yes," she said. "Please."

"I do like to hear you ask so nicely, especially when you're on your knees like a bitch in heat with your arse in the air."

Muttering, she shoved her hips back.

Rex's balls lifted, tightened. "Who gave you permission to move?"

He slapped her arse.

"You did!" she cried out, and pumped her hips back and forth, working herself onto him vigorously.

Rex stared down at his cock being sheathed and unsheathed by her cunt and he decided to wait a moment and enjoy the view before he argued the point. She was milking him hard and fast, and even while his body readied to let rip inside her—to flatten her to the floor and fuck her senseless—he knew without a doubt a month of Carmen Shelby would never be enough.

CHAPTER SEVEN

"Well, I wasn't expecting to see you in this early today." Estelle Black, the managing director of *Objet d'Art*, stopped to take a good look at Carmen as she arrived in the offices on Monday morning. Estelle had her coffee cup in her hand and appeared to be going to the kitchen for her first caffeine shot of the day.

Carmen's heels clicked as she walked down the corridor to join Estelle. She glanced into the open office doorways as she passed, waving in greeting when she caught anyone's eye.

"Came back last night, as planned." Carmen smiled. "I gave you my word. I'm determined these property negotiations aren't going to interrupt my day-to-day working schedule."

Estelle looked at her thoughtfully. "We can manage. This is an important family obligation you're dealing with. The world won't fall apart if you take some time away from the business."

"I know." Carmen knew what she was thinking. Estelle had been the managing director of *Objet d'Art* for many years, and had worked with Carmen's mother before her. She was always nagging her to take some time off and have a proper holiday. When Charles Carruthers passed on and his will presented an issue that had to be dealt with, Estelle had once again suggested she take time away. They were dear friends as well as close business associates. In many ways, the employees at *Objet d'Art* HQ were Carmen's family now.

Estelle stepped closer and scrutinized Carmen, smiling as she did so. "I must say, the country air seems to have done you good. You have quite the healthy glow about you."

Carmen's thoughts flitted to Rex. It wasn't just the country air. She'd just had the most stimulating weekend of her life, at Rex's hands. "The Oxfordshire countryside is very good for a girl's complexion, as you'll soon see. Once I get the house in shape you'll have to make plans to visit."

"Sounds heavenly."

"Bring the kids, they'll love it." It was what Carmen wanted most of all, Burlington Manor filled with visitors and happiness.

Estelle pouted. "Can't I leave them at home?"

Carmen chuckled. "Believe me, if you bring them with you, they'll have so much to explore you won't even know they're there."

"It's a deal." Estelle nodded at her coffee cup. "Give me a mo. I'll bring you your espresso."

"Thanks." Carmen headed into her office.

Was it really only a couple of days ago she was last here? It felt as if so much more time had passed. She deposited her personal belongings on the table inside the door and strode over to the desk. Before she sat down, she glanced out at the view, as she always did. The offices were in a busy part of Kensington, in an old Georgian building that had been divided up to create practical commercial offices in the 1980s. Sylvia Shelby had invested in the building and the company now owned all of it, occupying one-third and renting out the rest of the space. The interior had been remodeled twice since then, and had a much lighter, airy feel than Carmen's first memories of the place, when she was brought in here as a child to see Mummy's office.

It was a very different type of Georgian building to Burlington Manor but the similarity always struck her poignantly. It was the reason Sylvia Shelby and Charles Carruthers had met, their appreciation for Georgian architecture. Sylvia had gone to a lecture at Oxford University. Charles had been there to talk about Burlington Manor. At the coffee session afterward, they chatted. Charles had invited her to visit the manor and their shared interests had become the foundation of a beautiful relationship.

Now Carmen was dividing her time between the two places, so similar yet so different. *Like Rex and me.* The notion made her smile. There had been familiarity, but there had also been so much to learn. They'd both changed in between, and there were aspects of each other they never knew about. So much more to discover, perhaps.

Despite the fact they were sleeping together, she felt as if they were scratching the surface. They were definitely at odds, and keeping each other at arm's length while they negotiated. *Did I really sleep with him for Burlington Manor?* On the one hand, it was an inconceivable method of doing business. She considered herself morally upstanding in such matters. On the other hand, he was right. They had to burn out the attraction they felt for each other all those years ago, which had been left unfulfilled for so long.

It certainly wasn't unfulfilled now.

The nature of the exchange thrilled her. Aside from the sexual fulfillment, and the end reward—the manor itself—she felt empowered. Gloriously female, somehow. It never would have occurred to her that offering herself, and exploring her sexuality under such circumstances, would make her feel enriched, but it had. She felt more powerful, more feminine and more aware of herself in every way.

Is that what Estelle had noticed?

Do I have a healthy glow? Carmen stepped into her adjacent bathroom and checked her reflection. Well, it wasn't every weekend she spent at the hands of a sexual master, and Rex Carruthers had totally proved himself in that department. As she allowed herself to linger on the pictures of him she'd already stored in memory, the week ahead suddenly stretched endlessly like a barren wasteland. Her body already ticked faster in anticipation of Friday night and their next encounter. It was going to be hard to keep her mind off it, but she had to be practical. This was her life, and the arrangement with Rex was short-term.

She had to keep a handle on it, because once he was satisfied he'd be gone in a heartbeat. Like he had all those years ago when he'd got bored with the manor and everything it entailed. For a while there, she felt sure he was beginning to bond with the place again. When they'd walked the grounds, she'd noticed him looking around with fondness. His lineage was perhaps making him feel a tad guilty. By the end of the weekend, however, he only seemed concerned with her and their ongoing arrangement.

"Friday night," he'd repeated as they said their goodbyes, and it had sounded like a promise, "we'll pick up where we left off."

"Twenty-five percent deposit exchanged," she'd said, trying to match up to his cocky attitude. "Three more weekends and the manor is mine." She reiterated the terms to see if he reacted.

"Three more weekends," he repeated, looking her over as if he was anticipating everything that might occur between them. "I look forward to it."

He stood by as she got into her taxi, and then he climbed into his Maserati Gran Turismo, ready to depart. The Maserati had overtaken her taxi a while later. The fact he hadn't lingered at the manor after she'd gone reassured her it was just a diversion for him and he had no long-standing doubts about selling to her.

The erotic nature of their relationship was the biggest surprise. She'd always known he would be a good lover, but the taut dynamic between them was something she'd never experienced. It was a sexual nirvana that would be hard to forget, after the affair was over. Then again, she'd never forgotten him all these years anyway.

Had she always had an obsession? If she was honest with herself, yes. But he was right, this is what they needed, to burn the old flame out. For Rex it was simply a game, and he would walk away. She just had to stay focused on the fact it was a trade-off for the house. She would remain emotionally safe if she stuck to the plan.

"Espresso delivery for Carmen Shelby," Estelle called out from the office.

Carmen emerged from the bathroom. "Thanks. I need that."

When she took up her seat, Estelle lingered. "So, did your stepbrother agree to sign over his share?"

Estelle had gleaned the briefest outline of circumstances from Carmen after the reading of the will. It was enough to keep her fascinated.

Carmen reached for her coffee cup. "More or less. He wants to spend a few weekends there, to say goodbye to the place. That's all it is."

And me. Say hello, wave goodbye. That's all it is.

Rex parked his Maserati in his designated spot outside the workspace he rented for his business in South London. The rest of the lot was already full. He was running a bit late, because he'd been busy making plans for the following weekend.

Climbing out of the car, he locked up and headed to the entrance. The building was simple and unassuming on the outside, but inside, Rex had created an energized environment for the small team of Slipstream staff. When he'd first hired them, he'd asked them about their most inspiring moments from Formula One racing. The two design engineers who were the core of the company listed three events each. By the time they started work, Rex had installed larger-than-life photographic prints of their favorite memories on the interior walls.

Rex often wished he could do the same on the outside of the building so that it would appeal to potential clients on first sight. It was what went on inside the building that mattered. Pretty soon he wanted to open up the place to visiting clients. It was on the to-do list. Right now, he had other things on his mind.

Like Carmen Shelby.

He had a lot to prepare for the following weekend. He wanted to help Carmen enjoy their time together more. He wasn't worried about the sex. She really let rip then. All the barriers came down and it was spectacular to witness. However, she was often tense around him when they were chatting, or negotiating. She'd been most at ease while talking about the way things were in the past, when times were happy in the house. It would be good to recreate that, even if only for a short time. It would also be good to bring some atmosphere back into the old place.

"Morning, Jerry, how goes it?"

"Rex, good morning." Jerry looked up from his workstation with a grin.

"You look pleased with yourself," Rex commented.

"We've got news. Nikhil Rashid has taken the bait."

"Ah, that *is* good news." Rashid was an up-and-coming racing enthusiast, the sort of client they wanted to hook up with at an early stage. Rashid was looking to put together a Formula 3000 racing team and had contacted them about his design needs. "He's ready to talk business?"

"Yes. He said he'd like to book a meeting, two weeks from Friday." Jerry paused, and held up his hands. "Don't worry. I said we'd go."

"Excellent work." That gave them plenty of time to perfect their presentation and organize the best display for their components. "We're going to be busy."

In one sense it was great news. In another it was unfortunate timing. Aside from wanting to spend every moment with the lovely Carmen, he'd realized he was going to have to look into his father's paperwork. Mrs. Amery had informed him the library at Burlington Manor was sinking under the weight of old ledgers and accounts. His father had used the library as his office throughout his life, and he rarely threw anything away. Rex didn't want Carmen to have to deal with that when she took the place over.

He was also dealing with the unremitting challenge of breaking down the boundaries of the deal he'd set up. He wanted to get Carmen to see him in London. He'd asked her before they'd parted, but she'd refused, claiming she'd be too busy. It was a need that just wouldn't go away, though. Why? Because he liked the idea of being with her, not just more often, but also after their negotiations for the manor were over. He decided she would be happy there, but he didn't like the idea of a line in the sand after which he'd never see her again. Cutting all ties with her was becoming increasingly unrealistic.

Another greeting drew him back from his thoughts. Lance, the second engineer, emerged from the catering area with two large mugs. "The kettle's still warm, boss."

"Cheers. How are things with the little one?" Lance had become a father for the second time, three weeks earlier.

"Mother and baby are doing well, and I'm beginning to get used to minimal sleep patterns."

"Good man. I wouldn't want to find you asleep over your desk, though, so if you do need to take time off, flag it up."

Lance nodded. "We've got a lot going on here right now."

The entrance door clicked open again and Ayo joined them, several bags of take-out sandwiches clutched in his hand. He grinned when he saw Rex. Rex gave him a high five. Ayo—who more than lived up the West African meaning of his name: joy—could light up a room with his smile.

"Is Bertha ready to go?" Rex asked.

Bertha, their demo machine—a stripped-down racing car with which they could show clients their parts in action—was Ayo's responsibility. "Too right. I need to hire the trailer, but otherwise she's ready for her big show."

"Good stuff." Rex looked at his three teammates. "I'll be here as much as I can during the lead in, but I have to be back at my dad's place in between times."

Rex quickly calculated. If the meeting with Rashid was two weeks from Friday, that might impinge on his plans, but he'd have to fly with it. They'd been working toward this potential contract for a long while, and he would somehow make it fit together with his time with Carmen.

He couldn't afford to waste a second of that.

CHAPTER EIGHT

On Friday afternoon, Carmen darted along the platform at Paddington station, her heart racing. Once she'd boarded the train for Beldover and located her seat, she got comfy and tried to relax. It was impossible to do so.

As the train pulled out of the station she crossed her legs high on the thigh and closed her eyes, hoping that the rhythmic swaying of the carriage would help her relax. All it did was make her aware of the anticipation that had been building inside her all week long.

She let her thoughts wander. She'd been doing that a lot.

Scarcely five minutes had gone by without her thinking about Rex, and what they'd done—and what they would do when they were alone again. At night she couldn't sleep for thinking about him, her body wired and restless as she remembered every detail.

As the train passed out of greater London and into the Oxfordshire countryside, she kept glancing at her watch. By the time it finally pulled up in Beldover, she was already at the carriage door, bags in hand.

Andy Redmond was there to meet her.

She climbed into the taxi eagerly. There was no point in denying it; she could hardly wait for her time with Rex to roll around.

It was with dismay she found the situation different.

As the taxi approached the house she saw the front door stood open and several cars were parked outside.

"Mr. Carruthers didn't want me to say anything before we got here, but I took a carload up from the station earlier on," Andy informed her, adjusting his flat cap so that he could address her in the rearview mirror. "He wanted the party to be a surprise for you."

A surprise party. Carmen's heart sank. "How lovely," she lied.

She didn't like not knowing. What the hell was Rex up to?

"Mr. Carruthers made a block booking at the bed-and-breakfast in the village for your out-of-town guests," Andy continued. "Just like the old times, it is."

Why did that annoy her so? Because she both did and didn't want it to be like old times. She wanted the house and the happy memories, but she was surprised Rex wanted it to be like old times. Maybe it was part of him saying goodbye to the place. Whatever it was, it unnerved her.

Besides which she was massively disappointed they weren't going to be alone. Anticipation had been building all week, and she'd given up ignoring it. There was simply no denying she was horny as hell and dying for him to take her in hand again as soon as she got to the manor. On the train journey, she'd unleashed her imagination, which now meant she had to walk into the house and face a crowd of people while keyed up and ready for something entirely different.

Damn you, Rex.

The car drew to a halt. When she went to get her purse out to pay Andy, he put up his hand again. "Mr. Carruthers has booked me for the whole evening and paid in advance. I'll be ferrying some people back to Beldover later on."

Rex had thought of everything. She climbed out of the car and stared at the house. The front door was wedged open and she could see figures milling about inside. Music spilled from an open window. She tried to brace herself, to be prepared and not look too devastated, but with every step she took toward the door her unease grew.

How could Rex do this without consulting her? It was fifty percent ownership each at the moment, and he'd effectively organized a party in her home. And what did it mean? Was he bored with things already? Did he want to stir things up by showing he owned the place, too—or, worse still, had he changed his mind and this was a signal he was here to stay?

She climbed up the steps to the house, pressed her lips together tightly and adopted an amenable smile, in order to stop herself going in there and asking them all to leave—whoever they were. Most likely Rex's racing set, people she wouldn't feel comfortable with at all, taking over the manor. This was typical of him, though. Unpredictable Rex had pulled the rug out from under her feet again. She'd actually been looking forward to this weekend, anticipating being with him, and he'd gone and ruined it.

Andy tucked in behind her and deposited her weekend case inside the door. Carmen turned to thank him and, as she did, he waved beyond her. She glanced back, and saw Rex. There was a group of people chatting to him, but he must have been watching out for Andy to arrive with her in tow.

REX

As Andy headed out, she saw Rex give his excuses in order to make his way over to her. He embraced her with his hands around her shoulders and kissed her on both cheeks.

"Surprise." He smiled at her expectantly.

"Yes, isn't it?"

Rex's expression quickly changed. "What's up?"

"Apart from the fact we have joint ownership of the property and you have opened it up to all and sundry without a word of warning…apart from that, well, you've shifted the goalposts on the agreement."

"What goalposts?" He looked genuinely confused.

He really was expecting her to be over the moon because he'd thrown a party. She'd have been much more over the moon if they'd picked up where they'd left off the week before. As much as she hated to admit it, she wanted more of his intimacy instead of this public display. It smacked of possession. "I agreed to four weekends with you in this house, you and me, negotiating the property deal."

"We will be…negotiating…again very soon, my dear," Rex promised, and there was a wicked gleam in his eye. "Don't worry about that."

Carmen fumed silently and struggled to find the appropriate thing to say—something that wouldn't give him an even bigger ego. "What I mean is, I agreed to harangue this out with you, under certain terms and conditions, and now you've changed things. Filling the house with people was not on the agenda, nor do I find it conducive to our financial negotiations."

He arched his brows. "So businesslike."

She bristled. He sounded disapproving. "A pity you aren't, too."

"Hey, I did this because you said you wanted it to be like it was, with parties and people in the house."

Carmen had said that, but she meant her friends, her parties. "You should've asked me, or at least informed me of your intentions."

Rex frowned. "I thought this would make you happy."

Happy, to be invaded by his buddies? But as she glanced around— which she did to make a point—she realized she did recognize many of the faces he'd gathered. It was the old set, people they used to knock about with years ago when they lived at the house together. There were friends from Rex's university days, and neighbors, and people she knew from her final school days at the local secondary school in nearby Leamington.

"Our hostess, the lady of the evening, the lovely Carmen." It was Nathaniel Dean who said that as he approached, and his warm smile undid some of the unease she felt.

With her animosity to Rex temporarily shelved, she welcomed Nate's embrace. "Nate. I haven't seen you in ages."

"You look amazing." Nate looked her up and down and gave a sigh. "Carmen Shelby, totally the business diva. It's good to see you again."

Carmen looked at him and nodded. It was good to see him. Nate was Rex's best buddy from university and he often used to come to the manor during the holidays, for weekends. Nate was the cricket buff, and whenever he was around, the lads would gather people to play cricket on the lawns at the front of the house. "And you, what are you up to these days?"

"Followed in my dad's footsteps, sad to say. I vowed I never would, but boring old banking turned out not to be so boring, after all."

"And the rest? Are you married? Girlfriend?"

Nate pushed his hand through his hair. "Bit of a sore point…the fiancée and I split up recently."

"Oops. Sorry."

"Don't be. Besides, gives me a chance to chat up beautiful women like you."

Carmen laughed.

When she glanced back at Rex, he was looking at her with an expression that seemed to say, I told you so.

"Mingle," Rex instructed her when Nate moved on, "you might even enjoy yourself." With that he gave her a swift slap on the arse, propelling her in the direction of the large sitting room, the biggest reception area in the house, where most of the guests seemed to have gathered.

"You've got a damn cheek."

Rex grinned, and then left her to "mingle," as he put it.

In the large sitting room, Mrs. Amery was supervising, but there was a long table set out as a bar at the far end of the room, and a man she didn't know was stationed behind it. Had Rex hired catering in for the event? Carmen had spoken to Mrs. Amery earlier in the day, and she hadn't said a word about it. If Rex had come down heavily on them and made it sound like the treat he thought it was, Mrs. Amery wouldn't have thought twice about it.

"Miss Carmen, hello." It was Leanne, and she looked elated as she carried a tray of canapés through the crowd. "Isn't it wonderful? It's like a housewarming party."

A housewarming party the owner didn't know about, Carmen thought wryly to herself. "Isn't this outside your working hours?"

"Oh, I don't mind. In fact, we've had less to do this week. Mr. Rex brought people in, you see. Mrs. Summerfield said it was like having a holiday. They arrived in this amazing truck with these high-tech refrigerated shelves. Custom-made trays with delicious food ready to go." Leanne nodded at the canapés.

Feeling rather sheepish—given Leanne's enthusiasm for the event—Carmen looked down at the tray. It was top-notch food, first-class catering. She helped herself to some dim sum.

"Mrs. Amery said he was on the phone every day organizing things," Leanne continued. "He said he wanted it to be perfect for you."

Carmen's heart sank. He'd been trying to please her, he really had. And she'd been churlish and awkward, much like the week before when he'd given her the dress and she'd reacted so poorly. It was only to be expected, given Rex was unpredictable and couldn't be trusted. But both times she thought the worst of him when he'd been trying to do something for her. *Not without strings*, she reminded herself. Yes, everything came with strings when it came to Rex Carruthers. Strings and complications.

When he checked on her later in the evening, she'd been chatting with two of the Beldover women she'd known at school. Both were married with kids and were delighted to hear she was going to be in the area again. It felt good, and when Rex joined her, she clasped his arm. "Thank you, it's lovely."

Mercifully he didn't gloat. "I'm glad."

Did she see a shadow pass through his eyes? It disturbed her. Had he been upset by her reaction? "I'm sorry—" she lowered her voice for his ears only "—it was just such a shock when I was expecting to be...alone with you."

"As long as you're enjoying it I'm happy."

"I am." She smiled. She really was.

Then a familiar face beyond him caught her eye. She froze. "You invited Amanda Mason?"

Rex took a sip from the bottle of Italian beer he held. He didn't even look Amanda's way. "Yes, of course. You were best buddies at school."

He just stood there, nonchalant as anything, saying that. Carmen couldn't believe it. But he didn't know she was aware the two of them had some sort of relationship back then. Carmen had unintentionally discovered they'd slept together, here in the manor. It had broken her heart.

"Can I get you another wine?" He took the empty glass from her hand.

"No, thanks."

He looked so caring. She forced a smile.

Amanda was on her way over.

"Go, mingle," Carmen told him. There was no way she could face the pair of them together, not without a few minutes to prepare for it.

Rex strolled off.

Amanda's gaze went in his direction.

Carmen sighed.

Amanda Mason had been her best friend for a long while. When Carmen transferred to the secondary school in the neighboring town of Leamington, she and Amanda had hitched up because they were from Beldover territory, so they traveled to and from school together. They began to hang out, outside school hours. Amanda was a wild child, and they used to run her parents ragged up at their farmland, borrowing the quad bikes and churning up the lane when they were bored. They'd been good pals, but their close friendship had been hard to maintain after Rex slept with Amanda.

It was jealousy. Carmen hurt, plain and simple.

It would have destroyed their friendship completely if it had continued, but Rex split with his dad shortly after and then he was gone from their lives. Until now. Even after Carmen had left for university, she'd stayed in touch with Amanda for a while. Amanda had even come down to London and they went out clubbing, but once Carmen had committed to learning her mother's business inside out, that came first and she didn't have time for a lot else.

Amanda arrived at Carmen's side, even though she'd been watching Rex. She wrapped her arm around Carmen's waist possessively, drawing her closer. "It's wonderful to have you back," she said, and then glanced back toward Rex.

Carmen wondered, somewhat bitterly, if anything ever changed. Amanda had been a great friend, except when Rex was on offer. Then all she could do was push past Carmen to get to him. "How are you keeping these days? Still at home?"

Amanda grimaced. "Afraid so. I moved out for a while, when I got married."

"Married? I never heard."

"It didn't last long enough to talk about."

"I'm sorry."

"Don't be. I don't know what I was thinking, marrying a vicar."

Carmen couldn't restrain her reaction; she burst out laughing. "Amanda Mason, a vicar's wife?"

Amanda grinned. "I told you it wasn't worth discussing."

"Oh, no, I'm sure it is. We'll have to get together so you can fill me in on all the sordid details." Carmen was tickled at the thought.

"Yes, we ought to get together." Again Amanda's gaze sidled over toward Rex. "Life suddenly looks a whole lot more interesting now that you guys are back in town."

When Carmen followed her gaze, Rex looked over and waved at them both.

"Never was there such a fine man in Beldover parish," Amanda said, apparently to herself.

"Was it the Beldover vicar you got hitched with?" Carmen asked, hoping to blot out memories evoked by the silent communication across the reception room. She figured it couldn't be the local vicar because he was in his late sixties.

"Good Lord, no. He was the new vicar in Leamington last year. Everyone was talking about him, so I had to go check him out."

"Sounds as if you checked him out pretty thoroughly."

Amanda's attention was elsewhere, but it was mainly on Rex. "I couldn't resist. Biggest mistake of my life. Never mind, the divorce has come through now so I can do as I please again and I don't have to worry about shocking the Women's Institute or the upstanding members of the parish."

Carmen looked again at Rex. Biggest mistake of my life? She knew that feeling. How had she managed to fall into this situation when she knew what he was like? There were several women buzzing around him now, plus Amanda was waiting to pounce.

Carmen didn't torture herself by watching when Amanda gravitated in his direction, joining the scrum of women around him. She wandered away, took some time out before she mingled again. It was just like it always was, believing he was flirting with her, except now he'd taken things to a whole new level. Even though she'd vowed not to get emotionally involved, it was fast becoming apparent she was, and even a few weekends together was a big mistake.

Within the hour, Amanda was back at Carmen's side. She was loaded, and she had that look about her—a look Carmen remembered well. She was on a mission, and usually there was a man at the end of it.

"Tell me," Amanda asked, "is this a permanent arrangement, you two sharing this place?"

Carmen wondered if Rex had informed everybody of their personal business, or whether Amanda had wheedled it out of him. She did have a knack with men. "We haven't finalized anything as yet. At the moment this is just a temporary arrangement."

"It must be so difficult for you, poor love." Amanda peered into Carmen's eyes.

"Difficult? Oh, well, yes, deciding the future of the house is a big thing. For everyone involved. Even the staff are in limbo until we come to an agreement."

Amanda smirked. "No, no. I meant it must be difficult having to be around Rex Carruthers, especially after he rejected you so horribly."

Carmen froze. Every atom of her body warned her not to respond, not to let Amanda rile and provoke her. *Don't let her get to you.* She repeated the instruction several times over, but it wasn't working.

"Don't be silly," she managed to say.

Amanda knew about Carmen's crush on Rex, but that had been overruled now. Far from rejected this time—in fact, quite the contrary. It was a defensive reaction, but it was the truth. She wasn't going to broadcast it to Amanda, though. No matter how much her pride wanted to blurt it out, she didn't want her personal business spread all over Oxfordshire.

Amanda waited for more.

"We're adults, we're old friends, and we have to sort out an inheritance issue." She shrugged and took a gulp of wine.

Amanda snorted. "You can't fool me so easily, Carmen Shelby. Anyone with two brain cells to rub together can see you've still got the hots for him. It was written all over you the moment you walked in the door."

Amanda had been observing? Carmen felt trapped. "That's not the case."

She knew she could handle it and keep her facade, but the conversation was rubbing at old and familiar hurts. Most of all she wanted to react badly, tell Amanda exactly what they'd been doing and there had been no rejection involved. Luckily it was in her nature to be guarded and cautious.

"Rex is a free spirit, even you know that." Carmen couldn't resist the little barb, although it was likely too subtle for Amanda given her current state of inebriation. "He's not the sort of man to get tangled up with for long."

The comment was a lament, too. *I should've known better.* This sort of thing was inevitable when she let her emotions become involved with a man like Rex Carruthers.

Amanda knocked back the remaining wine in her glass and deposited the empty on a tray as one of the catering staff went past. "Oh, I'd happily get tangled up with him again. He was bloody good in the sack." She smiled smugly. "Of course, you wouldn't know that. Poor little Carmen, left on the shelf."

REX

Mustering every bit of pride she owned, Carmen braced herself. She'd had enough. "It's a good job I don't give a damn what you think. You really have become more cruel and twisted over the years."

The swipe about being left on the shelf was the last straw. She was alone out of choice. Besides, the only reason Amanda was able to use that as a weapon was because she had a failed marriage on her résumé.

Nevertheless, it took Carmen's deepest reserves to stand there and speak so boldly, when inside she was crumbling. Because everything Amanda inferred was true in one sense or another. Rex had rejected her, and now he was only sleeping with her to burn out the old desire between them. Circumstances had made it convenient for him to do. He hadn't pursued her before. He hadn't even kept in touch.

I know all these things, so it shouldn't hurt.

But it hurt because she wanted him. Carmen didn't want to be here with these people, not in their weekend time. She wanted to be here with Rex. Alone. *I want what I was promised.* Yes, whatever the circumstances, she wanted every moment of their time. Possessive, angry emotions threatened to overwhelm her. She wanted to run, but she forced herself to stay. She'd tough this out, and then she could step away having maintained her dignity.

"Oh, look, Rex is waving at me," Amanda said, swaying as she did so.

"Good for you," Carmen muttered.

Amanda swung around to face her. "Suck it up, buttercup. I'll be screwing him again before you even get off the starting grid."

It hurt too much.

Carmen turned and walked away.

CHAPTER NINE

The friendly wave and the forced smile Carmen gave Rex as she disappeared from the party didn't fool him for a moment.

Something was badly wrong.

She'd seemed to relax over the course of the evening, which was a mercy after the fraught tension she'd given off when she'd arrived. Things hadn't gone exactly to plan, and Rex regretted organizing the party. Later, when he'd seen her enjoying herself and happily chatting with the guests, he felt a bit better about it. He was still eager to get her on her own and explain things properly. He'd seen her expression change as she chatted with Amanda. He'd been watching. And when Carmen headed off, there was such a pained look in her eyes that he felt it physically.

It hit him like a lumbar punch.

What had Amanda said to her?

Amanda had always been out of control. In retrospect he probably shouldn't have invited her, but he thought she might have matured. Sometimes she used to screw with people's heads for entertainment. In his youth it had a certain appeal; he'd even identified with it. Now, it appalled him. It made him wonder if he'd been as bad as she was. His instinct was to boot her out, but Rex wanted to know what had happened. He didn't have to wait long to find out.

When Carmen slipped away, Amanda shrugged and sauntered his way, obviously trashed and on the prowl.

"I see Carmen's as frigid and frustrated as ever."

Irritated, Rex shook his head. "You don't know what you're talking about."

"Oh, I do. She used to share everything with me, sad little virgin that she was, fixated on her stepbrother."

Too much information. Rex tried to process it while he decided what to say. He was fuming. She'd obviously said something hurtful to Carmen. In fact, she was still running off at the mouth, loading on the insults about Carmen being a frustrated spinster because of her unrequited desire for the unattainable stepbrother.

REX

"Poor little rich girl, Carmen Shelby, harboring fantasies about the man she could never have, the one who never wanted her."

Conversations nearby ceased as heads turned in Amanda's direction. Her voice had been getting louder and she was getting theatrical with it.

Rex fought the urge to silence her by putting a hand over her mouth. Perversely, he wanted to hear what she had to say.

"Amanda, stop it." It was Nate.

Amanda's head swung in his direction and she gave a harsh laugh. "No way, I'm having fun. Me and sexy Rexy have to catch up."

"We're here as friends," Nate continued. "It's not long since Rex buried his father and he's trying to get things back to normal here. For God's sake, try to keep your twisted sense of fun under control."

Rex didn't need Nate to watch out for him, but right then his thoughts weren't ordered and he appreciated a second.

"She's too weak for a man like you," Amanda stated while looking up at Rex. Brazenly she met Rex's stare and smiled, ignoring Nate.

"Carmen's the strongest woman I know," Rex said. "She stepped in and took on the challenge of her mother's business when she was barely twenty-one."

"I'm not talking about business, Rex."

The woman was taking such pleasure in having all their attention on her. Then she grasped Rex's arm.

Rex jerked free, reacting. He no longer cared who saw and heard. "What the hell did you say to her?"

Amanda smirked. "Just pointed out what she was missing. Same as it ever was, poor frigid little Carmen, chaste as a nun dreaming about the event."

"Don't be ridiculous." Barely withheld anger beat at the back of his temples. "You're more wrong than you'll ever know and you're way out of line."

Amanda laughed. "Carmen had a crush on you for years and she was so uptight she couldn't do anything about it. From the look of it, that situation doesn't seem to have changed. Ask yourself how many lovers she's had."

How many lovers? There were so many things he wanted to deny, but the information was too sudden, too intense, for him to verbalize what he felt. His primary instinct was to protect Carmen, and it was more powerful than anything he'd ever felt. That confused him, because it wasn't something he'd ever known before.

Storm in a teacup, all you have to do is tell Amanda to bugger off and get Carmen back on side. It wasn't so simple, because Amanda's comments had raised so many questions for him.

Had Carmen wanted him so much, all these years? She'd seemed reluctant at first to satisfy the lust that'd been between them years ago, yet set on having the manor. He knew there was chemistry, they were attracted to each other. Sex simply had to happen between them, they both knew it. God knows he was playing into it now by bargaining with her for what he'd always wanted a taste of. Was it more, though, and if so why couldn't she tell him?

Amanda was on a roll, aware she had the attention of everyone in the room. Beyond, the music faded out of significance, the tension in the hallway so strong it seemed to muffle the sound.

"Her loss." She lifted her brows suggestively. "She got you all wound up and then couldn't put out the goods, but I managed to make it up to you, didn't I, Rex?"

Rex's hands fisted. *Jesus, is that what she'd said to Carmen to upset her?* He wanted to kick himself. This gathering was meant to be a surprise for Carmen, an event to bring life into the house again and make her smile. He'd made a major error. "Were you always this much of a bitch?"

He said it loud enough for everyone to hear.

Amanda's expression morphed from smugness to shock then spite.

"I think you should leave now," he added.

"Don't worry, I'm going. Men, dense as dirt." Amanda spat her parting comment at him and pulled her car keys out of her clutch bag as she turned away.

Rex arrested her with a hand on her shoulder. "Amanda, you're drunk."

"So what if I am?"

"You may have no sense of responsibility to people you call friends, but some of us do. You're not driving. Nate, would you care to escort Amanda home?"

"I'm not going home," she declared. "I'll find a better party."

Nate was already at her side, taking charge.

Rex nodded at him.

Amanda laughed. "Silly cow, she's ruined the party you put on for her."

"One person has ruined the evening, but it wasn't Carmen," Rex retorted. "It was you, and only you. You're a drama queen and an attention seeker and you don't give a damn who you upset along the way. Now get out and don't come back unless it's to offer an apology."

REX

The look she gave him was full of spite.

It didn't touch him.

Rex covered the upstairs of the manor in long strides, searching for Carmen. She wasn't in her room, or his. Thankfully she hadn't driven there, or he'd be checking on her car. Had she left the grounds? As soon as it occurred to him, he raced downstairs to the boot room and grabbed a flashlight from the storage unit there. Once he'd located it, he unlocked the back door and headed out into the night, sweeping the light back and forth as he went. He went down to the lakeside, where she sometimes used to go to be alone. No sign of her. In the moonlight, he saw the boathouse and made his way over. It was empty.

By the time he got back up to the manor, he could see headlights making their way down the private driveway beyond the house, the cars headed in the direction of the village or beyond. Back in the boot room, he locked the door and counted to ten.

Where are you?

He'd been all over the house. There was nowhere else.

He took one last glance outside, and when he looked along the building from the boot room, he caught sight of the low glow of light given out by the night heaters in the conservatory. They were left on timers for the tropical plants in there.

Of course, the conservatory.

Carmen often used to go there to be on her own and read. She loved the greenery more than anyone else in the house. Apart from a brief wander through it on his initial return to the manor—when he'd familiarized himself with the whole house again—Rex hadn't been back there. Could she be in there now?

He made his way back through the house and, as he glanced into the reception rooms, he saw Mrs. Amery and Leanne were already busy with the clean-up operation, even though a couple of the guests still lingered. Rex headed quickly down the corridor before they could waylay him.

The double casement glass doors were closed, and he peered into the gloom but couldn't see anything. Quietly, he opened the doors and went inside. The smell of earth and sap immediately filled his senses. He padded across the terra-cotta-tiled floor and down to the far end where he remembered she used to go. In the far corner of the space you could see right across the countryside beyond.

Sure enough she was there, perched on a work surface used for potting plants. Beneath the solid worktop where shelves lined with pots ready for seedlings. It was her favorite spot, and he berated himself for not thinking of it earlier.

It was also the place where they'd nearly made love. He'd found her there then, and they got stoned and she'd put her hand on his chest, looking up at him with an invitation in her eyes. They'd kissed—and a long-awaited kiss it was, too—and it tripped something in them both. Unbridled lust. She'd plucked at his clothing with her hands, and he lifted her and sat her onto that very work surface. He'd stood between her legs, his hands wrapped around her thighs. When he asked her what she needed, she told him how much she wanted him.

Just remembering the occasion gave Rex a semi.

Now they'd been apart one week and Rex wanted her badly. What had he been thinking of arranging for other people to be around? He'd put space between them. That had to be mended. These weekends were far too precious.

Nearby the place where she sat, a night heater glowed in the gloom, just enough to illuminate her outline in the corner. She'd abandoned her heels and sat with her stocking feet up on the work surface.

Rex put his hands in his pockets and walked closer, as casually as he could. As he closed in on her, she sat up properly, dangling her feet to the floor. Her face was still shrouded in darkness, but the light from the heater illuminated her legs, drawing his attention.

"I'm sorry I left you to it," she said when he drew to a halt some four feet away. "You must think me very childish, baling out like that."

"Of course not, you've never been that."

Even though he was aching to hold and comfort her, he knew he had to tread cautiously. One thing he'd quickly learned was she was a proud woman now, and she protected herself fiercely. The mature Carmen Shelby was independent and prickly. That she'd let him so close and submitted herself to him so thoroughly made him feel privileged, and yet he knew she could withdraw just as easily. He'd seen it happening already and he didn't like the way it felt. The look he'd seen on her face the week before, when she said she couldn't do this, made him fear she would pull away. Yet she'd looked so sure, so happy, at the end of the first weekend, happy to be back in Burlington Manor, and taking pleasure from their intimacy.

The need to make amends was great. When he'd seen her hurting it struck home how much she meant to him, but Carmen was a proud woman and it had to be handled right. He was afraid he'd take something away from her, something important. This was real now. When they were having sex it almost felt like role-play. Perhaps it was, perhaps it wasn't. He wasn't sure, but he wanted to know.

"You went to so much trouble," she said.

"I wanted life in the old place again. I wanted to see you happy. You used to love the parties." He felt her scrutiny.

"I know, and I appreciate your efforts." She hopped down from her perch, and stepped closer to the heater.

Rex didn't like the reserved, almost sad look he saw on her face when the soft glow lit her from below. "I'm sorry I did the wrong thing."

She gave a quick smile but he could tell it was forced. "You didn't do anything wrong."

There was no way around it. He was going to have to ask. "What did Amanda say to you?"

Carmen broke eye contact and glanced away, shifting closer to the window as she wrapped her hands around her upper arms. Looking out into the moonlight she took some time before she answered. "She told me I was a sad, lonely spinster, and she said you were one of the best lovers she'd ever had."

"Bloody hell." Rex hadn't expected that last part. It never even occurred to him Amanda would throw up a one-night stand from the past just to upset Carmen. Perhaps he should have thought of it, given Amanda could be deliberately provocative when she'd had a few drinks, but he scarcely even remembered the event and assumed she'd be the same. "I'm really sorry she told you."

Carmen laughed softly, and there was a wry tone to it. "Oh, don't be. I already knew you'd screwed her."

Rex reeled. *Carmen knew?*

Her tone was so wary, he wondered if he'd be able to get through the barbed exterior she emanated. "I'm sorry. And I'm sorry if it was awkward, her being here tonight. It didn't occur to me she'd be like that."

Women talked, he should have realized.

Carmen threw him a disappointed look, then turned away again.

"Yes, I know," he added, "expecting maturity, decency and a modicum of civility was a bit of a long shot, in her case."

"Too right."

"I didn't mean for that to happen, though. You're too precious to me."

Carmen's head jerked back. She seemed surprised. "Like I said, I knew you two had slept together. Unfortunately I nearly walked in on you mid-shag. I saw it with my own eyes."

Again, he was astounded. His thoughts raced. It had only happened once, and he struggled to place it. It'd been here at the house, he seemed to recall, and it was a Christmas party. The memory sharpened. His father had spoken to him in the afternoon, laying down laws, and he'd gone off the rails. Amanda had been a convenient distraction. Nothing more. The thought of Carmen seeing them, that she'd known about it right back then, floored him. It was the last thing in the world he would've wanted.

"I had no idea." Rex felt guilty. She was hurt. Why was she hurt by a one-night thing? Okay, Amanda had made something out of it, or had attempted to, but the lingering sadness in Carmen's eyes was something he didn't understand. A guarded, assessing look, a disappointed look. Betrayed, even. It'd hurt her back then, and now. Once again he had to force back the physical urge to pull her into his arms. It was a desperate need in him, but her wary expression warned him off.

"I'll get over it," she said, overly flippant. "It was just a shock having it thrown in my face right after she was fishing to see if we were—" she paused, as if she was trying to find the right description for their arrangement "—sleeping together, but she does love to tease people." She gave him another one of her lingering, thoughtful glances. "In fact, the two of you are a good match. Perhaps you should have stuck with her."

Rex supposed he deserved that, but he felt increasingly frustrated. "Stuck with Amanda? I didn't even want her, she was a distraction."

"She might have been a distraction to you, but you and I were close, even though we were told to act like siblings, there was much, much more. We'd kissed..." It came out in a rush, and her depth of feeling on the issue was suddenly stark and apparent, and she sounded as if she was trying not to cry. "Okay, so I was an ingénue, but it was bloody hard, Rex. I really cared about you. I thought we were going to be together, that you'd be my first, but you got with her instead. It broke my stupid teenage heart."

Rex couldn't hold himself in check any longer. He acted purely on instinct and crossed to her, taking her into his arms and holding her close against him. She kept her arms folded, remained rigid. Then he kissed the top of her head, and he felt her sob.

"Hush, hush now." He wrapped her closer still, resting his cheek against her hair. It shocked him how much he hurt for her. He couldn't bear it and wanted it to end immediately.

Then she muttered something into his shoulder.

He looked down at her and put his hand under her chin, making her look at him. Her eyes shone with tears, but she was pouting and looking at him with the resentful glance he knew so well.

"Now I've made myself look like even more of an idiot."

"No, you haven't." Something loosened in his chest. The tension, the resistance. It was a relief. Things weren't perfect, but at least she was talking to him.

"I have. I didn't mean to blurt that out. Now you're going to have an even bigger ego, knowing I had a stupid crush on you."

Rex laughed, because it was crazy. "Jesus, Carmen. This whole thing we're doing is because we wanted each other—that's hardly news. The only revelation here is you knew about my stupid mistake with Amanda. I had no clue you knew. I'd pretty much forgotten it ever happened, to be honest. It was a one-off and I immediately regretted it."

She listened, but she didn't look entirely convinced. "What did you mean she was a distraction?"

"I wanted *you*."

She continued to stare up at him.

He took a deep breath. "I wanted you, but I couldn't have you."

Her eyebrows drew together.

She didn't know. Rex had always wondered, but it was obvious now. *Carmen didn't know.*

He moved away, just slightly, but he needed space if he was going to have to tell her. It was hard, because he never spoke about it, not to anyone. He didn't even want to think about it. He'd cut all ties with his father and even his mother didn't know why.

Carmen's eyes flickered, and Rex knew what needed to be said. "It was a stupid thing to do, but I couldn't have you and you were what I wanted. I thought she'd make me stop thinking about you. It didn't work."

He pushed his fingers through his hair, remembering, taken right back. The frustration—the withheld longing for something forbidden to him—it was right there, resurrected as it was by the events of the evening. "Dad was watching me all the time. It'd got to the point where I couldn't even speak to you without him assessing the situation."

Carmen frowned. "I don't understand."

"Dad knew. He knew I wanted you, and he knew we were attracted to each other. When he confronted me, I told him I didn't want to be a big brother to you. I told him I was going to ask you on a date. He forbade me, in no uncertain terms."

"But I don't understand. We heard him, on the day you left. We heard him shouting after you. Mum and I were in the drawing room and the door was open and we heard. He said if you walked away from him—*him*—you wouldn't ever be part of Burlington Manor."

It was hard. He didn't want it to sound as if it was her fault, because it wasn't, but there wasn't an easy way to tell the tale without old wounds being opened up. "He'd already warned me off you, but I guess him doing so only made it worse. After that one time in here—" he paused, gesturing toward the spot where she'd been sitting moments before "—I knew I had to speak to him, tell him I was serious about you. He wanted us to play the happy family, and in his mind that meant we were as good as blood relatives, when it wasn't the case. He called me a freak, a deviant." The anger he'd harbored toward his dad was rising fast. "He said it'd be incest. Moron. He was a fucking control freak living in a dream world of his own making."

Now that the wound was open his repressed feelings on the matter spilled out. "The old bastard wouldn't let his new dream family be shattered. He said I was only doing it to make us all unhappy. He even told me that if I pursued you, your life here would be ruined. I knew he would make sure of it, and I couldn't do that to you."

"Are you saying you left because of me?" Her expression said it all. She was incredulous.

There was no point in denying it. "Yes."

"Rex, no." She looked shocked, disturbed even. "We wondered why you left, and I thought you got fed up because…" She gave him a sidelong glance. "Well, you know, we'd taken over your home."

"No. I tried really hard to be what he wanted me to be, for your sake. I didn't want him to punish you just because I couldn't play your brother. Right until the end of the year I stuck it out, then I lost it. I did try. At that age, I felt I could deflect it by being with someone else. But no other woman could drive you out of my mind for long."

She shook her head. "That Christmas was your last visit," she whispered.

Rex nodded. That Christmas, when he'd told his father he would not participate in his fake family scenario any longer, and then he'd bedded Amanda out of sheer frustration. "I talked to him again. Told him I didn't care whether he liked it or not. He was angry. He said I'd ruin your life. I had to walk away. I didn't want him to reject you, because it was more than a stepdad for you—you'd have lost your mum, as well, and he told me he'd make sure Sylvia knew. It spilled out, right through the house."

"You never came back. Because I'd seen you with Amanda, I thought it was because you wanted other girls instead of me."

"No."

Her hands went to her face, and she covered her mouth. It twisted the knife inside him. She was shocked. More shocked and upset than he thought she would be.

"Rex," she whispered. She looked shattered. "I'm so sorry. I never knew it was my fault, that I'd come between you and Charles."

"Christ, no, it wasn't your fault. The old man ruined everything for everybody." He sighed. "It's ironic, but I never expected him to leave me any part of it, not after I walked out on him that way. But he must have come to terms with the fact it was you I had to leave, not him. None of this meant anything to me, not without you."

He swallowed hard. In saying it aloud he'd admitted things he'd never truly acknowledged before. "I couldn't live with those boundaries, not when it came to you. I refused to compromise, refused to play the happy family."

He was going to say more, but suddenly she was right there in front of him and her hands were resting on his chest as she looked up at him, her lips softly parted as she studied his expression. "Rex." Her voice faltered when she reached up and stroked his hair back. "Oh, my God, Rex. I had no idea."

The contact was good, and she was soft and warm. It made him want to share it all, the deep subconscious thoughts he'd refused to acknowledge over the intervening years. "Walking away from him was about walking away from what he wanted—the ideal family he'd never had. With you and Sylvia here, he got closer to something he'd always dreamed of, and when I came back I was expected to fall in line and play the dutiful brother. But believe me, it was the last thing I wanted to do when it came to you."

He gave a gruff laugh. "Selfish bastard. He couldn't impose his will on me that way. All he cared about was having the perfect family and he didn't care whose emotions he screwed with."

"Why didn't you tell me? You should've told me back then. When you walked away you didn't even say goodbye. I thought you didn't care."

"I cared too much. That was the problem. And I didn't want to say goodbye. Not ever."

The way she stared up at him, lips softly parted, expression disbelieving, moved him, and he closed one arm around her waist. "I was crazy for you."

"That's why you never came back?"

He nodded.

"Oh Rex."

"It's okay. I got over it. Although I never got over wanting you, but you know that already."

She didn't respond with words. Instead, she stood up on her tiptoes and kissed him, her hands wrapping around the back of his head as she did so.

For a moment all Rex could do was experience it.

She was holding him so tightly. Her hands on his head, then on his back, clutching at him. There was no resistance and no resentment. She wanted him, openly, eagerly. Her hands were all over him, her kisses hungry and desperate.

"Please, make love to me," she begged as she broke the kiss.

Rex lost the ability to think rationally.

Grappling with his clothing, she tugged him against her, kissing him again.

A few steps and he had her up against the work surface that she'd been sitting on earlier. His cock was hard for her. He tugged her skirt up, groaning audibly against her mouth when he felt her bare buttocks, the slender line of lace resting between them a flimsy barrier.

Lifting her, he settled her onto the wooden surface. He put his hands on her knees, swinging them apart. Carmen shoved her panties down and he tugged them off. Tossing her hair, she maneuvered closer so she was on the edge of the work shelf, ready to receive him.

Rex held back, looked at her for maybe ten seconds to absorb her eagerness, and then his hands were back on her, one on her hip, the other reaching between her thighs to stroke her there.

Her pussy was warm and damp in its crease, and his cock grew stiffer still. At the base of his spine, the muscles grew taut. When he opened her up, her clit stood out, a firm ridge under his thumb.

She moaned loudly. "Please, Rex, I need you inside me."

He didn't need any more encouragement. Undoing his belt, he was ready in a flash. Before his jeans dropped, he pulled a condom packet from the pocket.

"You should've done this to me, right here, all those years ago."

The surge of power sweeping through him made him desperate to be inside her. "I couldn't agree more."

Carmen took the condom packet from his hand. She leaned over and purred her approval when his cock moved readily into her hand. The touch of her fingers on his erection—so eager and willing—made him whisper her name. He wanted her so badly it hurt.

She tore the condom packet open, even while Rex moved one finger inside her. She was so wet the movement of his finger made a sound. Rex nodded at her, and pushed another finger inside.

Rex's cock jerked against his belly, and his hands moved on her soft thighs. Her hips undulated. "Let me get this bloody condom on, Rex."

He huffed a laugh.

She got the condom into position on the head of his cock, and slowly rolled it on. Then she grabbed him with her hands around his head and kissed him passionately, one hand then guiding his erection to her, her body wriggling onto the edge of the surface to give him access.

Rex was against the work unit, the head of his cock just inside her.

"Give me more," she begged.

"Whatever you want." He clutched her around her hips, manipulating her as he gave it to her an inch at a time, stretching her open to take his full length.

Whimpering, her hands dug into his shoulders, her body clasping him tightly. His cock was home, deep, pleasured. Rex widened his stance for balance.

She rocked her hips, her spine straightening, her mouth open in a rush of pleasure, a loud moan escaping her. She bore down on him, pivoting on the edge of the work unit.

He cursed. The hot, moist grasp of her flesh on his was pushing him into another level of experience. Her fingernails roved over his back, sparking his libido. He had to hold on to her. He ran his hands down her spine, and curved them around her buttocks.

"I wanted you so badly, and I never knew," she said, her tone needy, echoing the eagerness he felt in her every move.

Rex had to fuck her harder. He grasped her around the waist, and eased her upper body back so she laid back on the work surface. In that position, her cunt felt like a fist around his cock.

Ragged sensation shot up the length of his spine. With effort, he focused on her, stroking her splayed pussy. Pleasure pulsed from his cock as he rode in and out in shallow thrusts.

It was intense, almost painful, his balls aching for release.

"Oh, oh. So good." Her voice was garbled as she tried to get the words out, and her hands reached for him.

Her body was primed for him, and seeing her that way made something inside Rex fracture. "I'm going to come soon. You've got me."

"More." Her head rolled back. Her body undulated, and she gripped his shoulders for purchase while she moved against him, fucking him hard, encouraging him to let rip.

He gave a husky laugh and found his rhythm, thrusting in and out of her, the muscles in his arms and neck cording with effort.

"Oh, fuck," she cried out. "This is too much."

His cock seemed to get even harder when she said that.

Carmen moaned, indicating she felt it, too.

Rex shifted, sliding out and then in again.

The hot fist of her cunt closed around him, rippling as she came, hot juices spilling from her sex. Her whole body vibrated and her moans were long and loud.

"That feels so damn good," Rex whispered. It was because she wasn't submitting this time. She was mirroring his lust, equaling it, and after his confession, it hit him hard.

She lifted her head and locked eyes with him.

He thrust deep again, then paused. "Never felt anything like this."

His chest grew tight. Tension was fast building in his balls. He exhaled loudly. The room seemed to darken completely while his balls tightened and released, and pleasure exploded through him.

He reached for her, holding her, encouraging her to put her arms around his neck, staying inside her for as long as he could.

That night, Carmen didn't go to sleep. Instead, she lay in Rex's arms while he slept, facing everything he'd revealed. Every aspect of what he'd told her had shocked her. Rex seemed to think she'd known, or had guessed. How could she have known? Should she have guessed? No, not after Amanda. That was a cold slap and it would have appeared the same to any woman. And Rex never attempted to get in touch afterward, to explain.

Most importantly, Charles Carruthers had shielded her from the information. It all fell into place now. Every time she'd asked about Rex, Charles simply told her Rex would rather spend time with his mother during vacations, and then he changed the subject.

Knowing how much Rex had wanted her, and how he'd tried to defy his father's expectations, made her heart ache. It also made her desperately needy for him, unable to shield her emotions. Hard lust had come upon them fast in the wake of his confession, as if fulfilling the past had removed some ghostly barrier still standing between them.

The significance of the evening's revelations was immense for them both. She'd seen the truth of their long withheld desire for the first time. She understood why he'd slept with Amanda. The truth had come out and it had created a new dynamic between them, resulting in unbridled mutual passion.

But for Carmen it also brought a new set of fears and complications.

Guilt swamped her. It was her fault Rex had been disinherited as a youth. Charles had gone back on that and changed his will more recently, thankfully, but the rift between father and son was because of her. No matter how Rex tried to turn the blame on his father, it came down to her.

She'd broken their bond.

It made her want to hand the house over to him fully, as recompense. But he didn't want it, not really. He'd lost it all because of her, but that's not why he'd come back. Rex admitted she was the forbidden fruit he always wanted. He'd also revealed so much else. The battle with his father was still important to him.

The closeness she'd longed for was shattered soon enough, because Rex said something that woke her from her reverie and reminded her of a few cold hard facts.

"The old man couldn't stop me forever." He laughed, as if he'd won some old game still being played with his father.

Her blood ran cold.

"When I heard the will," he added, sleepily, "I saw the way to do what should've been done a long while ago."

Carmen squeezed her eyes shut.

The opportunity to challenge his father arose, and he wanted to win his oldest game of all. The confession had revealed the deeper truth.

If he'd really wanted her, he could have sought her out after she'd left the manor. It wouldn't have been hard to do. An email. A phone call. No, it had just cropped up. *In a while, he'll move on.* Just as he always did, leaving a trail of heartache in his wake. He didn't want the house; he wanted to defy and beat his father, even after Charles had reneged on his promise to disinherit him.

Carmen closed her eyes and savored his strong arms around her and the feeling of his warm breath on her shoulder, because she knew it wouldn't last. Precious as it was, this moment was all the more transient because he'd now achieved the lingering goal his father had forbidden him.

And the house? For a while there she was sure she saw him begin to love the place again. At the party he'd seemed proud. Even the first weekend, she could see his expression change as he looked around and familiarized himself. But now she saw the truth of it. He'd never expected to inherit, and he'd only used it as a ploy to get the one thing he did want, to get one over on Dad.

And I've let myself become emotionally involved.

Reel it in, she told herself.

CHAPTER TEN

Rex always woke early. Previously he'd left Carmen sleeping, but he couldn't, not this morning. He kissed her awake.

She jolted and blinked.

"Sorry, I couldn't resist."

"I fell asleep," she murmured. "I didn't think I would."

"I didn't want to sleep, either." He kissed her shoulder. "Knowing you wanted me, and the way you were last night." He could hear the hoarseness in his own voice. "It's made everything different. It's made it so much better."

She looked at him, her eyes wide and yet strangely unreadable.

He drew her fingers to his lips, kissing them. "There's so much I want to do with you. I could spend a lot of time this way."

She tipped her head back and eyed him warily. "Last night was about the truth of the past."

"And since it's out now we can enjoy each other and make up for lost time."

"For two more weekends after this one, yes. Our arrangement can't go on indefinitely."

Rex didn't want to hear that. "Of course it can."

He shifted and kissed her neck, tenderly grazing her jaw with his teeth.

She sighed deeply, then grasped his head between her hands, stilling him. "Ever the privileged playboy. You're just trying to get more out of this deal than we agreed. Typical Rex, greedy and demanding."

"Not at all." He responded cautiously, warily lifting his head to look at her again. She was still thinking about the deal? He was surprised. Was it still just about that for her, even though they'd discovered the truth together the night before? Unwelcome doubts crowded in on him.

Was it why she liked him to take charge? Because she was only doing it as a means to an end? If she was engaging in sexual role-play in order to endure the deal, he had to know. A memory whispered in his mind. Her voice. "Easier, this makes it easier."

"There's something I have to know. It's been bugging me. Why the sub act? Why the whole role-play thing?"

Carmen stiffened in his arms.

Before he had a chance to undo that, she pulled away from him and sat on the edge of the bed with her back to him. "So, I call you on being a greedy playboy and you turn it on me and make me feel embarrassed about my sexuality. Nice."

He reached out and rested his hand on the soft curve of her hip. "No, for fuck's sake, Carmen, no. I want to know everything about you, especially since things have changed between us."

She rose to her feet and wandered the room.

Why was she pulling away now? Was it the question about her submissive nature or something else? What else had he said? The suggestion of more time together than what was originally agreed upon. Of course. She didn't want more than that. *Other than the bloody house, of course.*

Frustration ratcheted inside him.

What the hell was it about this woman? He stared at her, both irritated and offended. Never had a woman resisted him like this. If one would have, he'd have simply shrugged and moved on. Why did it have to be her, the one he really cared for? It annoyed the hell out of him.

She walked across the room, naked. The bright morning sunlight behind her body made her seem even more surreal and unobtainable than ever, slipping her in and out of focus.

She was looking for clothing.

Rex didn't want her to dress. He leaped out of the bed and crossed the room to her side. Grasping her wrist, he drew her to him. "Why? Why were you like this with me, why did you let me dominate you?"

She stared up at him, her eyes large and luminous in the morning light, panic and mistrust growing in her expression. "I don't know why."

Her glance fell to his hand on her wrist and he saw her mood altering immediately. He tightened his grip.

Sexual tension shot high between them.

"But you like it?" His cock was hardening. Silently he cursed it. He had to know the truth.

"I told you. I don't know why."

The fear he saw in her eyes hit him hard. It was different. When she offered herself, she wasn't afraid. She was resentful, but she was willing. The look on her face tore him apart. Did this mean the submissive side of her was her nature, and not a role-play? *Will I ever really know?* The woman was an enigma, and just when he thought they were getting closer, she clammed up good and proper.

What shocked him most of all was the fear. Why was she afraid to be honest about it? Did she think he would tease her, was that it?

"Rex, please, don't."

The sound of her whispering his name so breathlessly, so afraid, made him want to protect her, above all else.

"You do it because it makes it easier," he stated.

Silence. Then she nodded, grateful.

He'd said it to break the tension, and it had. Somewhat. Yet his nerves felt tauter than ever. Carmen was the important thing here, not his base reactions. He didn't want her to be uncomfortable around him. They'd done enough of that over the years. Far too much, in fact.

She didn't respond, but when she met his gaze there was a silent plea for understanding in her expression.

"I'm sorry." He stroked her cheek with his thumb. "I adore you that way. What man wouldn't—"

"You're not just any man," she interrupted.

He stared at her, surprised by her comment, but instantly needing more explanation.

"Oh, bloody hell, Rex. Do I have to spell it out for you?"

"I'm sorry, but apparently you do."

She meshed her hands, fingers twisting together as she spoke. "I haven't been like this before…not with anyone else."

"I don't understand." It was the honest to God truth. He didn't get it.

"It's just you. I don't know why. Maybe because I'd wanted you for so long. It just happened, and when it did, it felt right when you mastered me." Her face was aflame. "Fucking hell, Rex! It's what I wanted, what I'd always wanted, deep down."

The information seemed unreal and he couldn't take it in. But why would she lie? Stunned, Rex paced up and down the room and then sat down on the edge of the bed.

He stared across at her. She seemed dreamlike to him.

She folded her hands around her upper arms and her hair fell over her face, so he couldn't see her eyes.

Instinctively Rex knew what she needed from him right then. It wasn't rocket science, but it made him wonder. They did have a seemingly natural symbiosis in their sexuality; it was unquestionable. But he'd assumed this was the way she was, she had an inherent desire for the kinky aspect. Had she really not behaved this way with anyone else? He'd assumed she'd been introduced to submission by another man. Apparently not. It also wasn't the real problem here. It was part of the solution.

The notion made his possessive feelings for her multiply rapidly. He put out his hand, gesturing for her to come closer. "Come to me."

Without hesitation, she did so.

Stepping across the room, she paused in front of him. A moment later she lowered to her knees at his side and sat back on her heels.

The neat, folded posture she assumed was so simple, yet it stunned him to see her that way, like an elegant geisha, her head lowered yet cocked, as if to hear his request. What a prize, what a beauty.

He reached out and stroked her head.

She leaned into his touch, her forehead against his knee.

A tight, willful mood swamped him, weighing heavily on the moment. How much easier did it make sex for her? How hard would it be to balance the power, as they had in the heat of the moment last night? The questions made him want to know why she was really here, on her knees.

Was it for him, or for Burlington Manor?

"What if I asked something of you that you couldn't do?"

She looked into his eyes, openly, seemingly not afraid of that rather weighty question. The sight of her in such a way made him feel as if nothing else existed, except Carmen. She filled his mind, his every thought. It made him unsteady, because he was indeed possessive and greedy for her, just as she had accused him of being. But he craved clarity of meaning; he needed to understand what was happening between them, and why.

"I'd say the safeword." Her voice faltered.

"Say it," he instructed. "I want to be sure you can."

"Boo," she whispered.

A quick smile flitted across her expression and then she was still, entirely focused on him, alert and poised yet palpably keen to move forward in the sexual negotiation.

"I scarcely heard you, Carmen."

"I didn't want to use the safeword, that's why. You asked me to."

Rex was torn. He wanted her, wanted this to be real, not some kinky role-play session. Was she doing it because it was in her nature, or was this just her way of fulfilling the deal that he'd set out at the beginning? He was growing more frustrated. The night before, he thought they'd kicked down the barriers between them. They'd come this far; they'd peeled back so much of what was holding them apart, but there was more. Here in their nakedness and the honesty, it was time to test her.

Even if it meant he found out something he didn't want to know.

"I'm going to ask you to do something you might find very hard. You might even want to use the safeword."

The way she looked up at him made his blood pump hard. Like she wanted to be tested.

It frustrated him, because he did want to make her cry out in orgasm, to beg for him to fuck her, to plead with him to use her in every way—and he knew she probably would. God knows he wouldn't turn her away. That wasn't an option. But what he wanted even more right now was her honesty about why they were here at all. Even if it disappointed him.

"Are you on your knees for the keys to Burlington Manor?"

Her eyes narrowed. "This is all just a game to you, isn't it?"

It hit him like a hammer blow. He thought the night before was the most intensity he could be made to feel, until now. How did she do this to him?

Holding it together, he pressed on. "Not at all. I'm just trying to get to the bottom of your motivation, my dear stepling."

Her eyes blazed at him. "Oh, bloody hell, Rex. Don't call me that! You set out the rules here. You made the deal."

He clenched his jaw, took a moment to breathe. "It's the only reason you're doing this, isn't it? For the keys to Burlington Manor."

She squirmed, resistance pouring out of her.

"Yes." It was a blurted response. "Fuck it, Rex! You know this already. You're just burning out an old flame, proving something to your Dad. We both are. You'll walk away at the end of it, but you knew how much I wanted to take this place on, and that's why you knew I'd buckle and you could toy with me for a while."

"I'm not toying with you." He issued the statement from between his gritted teeth.

Her eyes flashed, as if in denial of his words.

That annoyed him immensely. She thought he was toying with her? She was the one who was performing. She was the one who was backing away. And more than that he was annoyed because he wanted her to need him now, not the bloody house. He rose to his feet. "Show me how much you want Burlington Manor," he demanded.

She tossed her head back and her eyes closed for a moment.

The way the light fell on her arched neck transfixed him. The pulse there beat rapidly. Was it anger, or arousal? He couldn't be sure.

"Why?" she asked eventually as she opened her eyes again.

"Because I want to know. You said you'd do anything for me, for a month, for this place."

"I didn't actually say that."

"I had your implicit agreement. I think we both know that."

Her lips pursed.

"I want to know how much you want the house. Demonstrate your commitment to Burlington Manor."

If looks could kill, Rex knew he would be dead already.

"It's all right for you to say that," she seethed, "but how in hell can I prove it to you?"

Her attitude triggered something dark in him. Something that demanded to be fed. "Crawl."

Carmen's head dropped back as if she'd been physically slapped.

The urge to push her some more roared in on him, taking charge. He strode to the chair where his clothes lay abandoned from the night before.

Swiping up his jeans, he fished into the pocket. He tossed the key chain out across the floor, holding on to the end of the long chain. "Get down on your hands and knees and crawl over here for it."

When the key landed on the Persian rug, she stared down at it.

Rex jerked on the chain.

The key flipped over on the floor between them, like bait. Like a lure.

"Show me what you want, what you came here for," he said.

Carmen shook her head.

"I want to know exactly what you wanted when you stepped through the door. The truth."

She stared up at him. "I can't do this. It's too hard!"

"You can, because you want me to sign it over, and you agreed to do whatever I said to get it."

He felt her buckling. Would she use the safeword? Would this push her humiliation trigger just that bit too far? He didn't care, as long as it got the truth out of her. He had to know. "Why are you here? What did you want? Just the property?"

"Yes." She dropped onto her hands and knees. Her voice was weak, forced. "It's a fair exchange, that's what you said."

The light outlined her body, drawing his eye to her curves.

She moved suddenly, jerking forward and crawling toward the key, but she was in turmoil. He could sense it. He could see it.

The sight of her that way made him painfully hard and yet his sense of frustration only grew. He wanted to understand this woman more than anything in the world.

When she got to it, her hand wrapped around the key, but she stayed there, shifting uneasily. The light from the window fell across her naked form, delineating the arch of her waist and the curve of her hip. Her soft skin glowed in the morning light. In contrast, her face was shadowed by her hair as it fell forward, and she looked up at him like a wild creature, her eyes blazing.

"Tell me why," he demanded, and he held tight to his end of the key chain.

Her body rippled, her back arching. Her head swung to one side. She whimpered. Taking a deep breath she moved again, gathering the chain up in her hand as she went.

"Just the house?" he asked. "That's all you wanted? You were that cold and mercenary?"

She froze, then sat back on her heels. Her breathing was labored. She was battling something.

He pressed her further. "Why is this so hard for you to talk about?"

"Because I'm scared." She stared up at him, and her eyes looked wild.

Rex swallowed. "Why are you scared?"

Her gaze roved over him, her jaw going lax when she saw his erection.

Sensing her giving way, he softened his tone. "Tell me why, please don't be afraid. I won't tease you, whatever you say."

Her eyes flashed shut. "Because I wanted you." Her voice was scarcely above a whisper "I didn't realize how much, at first, but I came here because I've always wanted you."

Rex had been holding his breath, and his chest felt tight and restricted.

He let go of the key chain, throwing it down on the floor, and clicked his fingers. "Then come to my side."

She moved fast, kneeling up at his feet, her arms wrapping around his thighs. The key and its chain lay abandoned on the floor. Rex stared down at it, assuring himself of what had occurred.

She clung to him, and he felt damp tears against his skin. "Please don't tease me about it."

Rex let his head drop back, relief barreling through him.

Grateful, and empowered, he stroked her head possessively, admitting to himself that a month would never be enough.

Never enough.

He never wanted to be without her.

CHAPTER ELEVEN

Rex noticed how different the country air was when he was out on his Sunday jog the following day. He'd risen early with the birds and was making his way around the lake. The air was so much more invigorating than back at his weekday jogging spot, a busy park in South London. Something about the atmosphere today really highlighted his connection to the place. He felt more engaged. That wasn't something he normally thought about, being very much a city man these days. Though he'd grown up here in the countryside he'd suffered what most young people did, a longing for the action of cities. He'd been happy to shelve the country life.

As he made his way back to the house he studied the building. The notion of hidden secrets and mysteries teased at his consciousness, as if every window shielded something he was unaware of. The concept was strange, but alluring. It was something he'd thought about before, but now he was growing familiar with the place again, his curiosity levels rose.

His gaze settled on Carmen's window. They'd reached some sort of plateau the morning before. An impasse, perhaps. She knew he'd always wanted her, and she'd admitted—finally, and very reluctantly—she'd wanted him, as well as the house. The whole thing had been emotionally exhausting, and at the end of it they'd been quieter, but closer. It was as if enough had been said about the past, for the time being.

He couldn't let her leave that way, though. No, before they parted and returned to London, he wanted more level ground.

When he got to the kitchen, he chatted with Mrs. Summerfield while he waited for Carmen to appear.

"So, tell me, what's your opinion of the newer members of staff?" Rex was aware Mrs. Amery would have been responsible for employing them, but Mrs. Summerfield had always been more generous with her opinions and didn't stand on ceremony quite as much as the housekeeper.

"Not a bad bunch. I miss the old ones who've gone, though. Leanne is a good girl, throws herself at things a bit too much but she'll slow down as she gets used to it."

Rex nodded. "She seemed to enjoy the party."

Mrs. Summerfield chuckled. "She did."

"What about the others?"

"The lads who help Bill seem to be reliable enough. I don't see a lot of them because they're only part-timers. They come up for a mug of tea midmorning, but they don't say a lot. There's also a chap called Jack Formby. He does a lot of odd jobs around the place but he's not a member of staff as such. Jack runs his own business in the village but whenever it's something that Bill doesn't have time for Mrs. Amery will call him in. He gets paid by the hour."

She seemed pleased he was asking and smiled his way as she chatted. "When you first came back, you said you didn't know what the long-term plans for the place were. Now you've had time to talk with Carmen, has that changed at all?"

She dried her hands on a towel, and rested her hip up against the range, an action he seemed to remember. It was something about the heat helping her arthritis, even though it was a warm day. It was odd, the sudden redemption of long-lost memories, but it kept happening while he spent time there. Little quirks about the people and the place kept coming back to him, like remembering exactly where to put his hand in a drawer in his bedroom to find the secret compartment, without even having to look.

"I think it's going to take us a bit more time," he responded. "It's not something easily done. Carmen is set on keeping the place, but I want to make sure it's the right thing for her. It's a big commitment for anyone to take on, on their own, and she's got a lot of business responsibilities in London to manage, as well."

Rex answered without thinking it through, and yet it was how he felt. If Carmen wanted the place, so be it. She was a grown woman and she could afford to run it. However, he wanted to make sure it wasn't simply some misguided sense of obligation on her part, and she could cope with it. God knows it wasn't the easiest place in the world to run. "Not much of an answer for you as yet, I'm afraid, but we both want what's best for the place."

Mrs. Summerfield looked at him, smiled and nodded. "I'm sure you do." She paused. "Now, you said you'd be returning to London before dinner this evening. Would you like me to prepare something special for lunch, for you and Carmen?"

Rex noticed she seemed satisfied with his responses. Yet he hadn't given her a real answer. It made him wonder how much the staff were speculating, above and beyond the future of the house, but about them, the two people who had inherited it. Perhaps they always had speculated. A woman like Mrs. Summerfield had probably noticed the standing attraction between them and would be intrigued to see where it might go while they were reunited at the manor. It was probably like watching a live soap opera for her. "What do you suggest?" he asked.

Mrs. Summerfield beamed and clutched her towel between her hands as she spoke. "Why don't you take Carmen down to the village for a nice pub lunch? Not that I mind cooking for you. Quite the contrary. But I think she'd enjoy it and I'm sure you would, too. Get away from the house for a while, be on your own without the big decisions hanging over you."

Intrigued by the idea, Rex nodded. "I'll take your advice, thank you."

"My pleasure."

Why did it sound so good, getting away from the house together? Because the bloody house was a nuisance, a millstone. Originally it had been a way to get to Carmen, but now her loyalty to it was making him hate the place. She'd admitted she did want to sleep with him when she'd returned, but the house was still her biggest concern going forward. It was as if she was in agreement with his theory about burning out the old flame when he was beginning to doubt it would ever burn out. It made him resent the estate.

Someone entered the kitchen from the hallway and Rex turned expectantly, assuming it was Carmen.

It was Mrs. Amery. "Ah, Mr. Rex. Is there anything specific you want me to do here while you're away this week?"

Rex had the urge to say he didn't give a toss about the house. The house could rot in hell for all he cared right at that moment. Carmen was his only concern. He paused and looked at the woman who anchored their home when no one else would.

She looked at him searchingly. Mrs. Amery needed to be given instructions, to be made to feel useful.

Nodding, he tried to look appreciative. "Is there something you think is important to schedule in soon?"

"Well, your father wouldn't let me into the library to give it a proper clean, called it his stronghold or some such nonsense. The place could do with a good airing, at the very least." She brushed an invisible piece of dust from her shoulder.

The barely withheld relish with which she anticipated the task was most amusing. If she'd been told to keep out, she'd have hated it. Rex had only stuck his head in there for a moment on his return, when he was reacquainting himself with the place. "Absolutely. I noticed the place was sinking under the weight of old papers."

Mrs. Amery nodded approvingly. "In that respect, your father was an absolute hoarder."

"If you can start shredding any of the more mundane estate account paperwork more than five years old, it'd be very helpful. Keep anything historically important, but I'm aware my father kept every invoice, every receipt, and we don't need to know the milk bill for thirty years past."

"My feeling exactly. I'll begin right away."

When she disappeared a split second later, Rex looked at Mrs. Summerfield. "Keen or what?"

She laughed. "It drove her to despair that she wasn't allowed in there."

"I'm surprised she waited for me to give permission."

"She's very strict about protocol. And she was loyal to your dad. He spent more and more time in there, too, after Sylvia's death." She stopped talking quite suddenly, as if she regretted mentioning Sylvia's death. "Skimmed milk?"

"If we have it."

She beamed. "We do."

Rex was busy eating his breakfast when Carmen eventually appeared in the doorway. Her damp hair clung to her head, making her look elfin. Cautiously she smiled his way.

What a mystery she was.

He noticed she closed her left hand around her right wrist for a moment before she walked past him to get to her seat. He reached out and stopped her, grabbed her hand and gave her wrists a quick examination. He'd kept her bound for two hours the night before. Two hours, while he observed her, stroked her and then talked to her about her sexuality—until she begged him to fuck her and he could resist no longer.

Seeing no signs of injury, he was relieved. He drew her hand quickly to his mouth and kissed it on the soft skin inside of her wrist, then gestured at her seat so she could continue on her way before Mrs. Summerfield noticed their interaction.

But Carmen didn't move. She stood still and stared at him, lips slightly parted, eyes bright.

Instantly he wanted her again.

Rex studied Carmen across the polished pine table in the snug at the local pub. Mrs. Summerfield's idea had been a good one. Carmen seemed more relaxed here in the Woolpack than she did at the manor. Was it the genial atmosphere or was it because there were other people milling about? Or was the tension up at the house due to the fact she still wasn't sure of him and his intentions regarding selling her his share? She wanted it badly, and mostly he was teasing her, but he didn't want to give up the option too soon because right now it was the only thing enabling him to be close to her. Much as he hated to admit it, he might never see her again once he signed the place over.

"This was a really nice idea," Carmen said.

"I can't claim full responsibility. Mrs. Summerfield suggested it."

"Oh, really?"

"She thought it'd do us good to get out of the house together, and I agreed." He looked at her, as if watching for her reaction.

The wary look returned for a moment.

"Is my memory deceiving me," he asked, deliberately changing the subject, "or did we do this before?"

Carmen broke into a smile. The sight of it warmed him right through. He liked it when she was all fire and brimstone, but it was good to see genuine warmth in her expression and—if he wasn't mistaken—fondness in her eyes as she looked across the table at him.

"It wasn't Sunday lunch, but yes. We snuck down here a couple of times when we needed an escape from the manor."

"You've got a much better memory than me."

"Apparently so. For both the good times and the bad."

She was obviously thinking about Amanda again. The hurt look he'd seen on Friday evening flickered briefly in her eyes. Rex wished he could push the event right out of her memory. He'd known it was a mistake as soon as he'd fallen into bed with Amanda, but he had no idea of the extent of the fallout until it had been recently revealed.

It was no wonder Carmen hadn't trusted him at the beginning of this reunion. They'd grown so close back then, and then she'd seen him with Amanda. Following that, he'd walked out of the house never to return. He hadn't said goodbye. He didn't want to. But she never knew the reason why. It was beginning to make sense, but he was cautious about discussing it again. He'd said his piece. As far as he was concerned that issue was shelved.

"Were the Beldover folk as intrigued with us back then?"

Carmen laughed softly and glanced about.

Rex followed her gaze. The village pub was a traditional local. The long wooden bar was the hub around which the villagers gathered, the old-timers sitting on the same high chair each night or propped on elbow chatting to their neighbors at the end of the day. Around the walls, snugs and tables filled the rest of the space—the table nearest the fireplace the most prized seat in the house and rarely vacant. The furniture was oak and pine, the fireplace surround formed from old wood beams studded with brasses. A shelf ran around the top of the walls and was lined with a collection of Toby jugs of all sizes and varieties. The appetizing scent of roasting beef and apple pie with cloves wafted by from time to time, like an aromatic invitation to stay awhile.

Everyone who'd come in since they arrived in the Woolpack had looked their way. Some had smiled and waved in greeting. Whispered conversations followed, but they seemed jovial enough. There was no animosity. It was just that he and Carmen were the center of attention.

"There was less intrigue about us back then," Carmen replied. "We were just the kids who'd come down from the big house on a sunny summer's evening. Now they're wondering what the outcome of our visits to the manor will be. I'm sure Andy Redmond will be passing on all the details of my comings and goings."

Rex noticed she seemed to enjoy speculating about the other customers.

"Are they placing bets?"

She looked at him pensively. "Should they be?"

She still doubted him.

"Hey, I'm not going to ruin the fun for them by announcing you're the new lady of the manor."

Her expression relaxed. She glanced away and smiled again when the locals who were gathered around the bar started arguing amiably about some local council matter. "Even if they're not really associated with Burlington Manor by employment or trade, it's the big house around here and they feel a connection if they know things about the people who live there. They know us, so they'll want one of us to stay on."

Rex nodded. They knew Carmen much better than him. Despite his lineage, Carmen had been around more recently and she'd engaged with the villagers more readily than he had. Even when his mother had been the mistress of the house he'd gone away to school. Carmen hadn't.

"If it sold to a totally new owner," Carmen continued, "they'd lose their right to gossip. They've gained that from long-held knowledge and they'd have to start over again, finding out stuff about the new people, sharing it."

"In that case I'm glad we came down here for our Sunday lunch to give them something to gossip about."

Carmen nodded and lifted her wineglass, sipping from it as she looked at him. Her eyes twinkled.

Rex wished he could capture it. He'd like to see it more.

"Why do you want the manor so badly?" He was beginning to think they'd both be better off without it.

"Because I was happy there."

"You think you'll be happy there again?"

"I hope so. I'd like to try. I love that place."

Why did that irritate him? *Surely I can't be jealous of her feelings for the house?* Rex frowned, confused. "But, alone? It's a big house."

Carmen looked at him with something akin to pity. "I might be self-sufficient but I do have friends."

Rex could have kicked himself. He'd been jealous, and he hadn't thought how his words might sound. Carmen was mostly a loner, but it didn't mean she was lonely.

"Besides, hard as I'm sure it is for someone like you to believe, I'd like to raise a family."

That shouldn't have surprised or unsettled him, but for some reason it did. He attempted to ignore it. "Why don't you let me drive you back to London this evening?"

Immediately she shook her head. "The taxi and train tickets are already booked."

"Next Friday, then. I'll pick you up. It's crazy us traveling here separately." In truth he wanted as much time as he could finagle with her. A couple of hours in the car at the start and close of their weekends seemed like a wasted opportunity to chat.

Again she shook her head. "I want to keep the boundaries exactly where they are, Rex." Her tone was adamant, and her expression had changed. The shutters had come down and the independent, controlled mask of hers had slid into place.

Frustrated, Rex wondered what on earth was going on in her head. It'd been relatively easy to compromise her sexually, compared to this. She was absolutely rigid about the time they spent together. Why? He knew he should hold back, but it was too much of a challenge. "Surely driving up here with me is preferable to the train?"

"I need time to decompress from my week's work, before we...before our time together." It was a perfunctory answer.

The more she denied him, the more intrigued he was. While this wasn't exactly part of the sexual challenge she'd originally been to him, he wanted to know her inside and out. He wanted to understand her fierce independence. Was she a loner as he suspected, or did she have a pack of friends she hung out with during the week in London? "Okay. Well, let's get together for dinner in the city, midweek."

"Thank you, but no." She sighed, then lowered her voice and leaned forward. "Rex, please. It's getting hard for me to keep my mind on my work in between these weekends."

"Aha, a confession. Does this mean you're thinking about me during the week?" Rex liked that idea.

She rolled her eyes. "Don't flatter yourself. I haven't had sex in a long while, that's all."

He wondered if that were true. Was there someone else she was seeing during the week? It was possible, probable even. A woman like Carmen Shelby had to have a string of admirers. Rex knew nothing of her life in London. Rattled by how much it got to him, he vowed to change that.

The food arrived.

"Thank you, Marilyn." Carmen beamed at the waitress.

"You're very welcome. It's so good to see you both. Enjoy your dinners." The waitress nodded at them meaningfully and then departed.

Carmen was right. They really did want one of them to stay on.

He looked across at her, then reached out and closed his hand over hers.

"What?" She cocked her head. "Are you attempting to give them something else to gossip about?"

"Maybe." *Maybe I just had to touch you.*

"Well, it worked." She slid her hand free and reached for her cutlery, smiling as she surreptitiously nodded her head in the direction of the bar.

Rex glanced over. Several heads had turned their way.

He shrugged. He didn't care.

He wanted them to know.

CHAPTER TWELVE

Rex watched the taxi depart. Then he turned around and walked up the steps, glancing at the house as he did so. He had such mixed feelings about the place now. It was so familiar, like an old glove that bore the imprint of his hand. It had also brought him closer to Carmen, the enigma of his life. But something about the place felt like an obstacle, too. *What kind of an idiot was I, agreeing to weekends here at the house, and nothing more?*

He glanced at his watch. He'd left his phone upstairs. Once he'd grabbed it, he could get on his way.

Mrs. Amery appeared as he crossed the hallway. She had half-moon reading glasses perched on the end of her nose. "Mr. Rex, I'm glad I caught you. Could I have a quick word before you leave?"

"Please, just call me Rex." The old fashioned ways grated. He knew it was because of his other frustrations, but he had to say something.

"I wouldn't feel comfortable calling you just by your Christian name."

"If you ever feel differently about that, we'd both be more comfortable."

Mrs. Amery looked at him, and arched her brows.

He lifted his hands. "No pressure."

He resisted the urge to tease her about it.

She nodded. "Well, I've been sorting through the old paperwork today, as you requested." A frown gathered between her eyebrows. "I found a partially written letter among some rather inconsequential household receipts. It was obviously personal. I knew once I started reading it, and when I saw the content I thought you ought to have it, and soon."

Rex didn't want to be dealing with whatever household issue she'd unearthed right now. He wanted to leap in his Maserati and follow Carmen, trail her to London and insist she spend time with him during the week.

"Forgive me for taking the liberty and insisting you read it right away, but it seems important." She widened her eyes.

It was the closest she'd get to ordering him about, but Rex felt her will.

"I left it on the desk in the library."

"Thank you. I'll check it out."

She looked at him strangely, then nodded and gave a quick smile. Whatever the hell it was, she didn't want to deal with it, so he supposed he must.

He went upstairs, pocketed his phone, then made his way to the library.

The room wasn't a familiar place to him. His father had used it as an office. Where there'd once been books that might have drawn him ledgers and box files containing fading, yellowing pages of estate accounts lined the shelves. The kind of paper documents obsolete in most offices these days.

Rex stood in the doorway observing the scene and shook his head.

His father really had been a relic of the old ways.

Mrs. Amery had pinned back the heavy curtains. One window was open and the late-afternoon air wafting in made it a more pleasant place than he expected. Beneath the earthy scent from outdoors the faint aroma of cigars still lingered. Rex noticed a patterned rug had been folded and pinned with a note "for cleaning." Mrs. Amery really hadn't been allowed in here until that morning, when he suggested she begin the overhaul of old paperwork. It made sense. As a lad, he was rarely allowed in here. This was his father's space.

Rex strolled in.

Above the fireplace hung a portrait of his grandfather. He wore his World War Two army uniform, decorated with medals. At the opposite end of the room, behind the desk, was a similar portrait of his father. It had been painted in the 1980s and Charles Carruthers was wearing a tweed jacket with a suede waistcoat beneath, a much more relaxed statement of self.

Rex walked toward it, eyeing the old man with curiosity. He saw a likeness there he hadn't considered before. Perhaps it was because he was getting close to the age his dad had been at the time of the portrait.

"I hope I don't look that bloody grim and austere," Rex muttered.

As Rex studied it he recalled the painting being done. He'd been about six years old and was allowed in for a few minutes at each session to see the portraitist at work. He recalled the artist telling him he would have his portrait done one day for the library. Rex had disagreed, said posing for it looked very boring indeed, and he'd run off. His father had laughed.

There never would be a portrait of him in Burlington Manor, Rex decided. A portrait of Carmen would look good in that spot, though. Would she rework this room, make it more functional? They hadn't even had time to discuss her plans for the interior yet. They might have done that this weekend if he hadn't wasted so much time on that disastrous party.

A large recycling bin stood by the old mahogany desk, where stacks of paperwork were being sorted. The bin was perched on a trolley, presumably for maneuverability. Several of the nearby shelves had been emptied. Mrs. Amery had really got stuck into the job. She was a whirlwind when she had a cause.

He was staring at the amount of paperwork still to be dealt with when he heard a sound and turned toward the window. A figure in a dark coat with an upturned collar shifted and then disappeared from view. Rex frowned.

Someone had been looking in at him.

He stepped over to the window, but there was no sign of anyone nearby. It struck him as odd, because if it had been one of the groundsmen he'd have expected them to acknowledge him, not just run off. Presumably they were as surprised to see him in there as he was to be there.

Shrugging it off, he returned to the desk. A box file lay open and papers were arranged in neat stacks as if they were being sifted.

A single page of handwritten, unlined paper had been set aside on the blotter. A brass paperweight held it in place. Rex sat down in the carved wooden office chair while he picked up the page. The letter was unfinished, but it was addressed to him. The humor he'd felt a moment before dissipated quickly as he began to read.

> *Rex,*
> *I never took the time to explain things, which I do regret.*

Unease ran over Rex. A confessional? He wasn't sure he wanted to give it the time of day. His curiosity was baited, though.

> *I messed things up with your mother, and I was lonely.*

Rex lowered the page. Lonely? What a joke.

The truth of the matter was Charles Carruthers had only ever been lonely right at the end. *What about the mistress you kept on the side when I was a child?* The woman, whoever she was, obviously hadn't meant much to Charles Carruthers. Rex had known about his father's mistress from a young age because his parents argued, a lot, and 'the other woman' was mentioned. For a while he'd wondered if it was Sylvia Shelby, especially when his father married Sylvia. He'd confronted his mother about it, but she assured him it wasn't Sylvia, she was sure. This other woman, whoever she was, was the real reason that his parents' marriage fell apart. That made Rex despise his father's attitude even more.

Sylvia restored my life; she lit all of our lives. She made Burlington Manor a proper home again. It was as if the house was alive, after several years of being a desperate place, after your mother had gone.

As he read, Rex's terse attitude to this after-death confession morphed from irritation to frustration. Even now, Charles Carruthers was exerting his presence on them.

Carmen was the daughter I never had and it felt more like a family home than before. But I was wrong when I expected you and Carmen to become brother and sister.

Initially I thought you were coping with the new adjustments better than I could've wished. Once I knew you had true feelings for her, it felt as if everything was going to be spoiled, and I was doomed to be unhappy. I couldn't let that happen. But now I see it was my fault, not yours, because my expectations were unrealistic. I see that, after all this time I've had to reflect on it alone. It pains me that I've left it this late, and I don't know if I even have the courage to send this letter to you, and ask you to forgive me, and come home.

I wish things had been different. Perhaps I can make amends. I know it won't be easy to

The letter ended abruptly and midsentence. It wasn't signed.

On first reading it made Rex angry. His dad hadn't even had the guts to send it. Rex despised that.

"It's all well and good being sorry now," he muttered, throwing the letter down on the desk, "or whenever the hell it was you had a moment to regret what you'd done."

When was it written? He dug through the accompanying accounts for clues. The papers seemed to be from around eight months earlier.

Rex picked it up and read it again.

It seemed the old man really had realized he'd got it wrong. What did he mean about making amends? Rex stared at the letter, turned it over and put it down. He sifted through all the other papers in that box, but there was no continuation and no other indication he'd given it any more thought.

The old man had probably been sozzled on whisky and feeling sorry for himself, trying to think of a way to gather his pitifully small tribe back together again. But it never would have worked, would it? Perhaps that's why he never finished the letter. In life, there was nothing he could do to make it right. If he'd tried, it would have been a vast humiliation for him, and Charles Carruthers would never have accepted that.

Rex's anger flared and he screwed the letter into a ball, spun the office chair around and hurled it at the portrait of his father. The paper bounced off the painting and dropped to the floor at Rex's feet.

Rex stared at the portrait again, transfixed, because a strange notion was evolving in his mind. Had Charles Carruthers found a way, in death, to make amends? Had he attempted to do so via the very structure of his will? It hadn't occurred to Rex before. He'd been too bound up in getting close to Carmen.

Had Charles Carruthers put the two of them together to deal with this problem because if they were meant to be together, the way Rex had been convinced they were—all those years ago—then it would happen? At least he'd given them the chance to reunite here, to try.

"Why the hell did you wait so bloody long?" Rex picked up the balled letter and returned to the desk, where he slumped into the chair.

Could it be true? It was exactly what was occurring whether Charles Carruthers had planned for it or not. They were testing a pathway that had been laid for them many years before. How differently his father could have handled it, though. Nevertheless, they might never have seen each other, apart from the brief sighting at the graveyard, if he hadn't structured his will that way.

The very thought of it made Rex long for Carmen.

When the circumstances of the will had been read Rex had been delighted—exactly for that reason, because it meant he and Carmen would have to spend time together. He'd been so elated, in fact, he'd barely stopped to think of the whys and wherefores of various aspects of the will.

Rex pushed the chair back against the desk, his hands going loose on the armrests as he contemplated it. He stared around the office with unseeing eyes and tried to imagine what he would do if he were in the same position as his dad had been, alone with his regrets. Had the need to right a wrong haunted the old man all those years?

If it was indeed intentional, how clever it was.

If they'd both moved on and weren't interested in each other, it wouldn't happen. No harm done. If it did, then the injustices of the past would be dealt with through the natural course of events—passion reignited while they looked at the future of the manor together.

REX

It angered Rex that his father still held power over them, even from the grave. *The old bastard, playing with people's lives like they were pawns. I don't want to be like him.* It had always been Rex's fear, to be self-centered and to hurt people close to him. Yet sometimes recently he wondered if it was inevitable. Several women had screamed their grievances at him when he'd decided he wanted to be alone. He didn't want to string anyone along, though. He'd never felt committed to a relationship; he always been clear about it when he slept with a woman. He just figured he wasn't cut out for it, because of his background, the broken home and all.

Since his reunion with Carmen he knew the real reason why.

Subconsciously he'd always known. There was no hiding from the truth now. Carmen was the reason why—because his hankering need for her had never gone away.

Rex looked at the portrait again with different eyes, saw again the likeness between them, but more than that, he noticed the thoughtful, inquisitive look in his father's eyes. Charles Carruthers had enjoyed a good mystery, and puzzles. Had he set one up in his very will?

Rex gazed into his father's eyes, wanting to know.

Why the hell did you wait so long?

It hit him then—a sense of loss. Totally unexpected and without warning, grief barreled up inside him. He leaned forward, rested his elbows on his knees and buried his head in his hands, his emotions churning.

His father had wanted to make amends, after all. It tore him apart.

Because it's about Carmen, and we should've been together long before now.

Somewhere in there, though, there was plain old sadness and regret. Finally, Rex felt something. *I'm sorry, old man.*

For a few moments he closed his eyes and imagined his father saying the words in the letter, aloud, to his face, and offering his hand.

Raw emotion buckled him, and he wept.

Darkness fell, but Rex remained there at the foot of his father's portrait, deep in thought.

Sometime later a light was switched on in the corridor outside and he heard Mrs. Amery's voice in the distance.

He swiped his hands across his eyes, pushed his fingers through his hair, then rose to his feet. Once he'd smoothed the letter out, he folded it neatly and stored it away in his wallet.

The following weekend, he'd show it to Carmen.

It meant they'd be forced to consider their relationship anew. Rex was ready for that. Was Carmen? He wasn't sure. Her fiercely guarded independence might force her to deny it was anything more than a sexual trade-off. That's what he figured she was doing, after these past two days together. They'd swapped places, in one respect. As a teenager, she'd wanted romance. Now, she wanted the house. And he wanted her more than ever.

The letter would force the issue. He'd find the right moment, and they could calmly consider it. Some groundwork would help. They'd already broken down one barrier—Carmen knew why he'd left all those years ago. Now they had to consider why they were back together.

Did it really matter? He just wanted to be with her, always had. Probably always would. Rex contemplated the question.

It did matter. It mattered because, if his suspicions were true, it was an apology of sorts—an apology to them both.

CHAPTER THIRTEEN

By Tuesday evening, Carmen was already planning what she would take with her to wear the following weekend. So far she'd dressed conservatively, her initial reservations about Rex's sexual agenda not allowing her to be overtly provocative. Since she'd accepted his argument about burning out the old flame, she'd begun to relax somewhat. She'd also thought about her appearance differently. At the back of it all, her newfound knowledge about Rex's history with his father made her thoughts more tender, and that led to her acceptance of his terms.

There was no reason why she shouldn't enjoy it. So long as she guarded her emotions and kept the relationship within certain bounds, then she'd always have it—the affair she'd craved as a younger woman. A passionate love affair with Rex Carruthers. And it was even more hot and wild and fulfilling than she'd ever dreamed it might be.

When it came to sex, Rex was persuasive, demanding and predatory. No surprise. What was surprising was the extent of his sexual prowess and his sensitivity to her needs. She hadn't expected him to be so responsive and attuned, and the edgy side to their sexual encounters was one hell of a bonus. She liked the way he pushed her for honesty and made her exhibit her needs. No matter how unusual, it was wildly empowering.

Rex hadn't been far from her thoughts since they'd said goodbye on Sunday afternoon. In the shower, it was his hands she imagined on her skin as she lathered herself, and her entire body pulsed with energy, responding to him. When she got out of the shower and wrapped herself in a towel, she closed her eyes a moment, and thought of his arms around her. As she slipped a flimsy nightdress on, she imagined it was his mouth she felt kissing her skin.

Nevertheless, when her phone rang and it was his voice at the other end, her pulse stalled. "Rex? How the hell did you get my number?"

"I asked Mrs. Amery for it."

That easy. Of course. Mrs. Amery wouldn't think there was anything odd about it. "I should hang up on you."

"But you won't."

The sensible thing would have been to follow through, to keep the arrangement on simple terms, email only. But hearing his voice thrilled her to the core. Carmen sat down on her bed, then laid down, picturing him while he spoke to her. They'd parted with hungry kisses two days earlier, both of them openly eager for the next weekend. And now he'd called, and the sound of his voice was too good. So she didn't hang up. Instead, she cradled the phone to her ear. "I suppose I could humor you for a while."

"I'm not interrupting anything, am I?"

Did he think there was someone else? "Luckily for you, no. I just got out of the shower."

"Shame I'm not there to towel you off."

"A girl needs a break from these full-on weekends you're subjecting me to."

Rex laughed. "So you're enjoying our time together at the manor?"

She'd walked into the trap. "You need to ask?"

"You're a hard woman to please. That's why I'd like to hear you say it."

His tone was teasing, but his voice seemed to move over her like sunshine, making her stretch out on the bed to enjoy the heat. "You're very demanding."

"But you like it."

There was something different about him, she noticed. She supposed it was because she wasn't used to hearing his voice over the phone. He sounded as if it meant a lot to speak to her.

"You know I'm enjoying it," she replied.

"So let's do it more often. Why stop at a month?"

Her heart missed a beat. Was it a trick?

There was no way she could do this for more than a month. If she did, she wouldn't survive the hit when he got bored and walked away. She'd tutored herself to cope with a month. No more. "What do you mean?"

"Meet me for lunch tomorrow."

She should've been relieved he meant a midweek meeting and not an extension, but she wasn't sure how it left her feeling. "You promised. A few days without contact so I can concentrate on my work and stay sane."

"I clearly can't be trusted."

She couldn't help herself. She laughed. "I've always known that."

"I can't help wanting you."

Oh, that sounded good, and there was tender intimacy there; she wasn't imagining it. "You admit it?"

"I thought it was obvious."

"You just have to have every woman who takes your fancy."

"Maybe, but some women are more elusive than others…and there's this one in particular who makes me want her even more every time I'm around her."

His tone had changed. There was an implied inner power struggle and it focused her, as if he'd flicked a switch and they were back trading sexual kinks at the manor.

"In fact, I want her so much I'd record my conversation with her so I could listen to her voice over and over again, if I didn't think it was creepy and she might accuse me of being a stalker if she found out."

Again she chuckled. "You should be ashamed."

"I can't help it. This woman is turning me into a crazy man."

"I find that hard to imagine."

"Seriously, we're talking stalker territory. I could watch this woman all day. I want to watch her dress, undress…get naked and crawl across the floor on her hands and knees."

Carmen's breath caught. She forced herself to respond as levelly as possible. "It's hard to imagine a man with such presence being able to stalk someone without being noticed."

The silence hung between them, heavily weighted with implication.

Rex was the one who broke it. "Would it surprise you to know I watched you swimming once, without you knowing?"

"When?"

"That first summer, at the lake."

He actually seemed to relish confessing. She countered it carefully. "I never went in the lake without a swimsuit, and you've often seen me in my swimsuit. So what are you saying?"

"I'm saying I watched you without you knowing. Does it freak you out?"

"No."

"Well, maybe it should. It sure as hell disturbs me that you caused me to do stupid things like that."

Carmen chuckled. "And you caused me to do stupid things, as well."

"Like what?"

She'd said too much. "Oh, I can't say."

"You're going to have to tell me or I'll come over there and spank it out of you."

The thought of his hands on her in such a way affected her wildly. She tried to stifle her moan of longing, but couldn't.

"Well, well, well. I can tell that's something I ought to consider adding to our repertoire." He let that hang in the void between them before continuing. "But you're not distracting me, madam. What is it I made you do?"

The pulse in her groin raced. She was so turned on by the prospect of him spanking her she wanted to tell him—wanted to provoke him the way he provoked her.

"Playing hard to get?" He sounded casual, as if he was lounging back in his chair with a wineglass in one hand while he discussed their strange relationship. "And here I was thinking we were getting somewhere after last weekend. Carmen, this conversation is almost comfortable."

He had a point, and it made her smile. "It feels like, it feels like…well, the old days when we were back at the manor. When you used to flirt with me."

"It does, doesn't it? Do you think last weekend's revelations might have bridged the gap between us?"

"Oh, no, I think it's much simpler than that." Carmen rolled on the surface of the bed, sure in this fact. "I've got you on the end of the phone where you won't be able to physically take charge of me the way you do on weekends."

"That sounds like a challenge."

Heat traversed her body,. He could easily rise to the challenge and it made her body palpate in expectation.

Before she could respond, he continued. "I won't be distracted. I want you to tell me every detail."

It struck her he'd already taken charge, even from the end of the phone. She swallowed down her anxiety when warnings flashed in her mind. She wanted to confess while he wasn't there to react. It was about bloody time he knew what he'd put her through. "I used to go to my bedroom wall at night, knowing you were on the other side of it. And I'd touch it, because I wanted to touch you."

It took him some time to respond. "You did?"

"Yes, sometimes I moved my body up against the wall, and I kissed it."

"What a naughty girl. And did you do anything else? Is there more to tell, hmm?"

"Rex…"

"Oh…so there is."

She couldn't answer.

"Tell me exactly what you did."

She squirmed on the surface of the bed. How was it he could turn her into a helpless piece of putty in his hands by the tone of voice? "I thought about you, and I'd lie down on my bed and shut my eyes and imagine the things I'd do if…if I weren't a gauche virgin with a stupid crush."

"Like what?"

"Like walking into your room and straddling you." She forced herself on, because the confession had now become a burden she wanted rid of. "And I'd imagine it happening…while I masturbated."

The rush she experienced when she said it aloud was extreme.

"If I'd known, you wouldn't have been safe in your bed."

She clenched her thighs together. "If you'd known, you'd have done something about it?"

"We came close enough. If I'd known you were touching yourself while thinking about me I'd have taken the wall down with my bare hands."

Silence hung between them, an aching silence. It felt like an echo of the longing she'd felt for him.

"Are you touching yourself now?" His tone had become more intimate, his voice even lower than before.

Carmen glanced down at where her hand rested on her hip bone, her fingers in the groove at the top of her right thigh. "Not quite."

"What are you wearing?"

"A silky red nightdress. Mid-thigh-length."

"Nothing else?"

"No."

"Do you have a floor-length mirror?"

He was looking to test her. Nevertheless, she was intrigued. "Yes."

"I want you to go to the mirror and do what you did the first weekend at Burlington. I want you to lift your skirt for me and I want you to look at yourself and see what I see."

Carmen slid off the bed and made her way across the room. The sight of herself with the phone to her ear was surreal.

"Are you at the mirror?"

"Yes."

"Tell me what you see."

Even though he wasn't there looking at her, it felt as if he was. It was the way he was able to control her so easily, with his voice alone. "I'm in front of the mirror, barefoot. Just this red satin nightie with spaghetti straps and black lace at the edges."

"You're avoiding the good stuff. Do you look aroused?"

She forced herself to do as he said. Staring at herself, she hardly recognized what she saw. Her eyes were dark with arousal, her nipples starkly apparent through the sheer slip of fabric she was wearing.

Is this what Rex sees? This breathless woman who hung on his every word. No wonder he thought he could have her so easily. She was weak with lust for him, and he knew it.

"Well, do you?"

"You know I do." She heard the resentment in her own voice, but Rex just laughed.

He left her standing there looking at herself for a moment longer. "Time to lift your skirt for me."

It was so hard to do the simple act, so out of her realm, yet she felt compelled to do it for him. "Damn you, Rex, it's so humiliating."

"That's why it's worth doing, because it's turning you on, isn't it? I can tell by the sound of your voice, and I could see it all over you at   Burlington."

126

Carmen pressed her eyelids shut, silently cursing him.

"It aroused you to show yourself to me."

He was so right, and it annoyed the hell out of her.

The resistance was like fuel to the furnace of her lust, as if doing something so blatantly rude for him hooked deep into her psyche. When she opened her eyes, she moved her free hand down to the hem of the nightie.

"I'm doing it now," she whispered

Lifting the fabric she watched as the tops of her thighs and her groin were revealed. The very act of lifting her skirt was both sordid and liberating at the same time, and it made her restless and needy. A whimper escaped her.

"And you look beautiful, don't you?"

Carmen stared at her reflection.

She was unable to reply.

Is this really what he saw, this aroused creature? No wonder he could take advantage of her. She looked like an open book, words screaming off the page: *I want him. I want this man.*

"You've never seen yourself looking like that before, have you?"

"You make me sound like I'm a gauche virgin again."

"That's not what I meant. I'm asking you if you've ever looked at yourself while you're aroused."

Carmen felt incredibly vulnerable. It was because he was edging dangerously close to asking her about her sexual history.

"It's not a difficult question, Carmen. Most people don't stop to consider what they look like when they're about to have sex." He chuckled into the phone and the sound made him feel even closer, as if he was there standing behind her, forcing her to look at herself, his breath warm against her ear as he gave instructions.

The notion didn't help. "I can't say I ever have. But, as you point out, it's not top of my to-do list when in a state of arousal."

"Do you think you look different?"

"Startlingly so, and yet…"

"What? Tell me."

"I look the way I feel."

"Ready for sex?"

"It's more than that."

"Tell me. I want to understand you. I've wanted to understand you more than any person I've ever known. You're an enigma to me."

127

REX

Carmen shook her head. He was ladling charm on her and it wasn't needed. "I'm not a complicated person."

"You've been the biggest mystery in my life and I need to know you."

The things he was saying tugged on her heartstrings. Could it be true?

Drifting on a tide of emotion, she found herself confessing; even before she'd registered the thoughts they came out in words, a confession that surprised her as much as it might him. "When we're like this, when you—" she paused, looking for the right words "—when you take control, I feel feminine, I feel like a woman. It surprises me how strong it is, but I like the way it feels.... And that's what I see now."

"Is that the appeal?" His tone was curious. "Of giving over the control to me?"

Had she said too much? Given him even more power over her? "I suppose it is," she said, trying to reel it back in, to make it an objective discussion rather than a confession about how he made her feel. "Allowing the man to take charge is a sacrifice of self, but it comes with certain rewards."

It was a vast understatement. She'd never experienced such undeniable male allure.

There was silence at the other end of the phone, but she could sense him assessing her, perhaps even planning his next move. She turned away from the mirror and grasped the brass bedpost on the footboard of her bed, worrying at it as she waited for him to say something.

"Are you close to your bed?"

"Yes."

"Put the phone down, get naked."

She pressed her eyes closed a moment, wishing she could deny him and hang up. It was a simple enough command, but it implied there was more to come. It left her body throbbing with longing, unwilling to be denied whatever pleasure he might give her. Silently she did as instructed, setting the phone down on her bedside cupboard before lifting the slip of fabric she wore, taking it up and over her head, and tossing it aside.

Before she picked up the phone, she sat down on the edge of the bed. From the corner of her eye she saw herself there in the mirror. "I've undressed."

"Do you have a vibrator?"

"Rex, please, stop winding me up." He couldn't be serious.

"Come now, you're an aroused woman and it's due to the nature of the discussion we've had. Do you agree?"

She said nothing.

He continued.

"I wouldn't be a real man if I left you in such a state. I'd like to bring the situation to some satisfactory conclusion. And as I'm not allowed to see you during the week, I'll have to help you with it in some other way." He paused deliberately. The commanding tone was back, the intimacy of his earlier questioning given over to a more direct approach.

Helpless to do anything else, Carmen lay back on her bed.

"So we've established you own some sort of sex toy. Is it close at hand?"

She swallowed down her embarrassment and distracted herself by imagining him standing there by the side of the bed looking at her the way he did. It was so much easier to submit to him when she could look at his gorgeousness. But still she found she wanted to submit, to please him. "It's called a Silver Dream Machine and it's in the top drawer of my bedside cabinet."

"Silver Dream Machine, huh?" He laughed softly. "Does it do the job?"

"It's…satisfactory."

"Satisfactory?" There was humor in his tone. "Somehow that doesn't sound good enough."

If he was fishing for compliments he was going to have a long wait. His ego didn't need flattering. He had her flat on her back and naked through the sheer power of his voice and his suggestions. Instead, she rolled on her side and opened the drawer with her free hand, reaching for the vibrator.

"The vibrator is now on the bed."

"Good." He paused, and then sighed deeply. "Phone sex with you is making me want a cigarette."

A cigarette? He'd got her all hot and bothered and now he'd taken his foot off the accelerator, leaving her hanging. She pressed her lips together, determined not to reveal just how desperate she was for him to continue. "Phone sex? Is that what we're doing here?"

"Oh yeah." His low chuckle assured he loved every moment.

"I didn't know you still smoked."

"I don't. Although I may have a packet stashed away in a drawer for emergencies like this."

She laughed, thinking back on a memory. "The last cigarette I recall was an illicit smoke…shared with a boy I had a crush on…"

"I remember it well. It was hella arousing passing it back and forth, watching you draw on it."

"What makes you think I was talking about you?"

"I *know* it was me. I tempted you with my smokes when I cam home from Uni. I led you astray."

"Just like you're doing now, huh?"

Silence hung in the air for a long moment. "I prefer to think we're on the right path and going forward together now."

Butterflies loosed from the pit of her belly, making her crave more intimacy. She squeezed her eyes shut, attempting to push away the memory. It wouldn't leave though. It never had.

"Touch yourself," he whispered, "and tell me exactly how wet you are. I need to know."

She didn't need to touch herself to know she was exceedingly damp. Yet her hand moved automatically to answer his request. Tentatively she stroked her fingers over her folds. It was torment. "I'm wet. You made me wet."

"Put your fingers inside."

She did as instructed and her sex quivered.

"Tell me how wet you are…wet enough to take something hard?"

"Rex…please," she murmured as her fingers thrust inside. Then lust unleashed her tongue. "I'm so wet, the sound of your voice…it does bad things to me." Shoving her fingers in and out, she burned up, embarrassed and aroused in equal doses. Her core clenched, aching for him to be there.

"Good. That pleases me immensely. Stroke yourself. Imagine it's my tongue on you. It'll be there as soon as I get you alone next weekend."

She panted aloud to relieve some of the tension she felt. Her hand was shaking as her fingers moved, but her flesh throbbed with longing for him, roused to distraction by his intimacy and his commanding tone.

When she moaned, he tutted. Loudly.

"I think you're ready for the lucky vibrator. Pick it up."

She reached for the vibrator.

"Turn it on. Let me hear it."

Carmen moved it close to the phone and switched it on.

"Very subtle. Now, are you comfortable? Would I be able to watch you masturbating if I was standing at the end of your bed?"

"Rex…"

"Make sure I could see everything, if I was there."

Aside from actually being there, he couldn't make his presence more felt. Swearing beneath her breath, she shimmied down the bed and latched her legs over the footboard. "Legs akimbo, bastard."

"I bet that looks good."

"You'll never know."

"I can just picture it."

She smiled. The tension in his tone revealed he was suffering too.

"Now, move it over your clit, nice and slow."

When she did, she wanted him inside her.

"Take it in, to half-mast, and then slide it   in and out."

"Do you have to be quite so detailed?"

"Obviously I do."

The humming vibrator slid easily into her damp cleft. She did as instructed, barely rocking it back and forth.

"Now push it deeper. All the way in."

She cried out when the machine hit deep against her sleek walls.

"Good girl."

She maneuvered the humming machine in and out on his command. Total submission bent her to his will even though he was several miles away, freeing her spirit to its every pleasure. When she felt the head nudging up against her center, she was open, exposed, moaning wildly, and there was absolutely nothing she could do about it. She pressed her thumb to her clit.

"I'm coming, I'm coming." A hot plume of sensation burst up through her pelvis and spine. Her head rolled on the pillow while she moaned with inescapable pleasure.

"Good girl. I can just picture you," he said quietly. Then he laughed softly into the phone. "At least one of us will sleep well tonight."

"Poor Rex. Have you left yourself high and dry?"

His laugh was husky. "Yeah. I really need that after-phone-sex cigarette now."

"Think of me while you're…smokin'…" She purred, knowing she'd delivered a bit of payback.

"Oh, I intend to."

She pictured him stroking his erection. "It was you I wanted," she added.

"Good. You can tell me all about it over lunch tomorrow. Be at the Fuji Hiro noodle bar in Hackney at midday."

Barely out of the throes of orgasm, she struggled to respond.

"I'll see you then," he added.

"No," she whispered, "I can't."

"Yes, you can."

He'd already hung up.

She stared at the phone. "Damn you, Rex."

CHAPTER FOURTEEN

Rex sat at the bench by the window at the Fuji Hiro noodle bar and watched the street outside, eager to catch sight of Carmen's arrival.

It was crowded, but as soon as he saw her, it was as if the rest of the people vanished and she was alone out there. She was walking along, looking up at the name above the noodle bar. Rex scanned her appearance. She was wearing stacked heels and skin-tight black jeans. Her filmy, long-sleeved top dipped low in her cleavage and swung out at her hips as she walked. It was dramatic dark red and suited her. Unusually, her hair was pinned up, making her neck appear even more graceful than he already knew it was.

When she paused and looked through the window, their eyes met.

Her smile made Rex glad to be alive. He waved, and she quickly came inside. Rex watched as she walked over. Thinking of what this elegant woman had been like with him—both at the manor and on the phone the night before—made him want to study her at length.

"Don't look at me like that," she said as she sat down.

"Like what?"

She arched her eyebrows. "I can tell what you're thinking."

Rex smiled, and kept studying her.

Her cheekbones colored.

"I'm admiring you, is that so hard to endure?"

"You're thinking about sex."

"So are you. That's why you mentioned it."

Her eyes flashed.

The waiter arrived and they placed their orders.

After the waiter had gone Rex leaned in and put his hand over hers where it rested on the table, then he drew it to his lips to kiss her. "It's good to see you here. Anywhere, in fact. Thank you for coming. I don't mean to make you feel uncomfortable. I can't help admiring you and wanting to be around you. You're a beautiful woman."

SASKIA WALKER

Carmen glanced away, scoping the place while she responded. "I'm never quite sure what makes me more uncomfortable, when you tease and toy with me, or when you use your charm as a weapon."

"You make me sound like a bad person." Rex meant it humorously but there was an underlying edge there, too. Did she really think that way?

She smiled. There was power in that smile of hers.

"Have I dragged you away from a hectic desk?"

"Luckily for you, it wasn't too bad. Otherwise, you might have been dining alone. It was very naughty of you to trick me into this."

"It was. But you can't refuse me anything. And that's such a tempting thought, I can't help taking a few liberties."

She laughed. "What about you?"

"I had a meeting nearby this morning." This felt normal. This is what they should be doing, Rex realized, sharing their day.

While they talked about commuting in London and office space and other work-related trivia, he realized he wanted all of this as well as the rest. He wanted to lock her away and keep her to be his and his alone. He couldn't do that with anyone, let alone a woman like her—so independent, so strong and able to run her own business—whatever her proclivities in the sexual department. Her private submissive nature didn't detract from everything else she was. Elegant, desirable and an exceptionally capable businesswoman.

When the food arrived, he noticed the way she ate, using her chopsticks effortlessly to flake her salmon teriyaki. She savored each morsel, dividing her attention equally between the food and the conversation. He also had the feeling she knew exactly what every other person in the restaurant had ordered and at what stage the service was at. Her attention flitted about, but with consummate skill. Her observations never interrupted their current discussion. This was a side of her he'd never studied closely before—the mature, sophisticated businesswoman she'd become.

It shouldn't be a surprise. Carmen Shelby was the director of a company with a healthy turnover, despite the hard times of the recession years. Everything he'd read about Carmen's work proved how much she'd pushed the business on, sourcing items everybody wanted for their homes, comfy furnishings, crockery and ornaments. Affordable but at the top end, so having these items still felt like they were classy and desirable. There was prestige when you carried an *Objet d'Art* bag among your shopping.

"Have you been okay," he asked, "since the weekend?"

"It's been so weird, thinking about what you said, about your dad's expectations of us."

133

The letter was in his mind, but he couldn't address it yet, not while she was still getting used to the previous information he'd shared with her. "You weren't aware of his perfect family dream?"

"I suppose I was, and in a weird way I could relate to it, because I'd always wanted a brother." She looked at him and smiled. "Then you arrived, all stroppy and surly. Stomping around the house with your long hair and your attitude."

It shamed him her memory for detail was so good. "I can't be blamed for my surly self. When I came home after our parents got hitched it was a total culture shock. I wasn't used to Burlington Manor being a happy place. I was a bit freaked out by what I found there."

She looked at him as if confused at first then she broke into laughter. "Oh, Rex, really?"

"Of course. My parents argued the whole time. Bitterly. It was a shock to me to come home and find…well, happiness. Dad was content with Sylvia."

She studied him. "I never knew it was such a change for you. I mean, I'd guessed it would be awkward, turning up to find us so thoroughly ensconced there."

"It's true. And I also felt a duty to my mother. I had to give my dad a bit of grief for upsetting her. It's in the contract for number-one son."

She chuckled. "So, to do right by your mother you came home stoned and then proceeded to get plastered on your dad's best whisky?"

"Like I say, duty." He lifted one shoulder.

The atmosphere between them felt so easy and warm. And the honesty, it was too good. He wanted to bottle the mood of the moment, to capture and keep it for them to enjoy always.

"Why did your parents split up?" she asked tentatively. "I always wondered."

Rex shrugged. It wasn't something he wanted to be totally honest about, not with her and not right now. So he lied. "My mother wouldn't talk about it, said it was in the past. Everything changed after that, when you came into our lives. It's why Dad was so keen to be the family unit, I guess. He'd made such a hash of it the first time around."

He'd be able to show her that in the letter, soon.

He smiled and tried to break the tension, hoping to steer her away from the more troublesome question. The last thing he wanted to tell her was his parents had split because Charles Carruthers had a mistress on the side while he was married to Rex's mother. Carmen didn't know, and he preferred to keep it that way. It would tarnish Carmen's image of Charles, and Rex didn't want to do that. When he did share the letter with her, he wanted them to be comfortable with each other. They were getting there and meeting like this, on neutral ground, was helping. "So you noticed that, me being a git?"

"I couldn't fail to notice, obsessed with you the way I was."

Rex wanted to respond with something easy, something witty, but her comments affected him so intensely he couldn't do anything else but reach out for her hand across the table.

Touching her that way felt precious.

She wasn't fighting. She also wasn't submitting. Instead, she was meeting him on equal ground. As much as he adored her when she offered herself like a gift—sacrificing all control to him—he also treasured these moments where they were stripped bare to each other. The honesty they shared was what counted most of all. They needed this time together, to edge it forward. *I want this. I need to be with this woman.*

"I was confused by you," she continued. "I'd wanted a brother, you see. But what I got was you…a stroppy, brooding bloke who somehow turned me into a puddle of lust every time he turned up and prowled around the house."

A puddle of lust? That triggered his libido dangerously. "Like I said last night, it's a good job I didn't know that at the time. You wouldn't have been safe."

She gave him a faux warning glance. "You did know."

Why did that make him feel like he hadn't done enough back then? He hadn't been mature enough to talk to her about their weird situation and the undeniable attraction between them. "I knew how it felt to be around you, and I knew it wasn't just me."

The look in her eyes made him want to hold her, badly. They needed to excise the demons that had been put in place around their desire for each other.

"The whole brother/sister thing." He shook his head. "I hated my dad for trying to enforce that on us. Both of us were the only child. Even if there hadn't been physical attraction between us, neither of us was equipped to take on a new sibling at the late stage of being a teenager."

"That's true." She blinked, and it was an accepting look she wore. "Just your average dysfunctional family, hmm?"

"Absolutely." He swigged from his iced Asahi. "I couldn't deny it felt good, though, what you and Sylvia brought to the house. And I didn't deny it for long. It was a new age. I began to enjoy it. Like I'm enjoying us there, together, now."

She didn't respond and to his surprise she seemed to pull away.

"Why can't we be like this all the time?" He asked the question because as soon as she pulled back, he felt crazy for her, desperate to hold on to her.

"Rex, please don't spoil it."

Was it a plea, or a warning? She'd shut off from him. It felt as real and stark as if she'd physically pulled a screen into place between them.

"I'm spoiling nothing. I'm asking a simple question."

She shook her head. "We're not at the house, so we're not weighed down by it all. That's all it is."

"But you love the house."

"I do. And you found out you do care about the place, after all."

"Maybe." He didn't want to pressure her too much, especially not now when she'd seemed so happy. Or was that beginning to dissolve before his eyes?

"You're going to renege on our deal," she accused, "aren't you?"

"No." Even as he said it, he wasn't sure he could stand by the deal. It was because he wanted her, and in his mind he couldn't take the two things apart. Even though it was illogical, he was stubbornly fixed on it now. If he signed the house over to her, he might never see her again – a risk he couldn't afford to take.

"You found you do care about the estate and your sense of responsibility has dropped into place." She sighed. "I can't blame you for that, but I feel duped."

Rex felt incredibly frustrated. He shifted, closing his hand around her wrist and holding her forearm to the table. "I never set out to dupe you. The first thing I said to you was why can't we share the place? Carmen, we want each other."

She glared at him. Even though she didn't pull away from his grip, there was vehemence in those eyes. "What? You want to come and go at weekends and use the shared ownership as a ticket to screw my mind as well as my body?"

Frustrated, he spoke very deliberately. "No. That's not what I want. I want something better than that, something normal, for both of us."

She stared at him for a moment, and he thought she was going to accept it, but her eyelids lowered, closing him out. "It's all too…"

"Too what?"

When she looked at him, he was taken aback by what he saw. Her eyes shone with withheld tears. "It's taking me back to my mother's death and all the pain that went down between all of us."

It hit him hard to see her hurting, but logic held him steady. "And you didn't think that'd always be there in Burlington Manor when you wanted it?"

"I suppose I ignored the possibility. I don't know. It's not being there so much as talking about the past."

"But we're both remembering the happy times, too. We remembered those first. I don't think talking about the past is creating this situation. We have to put the pieces together, the good and the bad. It's just something we have to get through, to get past it and be together."

She hung her head. "I don't know if we ever can."

"Carmen, I want you, and you can't deny you enjoy being with me. Why can't we do this?"

"So many reasons." She sighed and turned away.

Rex gave a wry smile. "The fact you haven't denied you enjoy our time together is a good start."

Her expression softened and she met his gaze. "I can't deny that anymore, can I?"

"Not since you tossed aside the keys to the manor to get to me, no."

She wagged her finger in warning. "Don't take advantage."

"What else is there that I need to know, tell me?"

She took a deep breath. "Specifically, when we talk about the past, it makes me remember how I felt after the car crash. I hadn't bargained for that."

He covered her hand with his.

"I didn't feel it when I arrived at the house. It was after you told me why you fell out with your dad. It made me think about when we were all closer, and why I chose to leave."

"It must have been a terrible time for you. I'm so sorry I wasn't there."

"So am I." She moved her hand, meshing her fingers through his.

The action was so simple yet so significant.

"I thought about you a lot," he said.

She gave a gentle smile, but the pain was there. Why hadn't he seen this aspect before? He hated himself for missing it.

"Your dad locked himself away." Pausing, she seemed to be picturing it. "I don't think we were in any state to comfort each other, though, so I went to my aunt's. I felt closer to Mum, with her sister. I wrote to your father every week at first, and he wrote back. I used to ask his advice about Mum's business interests, and he always offered an opinion."

"She's always with you."

Carmen nodded. "There's something else, though. I mentioned I didn't think it was an accident?"

He nodded.

"I told the police. She was a good driver. She never exceeded the speed limit. They looked into it but they found no evidence to suggest her car had been tampered with. I've never been happy with their explanation. It always felt as if there was more to it, and the suspicion never really went away."

Rex felt as if a window had been opened, and the view wasn't good. *Why didn't I think about this?* Because he'd been busy courting the racing circuit when it happened, most likely. Guilt crept in. "Did you tell my dad?"

"Yes. Well, actually, the police did." She had a faraway look in her eyes as she spoke. "He agreed they should investigate any concerns I had, but he couldn't think of a good reason anyone would do such a thing. I brought it up in our letters, and he reiterated that. He told me he felt guilty for bringing her out there to the country, where she died so tragically."

That was more tenderness than Rex had ever witnessed in his father, but he didn't resent it. He was glad they'd had the connection, before and after the accident. Had it been part of his father readdressing their own split, a cause for the letter he'd read?

He leaned forward, drawing her attention back to him. "You're bound to wonder exactly what happened, it's only natural."

"I know. I suppose it'll always haunt me. The important people do." She smiled then, and although her eyes shone and her lashes were damp, she looked at him with genuine affection.

"We'll talk more over the weekend, at the manor. We need to be there to address these issues and move on."

"I suppose you're right. I expected it to hurt, but walking in there, I mostly remember the happy times."

"You can't just blot it out. We need all the pieces of the jigsaw to make sense of the world. I hated the fact my parents split up at Burlington Manor, but I can't pretend it didn't happen, just as much as I couldn't deny how happy Dad was with Sylvia."

"You know, sometimes you're so sensible I barely recognize you, Rex Carruthers."

"That almost sounds like a compliment."

"Don't worry. I haven't lost my senses completely. I'm well aware you've rather cleverly got me lined up for another weekend of kinky sex at the manor."

"Guilty as charged."

"You're shameless."

"Utterly."

And this time there would be no partygoers to mess things up. Just him and her, the letter to discuss and the past to put to rest. Rex was ready to deal with it all, in the hope they could finally be together.

CHAPTER FIFTEEN

By Friday, Rex was counting the minutes.

A draft came down the tunnel into the tube station. Hopefully it heralded a train, Rex glanced back at the electronic information boards. One minute until the next arrival. He checked his watch impatiently.

He'd had a lot to deal with at Slipstream that week. The business meeting he'd had to attend took longer than planned and now he had to get home to pick up his car and drive north to Burlington Manor for his weekend with Carmen. After what had passed between them the weekend before—the understanding, and the mutual desire—all he could think about was being with her again. Weekends only was getting to be a burden. After his first call, they'd spoken on the phone every night of the week. Carmen drew a line when he asked her out to eat with him again, reminding him she needed the weekdays apart to stay sane, but it was driving him insane being apart from her.

The sound of the train approaching brought him back to the moment and he edged forward on the platform. It was crowded and he didn't want to have to wait for the next train.

Behind him the crowd thickened.

Rex felt a hand on his back. He was turning his head to tell whoever it was to back off when the hand pushed him. Hard. Between the shoulder blades, jolting him forward. The ground went from under Rex's feet.

The train loomed close.

Instinct kicked in. He scrabbled, keeling sideways.

A scream rang out and the crowd shifted.

The screeching of the brakes entered his consciousness as he hit the concrete platform. Grasping the edge of the concrete slab, he levered himself back before he could fall to the tracks below. The train ground to a halt, but not before he felt it, a mere breath away from his knuckles.

Bounding up, he stared through the crowd toward the stairs and he saw a figure racing away. Male, tall, wearing a hoodie. He was about to go in pursuit, but the crowd thickened again and he was surrounded by people quizzing him as to what had happened. Had he fallen? Did he intend to jump?

"I was pushed," he stated, anger fueling him.

"Sir, I need to make a report!" a uniformed supervisor shouted across as Rex headed off, but Rex shook his head.

Taking the steps two at a time, he raced up to ground level and vaulted over the turnstiles, craning his neck to catch sight of a navy blue hoodie as he went. Out on the street he looked both ways, but the late-afternoon commuters were thick on the street and his assailant had vanished.

Hands on hips, Rex caught his breath, taking a moment to absorb what had just happened. He'd acted on instinct, and he'd got lucky because he was already aware of the hand at his back and was twisting around to check the guy out. As a result, he'd gone down sideways instead of head-on.

What was the likelihood of it being random? Did he take a hit courtesy of a run-of-the-mill nutjob? Maybe, maybe not.

He recalled the figure at the window, last Sunday at the Manor. Unease crept up his spine. And the disconcerting event made him think of Carmen even more.

He hailed a taxi.

When Rex arrived at Burlington Manor he discovered a strange car parked on the forecourt outside the main entrance. He caught sight of the silver Audi and immediately wondered who was with Carmen. After the strange event at the Tube station, he was on high alert for the unusual.

It could be her taxi. She was due in much earlier than this, though, so the cab would be gone by now. This didn't look like a local cab. A delivery, perhaps? If so, it was after hours.

Parking next to it, he leaped out of his car and skirted the other vehicle to check it out. The only clue to the identity of the driver was a parking permit from the local hospital. With his sense of caution set high, he memorized the number plate before he went inside.

Mrs. Amery hurried down the stairs as he entered the hallway.

"What's going on?"

Mrs. Amery nodded her head up the stairs. "Dr. Ross is here from the village."

"Why?" Rex strode up the stairs.

"I called him. It's Miss Carmen, she had an accident."

An accident? Concern sent him into overdrive. "What happened?"

"She fell on the service staircase. Something must have worked loose and…"

Her voice faded away as Rex shot past her, his mood frantic.

REX

By the time he reached the doorway to her room, his chest felt constricted, concern for her almost blotting out the sound of voices chatting beyond. Grasping the door frame, he paused when he saw her, happily smiling at her companion. Only then did the noise register. It was her laughter.

Relief flooded him.

Carmen was sitting in her winged armchair, one foot raised and propped up on a large cushion on a stool. The doctor was fishing around in his briefcase, but paused, glancing up when Rex arrived. "Well, well, Rex Carruthers. I haven't seen you in a long while. You look well, young man."

The doctor reached out his hand.

Rex shook hands with the family doctor. It was comforting to find a familiar face with Carmen when he'd been so concerned. He stepped away from the doctor and knelt down at Carmen's side, looking at her searchingly. "I'll take care of you. I won't leave your side."

"Your sister will be fine."

"Stepsister. Ex-stepsister, in fact," Rex qualified sharply, clasping Carmen's hand inside his own. "We aren't blood related."

"Yes, of course, apologies." Dr. Ross looked from one to the other, then smiled. He nodded and picked up his briefcase. "It's a minor sprain but I'll get someone to deliver you a walking stick within the hour so you'll be able to get around easier."

Mrs. Amery, who hovered at the doorway, interrupted. "There's a range of walking sticks in the boot room. I'm sure one of them might do the job."

"Even better," the doctor responded. "Keep off it as much as you can for a day or two. If it's sore when you're moving around use the stick on the opposite side to help keep the weight off." He rooted about in his briefcase and came out with a prescription pad. "I'll prescribe some anti-inflammatory tablets, just in case there's swelling. Any other problems, give me a call."

Carmen smiled up at him. "Thank you, Doctor."

"I'll carry you everywhere," Rex said. "That's not a problem."

"You can't carry me everywhere." She chuckled.

"I can and I will." He heard the croak in his own voice. Responsibility and concern weighed heavily on him. It was more than responsibility he felt, though. He cupped her face in one palm, studying her.

She looked at him as if spellbound by what she saw in his eyes.

The look on her face was so precious. Somehow, it made him feel even more protective of her. Why had she fallen at all? Suspicion filled him. He'd had a near-miss himself earlier in the day, and now this. Vaguely he heard

Mrs. Amery ask if they needed anything urgently, but he couldn't tear himself away from looking at Carmen. If anything had happened to her...if anything did happen to her, he'd never forgive himself.

Mrs. Amery escorted the doctor out. Their footsteps and voices faded away on the landing.

Rex stroked Carmen's cheek with his thumb. "I'm going to check the stairs. Find out why this happened."

She blushed. "Just a silly accident."

Was it, though? He'd almost convinced himself the incident in the tube station was random. Not anymore. Were the two incidents not as coincidental as they might appear? But who would do such a thing? And why? The events of the weekend before came to mind. The scene Amanda had made, her drama-queen vocal attacks. The man lurking in the grounds by the windows. Had the gift his father had set up for them been a poison chalice? Rex frowned heavily, sure now.

Rex shook his head. "I'm not going to let you out of my sight. Get used to the idea."

CHAPTER SIXTEEN

There was something preoccupying Rex. It took Carmen a few minutes to realize, but as soon as she did she wanted to know what it was.

At first she'd been overcome by the sight of him racing to her side. The familiar sense of longing and desire flooded inside her as soon as he entered the room. The concern he expressed over her injury made her warm right through. It was so unexpected, to see Rex worked up over such a small thing. Because she craved him so, there was a sweet sense of indulgence in just seeing him that way, absorbing the feeling of being treasured and cared for.

Then she noticed he didn't lighten up.

After Mrs. Amery escorted the doctor out Rex left the room she heard him having a discussion with Bill Amery out on the landing and then the two voices faded away. When he returned, he paced about her room, checking the windows and doing the oddest things.

"Rex, whatever's the matter?" She shifted in her chair, rearranging herself.

He turned back immediately. "I'll get Mrs. Amery to bring you a cup of tea." He shifted a table from its place by the window closer to the bed. "In fact, we'll have dinner up here."

"Don't fuss about me, no need. Mrs. Summerfield has gone to a lot of trouble preparing the dinner and she's providing a full service before she heads home for the night. You know how she adores cooking for you. I'm not going to spoil it for her."

Rex frowned at her.

"If you insist, you can carry me downstairs, but I can easily use one of the sticks and I'll be able to get about quite easily. It's really not bad. Mrs. Amery rang the doctor as a precaution. It's only a little sore."

"I'm not going to risk you having another accident."

That annoyed her. "I already feel like a clumsy fool, there's no need to make me feel as if I'll injure myself again."

"That wasn't what I meant." His handsome mouth tightened. It was almost as if he didn't want to say what was on his mind.

144

He came back to her side and squatted down there again, an action which caused her to melt a little more because he was close, and so caring. He rested his elbows on the arm of the chair and looked deep into her eyes. "I want to get you out of here."

Get me out of here?

"What do you mean?" He might look like charm personified, but the statement immediately set off alarm bells for Carmen.

"I've checked out the stairs. Frankly, it's a miracle you aren't more seriously hurt. One of the banisters had been tampered with, and several of the carpet tacks had been removed."

"Tampered with? You can't be serious." His expression assured her he was. "I know the house needs work, but surely, that's all it was."

"Either way, it's not safe. I want to get you out of Burlington Manor, preferably tonight."

Carmen's jaw dropped.

"I know we set ground rules about our time together," he continued, "but given the circumstances, I want to take you back to London, to my place or yours, whichever you prefer. We could even go to a hotel." He ruffled his fingers through his hair. "Yes, somewhere anonymous might be better."

"No way." This was some sort of trick on his behalf, a ruse. He was trying to use this accident to unnerve her in order to get her out of the house. He'd engaged with the house again. He'd found out he was indeed fond of the place.

His eyes narrowed. "We're still inside our month, and you promised to be with me," he said, and he looked positively ruthless. "What difference does it make whether it's here or somewhere else?" He stood up and gestured dramatically with his hands, as if laying down law.

"It makes all the difference in the world. And anyway, we need to discuss the details of the property transfer this weekend. You've been busy playing your games but you haven't hoodwinked me, Rex Carruthers. I haven't forgotten the deal."

"The deal will be done. I'm not hanging around here to do it, though, not if you're in danger." He paced up and down the room as he spoke.

The change in him was unbelievable. Yet at the very same time she found herself overwhelmed by his presence and his powerful will. It affected her so profoundly she wondered if she would ever be able to deny him anything, no matter how ludicrous. It frustrated and angered her. She had to keep her head when it came to this man and the supposed deal between them. "Stop talking nonsense, you're overreacting."

145

There was no way she was going to let him push her out of the house now. Besides, she only had her emotions under control because the situation was limited to a time and a place that would eventually end. If they continued to see each other outside of the agreement, in other places, it would be more like dating and she couldn't risk falling more deeply than she already was.

Is that even possible?

Rex stared at her. "You've let me take charge in this situation, and that suits me fine. You will do as I say, even if I have to tie you up and throw you in the back of my car. I'd much rather you agreed and sat in the passenger seat."

Carmen stared at him. "What the hell is wrong with you? Why are you being like this?"

Her comments seemed to take a bit of the fire out of him and he returned to her side and shook his head. "Promise me you'll come back to London and spend the weekend with me there, if I explain."

Carmen frowned. "This better be good."

"Promise me."

She sighed with frustration. "I promise I'll travel back to London with you. I'm not sure I can spend time with you there, though."

Rex clasped one hand over the arm of her chair. He was looking at her as if she was mad. "Why the hell not?"

"Because…we agreed." She couldn't confess the real reason why—her fear of falling deeper if they spent too much time together. She'd already taken stupid risks that week, meeting him for lunch and entertaining him on the phone. He was beginning to seep into her everyday world, and she couldn't afford to let it keep happening.

"But the situation has changed." His eyes were wild.

"Has it? I need to protect myself." She glared at him, because he was confusing her and he was making her feel vulnerable and unable to keep emotions in check.

"That's what I'm trying to do, protect you." He cupped her jaw and then ran his fingers into her hair. "If anything happened to you here, I'd never forgive myself."

Carmen tried to make sense of it all. Could it be true, that someone had tampered with the stairs? She felt dizzy, confused and desperately vulnerable with him acting so tenderly toward her.

"Look—" he took a deep breath "—I need to figure out what's going on, but until I do I just want to get you the hell out of here and somewhere safe."

He spoke in a low voice and then glanced back at the open doorway as if checking they weren't being overheard by anyone.

"Okay, now you're scaring me." Suddenly she did want to leave. He'd rattled her. Maybe it was his goal, to get her out of the house. Had he pounced on this silly sprained ankle of hers to use it to gain the upper hand with her? He was such a charmer, such a smooth talker, for a minute there he'd almost got her convinced her safety was uppermost in his mind, but surely moving her out of the house was unwarranted. She would have put up with him forcing her to have dinner in her room while he fluffed her pillows. That might have been entertaining. But using it as an excuse to get her out of the house?

Mrs. Amery appeared with a carved wooden container filled with walking sticks. She deposited the stand in the middle of the room and then began to look among them. "Some of these aren't very practical. The doctor said the handle should be at hip height." She pulled some sticks out of the pot, started measuring them against herself, then brought them over.

Carmen scarcely heard what she was saying, fixated as she was on Rex.

"One of these should do the trick, but I'll leave them all so you can have a look at them."

Rex took the selection of canes from the housekeeper. "Thank you, Mrs. Amery. I understand dinner has been prepared."

"Yes, it'll be ready for service whenever you are."

"We'll dine as planned, but then I'll be taking Carmen back to London immediately afterward. It'll be more practical for her."

Mrs. Amery nodded. "That's a shame, but I do understand."

"Rex Carruthers, do *not* speak on my behalf."

His eyes flared as he looked at her. Never had she felt his dominance more directly than in the short, powerful glance.

Even though she was angry, her body responded instantly and intimately. She grew hot and restless and her thoughts went back to where they'd been before she slipped on the stairs. Preparing for his arrival, wanting to be his the moment he got to her. The need to feel him inside her had been building since the last time they were together. So she'd got there early, and run about the place, unpacking her bag and getting dressed for his arrival. It was that eagerness that landed her in this situation, but the desire hadn't gone away, and the way he was looking at her now—possessively, determined and oozing self-assured confidence—made her desire for him grow tenfold.

Rex stepped aside and let the housekeeper leave the room, then closed the door behind her. When her footsteps faded away, Rex locked the door.

Carmen swallowed. The mood in the room intensified, alone as they were. "You can't make me leave."

"That first night, you agreed to anything I wanted." He strolled closer and put his hands in his pockets. The casual pose was affected. The tension in him was obvious as he loomed over her.

"What I agreed to was a sexual negotiation. Anything, sexual, here in the manor."

He shook his head. "Funny, I don't remember you issuing any small-print details. All I remember is your agreement for me to have full control of you, every weekend, for one month. And if I recall, you were pleading, as much as agreeing."

"How dare you use that against me!"

He was so forceful, so utterly devastating in his command, she almost lost sight of what they were arguing about. It would be easy to revel in this moment and let him have his way. However, she suspected this situation was manufactured in order to break her down.

Carmen attempted to rise.

As soon as she did he, lifted her easily into his arms.

"Let me down," she said, wriggling and thumping her fists against the wall of his chest.

He quirked an eyebrow. "Tut-tut, my dear, you can't keep going back on your word like this." He carried her to the bed, where he laid her down. He did not, however, let her go. "Just moments ago you said I could carry you around."

He kept her pinned to the bed with his hands on her shoulders.

"You can't shift the goalposts on an arrangement like this," she blurted. "You keep trying to up the ante but it's really important there's absolute trust in the agreement."

"You say that, and yet you're the one who won't trust me when I'm trying to take care of you."

She wriggled her hips from side to side, trying to roll free of his hold on her. He wasn't having any of it. When her lower body rolled away, he moved one hand. Easily latching it around her thigh, he rolled her back. He kept his hand there between her thighs, bunching the fabric of her dress in her groin. His fingers were tantalizingly close to her sex, his thumb pressed against her mound. She had to keep completely still in order not to rub against him.

His expression grew dark and brooding as he watched her wriggling and trying to escape him on the bed. Then he shook his head, challenging her.

"You really are a little spitfire, Carmen Shelby. There seems to be only one way to get your attention for any length of time these days, but if you insist…"

He removed his hand from her shoulder and pulled up her dress. Moving his hand between her thighs he locked it over the surface of her sheer panties, cupping the mound of her sex easily in his palm.

Carmen moaned loudly. She couldn't help it. His hand on her there was too good. Immediately he began to knead her sensitive flesh, making her clit swell and tingle, her body heating through in a flash.

"Who'd have ever thought you'd turned out to be such a sexually voracious submissive." He shook his head.

"I'm not being submissive now," she shot at him.

"Are you sure?" A wry smile crossed his face as he looked down at her hips, where she was rubbing against his hand even while she argued with him.

Too much. With all her effort she pulled free and rolled away, quickly climbing onto her hands and knees as she tried to break free from him.

He grabbed her, holding her there. "You claimed you wanted to be mastered by me, and yet here you are, defying a simple request."

Her stomach flipped. She felt dizzy. *How is it my psyche is so in tune with that notion?* She wanted to fight with him, to argue about what he was asking of her, but when he demonstrated his will and his intention to have her, she lost the power to resist.

He took advantage of her brief pause and flattened her to the bed.

Before she had the chance to even wonder what he might do, the back of her skirt was lifted, and she felt his hand on her bottom. Hard.

Carmen yelped.

He spanked her again.

Her buttock stung. She tried to pull away.

"Facedown!"

She was about to deny him when the sting in her flesh turned into pleasure, the afterburn setting loose a heady sexual thrill. Her sex throbbed with longing, the pulse in her clit beating wildly.

"Carmen," he warned.

She did as instructed, staying facedown.

"That's better." He delivered another slap.

She groaned. Reaching out, she closed her fingers around the struts of the headboard.

"You really do have the most gorgeous arse." He slapped it again.

"It won't be gorgeous by the time you've finished with it," she blurted, unable to hold back the words.

He paused and she could feel the tension in him. "The way you're wriggling about is quite the turn-on. It's like you can't get enough of being spanked and want me to see how much it's turning you on."

She squeezed her eyes shut, wondering how she'd ever manage to endure the humiliation. But it was true; she was turned on by it, vividly so.

He slapped her again, and again, this time catching the underside of her buttock and the top of her thigh. The shock made her cry out. She panted, her whole nether region aflame. Heat shot through her from the points of contact, each strike connecting with the place at her center—the place where she craved his thrusts. Pleasure, pain and shame quickly engulfed her.

Moaning loudly, she arched her back, anticipating the next smack.

He changed his tactics and stroked the underside of her buttocks instead, his fingers making brief, maddening contact with her swollen sex.

While he toyed with her, running his fingers over her burning buttocks, the heat spread out, heightening the arousal she felt. Her breasts were tight, nipples hard against her bra. Her thighs were damp. She could smell the aroma of her own desire.

His fingers moved lower, pressing against her swollen, sensitive folds until he reached her clit. When he touched her through her panties, she panted aloud.

"You need a little relief, or so it seems," he commented. He tugged her undies off.

Carmen rolled helplessly on the bed as he did so, unable to resist or assist. She was already close. She felt it brimming inside her, burning hot and pulsating. He thrust his thumb inside her while his hand curved over her mound, crushing her clit. When he rocked his hand, she bore down on it, moving frantically, desperate for release. Her body was so wired she reached orgasm moments later, crying out as she came.

Then he was on the bed behind her, pushing her legs farther apart with a demanding knee. Cool air ran over her inflamed sex. Then she heard the rip of a condom wrapper. Her core clenched in expectation.

He slapped her on the buttock and positioned her hips, pulling her onto her hands and knees. That action—so brief, so commanding—made her weak. She was still swaying when he opened her up with two fingers and thrust his cock inside her.

"Rex," she cried out in relief, suddenly filled with him.

He pulled her hips hard onto him, lifting her physically, his cock buried deep. Every bit of her was singing out with pleasure at his penetration.

When his hands moved over her tender, inflamed buttocks she grasped at the headboard to stop the world spinning.

Pinning her there, he stayed still.

"You're mine for a month," he told her, "and I'll not endure any submissive of mine defying or subverting any of my instructions or needs. Not one!"

The very tone of his voice had her close to coming again. She tried to move, tried to respond to the pressure he was maintaining inside her, but he wouldn't let her.

"Do you understand?" Tension was evident in his voice.

Frustration built, her body craving friction, her sex so stretched and full with him something had to give.

"Carmen, I will not fuck you until I have your agreement, and I think we both know this has to happen."

"Yes, I agree," she cried out, unable to do anything but.

Then his hips began to roll into hers and the ability to think or negotiate was gone.

CHAPTER SEVENTEEN

It was near nine o'clock by the time Rex got Carmen organized and in the car. She sniped at him throughout dinner. She ate heartily, though, which amused him, despite the weight of concern he carried. The fact she sat down rather tentatively said it all. Her adorably pinked derriere was keeping her on edge. It also made her face flush whenever she moved.

She glared at him each and every time, despite the look of sheer and utter satiation also apparent on her face. It didn't bother him she was still disagreeable, as long as she wasn't in the house where she'd been in danger. Since he already had her agreement to obey him—given in the throes of orgasm—was all he needed.

The coincidences of the day were too worrying, and he kept thinking back to the time he'd spotted someone watching him when he was in his father's library. Once he'd examined the stairs where Carmen had fallen, he was convinced he had real cause for concern. The banister looked as though it'd been deliberately sawn so it would give way. The tacks holding the carpet in place had been carefully removed, and one of the old carpet braces—a relic from the 1930s—had been pried free. There was only one inevitable result there. The carpet would buckle up and become a death trap for whoever came down that way. It was a minor miracle she hadn't fallen all the way down. The marble floor in the service hallway below would have been an unforgiving landing pad.

When he quizzed Mrs. Amery as to why Carmen had used the staircase, the housekeeper informed him she always went down that way after she arrived back at the house, to go outside and look at her favorite place, the lake.

Why didn't he know that? It annoyed him her habits were so elusive and mysterious to him. Someone else knew, though. Someone who'd timed it to perfection. Could it be the same person—or persons—who had ambushed him in London? Whoever it was, they were rank amateurs. Neither prank had come to much of a result, but it had been enough to worry him about what they might be after. Was somebody after Burlington Manor and willing to do anything to get it?

As far as he was aware, neither he nor Carmen had any real enemies. Amanda's actions the week before kept coming back to his mind. Could she have something to do with it? He wouldn't rest until he was sure. Even though he was frustrated by the unanswered questions, it was with relief Rex drove the Maserati out of the grounds and headed in the direction of the main route southwest, back to London.

They drove in silence. Rex knew she was still battling inner demons over agreeing to this. Why was she so adamant not to be with him during the week? He thought she'd enjoyed their time together at the noodle bar in London. She'd certainly enjoyed their time together this evening, despite her protestations. He couldn't help being amused, despite the effect she had on him. He meant only to spank her into submission, but once they got started and she'd let rip with those moans of hers, his cock was rigid and there was no turning back. He had to be deep inside her while she was so helpless and shuddering with release under him. His orgasm had been intense, stimulated as it was by the tight fist of her delicious cunt gripping him in welcome. She was so slick and hot from what the spanking had unleashed. For a moment he'd lost touch with reality and the reason why he was spanking her in the first place.

Then she sat docile yet smarting at the dinner table. Her face was flushed and her eyes black. There was something so mesmerizing about the way she looked after he'd taken charge of her and given her a good seeing to. It made him want to do it endlessly.

Annoyance poured from her, even now, while she sat staring ahead in the passenger seat, her hands neatly folded on her lap.

Rex reached out and put his hand on her thigh. "You'll be rewarded."

She didn't reply. However, Rex sensed her reluctant interest.

Using his hands-free car phone, he called Lance. "Sorry to disturb you so late. I have a favor to ask."

"What can I do for you?"

"Your sister-in-law's apartment, is it still available to rent?"

"Yes, I believe so, but it's only available for a couple of weeks."

"That's ideal."

"You know someone who needs a luxury pad for a short-term let?"

"Yes. Me."

"Oh. Are you okay?"

"I've got a problem on the home front. Need someplace else for a short while. Listen, I'll reach London just after ten. Can you put me in touch with your sister-in-law so I can go straight to her to collect the keys?"

"How about I fetch the keys and text the address to your sat nav. We can meet there."

"Sounds good. Are you looking for a bonus?"

"Once we secure the Rashid contract, yes."

Rex laughed.

When he disconnected the call Carmen was looking at him with curiosity. Immediately she turned her face away, refusing to ask.

Rex smiled. She didn't want to accept someone might want to harm her. Understandable. Until he found out what was going on, he was happy to let her think it was just some little sex game he had going on. Besides, she enjoyed it. He could see it and he could feel it. She was secretly intrigued by his latest demands.

Upping the ante, that's what she'd called it.

Yes, it suited Rex perfectly.

Carmen's silent objection didn't last.

Their first night together in London she only reproached him with her eyes, withholding comment but making her mood felt in the way women could. By the time they got back to London and found the place, they were both tired and edgy. Sensing another argument brewing, Rex gave her the master bedroom and assured her of her privacy for the night.

The following morning he skipped out early to find fresh coffee and breakfast takeout. Luckily there was a nearby Italian coffee bar serving pastries and breakfast wraps. By the time he got back to the apartment with the goods, she was in the shower. She seemed impressed he'd gone to some effort and they ended up in each other's arms. They made it through the weekend drifting on a tide of sexual indulgence and intimacy. Thankfully her ankle didn't get any worse, although it had helped keep her in check. By Sunday, she was able to move around without his aid.

Monday morning, however, brought about a complete revolt and she made it quite clear that once she was back in business mode she didn't want to be controlled in any way.

"Too bad," he said, daring her to defy him.

She stared daggers at him.

It was going to be a demanding week, Rex decided.

She hadn't complained about the apartment, which was a relief. It was comfortable, anonymous, and it did the job. Nobody knew where they were. At least, nobody he couldn't trust. Then he asked himself who he could trust? *I can trust my people.* Lance was the only one who knew. No doubt he'd share it with the other guys by the time Rex got in to Slipstream. They'd be looking for an explanation as to why he wasn't in his own home, but he knew them inside out and he had no reason to doubt their discretion—which he would ask for as soon as he got to Slipstream.

It wasn't until Rex told Carmen he had no intention of leaving her until he made sure she was safely inside a secure building where visitors had ID checked when they came in and out that she flipped completely.

"What, are you insane?"

He shrugged. "Possessive. For now you're mine. It's my prerogative."

She stared at him with a mixture of horror and fascination. "It's just silly."

Rex stood his ground. He intended to take her to work and collect her from there at the end of the day.

"New rules," he stated.

She muttered in disbelief.

By the time he got her down to the car in the underground car park, she was seething. She practically stomped away to the car, forcing him to hurry to keep up.

"Be careful, you might hurt your ankle."

She glared at him across the roof of the car while he retrieved the keys from his pocket. "This is not what I agreed to. You keep shifting the goalposts to mess with my head."

"You were hurt. I'm caring for you and taking you to work. Big deal." Rex nodded at her. "Get in."

She wrenched open the door and climbed in, practically slamming the thing off its hinges when she shut it.

Rex rolled his eyes and looked up at the ceiling of the underground car park, praying for strength. For a woman who enjoyed playing the submissive in the bedroom she sure could turn into a spitfire when the mood took her. He couldn't help wondering if that's what had happened to her. Even though she'd said it was just him she'd been submissive with, he had a mad image of her being hog-tied by some bloke because she was letting rip with her feelings about some issue or other, and then she'd got off on it. The idea amused him greatly. It broke the tension he felt and as he got into the driver's seat he smiled her way.

"What?" she snapped.

"I was just picturing you hog-tied, which I assure you I'm quite willing to do, if necessary."

"Hog-tied?" She looked at him aghast. "What the hell sort of kinky freak pervert are you?"

"This, coming from you, who instigated the whole submissive thing in the first place."

"If I'd known it meant being hog-tied whenever you took the fancy—"

"Don't get too excited," he interrupted with a laugh, "it was just a passing comment."

"Oh, bloody hell, Rex. Fuck you!" But a moment later she laughed, too, and then her face fell. "You don't really think someone wanted me to trip and fall on purpose, do you?"

He hated to see her worry. That was his job. "I can't imagine anyone wanting to do that to you, Carmen. You were probably right in suggesting it was a maintenance issue." He reached out and squeezed her hand. "The stairs will be repaired this week."

That seemed to reassure her. "There's a lot to do at the house," she commented, brightening. "I started a list."

They parted on good terms. She even kissed him goodbye.

Once he saw her inside and noted the security system, he raced back to his car. He had a lot to do before he collected her at five. He'd worked through everyone who might hold a grudge against them, and he had a mental checklist and a plan of attack.

When he got to Slipstream, he hit the ground running.

The first thing he did was contact a reputable private investigator. He outlined his concerns and requested an appointment for as soon as possible. Once the meet was organized for the following morning, he left a message for Nate to call him back. Rex needed to know how Amanda had been after the party, but there was something else he had to ask his old friend, too. He needed a contact who might help shed some light on the dusty skeletons in the cupboards at Burlington Manor.

Nate rang within the hour. "Rex, what can I do for you?"

"Thanks for getting back to me so quickly. Listen, there's some stuff I want to find out about my dad. Can you put me in touch with your old man?"

"Of course. You're in luck actually. He spends a lot of time in Italy since he retired, but he's back for my cousin's wedding so you can catch him in London this week. I'll email you his number."

"Cheers." He tried to keep his tone light and conversational. "Hey, did you manage to keep Amanda in check after you left the party?"

Nate laughed. "She's a bit of a handful, but yes, I did."

"Was she still angry with me, or Carmen?"

"She had a bit of a rant, but it was fleeting."

A fleeting rant? It didn't sound like someone who had grounds for two physical attacks, but Rex didn't dismiss it.

"I managed to charm her," Nate continued.

"Good to hear. I owe you one."

"Not really, I always liked her but years back she terrified me."

Surely not? If Nate's thinking of taking Amanda on, he's even more bonkers than I am.

"I think I'm man enough to deal with her now," Nate was saying. "Besides, back then it was you she wanted. No one else but you."

Rex groaned internally. Who else's life had he messed up when he fell into bed with Amanda? "Sorry, mate, I hadn't realized."

"Water under the bridge, but before you go, there's something I should mention."

"Go ahead."

"I bumped into Kelly the other day. She was asking about you. She'd heard about the funeral."

Rex stifled a sigh. The last thing he wanted to think about was his ex. "And? I sense there's more."

"She seems to think she still has a chance with you. Um, what should I have said?"

"I think I know you well enough to know you said the right thing."

"Yeah, maybe. I told her you were fine, but I didn't encourage her."

"You're too nice for your own good, Nate. It was over weeks ago…or are you mentioning it because you're thinking about asking Kelly out yourself?"

There was an awkward moment. "No, not at all. I've been rather busy with Amanda since you charged me with her care."

Rex shook his head. "I didn't mean it to be a life sentence, man."

"My mistake." Nate paused. "Actually, it's okay. She needs someone."

"And you're the man?"

"Maybe." It was tentatively offered. "As I said, I always liked her."

"Watch your back. She can be mean."

"Fuck off."

Tersely delivered, the response made Rex shake his head. Nate was a goner. "Happily."

"Whatever. Look, I really don't need your opinion."

"I didn't give you my opinion. I gave you a heartfelt warning. Believe me, my opinion would have been a whole lot harder to hear. You're my buddy. I care what happens to you."

Nate sighed, clearly losing his patience. "She's damaged, for sure, but…well, she might be worth mending."

Damaged. Rex thought about it after they leveled up and said their goodbyes. It wasn't a term he associated with people, but he remembered his mother using it. She'd been talking about his dad at the time, of course. "Damaged people do damage to others," she'd said. "They can't help themselves. It's what they've learned to do."

Rex had argued, thinking it an angry lash back from a woman who'd been cheated on and wronged. It was also too much of a generalization to earn his agreement. Thinking about it now, however, he could see the sense in it. At least, to some extent. His father had done damage to pretty much everyone around him. Either directly or indirectly. Charles Carruthers had hurt all of them, beginning with Bea Swanitch, Rex's mother.

She'd had every right to leave Charles Carruthers when she found out about his mistress. It had been harsh for her. She'd loved Charles deeply, but she rebuilt her life. Returning to her family and friends in South London, his mother rejoined the life she'd had before. She'd come from an arts background and found her way there again. Nowadays she lived with her partner—a Swedish architect who Rex got on with well—and she managed a small art gallery near Sloane Square.

Rex tapped his lips thoughtfully.

Maybe his own mother would be a better source of information than his dad's buddy. Would she open up about the mistress? She'd refused to speak to him about his dad for years, but Charles Carruthers was gone.

And I need to know.

CHAPTER EIGHTEEN

"Come in," Carmen called out when there was a knock at her office door.

Estelle was there with two of the girls from marketing. "We're heading down to the Asian buffet for lunch, want to join us?"

Carmen gestured at the take-out bag on her desk. "I'd love to, but I had food delivered. I've got something specific I want to take care of."

"We'll bring you a fortune cookie."

Carmen waved. She needed more than a fortune cookie to help sort her head out. The task she'd set for herself was to go through every photo she could find on the internet of Rex with another woman, every bit of gossip and evidence of his philandering nature. It wasn't as if she didn't know about it already. She was simply going to drum it into her head, forever, because it was so easy to forget when subjected to his seductive charms.

Plus he was keeping something from her. Playing house wasn't all there was. He wanted her by his side, but he didn't want to take her to his home. On Sunday morning he'd taken her to her place to pick up some of the things she'd need for the week, and he'd peered around, curious about where she lived and her belongings. But he hadn't taken her to his place. He said he'd go during the week. Was there another woman's things there, or evidence of his past lovers?

After the situation with Amanda, and what followed, she knew she had to face up to it. This was a temporary arrangement, and the sooner she got used to the idea that he'd be with other women in the blink of an eye, the better it would be for her. Somehow, her guard had slipped. She was entertaining foolish fantasies about him, when what she really wanted to do was be level-headed and just enjoy it while it lasted.

In order to help her fix that goal in mind, she entered Google searches on his name and business, scanning photos. Most recently was the Australian model, Kelly Brown. Touted as the next Elle Macpherson, leggy blonde Kelly had lasted several weeks with Rex, months even. It hurt, stupidly so, but Carmen forced herself to look at the glamorous photos of them together at racing events and after-show parties at Paris fashion week.

REX

The farther she went back, the more a pattern emerged.

Rex only entertained short, intense affairs.

Short. Like two weeks, or a month?

Yes, he liked to play hard and move on.

Carmen realized she had to grow a thicker skin, and fast.

Rex stood outside the Lomsdale Gallery and looked through the large plate-glass window at his mother. Bea Swanitch was closing on her fifty-fifth birthday, but would easily pass for a woman a decade younger. He observed her as she dealt with a delivery person. She was impeccably dressed and unflustered even though there was some problem with the papers.

When she was done and had caught sight of him, she waved and then spoke to her assistant. A few moments later, she joined him on the busy Sloane Square pavement and they headed toward her favorite nearby restaurant. Rex glanced over his shoulder as they went, as he'd done since Friday.

"I didn't think you'd have time for a lunch date this week."

Rex noticed how carefully she worded that. She was aware he was dealing with his father's estate, but wouldn't refer to it directly. "Things are turning out to be a little bit more complicated than I anticipated."

"Is there a lot of paperwork to sort out before you can put the house on the market?"

"I'm not sure I'll be putting it on the market."

They were within five feet of the doorway to the restaurant, but his mother stopped in her tracks. "Please tell me you're not considering living up there."

Rex had anticipated that reaction. "Don't look so dismayed." He put a reassuring hand on the back of her shoulder and ushered her on, opening the door to the restaurant as they went. "I don't know what I'm doing at the moment."

Never a truer word said, he thought wryly.

"Maybe you can help me sort a few things out," he added after the manager had directed them to a table close to the window and they'd taken up their seats.

She gave him a suspicious glance. "It's not often you ask for my advice, but since you have, I think you should get rid of the place as quickly as possible."

"Lighten up. Dad's gone now." Everything associated with his father was shrouded in negativity for Bea Swanitch, apart—luckily—from himself. "I know it's difficult for you, but the house wasn't always an unhappy place."

She pursed her lips and concentrated on reading the menu for a few moments. The waiter appeared and took their orders. Once they were alone, she responded. "Rex, have some sense. It's not a working estate. It's a money sink."

"I never understood why he didn't change that. Why didn't he look into ways to make the house earn a living?"

She gave him a shrewd glance.

Rex gestured with his hands. "I know you hate talking about him, but there are a few things I need to know, just to sort out…some issues I'm having at the property."

"So this is the real reason we're having lunch." She wore a vaguely amused expression, indicating she wasn't too bothered.

"I always enjoy taking you to lunch, but I honestly could do with some information. My father hasn't exactly made it straightforward, and while I can't blame him for that, it's not altogether easy for me to deal with." Rex felt as if his father had presented them with a dubious legacy, one with mysterious complications attached. At first he'd been amused by the deal with Carmen, and he relished the prospect to get close to her as a result. But the subsequent events and emotional ties meant he was delving deeper into the past than he'd planned.

His strategy worked. His mother nodded. "Well, that doesn't surprise me at all. His life was a mess so why should his passing be any different?"

Their drinks had arrived and she took a sip of her chardonnay. "Charles was old school. There was money in the coffers when he inherited, and he used it to maintain the manor. When it ran out, and after we split, he married money."

Rex didn't want to give his opinion on the matter. Perhaps Charles Carruthers had married Sylvia Shelby for the money—they would never know for sure—but the two of them were happy together.

"Charles kept me out of the estate affairs, but it doesn't take long to notice the immense upkeep a property like that demands. Coal mining had funded the Carruthers family for decades, but when the mine closed down in the 1980s it soon became apparent that things weren't looking quite so rosy for Charles. After you were born I did suggest he open the grounds for private clay pigeon shooting parties and the like, but he said Burlington Manor was his home and he wanted it to remain a family home as it always had been."

She rolled her eyes. "Albeit without me in it, once I found out about his mistress."

Rex was about to ask about the mistress, but now she'd got started his mother was on a roll.

"I thought he might hitch up with his bit on the side, but he didn't. Instead, he married wealthy businesswoman Sylvia Shelby, which meant Charles didn't have to contemplate opening Burlington Manor up." She forced a smile. "Clever that."

Rex sat back in his chair and thought about the implications. He'd always accepted he came from a broken, dysfunctional family. Yet those years when Sylvia Shelby-Carruthers had been mistress at the manor had been the happiest of all. Growing up there as a child, his parents had argued. Then came the divorce. When he was told his father was marrying again, he'd expected the worse and rebelled against his father, majorly. As a result, his father hadn't allowed him to come home from boarding school for the holidays until Sylvia and Carmen were well-settled and the renovations Sylvia funded were under way.

It wasn't an immediate acceptance, but when he walked into that house the year he finished school and had some months to wile away before university, it felt so different it was hard to cast aspersions on the new arrangements. He tried for a while, solemnly resenting the happy family he found ensconced there. Sylvia had a knack with people, though, and then there was Carmen. Just thinking about her made him feel more focused on making this right.

Carmen must've found it difficult, too, back then. *Why did I never consider that?* The first summer he'd given her a hard time and treated her like a spoiled brat. By the following Christmas, however, the time they spent together had a decidedly different mood to it.

"It's a big burden he's left you with." The sound of his mother's voice snapped him back to the moment. "I can see it's taking its toll on you. You didn't even look this distracted when your first prototypes were being put to test."

Rex smiled. "Sorry. It's pretty weird going back there after all these years and trying to piece together what happened."

She rested her elbows on the table and meshed her fingers. "Rex, you know your own mind, and I've always been able to rely on you to make the best decisions in life. I will, however, remind you that your business should be your first consideration. Don't let that pile of old stones and its weird history drain your energies. You can't afford to let Slipstream suffer."

"You're quite right, and I do appreciate your wisdom on this."

His mother relaxed visibly. "So, you're going to get the Manor on the market as soon as possible." She opened her bag as she spoke. "Auctioning it off will be the quickest route, and you'll be able to invest the proceeds in your business, which is a much more viable and creative pursuit than anything your father ever did." She smiled at him proudly. "You'll be done and back in London within the month."

Rex lifted his eyebrows at her. "As I mentioned at the outset, it's not so simple. I don't have sole ownership."

His mother had been looking for something in her handbag but she stopped. Her head jerked up to look at him. "Really? Who did he…" She paused and then nodded. "Sylvia Shelby's daughter. Carmen, isn't it?"

"Yes, Carmen."

She cursed under her breath. "Second wives always benefit. They get it easy, while first wives get the tough years followed by the wreckage that comes with a man's midlife crisis."

Rex suddenly remembered why he'd been agreeable to the ban on discussing his father all these years. The bad feeling was never far way. He sympathized with his mother, and for many years he'd also been angry at his father. It was hard for her, finding out her husband had a mistress, but Rex didn't like the bitterness he saw in his mother's expression. It was still eating away at her even after all these years. "Sylvia Shelby died a tragic death. She's hardly benefited."

"You know what I mean. Her daughter benefited."

"And so has your son."

"Of course, you're Charles's heir."

"And, as you so rightly pointed out, Sylvia's financial support and the work she did on Burlington Manor kept it afloat."

His mother shrugged and went back to her handbag, pulling out a powder compact and opening it up to check her appearance in the mirror. "From what I've heard, Carmen Shelby doesn't need the money. Her PR person is a friend of a friend. Her business has an excellent turnover and keeps her very busy."

"That is the case, yes."

She tucked her compact away and then studied him.

Her scrutiny was top form. He shuffled in his seat and fiddled with his wineglass. "Carmen doesn't want to sell."

"I'm surprised. But what's the problem? Why don't you just let her buy you out?"

"Because I don't want to let her buy me out."

"Good grief, Rex. It's the past, let it go."

He stared across at her, wanting to tell her it wasn't just the past. He never discussed his relationships with his mother.

Her eyes narrowed as she studied him." Surely you can't be serious…you haven't got the hots for your half sister? "

Rex's mood shifted in an instant. "Stepsister! Ex-stepsister even. We're not blood related."

"Well, clearly you do have the hots for her."

Damn it. She'd phrased her question in order to trap him into a confession.

"What about the attractive model you're seeing, Kelly, isn't it?"

"I didn't even know you knew about her."

"A mother keeps tabs. And with you it's not hard. If you look in the right places."

Rex frowned. What right places? Aside from the occasional publicity shot he'd taken with Kelly—mostly when he'd accompanied her to events—he kept his press appearances solely to those associated with his business.

"Your mother can use a computer," she continued. "I'm not that old, you know. Don't look so surprised."

"I'm not surprised, and no, you're not old. I just didn't know you—"

"Oh, yes," she said proudly. "In my line of business we need to know who to invite to exhibition openings, and the internet is the fastest, most comprehensive grapevine I've witnessed in my life."

"True enough." It had never occurred to him his mother was tracking his affairs online.

"Kelly was a very presentable young woman, and you lasted several months with her. I was beginning to wonder if I might get a call telling me to budget for a decent wedding outfit."

Why did that rankle him so? "I hope you didn't put money on it."

"I know you too well." She smiled somewhat sadly. "So is it Carmen Shelby I have to blame for making you sentimental about the old place?"

That annoyed him even more, especially because it came so close on the heels of Carmen's accusation about him being fond of the house. "Sentiment has nothing to do with it. I'm trying to tidy loose ends."

The food arrived and Rex chatted about other things while they ate. Then he had to get to the point.

"There's something else I wanted to ask you," he broached. "Something I can't find out on the internet. This is a bit more personal, but I need to know."

"That sounds like a warning, but I confess you're intriguing me." The food and wine had mellowed her attitude to the subject of her ex-husband and his estate. That might be about to change.

"Did you ever know her name, his mistress?"

She paused as she was about to take the last sip of her wine, and returned the glass to the table. "Well, that wasn't what I expected you to ask." She eyed him across the table, her brows gathered. "Have you found some papers or something?"

"Something like that."

"Well, there's bound to be documents. He bought her a place to live. Nothing shabby, either. I heard it was a top-floor conversion overlooking Regent's Park. It's bound to be there in the papers."

Rex had no idea, but if she was right it meant he could find out the address by going back through the records. She might not even be living there anymore, but it was a starting point. He made a mental note to call Mrs. Amery and tell her to leave the paperwork to him. He couldn't risk the address going into the shredder.

"I never knew her last name, but her first name was Olivia."

"You've been really helpful, thank you."

"You'd be mad to keep the place. Don't let it get to you now Charles has passed on. Your whole life and your business are in London. Just think of the commuting."

The real reason flickered at the back of her eyes. She was concerned because she believed she might not be able to visit the manor if he took up residence there. She'd always said she wouldn't go back. Nothing was too great a challenge for Rex, though. He could think of a few circumstances that might make her change her mind.

"If your father has somehow made you feel responsible, or guilty, I won't be very happy."

She'd never stopped being angry with him. A strange kind of love, but Rex saw it then. She was driven by a broken heart.

"Did he leave you a letter or something?"

"Just basic legal instructions." He wasn't sharing the letter with her. He hadn't even shared it with Carmen yet. What with everything that had happened in between, it was still folded away in his wallet.

"So don't let him get to you with any sense of obligation or sentimentality."

Rex felt disturbed. It touched a nerve. He had felt for the old man when he'd sat in his father's chair in his stronghold in the library, holding the letter, looking at his portrait. "I'm not sentimental about the house. Don't think that."

"Carmen, then?"

"I do care about her." *Care about her enough to put you through questions I wish I hadn't had to.* "Look, we're just enjoying some time together while we deal with the property."

She studied him in silence and refrained from further comment, but he could tell she was uneasy. She glanced at her watch. "I'd better make tracks."

Rex gestured for the bill. "I'll walk you back."

Once again Rex scoured the busy London pavements as he escorted his mother back to the gallery, always watchful. It was difficult to concentrate, to keep in mind he might be being followed, when his mother had given him so much to think about. He already had enough on his mind.

When he bent to kiss her goodbye outside the gallery, she reached up and touched his cheek briefly before they separated, studying him again. "I hope this Carmen is worthy of you."

More like I'm not worthy of her. "It may never happen."

"You have got it bad, poor Rex." She smiled, perking up. "I can tell I better get online and find out more about Carmen Shelby."

Rex gave her a final kiss and then waved as she walked away.

Got it bad? He supposed he did have it bad. One way or the other, Carmen occupied all his thoughts. Between his insatiable desire for her, and his more recent concerns about her safety and well-being, it was as if everything else in the world had become far less important.

He hailed a taxi, giving the driver directions to Slipstream. Then he pulled out his phone to check on Carmen. He thought it might irritate her, but she laughed casually and poked fun at him.

"Promise you won't leave the building until I arrive."

"It's barely even a sprained ankle. Really, I can manage. It doesn't hurt at all, honestly."

"Hush now, you're ruining my excuse to carry you everywhere tonight."

She laughed softly.

After their call ended, he phoned the manor.

"Good afternoon, Mrs. Amery, it's Rex. I'm thinking of going through those papers in the library myself, so I wanted to ask you to leave the job to me."

"I can understand that. Rest assured of my discretion, sir." She was thinking about the letter she'd unearthed.

"I know."

"Is there something you're specifically looking for, Mr. Rex, I mean...Rex. Surely I can help."

Rex pondered. He didn't really want to tell her exactly what he was looking for. Then again, she might be well aware of his father's other property interests and the woman called Olivia. Perhaps Charles Carruthers had even taken the affair to the house, before he met Sylvia Shelby. "Yes, perhaps you can. I'm looking for any paperwork relating to an apartment in London. He bought it ages back, possibly in the late 1990s."

"I'm making notes."

He could hear the pen scratching. She hadn't reacted and didn't seem to know anything. "What I need is the address and any other contact information, names or telephone numbers."

"What I've been looking through is mostly old accounts for the estate, but I'll have a good hunt for you."

"Thank you. Call me back if you locate anything."

"Immediately, of course."

There was something else he wanted, but he hadn't decided quite how to go about it. His intention was to have the private investigator check out the house, but he had to make a cover story to introduce the person into the manor. He couldn't trust any of the staff at the present time, but he'd find a way. "I've got some other business in mind. I might want to bring in contractors for some maintenance and renovation work, but I'll phone you later on in the week regarding that."

A wary silence emanated from the other end of the phone. "We may not be the workforce we once were, but Bill and his men are very capable."

"I don't doubt it." He had to tread carefully. He didn't want to offend them. "I've given Bill permission to make the necessary repairs on the service stairs, but I'm thinking about drafting in some people to look at other renovations. Don't worry, Mrs. Amery, no one is criticizing your work. Think of it as a few extra hands."

She didn't sound convinced, but at least he'd broached the subject.

When he hung up, he looked at his watch. He had a couple of hours at Slipstream, then he'd head off to collect Carmen. He couldn't help wondering what her mood would be. There was no telling, but at least he knew how to keep her in check. The thought made him smile.

CHAPTER NINETEEN

"I still can't believe you managed to force me into this around-the-clock thing," Carmen said as Rex slowed the car down, ready to turn it into the underground car park beneath the rented apartment.

"It's not so bad, is it? I really wanted to keep you safe, but I am enjoying playing house."

She laughed.

"I'm serious," he continued. "I wanted to see how we might get on, on neutral ground. Perhaps it's just a whim, as you would call it. Humor me. Let's be anonymous for the week."

"Anonymous?" She stared across at him with an amused look in her eyes, making the most of the time it took for the security gate to scan his number plate, roll up and allow him to drive in. "The whole point of this arrangement is Burlington Manor, and my part of the bargain was to give you a certain number of weekends." Her tone was teasing. "Now we're no longer at the manor, and you're taking liberties with my time beyond what we agreed."

Rex drove the car quickly into its designated parking space, pulled on the brake and switched off the engine. He turned to look at her. "Tell me, is it so awful being with me? Are you pretending to enjoy yourself when you occasionally let rip?"

She pouted. "No, I've enjoyed being with you. You know I have. I'm just used to my own private space at the end of the day—"

"You can be alone tonight if you want to," he interrupted. "I'll sleep in the guest room."

"I don't have any of my things around me," she continued, ignoring his offer to sleep alone.

Rex restrained a smile.

"I really don't understand you," she added. "You're lucky you're so good in bed."

"Why, thank you."

She rolled her eyes. "Oh, God, your ego is so huge!"

"Hey, there's a reason I'm doing this. I wanted to be sure you were safe." He reached across and covered her hand with his, forcing her to let him in. "But there's more. I've only got a short lease with you," he said, and noticed she rolled her eyes in response. "I've been enjoying our time together immensely. It's been very special."

He lifted her hand to his mouth and kissed it. It was true. He was planning to get her on board no matter what, but the words were what he felt. "Sometimes being at Burlington Manor feels like too much of a compromise, or a barrier, and I wanted to know what it would be like without that influencing our behavior toward each other."

She stared at him in silence for a long moment. Reaching for him, she kissed him full on the mouth. It took him by surprise, but he responded instantly, and when she moved closer his arms went around her, his hands automatically trying to lift her into his lap so he could feel her against him. When his hand curved around her bottom, he groaned with longing.

She drew back and laughed. "We can't do it here in the car. Someone will see."

Rex didn't really care who saw them as long as they got close again. The tension between them was evaporating, for which he was immensely grateful. "If you're so fussed about it, I'll take you inside first."

"Inside our anonymous apartment?" There was laughter in her eyes.

It warmed him through. "Yes, let's have anonymous sex in our anonymous apartment."

"Okay, then." She moved fast, climbing out of the car.

Rex did the same.

When they walked to the elevator and stepped inside, he looked at her. Her lips curled. She looked aroused and mischievous.

He dropped his laptop bag to the floor and grabbed her into his arms, kissing her.

She moaned into his mouth, clutching at him eagerly. He backed her against the wall of the elevator, pressing himself hard against her. She shifted him back. They ricocheted back and forth, and she chuckled as they drew apart. The elevator pinged. Rex ducked down and snatched up his bag, then grabbed her by the hand and led her to the apartment, fast.

Once inside, he started taking off her clothes.

Carmen laughed. "This place may be anonymous but you're not, Mr. Rex Carruthers, and you never will be."

The teasing tone in her voice set him alight. "What if you couldn't see me?"

Her attention sharpened. Desire poured from her. "Are you going to hide?"

"Kind of." He pulled off his tie, and held it over her eyes.

Carmen inhaled sharply. "Oh."

"Anonymous enough for you?"

She nodded.

Rex stepped behind her and secured the tie. Then he finished undressing her and led her to the bedroom. "We're in the bedroom now."

He stationed her at the end of the bed.

Rex quickly undressed, kicking off his shoes and flinging his clothes aside. He climbed onto the overly wide bed, punched the pillows into position and folded his arms behind his head.

Carmen stood where he'd left her at the end of the bed, entirely naked, but for the blindfold. She cocked her head and he could tell she was listening for audio clues on his actions.

The room was lit by two lamps, and her body was cast in a mix of light and shadow. She looked beautiful.

"Your anonymous lover is on the bed, admiring you."

She smiled nervously. Her fingers moved, as if unsure whether to reach out. She captured her bottom lip between her teeth.

Rex had meant to remain in position and simply observe her, but seeing her focused him in a way he hadn't been expecting. He'd been planning to enjoy her, without her knowing his reaction. It would be interesting, but for some reason it wasn't possible.

It was her vulnerability. She affected him strangely. It was as if he couldn't bear to leave her there without assisting. "Step forward. You're about ten inches from the end of the bed, and then you'll find what you're looking for easy enough."

Her expression changed. She smiled.

Seeing her smile caused an instant feeling of mellowness. That wasn't part of the scheme, but it didn't affect his libido. His cock was long and hard. Ready for her. He didn't like to see her too vulnerable, though. Was that because of the potential danger she might be in, the accident she'd experienced, or would he respond like that, anyway? Rex frowned. It wasn't the time to be thinking on those sorts of questions. They were anonymously hidden and now they were going to have anonymous sex. Except it wasn't anonymous, and he was in the curious position of being able to enjoy her without her being able to see him. It made him aware of how deeply he cared for her. He wanted and needed her. Above and beyond that, he wanted her to be happy, as well as safe.

When her legs moved against the edge of the bed, she came to a halt. Her breasts bounced and she laughed breathlessly. She turned her head from side to side, trying to get her bearings.

Rex shifted, rising up onto his elbows. Stretching out his left foot he touched her with his big toe and drew it down the front of her thigh. She smiled, and then reached down to close her hands around his ankle.

"Oh, my, what big strong calf muscles you have," she whispered as she stroked her hands underneath his legs.

"All the better to chase you with."

She inhaled, and her hands paused in their exploration.

What was she thinking?

How beautiful she looked. Had she really never been submissive like this with another man? It could be true, because she was so often unsure about it. Rex had never known a woman so deliciously conflicted by her sexuality. It was a pleasure edging her toward an understanding of it, but it was also dangerously close to becoming an obsession for him.

She climbed onto the end of the bed, knees on either side of his lower legs, then reached out and trailed her fingers over his erection.

It jerked in response. "Found what you're looking for?"

She ducked down and rested her cheek against his knee in silent request. "Rex, I want you…I want the taste of you in my mouth."

When his knee shifted, she nudged her face between his legs, seeking his cock. It was eager for her mouth. "Permission granted."

The sight of her crawling to his cock with her lips parting was so damn hot. Then she wrapped one hand around the thick stem of his erection and drew it to her lips. She ran her tongue over the swollen crown. With her other hand, she lifted his balls, clasping them as she took him fully into her mouth, riding the large crown of his cock against the roof of her mouth, her tongue lapping against the underside.

Rex's blood pounded, pleasure roaring over him with every suck, squeeze and stroke she gave him. Taking him deeper, she began to move up and down, swallowing a little more of his length each time. When he released a guttural moan she moved faster still.

"Enough, I want to be inside you." With one hand on her shoulder he eased her away, his breathing labored.

He rested one hand around the back of her neck, staring down at her.

"Get up here and sit on me," he instructed, then grappled for the condom he'd left on the bedside. He couldn't pull it on quickly enough.

Carmen climbed over him with her knees either side of his hips.

The sight was too good. Her pussy, open and ready, her body primed, her lips parted and damp from his cock.

"Okay, I'm ready for you."

She grasped his cock, directed it to her and then flexed as she took it inside. "Rex…" She paused halfway, and she was panting loudly. "It's so good."

She worked herself down his length some more, and he felt her give, stretching to accommodate him. She cried out.

"Tell me what you feel," he demanded, and he could hear the gruffness in his own voice.

"Everything. I feel everything."

Desperate for her, he sat up and buried his face against the base of her throat where he kissed her so heavily he sucked her skin into his mouth.

She jerked but then sank into his harsh kiss.

"Bite me harder," she cried out.

He sank his teeth into her shoulder.

Her hips rolled. "Oh, yes, yes…it hurts, but it feels so good."

They were wrapped in each other, raw and uncompromising, and the artifice had gone, the role-playing. He knew this was real, and it sent him into overdrive. He bit her again. When she responded by digging her nails into his back, he looked at her, and even though her face was partially obscured, he saw her pleasure in the pain.

The scratch of her nails seemed to tug at his balls, priming him for the climax. He stroked her breasts, cupping them in his hands.

Her cunt tightened on his length.

Rex cursed and grasped the soft flesh of her breasts more firmly, molding it in his hands. Just a tweak of her sensitive nipples and she bucked her hips, her body clutching his erection so tightly that her hot juices spilled down around the base of his cock.

"Take your pleasure now," he instructed, knowing he wouldn't last long. Not with her like this.

She rode him faster.

Desperate for release, Rex clenched his jaw.

She leaned forward, rubbing herself against him with every thrust and roll of her hips. She was close. He could see it. While she ground down on him, his cock was solid and he wasn't going to come until she did—but, bloody hell, it was hard not to.

"There's nothing like this in the whole world," he whispered, and his hands locked around her hips, holding her in place as his body bowed up beneath her, thrusting into her.

She gave a wild cry, and her body tightened on him as she reached her peak. Rex let rip, ejaculating hard while her body shuddered to completion.

CHAPTER TWENTY

Rex had never hired a private investigator before, so he wasn't sure what to expect. Samuel Jacobson immediately dispelled any concerns Rex had.

Neatly dressed, wearing glasses and carrying a standard briefcase, there was nothing out of the ordinary about him. He was an unassuming character, a person you wouldn't look at twice. Rex shook the man's hand and gestured to the casual seating in the corner of his office. "I appreciate your coming to me."

"From what you told me on the phone, I understand your concern. My first question is, why haven't you gone to the police?"

"No real evidence of any misdemeanor outside of the tampering with the banisters. Not a lot to go on. But the two events can't be a coincidence, and if we assume it was carefully planned, how many were involved? It'd be almost impossible for one person to be behind both events because of the timing and the distance between where I was and Burlington Manor, where the other incident occurred."

Jacobson nodded. "The manor is the best place to start the investigation. Have you any suspicions about the staff there?"

"Nothing significant, but only three of them are well-known to me. The rest of them have been employed over the years I've been away from the place. I figure if someone had tampered with the stair carpet—and it looked that way to me—it had to be someone who knew Carmen's movements when she returned to the property. Apparently she always uses the back staircase shortly after her arrival. There are gardens and a lake beyond the house and she takes a walk there."

It still bugged Rex he hadn't known that about her. He wanted to know more about Carmen, everything there was to know, in fact.

"We need someone to talk to your staff. As you suggested on the phone, we could send a couple of men in under the guise of looking at renovation work."

"Absolutely. I can arrange that to begin by tomorrow morning."

"Two of my men have a particular knack—they can ingratiate themselves into a situation to find out what they want to know." Jacobson smiled. The man enjoyed his work. It was a good sign. Rex wanted to get to the bottom of this and fast.

"I need to visit the property next weekend as usual. I want to be sure the place is safe."

"You also mentioned your solicitor."

"I'll speak to him this afternoon, give permission for you to access the paperwork. There was a clause in my father's will that stated what should happen to the estate should both myself and the other part-owner be deceased. To be honest, I didn't take much notice of it at the time, seeing as we were both sitting there in fine health. However, since this happened, I want to be absolutely sure what's going on with that clause. More than my own safety, I'm very concerned for the other co-owner. At the present time I haven't alerted her to my fears, but I'm keeping her close by my side until we get to the bottom of this."

And for a long time after, if I have my way.

That afternoon Rex stood on the wide marble steps leading up to the apartments where his father's mistress lived. Once he had her first name, the rest was easy. Nate's father hadn't wanted to bad-mouth this Olivia woman, or Charles, but when Rex explained why he wanted to know, the situation changed.

Olivia Fordyce was her name.

According to Nate's father, Charles had bought his mistress a home of her own years ago. It was in her name, and that's why there had been no mention of it in the property listed in Charles's will.

Rex went up to the intercom on the right-hand side of the massive front door to the building. Her name was proudly displayed. He pressed the buzzer. Several moments later the intercom crackled into life.

"Yes. Who is it?" The voice was female.

Behind him, he heard the closed-circuit camera whir as it moved in his direction. He kept his back to it.

"Rex Carruthers. I'd like to have a word with you…about my father."

He had to force the last part out.

The intercom crackled, then went silent.

At first he thought she wasn't going to let him in. Then the camera began to whir again. Rex turned to face it. Staring at the small mounted camera above his head, he forced a smile. It wasn't an easy task.

The intercom crackled again. "Second floor, top of the stairs."

The door buzzed. Rex pushed it open. Crossing the hallway he made his way up the stairs. On the second-floor landing a door flanked by potted plants opened as he approached.

The woman standing there put up her hand as if to stop him. "Oh, please just let me admire you from a distance."

The comment, so blithely delivered and so odd, drew Rex to a halt, as she had no doubt intended. Olivia Fordyce looked sprightly, slender, possibly in her early fifties. She was elegant and refined and she had a beady look in her eyes he didn't like.

"Oh, yes, you do look like Charles now that you've filled out, how lovely." She offered him her hand.

Rex had known he would find this difficult, but he hadn't expected his feelings of distaste to be quite so sudden and strong. He didn't want to shake her hand. He didn't like the way she spoke about him, as if she knew all about him. Moreover, this was the woman who'd caused his parents to break up. But he had to speak to her, so he resorted to politeness, giving her cold hand a small and perfunctory shake.

"Do come in."

He followed her inside, into a grand sitting room overlooking the park. Prestige London property, for sure. When Rex was a small boy his father had owned a London house, but he'd sold it. Had he done so to fund this bit on the side?

"What can I do for you, Rex?"

The way she said his name held an implied intimacy, as if she knew him well. It irritated Rex immensely. "I understand you knew my father."

Her carefully plucked eyebrows lifted and she smirked. "Why are you here?"

She obviously didn't intend to ask him to take a seat. Presumably she didn't trust him or his motives. Then again, she had every reason to wonder why he was here. His dad had left him with this dubious task lurking in the background, and he resented his father all over again.

Rex forced himself to focus on the task in hand. He had to check her out because, as far as he could see, she was the most obvious person on his list of people who might hold grievances. "You're aware of my father's death?"

She nodded. "Regrettably so, but I hadn't seen Charles for many years before that."

For whatever reason, it pleased him to see she was upset by the fact she'd been dumped, too. "I understand you were old friends?"

She smiled wryly. "Yes."

"As you might imagine it's quite a task dealing with my father's paperwork and it's brought about a number of questions." He paused.

Her expression didn't change. She was wary and assessing. Was it a sign of guilt? He had to keep reminding himself she would be wary. He could have come here to have a right royal rant about her splitting up his parents, now he'd got hold of her name and address, and a look at her cushy little apartment. Right then Rex didn't want to address anything other than Carmen's safety and his ability to protect her. That's why he was here.

"There was paperwork that related to this property purchase, you see." That was a lie. Charles Carruthers had covered his tracks well there.

"And you want to know why your father bought me a place to live?"

Suddenly he didn't want to hear it. "No, I know why."

"That saves us a lot of time, then, doesn't it?" She gave him a sickly sweet smile, as if proud of her status as Charles's kept woman.

"It does. My concern is my father felt responsible for you and your income has come to an abrupt end because of his passing." It was a more probing question.

She took a deep breath, as if surprised. "You're far more direct than your father ever was. I'm impressed." She seemed to relax, and she looked at him with more open curiosity. "Your father once took me to see you." Her focus became distant, as if she were remembering.

Stage like, that's what she was, Rex decided. Amateur dramatics level.

"You were about thirteen years old at the time and he was on his way to meet you. It was your half-term holiday from Eton."

It was disturbing. Why was she telling him this? Did she want him to be disturbed? If so, his suspicion might be well founded. Rex stood his ground.

"He parked a distance along the driveway. Nobody noticed amid the chaos of the cars arriving. Charles pointed you out when you came out to be collected. I was curious, you see." She looked directly at him then. "Just as you're curious to see me."

She was deliberately letting him know she was around before his father had married Sylvia Shelby. She wanted a reaction.

He wasn't going to give it to her.

"Once I'd had a good look at you I got out of the car and went in the other direction, back up the driveway toward the town while he collected you. You were none the wiser."

The smugness in her smile turned his stomach.

"As I always said to him, what they don't know won't hurt them."

"Nothing stays secret forever." He hadn't meant it to sound like a threat but it came out that way.

She seemed unperturbed by his reaction. "Oh, you'd be surprised."

Her bitterness was obvious, but was she capable of anything more? She had her apartment and she didn't seem to have come upon hard times. She hadn't answered the question, though.

"My purpose in coming here was partly because I was curious, but also to ensure my father's demise has not left you in need of anything."

"It'd be nice to have seen him one last time, but I don't suppose you can organize that now." She gave a sad smile. "There was no ongoing income, if that's what you need to know. He used to pay my bills…when he was fucking me." She paused for effect.

Rex didn't react. He refused to allow himself to do so.

"Then the relationship ended. He gave me a lump sum to invest. To keep me quiet, as it were."

"You stuck by your promise."

"I did. Until now." Another sly smile passed over her face. "Once he met Sylvia Shelby he wasn't interested in keeping another woman on the side. She must have been 'the one' as it were. Unlike your poor old mother."

What a bitch. She really meant to hurt him. Aside from anything else, her comment made it obvious she'd been kept on the side throughout his parents' relationship. "It must've been so disappointing for you, being replaced by Sylvia."

"Very perceptive. You're a bright young man…considering you came from a broken home." Every comment was deliberately barbed. She wanted someone to feel her pain. "I loved your father."

Rex had the urge to tell her he didn't give a toss. He resisted comment. It would probably be right up her alley. He couldn't shake his suspicions, though. She was the obvious candidate. But why seek revenge on them now? She would have to have an accomplice, but he already suspected there was more than one person involved, because of the timing of events on the previous Friday.

He'd had enough. They were going around in circles here, with her taking a dig at him at every opportunity. The important thing was he knew enough to encourage Jacobson to dig a bit deeper with Olivia Fordyce.

"Well, thank you for your hospitality," he said pointedly. "I've done my duty to the old man's affairs so I'll leave you in peace."

He turned away quickly. He didn't want to feel her icy hand in his again.

She followed him to the door. "It's been intriguing, Rex. I enjoyed meeting you."

I wish I could say the same.

Rex didn't look back.

Outside, he hailed a taxi. The tube would be quicker but he didn't fancy looking over his shoulder all the time. Once he got into the cab, he realized the bad vibe hadn't been left on the pavement outside Olivia's home, as he'd hoped it might.

What disturbed him most was the uneasy feeling he'd had after speaking to two women who'd been wronged by his dad—Olivia, and his own mother, Bea. Charles Carruthers had left them both unhappy.

Rex had never wanted to be like his father. One of his life rules was he'd never cheat on a woman because of what adultery had done to his family. Yet he'd found himself being more of a womanizer than he liked. It had dissatisfied him. He was already beginning to change when Carmen came back into his life.

After the second weekend with Carmen his aims for their affair altered. He began to see she could be his redemption. As she constantly pointed out, however, he had a poor track record, and it meant she was keeping up her guard. He also didn't want to betray Carmen's memory of his father by telling her about Olivia—although ultimately he supposed he might have to.

It was time to show her the letter.

That would be a good place to start, and it was something that might force the issue of an ongoing relationship. Which he needed, badly.

CHAPTER TWENTY-ONE

Carmen cleared the plates and leftovers from the Chinese takeout they'd enjoyed that evening. He seemed preoccupied. "I think I'll call Mrs. Amery to see if the stairs have been fixed yet."

Rex frowned. "I sent some people up there this week. Professionals."

"Oh, so now you're having things done at the manor without telling me?" She couldn't resist teasing him. "Might I remind you I own fifty percent of the property, which means you're not in a position to take charge of it or do anything without discussing it with me first?"

He stopped dead and looked at her.

"For fuck's sake," he mumbled to himself.

Carmen chuckled. "I don't think I've ever seen you lost for words, Rex Carruthers."

He ruffled his fingers through his hair and looked as if he was as annoyed with himself as he was with her. That made her curious.

"I wanted to talk to you tonight," he said, "not about the house, but about us. I want us to be together. Like this." He gestured around the apartment, which they were sharing, but which was completely strange and alien to the pair of them. "I want us to be like a regular couple. Dating, living together or whatever."

Carmen burst out laughing. Never had she seen him so befuddled. She couldn't resist teasing him some more. "You want us to live together? Here?"

"Not here, but somewhere."

"That's a relief. My place is way nicer than this."

"You know what I mean. Somewhere mutual. This week has been great, hasn't it?"

"It has, once I let you off for changing the ground rules."

He strode over to where she sat on the sofa, squatted down in front of her and held her hands in his. "I want to be with you. I'm trying to do the right thing here. Why is it so hard to ask you out on a date?"

He looked desperate.

"Maybe we're not the dating kind?"

He sighed. "You're just trying to wind me up."

"No, I'm not. Seriously, consider this. You could have any woman you wanted. You weren't allowed to date me so it got stuck in your head you couldn't have me. Which made you want it more. That's what this is all about. I've come to terms with it. But you've done it now. You've achieved the sexual possession of Carmen Shelby. Many years overdue, I agree, but you can now add the notch to your bedpost and move on, as you planned at the outset when you put a strict time limit on it."

She hadn't meant for it to come out that way, but once it was out and she saw the expression on his face, she realized she might have gone a bit far.

He hung his head, but his fingers were worrying at her hand. "Something changed."

His posture and his mood informed her he was serious. The realization made her chest ache, suddenly and painfully. "You really are asking me out, normal style, aren't you?"

He lifted his head.

When she saw his expression, the world as she understood it seemed to crumble, leaving her strangely adrift.

"I am. Just think, we could be together in the city during the week and then go to Burlington for the weekends."

It sounded idyllic, but it wasn't Rex. He'd never lived his life like that, and he was far from comfortable with the notion, even though he was voicing the proposal. He looked as if he had pressing problems, and it wasn't how she'd expect a man to look while making a suggestion like that. "You don't do relationships, not for any length of time."

"I know, but it doesn't mean I can't. Besides, from what I can tell, you're not flush in the relationships department, either."

She pulled away.

Rex shifted, grasping her hand again. "Wait, why do you keep doing this? Why the withdrawal? I'm not blind, Carmen. We get to a certain point and then you cut off from me."

Carmen stared down at his hand covering hers. *I can't risk it.*

"Do I have to tie you up and torture it out of you?"

Knowing he probably would, Carmen buckled. "No, you don't. Look, it's not hard to figure out. I had to become independent. I had to get used to being alone."

Rex frowned. "After you mother died?"

"It wasn't just that. My dad died when I was very small, but I remember it, and the feeling of loss never went away. At the time my mum was trying to build the company up, and when cancer took him she threw herself into that for a while. I got used to being alone. Then came the golden years at the manor. And you." She met his gaze. "Then you left."

The wounded look in his eyes spoke volumes. "I'm sorry."

Carmen had never seen him look so serious, so sincere. "You know the rest. The accident…Mum died, and then Charles withdrew from me, as well."

"I didn't think. Throughout it all, I've always had my mother and her family to go back to. It really pains me to think you didn't have anyone, and I could've been there for you."

"I understand why you weren't, Rex. Don't worry. I don't blame you. It's just for a good while, I felt I couldn't trust anyone to be there for me for any length of time and I had to be strong. I had to be brave and live up to the ideals my mother set out for the company. Part of me has always held those golden years at the manor sacred. That's why I wanted to go back. I know I can't recapture it—"

"You can recapture it," Rex interrupted, "you can make it different, you can make it better. Maybe we can do it together."

Carmen wanted to believe, but it was so hard.

She studied his handsome face, and every part of her being craved him, longed to be held in his arms forever.

"What do I have to do to prove I will be there for you?"

"You can't always be there for me. Nobody can. That's what life has taught me." The ache in her heart tugged down into the pit of her stomach. Loss was too hard; she didn't want to open herself up to it again, and especially not with Rex, the only man she had ever loved.

"And what if I say different? What if I think we can do this?" The look in his eyes begged her to trust him.

"Do you really believe it?" It was still too hard for her, the impossible dream she'd tutored herself to dismiss.

"I do." He drew away, went for his back pocket. "There's something I need to show you." From his wallet, he pulled a folded page and opened it. "I found it, well, Mrs. Amery did, and she gave it to me." He handed it to her. "It's written by my dad, maybe a year or so ago. It was after you left, for sure. He never sent it, but it's an apology of sorts. To us both."

Carmen stared down at the page. The handwriting was instantly familiar because she'd often exchanged letters with Charles Carruthers. Once she moved out, it was how they stayed in touch. He was old-fashioned and didn't own a computer or do email or texts. In fact, the familiarity made her smile.

Once she began to read, the tone of the note stripped her smile away, fast. It was a familiar voice, but it was so sad and filled with regret it killed her to read it. When she got to the end, Carmen dropped the letter in her lap and covered her eyes with her hands.

She tried not to let it happen, but a sob broke loose.

"Hey." Rex reached out for her.

She shook her hair back, trying to get a grip. "I'm sorry. He just sounds so lonely here." It was hard to witness Charles's words, because she'd felt that way, too. Rex did this to people. "He wanted you back."

"That wasn't going to happen."

She understood why, but it sounded so harsh. She blubbed again.

"Carmen, please don't cry, love." He wiped her cheek. "Oh, I don't know, maybe it would've happened if he'd actually sent it. But he didn't send it. However, he did do something—he gave us this time together to make amends. He led us back to each other."

Carmen looked at him, wiping her eyes as she did so, trying to understand.

"Do you see? He brought us together, by the terms of his will. I figured, for him, it was the only way he could really apologize."

Carmen listened, and read the letter again. "I suppose it could be true." It was a grand gesture, all right, if it were true. She looked at him. "Did it change the way you felt about our situation?"

"About you? No. I already wanted more than what we'd agreed."

She stared at him, afraid to say anything, afraid to acknowledge what he seemed to be saying in case she was wrong.

When she didn't respond, he scrubbed his hair with his hand. "I guess it made me feel a bit differently about the old man."

She was going to say something, but he looked so disconcerted she just let it float. How strange it was. Minutes earlier she'd been laughing, and now she felt like an emotional wreck. This week of all weeks, this emotional roller coaster had to happen.

It was the anniversary of her mother's death the next day. Weary and vulnerable, she glanced away, suddenly wanting to be alone. "I was going to take a bath tonight, to chill out."

"We can do that."

"Not we. Me."

He stood up and lifted her in his arms, carrying her again. "I'm not going to let you run away and hide. I know you, you'll go off and brood and make up some daft reason why we can't be together."

Was that true? Is that what I would do? She fought it for a moment, then the feeling of being held in his arms won her over. She clung to him, looped her arms around the back of his neck and meshed her fingers together there.

He carried her into the bathroom, carefully easing her through the doorway. He stood her on the bath mat and undressed her. Within moments the bath tap was running and he poured bubble bath liberally into the tub. With consummate care, he lifted her and eased her into the warm water, keeping his arms around her.

Carmen dissolved.

Lowering to his knees beside the bath, he began to lap the warm water over her upper body.

She got dangerously near tears again, but he smiled her way and it touched her. "I feel pampered."

"Good." He cleared the bubbles here and there with his hand as if to see her better, then he reached for a sponge and soaped it.

He moved the sudsy sponge over her skin, taking his time to wash her.

Carmen's emotions leveled as he paid such close attention to her. The way he looked at her with those intense blue eyes of his made her ache for him. She was glad he hadn't let her bathe alone.

With each sweep of the sponge over her skin, she mellowed.

When she rested her head back, he set aside the sponge and massaged her shoulders, shedding more of her tension.

She sighed. "Mmm, you're good at this."

"I aim to please." He smiled and stroked his hands over her breasts.

When she moaned softly in response, he brushed his thumbs over her nipples. She gripped the sides of the bath while her desire for him flared with each suggestive touch against her sensitive skin.

Their eyes locked and he rested his fingers against her pussy, paddling beneath the water. She moaned again and he eased one finger into the groove of her sex, rubbing over her clit.

"Feeling better?"

She could barely speak because his touch was so direct. "You know I am."

"Just want to be sure." He smiled, and continued to work her, pushing one finger inside while he rocked the heel of his hand over her clit. "Looks good," he added.

She wanted him to want her. Latching one foot over the edge of the bath she opened her legs.

"Lovely."

The improved access meant she was closing on orgasm, quickly.

"Rex," she whispered when it hit, and she clung to his arm with both hands, the water splashing up around her.

He pulled the plug.

"I'm taking you to bed now." It was softly said, but there was tautness in his posture, and she knew what he wanted.

He wrapped her in a fluffy towel and rubbed her down, then carried her to the bed.

Carmen watched him strip. His cock bounced free as he shucked off his jockey shorts. He went straight for a condom, and when it was on he climbed over her, lifting her legs apart as he did so.

Carmen's heart raced. He was so sure, so strong, and she wanted him.

He paused and stared down at her.

She took in the image of his handsome face, the chiseled cheekbones and heavy slash of eyebrows. She breathed him in, the musk of his body filling her senses. The powerful shape of his muscled chest lured her and she stroked it with her hands, then kissed his breastbone.

Rex shifted, opened her up with his fingers, then thrust his cock deep inside her, claiming her.

"Want you so badly." His voice was husky, and the muscles in his neck corded.

Carmen's breath caught in her throat, her back arched as her hips rolled to meet his thrusts.

His gaze urged her on. "Why would either of us want this to end?"

Her body rode up on his vigorous thrusts, her every intimate place alight from the skin-to-skin contact and the intimacy in his words and his touches. She nodded, her arms tangling around his neck.

Rex groaned in response and his cock grew ever more rigid. He kissed her, holding her as only he could, his cock buried deep inside her where she craved him, where she would always crave him and him alone.

Breathless, mindless, she latched her hands over his shoulders as her body rolled to meet his each and every thrust.

His hands moved under her, as if he couldn't get close enough.

Her nipples flamed, the brush of his chest needling her from breasts to thigh and everywhere in between.

"Going to come," he murmured, kissing her face frantically.

Carmen shuddered. She was close, too. His cock stiffened, jerked hard, and again. Her body clasped it and he stayed with her, urging her to come.

When she did, a sob broke in her throat.

Pleasure rolled through her, wave after wave, and she clung to him. Only when she finally stilled did he slip from her, and when he did, she found herself wrapped in his arms again moments later.

CHAPTER TWENTY-TWO

"This feels far too much like camping to me," Carmen stated.

"You don't enjoy camping?" Rex grinned at her, glad that they were at ease with each other again.

She stood with one hip up against the breakfast bar in their rented apartment, eating the wrap he'd picked up from a nearby takeout.

It was Friday and Rex had woken with work nudging into his thoughts. Specifically, the meeting the Slipstream team had with Nikhil Rashid later in the day, but once Carmen moved in his arms his attention was all hers.

She was looking at him differently today. There was still wariness there in her eyes, but she was more like the old Carmen, more open. Curious. Last night had been tough on them both, but Rex felt they'd come to an understanding. All week long she'd kept telling him she disapproved of this setup and they should go to her place, but he was determined to stick to his guns until he heard back from Jacobson, at the very least. He was taking no risks whatsoever. He wasn't even sure if he wanted to take her to the manor for the weekend, not until Jacobson had cleared his doubts. Jacobson's men had been there the day before, and he was expecting a report.

He removed the lids from the take-out coffee cups, set one down next to her and then tucked into his own wrap.

"I'm woman enough to admit camping is not for me," she said, amused. "I like my home comforts."

"I never would've guessed." Rex took a sip of his coffee and admired her. She was wearing a business suit for work, and although it was very simple, she still managed to make it look elegant and feminine.

"Are you suggesting I couldn't actually cope with camping?" Her eyes twinkled.

It was so good to see. "I daresay you could do anything you put your mind to. I'll be honest, even though the idea of you crawling around on your hands and knees in a tent appeals to my base nature, I'd rather see you on your knees in Burlington Manor."

"You're so bad, making me think about that right now while I'm trying to get ready for the day ahead." The look in her eyes was mellow and inviting.

"My task is to have you think about it all the time, especially because I can see you like the idea."

Carmen put down the remains of her breakfast wrap and picked up her coffee, looking at him from under hooded lids as she sipped it.

They'd got past something the night before, and this was the easiest they'd been around each other. She hadn't exactly agreed to his suggestion of seeing each other as a more permanent arrangement, but she also hadn't outlawed it completely.

Rex was determined to make it work. He couldn't have it any other way; he needed this woman. Part of him had always known, but he hadn't realized how deeply it ran, and that it wouldn't just evaporate after they'd addressed the attraction between them. No, this felt different.

"Have you got a busy day today?"

"I'm glad you brought that up." Her expression grew serious. "I have a meeting first thing, but I was wondering if you could maybe finish early today?" She asked the question tentatively.

"If I could, I'd cancel the whole day to be with you, but we have an important pitch with a key client later this morning. I expect it to run until after lunchtime, but I'm sure I can finish up by three and be back to collect you from work by four."

She studied him for a moment, then nodded. She seemed wrapped in her own thoughts.

Rex felt uneasy. It was odd, because this was the closest they'd managed to get. But there still seemed to be obstacles he couldn't shift, barriers he couldn't even discern.

How could he prove his loyalty to her?

Grand gestures, it's what men did at times like this. Flowers and chocolates and gifts and stuff. Apart from the dress he'd bought her in Milan—which had made her wary about his motives, and she hadn't been sure about accepting it as a result—perhaps he hadn't demonstrated his intentions to her in the correct way. Was that the missing element?

There was no denying the sexual dynamic between them was powerful. He'd told her he wanted to be with her, but it wasn't enough.

While they made their way into the underground car park, Rex pondered it. He had time to think about it because Carmen was the quietest she'd been all week. He'd got rather used to her berating him for escorting her like a child who needed to be taken to school. Instead, she switched the radio on to the classical station. The music was calming despite the London traffic and freed up his thoughts. Carmen was wise, she was sensible. Left to his own devices he'd have the city radio station on with all the bad news and traffic reports he didn't need as well as the stuff he did.

I need someone like that in my life, an anchor.

Perhaps it was the fact she wasn't speaking to him, perhaps it was where his thoughts were going, but he felt unreasonably possessive about her. It had begun to irritate him their relationship wasn't more simple. With her accident on the stairs and his near-miss, he felt pressure all around, the pressure of unanswered questions. The issue of ownership and the manor was also complicating what might otherwise have been an uncomplicated reunion. Brooding, he remembered the staircase, the bunched carpet and how it had made him feel. He resented the manor, hated it for doing that to her, hated it for tearing them apart all those years ago. But if it hadn't been for the house and the contents of the will, would they have had this opportunity to be together?

The sound of a horn blaring snapped him into the reality of the moment. He slammed on the brakes.

"Rex!"

Her voice reached him. His hand instinctively went to hers while he scoped the situation. Someone had been trying to pull out on the opposite side of the road. The car on the nearside had stopped to let them out, but Rex hadn't seen it. "You okay?"

"I'm fine."

A black London city cab pulled out from behind them, blaring its horn, apparently aggrieved at the momentary pause.

"And the same to you, as well," Carmen shouted in the direction of the taxi.

Rex laughed. Shifting the gear stick, he signaled, indicating his intention to move on for the benefit of the car behind. It was the usual rush hour commuter chaos, but the way Carmen had looked at him with concern and then shouted at the cab made him relax a bit.

Minutes later he pulled the car up at the curb outside *Objet d'Art*. He turned and cupped her face, kissing her gently. "I'll call you as soon as I get out of my meeting."

"I hope it goes well," she responded.

Rex left the car and walked to the main doors where the security guard watched on, giving him some level of reassurance.

Amateurs, he reminded himself, they are amateurs. Maybe it was just a coincidence. He was determined to be sure before he let her go about her normal routine without precautions.

Once she was inside the building Carmen turned and waved, and she smiled fondly at him. It triggered something, the wave goodbye, and a notion struck him. A weekend away, away from Burlington and away from London, completely freed from their lives and the fear of a mystery stalker. *Somewhere romantic*, he thought as he strode back to his car.

Climbing into the driver's seat, he pulled on his seat belt and signaled.

Paris, the weekend in Paris. Yes. He had time to book them something before he left for the meeting. If he picked Carmen up at four, they could fly out of Heathrow by eight, away from the difficulties that had made the past week so fraught. "And whoever the hell these amateurs are, they won't have a bloody clue where we are." That was the seal on the deal.

He kept an eye on the clock. He had to do a last run-through of the presentation with the guys before they left, and the drive out of the city to Rashid's venue outside of Oxford would take a good hour. The presentation involved them all, as did the creation of carefully designed and built Slipstream parts. He'd only have twenty minutes free, tops, but it was enough to get flights and a hotel booked. If he was collecting Carmen at four it would give them time to go get their passports and grab a few things. Anything else they needed they could pick up along the way. Satisfied, he concentrated on the important day ahead.

Nikhil Rashid was a sophisticated guy who exuded calm, style and efficiency. He also didn't give a lot away. Their presentation had gone well and now they were all gathered, Bertha's engine purring, while Ayo sat in the driver's seat running the demo car through its paces.

Rex attempted to stand back at this point, let the designs speak for themselves. Instead, he looked around. Nikhil Rashid was an interesting man. He had a home in Oxford, but he'd bought a field in the countryside and built his business site there. Which meant they had room for their own racing track. A clever move.

Why didn't I think of doing the same at Burlington? It was a great idea.

He tried to gauge Rashid's response. He wore sunglasses the whole time, which didn't help, and his goatee beard also seemed to disguise his responses. "Have you got any other designers to meet with, Mr. Rashid?"

"Nikhil, please." He took off his shades and folded them into the top pocket on the jacket of his suit, then rested his hands on his hips. His eyes were intelligent, and he regarded Rex with a half smile. "I've met with two other teams."

Rex's hopes waned.

"Your designers are the best. You'd be my top choice." He stated the approval quite simply. "However, I have a proposition for you that you may need time to consider."

Rex lifted his brows. "Go on, we're listening."

"I don't want to limit any working relationship we have to a few bespoke designs. I'd like you to work directly with my team of drivers. I want Slipstream as a partner."

Rex didn't break eye contact with him. "That'd be a big step for us. We freelance design for a number of teams."

It would be a big leap of faith, but this development could mean great things for his business. It was the sort of opportunity he'd hoped for maybe five years down the line. If Rashid's team took off and they were directly involved in engine design, with Slipstream's flag flying on the cars, it was a whole new level of opportunity and growth.

Nikhil nodded. "Yes, but your contracts with them are flexible. We can get more manpower to deal with your bespoke part designs. If we unite we'll have an exceptional team to create our own exceptional vehicle."

Rex laughed. "You've done your homework."

Rashid nodded. "As I'm sure you have, too."

"Indeed." He'd found out Rashid was a serious businessman with clout, and he was pursuing his life dream.

"Take some time to think about it," Rashid offered.

Rex glanced around at his team and wondered if he looked as starry-eyed as they did. It was a big surprise, way above and beyond what they'd been hoping for, and it would be a lot of work. But it was very tempting indeed. "At Slipstream, we do everything as a team. We'll discuss it and get back to you."

"I'll email my investment profile and what I'm offering in terms of shares. I have high-profile sponsors lined up. I'm sure the information will help you make a decision." Nikhil Rashid put out his hand, and Rex grasped it firmly.

"Does this mean we get to crack open the bottle of champagne you stashed in the office fridge yesterday?" Lance asked when they were on their way back to their vehicles.

Rex laughed and switched on his phone. "You're like one of those kids who hunt down their Christmas presents in their parents' wardrobe."

The screen on his phone flashed a text message from Carmen. The sight of her name alone made him smile. It felt good when she'd asked him to leave work early. Perhaps they were getting close to a comfortable routine.

His smile faded when he read the message.

Rex, it's the anniversary of my mother's death and I visit her grave every year. I'll get the train up to Beldover as usual and—if you're willing—I'll see you at Burlington this evening. I could tell you wanted us to stay in London, but the manor is important to me. I have so many plans and I don't want to miss a single weekend there. I let Mrs. Amery know I'm coming and you might be, too. I've abided by all your requests and demands this past week. This is what I'd like: meet me at the manor this evening. Carmen. x

Rex looked at his watch. The meeting had gone on much longer than he'd expected and it was already past two. The message had been sent at eleven. He'd had his phone off for the duration of the meeting. Rashid's track was based twenty miles south of Oxford, so he was already on the right side of London. If he went straight to Beldover he might be able to catch her before she got to the manor.

He folded his phone into his pocket. "I'm going to have to postpone the champagne. Something's come up at the manor. Sorry, guys."

Lance lifted his hand. "No worries, we can make a session of it next week when you get back."

As soon as he drove the Maserati onto the main road, he instructed his hands-free to call Carmen. The call went straight to voice mail. Would she check it while she was traveling? He wasn't sure. It annoyed him he couldn't gauge her behavior more readily. She might have turned her phone off because she needed some alone time as she visited her mother's grave. Alternatively it could be a bad sign. He left a brief message, asking her to get back to him as soon as she switched on her phone.

"I'm on my way," he added before he ended the call.

Then he put a call in to Burlington Manor.

"Mrs. Amery, Rex here. I'm on my way to Beldover now. Has Carmen arrived at the manor?"

"Not as yet, but we're expecting her. She didn't know whether you'd be able to come this weekend, but I'll tell Cook to expect you, as well."

"Thank you. If Carmen arrives there, could you ask her to phone me immediately?"

"Yes, of course."

"Thank you. Tell me, has there been anything unusual about the manor this week? Have you seen anyone drifting around the place who concerned you?"

A weighty silence emitted from the other end of the line. Eventually she replied. "Do you mean those two louts you sent from London, or somebody else?" Her tone was overly austere and defensive.

Rex grimaced. He hadn't worded that very well. "I meant outside of them."

"In that case, no. However, they were disconcerting enough."

Rex clenched his jaw and his hands tightened on the wheel. "It wasn't meant to be disconcerting. It was meant to bring support in the running of the manor."

"We're well aware things need doing, and we'll get to them. We're working at full capacity."

"Mrs. Amery, I asked for outside people to assess any urgent repairs in order to take the burden off you."

"Running Burlington Manor has never been a burden and it never will be."

Rex groaned internally. Apparently he'd sprung open a real can of worms here. "As I said, it wasn't meant to undermine any of you. It was done in good faith. Two weeks ago, Bill told me more hands were needed."

"I expect he probably did, but he meant local people who we know we could trust, not some fly-by-night people up from the city."

There was the real grudge. Rex really didn't need this now. However, he wanted to keep her on side. "I apologize unreservedly. I promise I won't dump anything on you again without discussing it first. I was in a panic because of Carmen's fall."

"Oh, I'm so sorry. I hadn't realized."

"Don't worry. I know I didn't handle it very well. We'll chat about it when I get to the house."

When he hung up he asked himself how much he could really say to her. He couldn't rule out anyone in his hunt for the amateurs who were trying to scare them off the manor. There was no reason why the Amerys should be under suspicion, because his father had provided for them well. But he wasn't going to rule anyone out until he had some more solid information. He couldn't afford to. Carmen's safety was at stake.

He put his foot down.

By the time he reached the church in Beldover he was frantic.

The church was built on a hillside and the graveyard was beyond it. Rex scanned the area as he parked. There were no other cars around. He got out and jogged from his car to the row of thick, dark pines lining the church boundary. The old wooden lych-gate creaked open and he passed under its canopy. Looking ahead, he saw and heard no sign of visitors. Praying she hadn't been waylaid, he ran up the meandering path and skirted the perimeter of the church, his heart thumping in his chest.

When he turned a corner and arrived at the spot where the rolling hill flattened out beyond the church and the graveyard began, a flash of fabric moving in the breeze caught his eye.

Relief flooded him.

Carmen was there, her overnight bag sitting on the grass nearby as she stood at the grave. Rex stopped in his tracks. It was a poignant image, the sight of her standing there with her hair lifting on the afternoon breeze while she looked down at her mother's grave.

He recalled her saying she'd done this each year since her mother had passed on. Up until this anniversary, his father had joined her. Rex didn't want her to be standing there alone, so he walked to her side.

"Rex, you startled me." Her eyes were wide but she broke into a smile.

Her smile made him feel as if everything was right in the world, even though he knew it wasn't, not yet. He put his arm around her shoulders and drew her into his embrace. He kissed the top of her head. Her hands went against his chest and she rested her head on his shoulder.

He wanted to hold her forever. He looked across the rolling downs toward the clouds shifting over the distant hills. Centuries of tradition stood behind them within the church. Generations of the local villagers and people from the surrounding countryside were buried here, their headstones testifying to the lives they'd led.

The two of them had been here just weeks before for his father's funeral. At that event he'd felt like an outsider. Then he'd looked up and saw Carmen standing there, her expression concerned and curious, and the whole world fell away. Finally meaning took hold, as if the very sight of her drew the jigsaw pieces of his life together. Studying her face, he acknowledged how much he cared. *This is where I'm meant to be.* He'd come home, but it was because of Carmen.

He looked down at his father's grave—turfed now but still awaiting its headstone—and he felt both grief and regret. How different it was to the last time he'd been there. *Because of Carmen. Because we're together again.* Staring at his father's grave, Rex felt gratitude surge inside him. Despite the complications, the mysteries and secrets, the old man had put this woman back in his arms, and Rex couldn't have been more grateful.

"You didn't need to rush up here."

"I wish I'd known it was the anniversary today. You should've said."

"You had an important business meeting. I know you'd have taken time off if you could have." She moved, and wrapped her hands around the back of his head, stroking his hair as she smiled at him.

He wanted to see her smile that way forever.

"I still wish you'd told me it was today." He nodded his head at the grave.

"Hey, I'm a businesswoman. Your pitch had to come first and I knew it."

"If I'd known, I could have rearranged things." Why did he sound like he was making excuses? Because he felt as if he should've been there—should have at least driven her up and made sure she was okay and cared for. "I don't want you to have to do stuff like this alone."

Carmen gazed up at him, and her utter serenity impacted on him somehow, making him feel clueless.

"I've done just about everything on my own for a long time now, especially dealing with my mother's death. Your father came on the anniversaries, but it was an odd thing, barely rubbing shoulders with each other, all the regrets. It was a shared experience, yes, but…" She paused and shrugged. "I don't know, maybe it's me, maybe it's ingrained in me to be alone."

That hit Rex like a punch to the gut.

Was it true, was that what was stopping them being together?

"You weren't always that way." He knew it sounded shallow and childish, as if he wanted her to be the way she had been before. He couldn't help it. He loved the mature Carmen, but it pained him to think of her alone, ever, let alone always.

"I know." She smiled up at him and the smile was there in her eyes, too, which was a huge relief to Rex. "I need to be more sociable outside the workplace again. I'm hoping the manor will be part of me getting that back again."

She wrapped her arm around his waist as she turned away from the grave. It was an indication she was ready to go.

Rex grabbed her overnight bag from where it sat in the grass, slinging it over his shoulder before pausing a moment. There was something special about being here. They were alone with the glorious countryside and the sky, and what he felt for her seemed somehow more immense here. He kept his arm around her as they walked down the path, between the lush green borders and the lichen-covered gravestones that went back centuries.

"Mrs. Amery will be so pleased when we arrive together. I wasn't sure you'd come."

"You should've been sure," he replied gruffly.

"Well, I was rather demanding."

When he glanced down, her expression was mischievous. "I'm not sure I agree, about Mrs. Amery being pleased. I rang her on the way up here and I'm not in her good books."

"Why not?"

The confession was overdue, and the rest of the story had to be shared. It was a good place to begin. "As I mentioned last night, I sent a couple of people to check out the state of repair on the place and see what might need to be done immediately. I mean, after the business with you slipping on the staircase, it made me wonder."

Carmen responded by chuckling. "Ah, yes. No wonder you're in her bad books."

"I know," he said, resigned to the fact. "I've got a lot to learn." He scarcely withdrew his arm from around her as they passed under the lych-gate.

"I like your car," Carmen said as she settled into the passenger seat. "You do?"

"Yes, it makes me feel safe."

"That's good."

"The car, not you. I'm never safe with you, Rex."

It was meant to be a joke, he knew that, but it was too close to the bone.

Rex turned the key in the ignition. He didn't want to go to the manor, but he also didn't want to talk to her in the car, where he couldn't hold her and explain things properly. "We need to talk. If Mrs. Amery is expecting us for dinner, we'll talk then."

Then I get you out of there.

CHAPTER TWENTY-THREE

They were close to the manor when his phone rang. Rex looked at the display and saw it was Jacobson. "Sorry, I have to take this. It might be important."

Instead of putting it on speaker, he pulled over to the side of the road and brought the phone to his ear. "What have you got for me?"

"First up, I'm afraid your staff were a royal pain in the arse to deal with. Apparently they did everything bar getting the wagons in a circle. The housekeeper actually asked my men to leave. They'd only been there two hours."

"Jesus, I'm sorry."

"It's one level of security check, I suppose." Jacobson gave a wry laugh. "However, my men said the house really isn't very secure at all. You need to look into that."

Rex decided they definitely weren't staying past dinner. "I will. Thank you. Anything they picked up among the staff at the manor?"

He could feel Carmen's scrutiny. It was difficult to talk without letting some of it slip.

"They said it was hard to tell. The housekeeper turned into a Rottweiler and stalked after them everywhere they went. Let's just say the atmosphere wasn't conducive to chatting. I'd recommend more overt tactics. They can go in again next week and question them directly, if you prepare the way."

"I'll consider it. What else?"

"Well, and this was more worrying—your family solicitor was also very reluctant to share anything with me. I'd go so far as to say he deliberately avoided my calls and requests for access."

Rex's suspicions lit. Chris Montague. Could he have anything to do with it? Rex found it unnerving that he mistrusted everybody, but it was inevitable. Chris and his father had been old friends, University buddies. Had he known about Olivia Fordyce? Probably. What more did Chris know and what was he concealing? "Do you want me to speak to him?"

"No, I got through in the end. I'm tenacious, but his reluctance did put him in the spotlight. My conclusion is he knew there was something odd in the will and he possibly felt a little guilty because he hadn't made more of an effort to draw your attention to it." Jacobson paused. "I'll leave you to take it up with him, because I think you'll probably want to. In the meantime I can go over the clause now."

"Please do." Rex glanced at Carmen. She was making no effort to hide her curiosity.

"This charity you mentioned, it's a small affair. It provides support for people who are suffering from a rare form of cancer. It was named Wilmington's after the founder. His wife had the condition but he's passed on now, too, and the charity's run by a small team of volunteers."

"Right," Rex responded, his mind working overtime. He'd never heard of the organization and as far as he knew his father died of a heart attack. If the charity had been supporting him in some way, the solicitor would have been aware of it.

"The interesting part is the chief financial officer for the charity is the beneficiary and it's one of the names you gave me, this Olivia Fordyce."

So, there was a connection. Was the charity a front? "That's very interesting indeed. I've located the woman in question already. I'll email you her details."

"Your suspicions were grounded?" Jacobson asked.

"I think so. Anything else?"

"Not right now, but I'll keep on it."

When he ended the call, Carmen was sitting with her arms folded, studying him. "You're keeping things from me about the house and the staff?"

"I have been, yes."

Her eyes narrowed. "Just because I've been pliable in the sex department doesn't mean I want to be treated like a helpless child. We both own the house."

Rex took a deep breath. "There's something I need to tell you. It's not going to be easy." He really couldn't afford to have her running around oblivious and vulnerable anymore, especially not now that he had concrete suspicions he could go to the police with.

"What is it?" She looked wary, but undaunted.

"When we had lunch in London, you asked me why my parents split."

"Yes."

"I didn't want to tell you because I knew the reason it happened would upset you."

A frown developed between her eyebrows. "But you're going to tell me now?"

He nodded. "I have to."

"So tell me."

He admired her resilience. He hated to crush it. But this thing had gone too far and it was necessary. "My father had a mistress. It was a full-on thing. He set her up in her own home, the works. It broke my mum apart when she found out."

"Seriously?" She looked astonished. "I can't believe it."

"You had great admiration for him and a good relationship, that's why I didn't want to explain before now."

She stared out of the car window a moment, eyes focusing on a midpoint while she thought about it. "Are you telling me he had a mistress even after he married my mother…I mean, if he bought the woman a home and everything, was she a permanent fixture?"

Rex rested his hand on her arm, squeezing it gently. "I can't be entirely sure when it ended, but I don't think so."

She rested back against the headrest. "If it's true, I'm glad my mother never knew."

Rex could see it raised all sorts of questions for her. He looked out of the car. It was getting overcast, and he wanted to get her to the house. He felt increasingly uneasy. Jacobson's call had set his mind running with questions. "Do you remember when Chris read the will? He mentioned a clause that would come into action if we both passed on."

She turned back to him. "Vaguely."

"The estate funds would go to a charity. It wasn't something I'd ever heard of, so I've had someone look into it. I didn't think it was entirely above board. It turns out my father's mistress is the finance officer. I can't be sure yet, but I've got a private investigator on it."

Carmen's frown deepened. "I don't get it. Why on earth are you worried about what'll happen if we're both dead?"

This was it, the crunch. "Because an attempt has been made on both our lives."

"What do you mean?"

Slowly, carefully, Rex summarized what had happened to him on the day of her accident. When he delivered the information, he waited for her response. He expected her to be shocked, afraid even. Instead, she folded her arms tighter across her chest and glared at him.

"Unbelievable!"

"I know it sounds far-fetched, but believe me, I've got grounds for my suspicions."

"No, *you* are unbelievable. Why didn't you share all of this with me before now? It's just typical, you think you can take control and you don't think about the implications. You just do what suits you regardless of the consequences to other people."

Rex had to unclench his jaw in order to respond. "I was trying not to worry you any more than was necessary."

"Well, you sure as hell have me worried now."

"Believe me, I would've dealt with it all and protected you without you ever knowing the sordid details of my father's previous love life, if I could've."

"You just don't get it. Just because I like you to take charge in the bedroom, doesn't mean you can take charge of every aspect of my life since you've walked back into it." Her eyes glittered.

He could see she was afraid and it made her lash out.

He reached for her, but she drew back and nodded at the house. "Take me to the manor, please. I'll phone for a taxi and get the train back to London."

"No way. You aren't going anywhere on your own." It wasn't the only reason, but he was getting irritated by the way the conversation was evolving. "I don't intend to let you out of my sight, so get used to the idea!"

She sighed pointedly. "Didn't it occur to you all this information you just dropped on me might be upsetting and I might need some time on my own?" She turned and glared at him. "It's a lot to take in, the man we trusted, my mother's husband, had a mistress all those years."

"I know."

She shook her head at him. "And you lied to me. You told me you didn't know why your parents had split up."

Increasingly frustrated, Rex shook his head at her. "I'm beginning to regret telling you at all."

He turned the key in the ignition and revved the engine. "I should've just let you run loose and break your neck on some booby trap on the stairs?"

He pulled the car back onto the drive and set off at a pace.

"If you had any faith in my intelligence, you would've told me so I could have been prepared."

"Maybe I have gone the wrong way about it, maybe I should've told you. But I acted as I did with the best of intentions."

They were still arguing about it after he'd parked the car and they reached the doorway.

REX

Rex barely paused to grab his laptop bag from the boot of the car before darting after her. "Some women would be glad they had a protector."

"Okay, so now you want to be praised to the high heavens for keeping me in the dark and feeding me bullshit. Why doesn't that surprise me?"

They were standing on the steps outside the door.

Usually Mrs. Amery would be there, ready to greet them, door open. Rex tried the door handle. It was open.

Carmen gave him a terse look as she stepped past him into the hallway.

As soon as he stepped inside he registered the place was eerily silent. The chandelier in the hallway was lit up, as was the one on the floor above. "Why is it so quiet? Where's Mrs. Amery?"

The door was open and the housekeeper was expecting them. Mrs. Summerfield, too. Something was amiss. He set his bag down on the floor and stuck his head out the front. The CCTV camera didn't appear to be damaged in any way. Back in the hallway, he strained his ears, and heard nothing.

"What's the matter now?"

The lights flickered off and back on again.

Carmen was so upset she didn't seem to notice.

Rex put his fingers to his lips. With his arm around her shoulders, he directed her back toward the front door. Lowering his voice to a whisper, he gave her instructions. "Call the police, tell them we just arrived and we've found the property open with no staff around."

"They'll be in the kitchens. Don't be ridiculous."

"I hope you're right. I'll go and check. Now make the call and don't move from this spot." He paused. "If you hear anything unusual, head that way, fast." He nodded his head outside.

"What the hell do you mean?"

"Anything unusual, run, as fast as you can. Promise me."

Her eyes widened. "Rex, you're really scaring me."

"Good. Now make the call."

She nodded and went for her shoulder bag.

Once he saw her open it up and withdraw her phone, he touched her gently on the shoulder, then turned and made his way across the hallway toward the kitchens at the back of the house. Still he heard nothing.

The corridor running along to the kitchens was in darkness and he left it that way. When he reached the kitchen, it was empty, though everything appeared to be normal. Then he noticed the back door into the adjacent lobby was ajar. Stepping closer, he peeped into the lobby and saw the back door there was wide open.

Turning on his heel, he headed back.

When he reached the reception hallway he found it empty.

Carmen had gone.

The front door still stood open and he broke into a jog, assuming she'd gone outside. There was no sign of her anywhere on the lawns or pathways and he couldn't hear footsteps on gravel. Turning back, he jogged quickly up the stairs, wanting badly to find her on the way into her room, having ignored his instructions. There was no sign of her. He made his way back downstairs, eyes scanning the hallway.

As he reached the bottom of the staircase, he saw her phone in its electric-blue case lying near the doormat. Rex could barely stop himself screaming out her name, but instinct told him silence and stealth were his friends.

Frantic, Rex scanned the hallway again. He hadn't been gone long. Thirty seconds maybe, less than a minute. The doors to the reception rooms at the front of the building were open and at first glance those rooms seemed empty. There was only one answer; she was still in the hallway, but he just couldn't see her—oldest magician's trick in the book. She claimed his words had frightened her, though. Perhaps she'd hidden somewhere. Rex hoped so, but he couldn't take the risk by calling out her name.

Had she even had time to make the call? He was on his way to pick the phone up when he noticed something on the far side of the door, neatly positioned behind it. It was the pot of walking sticks that Mrs. Amery had dug out the week before. She'd obviously left it there in case Carmen needed one on arrival. As usual, Mrs. Amery had thought of everything. Instead of reaching for the phone, Rex reached into the pot and pulled out the most brutish-looking walking stick he could find.

Facing the hallway, he asked himself: *Where would I hide?*

He'd played hide-and-seek in this house as a child when his friends came to visit, and quite often with the staff, too.

Under the stairs. There, beneath the massive crescent-shaped staircase was a dark corner. If she was there, though, she'd have seen him looking for her. Heart thumping, he made his way over. When he rounded the corner and squinted into the dark shadows under the staircase, he saw her there.

A man stood at her back. He had his hand over her mouth.

"Back off," the man warned gruffly.

Carmen's eyes widened when she saw Rex. Then her gaze shifted, and he saw she was trying to indicate something. Before he had a chance to get any closer, she moved and whacked her assailant in the groin. When she broke free, Rex pulled her to one side.

The bloke straightened up and tried to make a run for it.

Rex used the stick. The man slumped to the floor, out cold.

Rex dropped his weapon, grabbed Carmen into his arms and kissed her head. "That was some move. Remind me never to hold you against your will."

"I'm perfectly capable of taking care of myself. I've told you that. I've had self-defense training."

"I'm glad." He never wanted her to be in this position again, though. He pulled his phone from his pocket. "You call the police. I'll try and see what's going on here. Stay under the stairs, out of view."

The sound of footsteps stalled them. Rex pulled her back into the shadows beneath the staircase and put his fingers on her lips. She nodded.

A woman's voice called out. "Charles?"

Puzzled, Rex craned his neck. The bizarre sight that met his eyes made no sense. Olivia Fordyce was walking across the hallway. She had Bill Amery at her side and was holding a gun to him.

"Charles?" she said again, calling it out quite loudly.

It was too surreal. Why was his father's mistress calling out the name of a man she knew was dead?

The man at their feet stirred.

Rex stared down at him, horror-struck. Was this Charles? If so, the possible implications of the name choice made his blood run cold.

He had to act fast. Bill was being held at gunpoint. This Charles bloke was about to wake up, and it wouldn't be long before Olivia looked their way.

With a hand on Carmen's shoulder, he indicated she stay put. Then he ducked down and picked up the stick. Stepping out from the cover of the staircase, he rapped the stick loudly on the floor as he went.

As he hoped, Olivia turned in his direction, arm swinging out wildly as she did so, gun pointing in his direction. He had a split second to incapacitate her. Breaking into a run, he batted her raised arm with the stick.

She crumpled, but she squeezed the trigger as she dropped.

The gun discharged, then skated across the marble tiles.

Olivia buckled to the floor, crying out.

Bill Amery staggered backward, bending double. He gripped his thigh and a bloodstain appeared on the fabric of his trousers.

Rex lunged for the gun, then stepped behind Bill, supporting him, slowly lowering him to the floor. When he had Bill safely down, his head snapped back in Carmen's direction. The man at her feet was slowly rising. Rex pointed the gun in his direction. "Don't move."

"I found them in the electricity generator," Bill said. "Tampering with it. Then she came at me with a gun."

"Take it easy," Rex stated. "Carmen, call the police and request an ambulance, as well."

Footsteps sounded in the corridor leading to the conservatory. Mrs. Amery appeared, cried out and ran toward her husband. Behind her was Jason, Bill's assistant. Hedging his bets, Rex pointed the gun in Jason's direction. The young man lifted his hands.

"The inside man," Rex said.

Jason had the decency to look ashamed.

Rex could hear Carmen speaking to the emergency services.

At his side, Mrs. Amery had taken off her jacket and folded it under Bill's head. She was crying and fretting as she removed the belt from his trousers to use as a tourniquet.

Olivia was writhing on the floor nearby, attempting to get up. When Rex looked her way she bellowed at him. "You've broken my arm, you monster."

Monster? Coming from her that was most amusing. "I'll break every bone in your body if you don't tell me why you did this."

She snarled at him.

Rex stepped closer and put the toe of his shoe on her forearm.

She screamed.

"You want the manor?"

"This old pile of rubble? No way."

Carmen waved his way and nodded, indicating the call to the emergency services was done.

"I'll have you know we love this old pile of rubble." Rex said it loudly and for Carmen's benefit, too, then he pressed his toe harder against Olivia's forearm.

Olivia cursed. "He promised he'd leave a share to my boys. My sons. He left it to her instead."

Her sons? Were her two henchmen her sons?

She threw a disparaging glance in Carmen's direction. "Charles went back on his word, so I decided to burn his pretty house down. If my boys didn't get what they're owed, why should you?"

Rex almost didn't want to know for sure, but it was staring him in the face so he had to hear it said aloud. "By 'your sons,' surely you don't mean…?"

"Charles's sons," she hissed at him, and her face twisted in an ugly, vengeful smile.

Carmen was close by and Rex looked at her in order to ground himself, to convince himself she was safe. He was suffering from information overload, and all he wanted was Carmen—to know she was real, to hold her.

When he caught her eye he saw the horror there in her expression, but also the concern. She reached his side and clung to him. "The police are on their way."

Never had Rex been more glad to feel her soft warmth against him.

CHAPTER TWENTY-FOUR

"I'll need to take a statement from you now, Ms. Shelby."

Carmen stared at the constable who was speaking to her, and tried to focus. She was a mess of emotions. Shocked by what had happened, and bewildered by the aftermath—the arrival of ambulances and police cars, arrests and medical treatment going on throughout the manor—she felt dizzy and nauseous. The ramifications of all that had been revealed left her reeling.

"Yes, yes, of course," she managed to reply.

The constable gestured into the drawing room, and she followed, walking alongside him. "I apologize for being so vague. I'm just so shocked," she said as they went.

"You're bound to be. This won't take too long."

The police constable—thankfully a vaguely familiar face from the Beldover area—took her into a quiet corner of the room where he pulled two chairs together so they could talk. While he made notes, Carmen kept looking out at the reception area beyond, the hallway where it had all taken place. It had been so sudden, and although she'd had some warning, it was so outrageous she'd hardly processed the information Rex had given her before the situation got out of hand. For a few minutes there she'd really feared for her life. And Rex's, too.

Yes, even though she was furious with him for keeping her in the dark this past week, she'd kept quiet and done exactly what her assailant had told her to do, out of fear for Rex's safety. When he'd found her and taken over the situation, she'd never felt more relieved in her life.

Now the relief had morphed into a battalion of questions—and overwhelming doubts. She was currently going through the motions, acting according to social norms, when what she really wanted to do was go out there and demand an explanation, tell all these people to get out of their home and then confront Rex. She was still angry with him for keeping things secret, for hiding the danger. He claimed to be protecting her from it, but she'd been kept in the dark. The black clouds of their history had gathered into a perfect storm while she'd been blinded by his brilliance.

Too much had unfolded, and she felt herself withdrawing from it all, estranged by things beyond her control and outside of what she knew and understood. The reaction brought about the most overwhelming emotion of all—heartbreak. They weren't close enough for him to confide in her, that was the bottom line. Those past two days had been so different. She'd begun to believe him, to trust him, and hoped the way she used to, for something more than the physical affair. But Rex was a lord unto himself, and she was alone.

She felt it as she looked around the house after the police arrived. Things were happening. People were talking to one another, and she was alone and bewildered and she had to slide her emotional armor back into place in order to cope.

"Were you aware you were under threat before you arrived at the property today?"

"Yes and no. I had a small accident the week before and Rex was concerned. In fact, we didn't stay here last weekend." She pieced it all together as she spoke, realizing he had indeed been trying to protect her all along. "I came up from London today because it was the anniversary of my mother's death. Rex met me at the church. On the way to the house, he was trying to warn me, but it was already too late."

"Did you know this woman, Olivia Fordyce?"

Carmen shook her head. "No, I'd never heard of her before today."

Rex had known all along, though; he said she was the reason his parents split up. "I'm sure Rex can shed more light than I."

The constable went over the details of the actual attack, checking each point with her before ticking it off. She watched as he made notes. At one point she heard the ambulance leaving the property, the lights flashing outside the sitting room window fading away.

Mrs. Summerfield appeared at the door.

"I'm making tea for everyone," she called in. "How do you take yours, Jim?"

The constable nodded and waved. "Two sugars please, Mrs. Summerfield."

Carmen looked from one to the other. There was something stoic about people who lived in this part of the world. It was the village life, because they knew one another so well, that in times of calamity it was all hands on deck.

When she signed the statement she rose to her feet and took a deep breath. "I'll fetch the tea for you."

Rex was standing beneath the crescent stairs in the hallway, demonstrating his actions to an officer. As she passed, he paused and locked his arm around her waist, drawing her in against him. "You okay?"

Carmen stared at him and felt as if her chest wrenched apart inside.

It was the same concern she'd witnessed all week, and yet she'd been unable to place it, mistaking it for a greedy possessiveness and his need for power over her. It made her knees weak to experience it now, knowing he'd been so worried about her.

Despite the tenderness in him, the secret legacy surrounding them all these years pressed down on her as she looked up at his handsome face. It was a legacy of jealousy they'd been left, a trail of bitterness and betrayal. Their family history had been hounded by ill fortune long before her mother's car crash. They were doomed to unhappiness, all of them. Falling in love with Rex was a cruel twist of fate, and the last straw.

"I'm okay," she managed. "I'm still angry with you, though."

"We'll talk, soon." He let her go and returned to the conversation with the two police officers he was dealing with.

Talk soon?

I can't. Not yet.

Finally the police were done. Rex quickly tracked Carmen down in the kitchens, where she was talking with Mrs. Summerfield.

As soon as he entered the room he noticed Mrs. Summerfield was comforting Carmen. She was bound to be upset, Rex knew, but the look on their faces gave him a bad feeling.

Mrs. Summerfield took off her apron. "I'll leave you two alone now. I'll be back in the morning."

The resigned look on the cook's face worried him even more. Was it just the events of the day, or was it something else?

Once she'd gone, he strode to Carmen's side and held her. For a few moments she clung to him.

"We're safe to stay here tonight, since they're under lock and key now." How long that would last was another question, but for now they could breathe easy.

Carmen pulled free of him. "No, I'm leaving, too."

Rex was dumbfounded. "Leaving? Now?"

"Yes, now." She picked up her handbag from the table and walked away quickly. He followed her, hanging on every word as she continued.

REX

"While you were dealing with the police, I arranged for a taxi to call at nine-thirty." She paused in the hallway and glanced at her watch. "It'll be here any moment. The last train for London leaves Beldover at ten."

Rex closed the space between them in four long strides and wrapped his hands around her shoulders. "There's no need to be concerned. We can be together now, we can relax."

"Rex, it's over. The house. You and me. Everything." She glanced around the hallway and then back to him.

He saw the resignation in her eyes and it cut him up inside. Her lashes were damp, a smudge of mascara darkening her lower lids. He couldn't bear it. "I want you to stay. I thought you loved being here."

"I do love the house. And what you've given me these past weeks—" she paused and inhaled deeply "—I'll be forever grateful for what you introduced me to. It was a side of myself I was unaware of."

Unaware of? Rex struggled to accept what she was saying. All of it.

"I need time out to get my head together. I need to get my life back on track." She broke free of his grasp.

Rex stared at the back of her head when she turned away.

She was still talking. "You found out what you needed to know. You really do care about the place, after all. You fought for it, you protected it. It's yours. You're the new custodian of Burlington Manor."

"No. Not without you."

She turned back, shook her head. "It won't work. Can't you see that? We were doomed before we even started. It should've been obvious to us even before all this horrible history came out. But come out it has. The sins of the fathers, Rex." Her eyes flashed. "False expectations and secrets kept us apart years ago when we might've had a natural relationship. When we came back here there was so much we didn't know about the past. Hell, there is still so much we don't know."

The haunted look in her eyes angered him. He wanted to push the shadows away, but if she left now that wouldn't happen. "But the danger is over."

"I know, and I thank you for all you did to protect me—I see it all now. But it's like a curse. We were nearly killed because of the history here."

He shook his head vehemently. "We were nearly killed because my father kept a crazy nutjob for a mistress."

"But don't you see? You found out you have two half brothers of Charles Carruthers's blood. They were cut out. I wasn't. They have more right

210

to this place than I do. From what you've said this week, it was only your father's guilt about keeping us apart that puts me here at all."

"That's not the case."

"It's why two men felt they had to take action. They were owed. That's what she said."

"They tried to hurt you. They're getting fuck all!" His self-control was slipping away.

She swiped back her hair. "Rex, my mother died here. For all I know she could've been a victim of that mad bitch."

Rex was stunned. It hadn't even occurred to him, even though Carmen had expressed doubts about the car accident. The possibilities roared in on him, making his mind reel. Could it be true? "If that's the case I'll get to the bottom of it." If it was the last thing he ever did, he'd answer the question. "I'll find out the truth. I promise you."

"Don't you think that's enough tragedy for a person to bear? For crying out loud, Rex, you've got two neglected half brothers you didn't even know about. That's going to take some time to come to terms with. I can see it, even if you can't."

"Okay, we all need time, but if you love the house we can work at it and live here."

"No."

"Why the hell not?"

"Because we're cursed to be unhappy. We proved it tonight. My mother loved your father. She gave everything to him and this place and look where it got her. A lonely grave, and your father grieving while his bitter mistress plotted against us all."

Once again the need to protect and cherish her pumped hard in his blood. He snatched her against him, one hand at the small of her back pressing her fully to him, the other cupping the back of her head as he kissed her heavily, trying to make her see, trying to kiss the denial out of her.

She was tense in his arms, rigid and fiercely resistant, but her lips softened and he felt her give, just for a moment.

Then she pulled away. Her eyes were luminous. She wanted him—he could see it, he could feel it—but she was resisting him more now than she ever had.

If they had time apart, she might withdraw again. She would become the elegant but fiercely independent woman he'd seen across his father's grave. It had been so much effort on his part to undo her tightly guarded ways and encourage the sensual woman to reveal herself. After all that, he couldn't take the risk that she would walk away and forget him. *I love this woman.* "We can get past it. All of it. Please don't walk away."

"I'm sorry, I can't stay. Nothing ever works out for this family, and it's the same for us. We're only here doing this because we wanted each other years ago. Like you said, we had to burn it out. There was only one way."

"It never went away, and you know it."

"Maybe not yet, but it will. Now you've had what you wanted you'll soon get bored with the whole situation."

He shook his head. "It'll never happen."

He'd never been more sure of anything. "God knows I don't have a good track record, but that's because it was always you in my head! It's always been you I wanted."

She stared up at him and her lower lip trembled.

"I'd dedicate my life to making you happy," he said, and stroked his hand down the length of her hair. "Carmen, I *will* make this right."

She shook her head. "You're better to start fresh with a new life, a new woman, not someone who reminds you of all the past mistakes made here."

"I don't want that, and I can tell you don't mean it."

"I do mean it. I think Burlington Manor deserves a fresh start, not two people who are totally screwed up by their past."

"Fuck the past!"

She shook her head and pulled away. "We can't ignore it, not after everything that's happened."

"Okay, we can't ignore it, but together we can get past it. You love this house and I'll only be happy with you here. We can make it work. Carmen, you have to be part of it."

She paused, looked back.

"I can't do it without you," he stated.

"That's blackmail."

"No, it's the honest to God truth."

She seemed to teeter on the edge, visibly torn.

The sound of tires on the gravel and headlights flashing through the windows on either side of the front door told him time was short. Carmen looked back, alerted to the presence of the taxi.

"I forbid you to leave," Rex blurted, his entire being opposed to the idea. It was a crazy move, but he couldn't help himself. He was desperate.

"This isn't a game, not anymore. And I'm not a possession you can order about, not now." She gave him a sidelong glance and it held a warning. "It's time to say goodbye."

She stared at him, determination and sadness showing in her expression.

He gritted his teeth, massaged his temples and forced himself to face up to everything that had happened in the past few hours. He had to get some form of compromise from her. "So, you need time out, a break away from the house. I understand. It's been hard on us both, but it doesn't mean we have to lose what we have."

"What do we have?" She looked at him, leveling him as she asked the question.

"You said it yourself—it's been great between us. I want to be with you." He heard it in his own voice, the sound of a relieved laugh, and wondered why it'd been so hard to say that. What had started as an interesting challenge had become so much more. "We've been through so much."

"That's it exactly. There's no need to put ourselves through any more."

It wasn't what he wanted to hear. *I want you, I want you.* The words echoed around his mind. The weight in his chest grew heavier, leaving him thwarted and angry.

"It won't always be like this, you have to see that." This was tearing him apart inside. He gripped her shoulders tightly.

She tried to wrench free.

"I can't let you go."

"You have to."

"I won't!" His grip on her tightened, his anger and denial a swelling tide obscuring everything but his goal.

Color flamed across her cheekbones and her eyes looked wild with anger. "Boo, damn it! Boo!"

Rex froze, as did she. The safeword. She'd used it, after all.

Her eyes glittered with tears.

He could hear the sound of his own angry heartbeat in his ears, the physical evidence of his volatility shattering the silence.

"Boo," she repeated in a strangled whisper, and a tear fell to her cheek.

Rex released her. It was the hardest thing he'd ever done. "Fine. Go, then. But you'll be back."

"For more of your fun and games? You think you can wish it all away with a session in the sack?"

"I know it'll take more than that. Give me a chance to prove it."

She put her finger to his lips. "Please. If you care for me at all, allow me some space."

He covered her hand with his, turned his face into her palm where he kissed her briefly. "I'll agree, but only because I want you back."

She stared at him a moment longer, eyes glistening, and then walked away. He followed her to the door and watched as she climbed into the taxi.

Feeling like a condemned man, he slammed his hands against the top of the door frame. As the car turned away, he caught his last glimpse of her.

I bought tickets to Paris, he thought as he turned away and paced up and down the hallway. He had to stop himself from jumping in the Maserati and chasing her down to announce what he'd planned.

She needed time alone. She'd hate him for not respecting that.

If only I'd done it earlier. He'd been so wrapped up in making the most of the situation between them, wielding the manor as his bargaining tool, he forgot how to do things properly. By the time he'd realized he should be courting her, it was too late.

"This bloody house," he muttered, and glared around the walls of the hallway, resenting the place. He thought it was a chance for them to be together, but now it had unveiled the secrets of the past, he wanted to tear it down brick by brick. The urge to pick up the weapon he'd used earlier and smash the carved banisters to smithereens was overwhelming.

But something stopped him. Reason. Carmen still loved this place, and deep down he did, too. *It's our home.*

He turned back to the door. Gripping the frame he stared at the fading lights of the taxi. "You belong here at Burlington Manor, Carmen Shelby. I'll show you it's meant to be."

Carmen was the heart of this place for him. She always had been.

And she's everything I ever wanted and always will be.

It was time to pull out all the stops.

CHAPTER TWENTY-FIVE

After three days of hell, Rex's emotions finally crystallized. He knew what he wanted and how to get it, and he believed his thoughts and actions would now be more precise and considered. Which was just as well, he reflected, because he was currently in a court of law.

He stared across the Oxford Crown Court room at the dock, where Olivia and her two sons awaited their initial hearing. Just seeing them again made his blood boil. Justice would be done. The date for the trial would be set by the end of this session and the prosecution barrister had assured him all three would be held in custody until the time of their court case.

Olivia looked every bit as prim and proper as when he'd first met her. Her gaze was set in the middle distance and her expression showed distaste, as if she was above it all and saw no reason for her incarceration. Rex shook his head. It was some delusion she'd woven for herself.

He still found it hard to accept the two men in the dock were his half brothers, but when he studied Charles, he saw the likeness to their father. Charles stared back at him, steely eyed. Only Jason, the younger man—the one who'd had the damn cheek to obtain employment at the manor—looked suitably penitent. With head lowered and loose hair hanging down around his face, he made a sorry picture.

At least one of them had the decency to look ashamed.

"Court in session, all rise," the usher announced.

The judge entered and took his seat.

Despite his intention to make Olivia and her sons feel his wrath across the courtroom, Rex glanced repeatedly at the entrance in the hope Carmen would appear. She wanted nothing to do with it, yet he couldn't stop looking for her. Even while the prosecution and defense presented their statements, his attention was divided. It had been the hardest three days of his life. The deep, profound need to contact her was unremitting. Even though he'd been working around the clock—his time divided between negotiating with Nikhil Rashid and pursuing the investigation into Sylvia Shelby's death—his thoughts had never been far from Carmen.

He forced his attention back as the charges were read. Olivia Fordyce didn't flinch when her crimes were listed. Not one iota of remorse. *Would that change during the actual court case itself?* Rex wondered. He wasn't inclined to think so.

"In view of the criminal and vindictive nature of their actions," the prosecution barrister stated, "I request your honor does not grant bail."

Rex frowned while he listened to the defense, who suggested Olivia had made misguided attempts to gain her sons' recognition, which had got out of hand. Muttering beneath his breath, he looked at the judge, hoping to God he wasn't going to be swayed.

"After due consideration of the circumstances," the judge concluded, "Olivia Fordyce and Charles Fordyce will be held in custody until the case is heard. Given the gravity of the crime—including attempted murder, possession of a weapon with intent to harm and actual bodily harm of an innocent bystander—the charges are serious enough to warrant no bail. However, with regards to Jason Fordyce I'm inclined to be more lenient."

Rex cursed beneath his breath.

"If the circumstances of the statements are true," the judge continued, "Jason was an unwitting pawn, manipulated for information and to gain access by his older brother and his mother. Bail for Jason Fordyce will be set at £5,000."

Rex stood and watched as Olivia and Charles were led back into custody. Would there be anyone there to provide the bail money? He observed as Jason was taken in a different direction. Nearby, on the observation bench, an elderly man rose to his feet and gestured at Jason. Rex studied the man. A relative, he surmised. Damn it.

As the court dispersed, Rex approached the prosecution barrister.

"Mr. Carruthers." The barrister nodded at him as he put his file into a briefcase.

"I was under the impression all three would be held?"

"The defense played on the youngest defendant's lack of knowledge." The barrister studied Rex as he spoke. "Do you think he'll attempt to skip bail?"

"I'm more concerned he'll try to see through what his mother set in motion. How quickly can I get a restraining order in place?"

"You're concerned for your safety?"

"Not mine. Carmen Shelby's."

The barrister nodded. "Of course. Let's take this to one of the meeting rooms and I'll advise you how to proceed."

When Rex eventually emerged from the courts, his mood hadn't lightened. He needed Carmen's agreement to proceed with a restraining order. He already had a reason to contact her, but he wanted the meeting to be kept as simple as possible. He couldn't take any risks. The sooner the restraining order was in place, the better.

He made his way quickly to the nearby car park, reaching into his pocket for his keys as he walked through the entrance. As he did, a figure emerged from the shadows inside.

It was Jason.

Rex cursed audibly, then pressed on.

"So the old guy sprung bail for you," he stated as he strode past the younger man. "Who is he, your grandfather?"

"My uncle." Jason hastened behind. "Please, Rex, can I speak with you?"

Rex paused and ground his jaw, his mind working fast. He wanted to thump the guy and tell him to get lost, but he also knew he had to tread carefully. "Go ahead, talk. I'm happy for you to add 'attempts to influence a witness' to your case."

"That's not what I want to do." Warily he met Rex's stare. "I don't blame you for thinking badly of me. I just wanted you to know when I first went to Burlington Manor, there was no malicious intent."

"Why should that even matter to me, given the end result?"

"I just want you to know, because it matters to me…what you think."

Rex's irritation grew. The lad was attempting to appeal to him, to gain sympathy. *Not going to happen.* He didn't care what their individual motives were, but he bit his words back. The man was panicking; he might let something useful slip. "Convince me."

"I wanted to see him again, that's all. He used to visit us, when we were kids he came once a week. We had a dad and we didn't feel any different than the other kids. Then he stopped coming. I'm not sure of the timing." The lad's discomfort was tangible. "I'm told it was after he married his second wife."

"That fits." Rex was determined not to feel sympathy for the guy, but there was something there he related to—being cut out when his father changed direction. "It's no excuse for attempted murder."

"I know, and that wasn't why I went there. I just wanted to know him again. I spent time in the village looking for work. Bill took some convincing because I wasn't local, but then he gave me a chance. I enjoyed working with Bill, and I didn't see much of Dad, but when I did, I felt sorry for him."

"Why?"

"He was lonely."

"He was surrounded by people, staff, whoever he wanted."

Jason shook his head. "No. Not really. It was awful to see." Jason eyeballed him briefly before looking away. "He was one lonely old man."

"He made it that way," Rex replied angrily.

"I know. Even if I hadn't experienced it firsthand, I know he abandoned people when they didn't fit his master plan."

It shook Rex, because it was a truth they shared.

"The staff said stuff," Jason continued. "I couldn't help hearing it. Bill Amery never stopped talking about what had gone on there in the past."

Rex's irritation hit a new level. Swiftly he got a hold of Jason, hands on the lapels of his jacket, and held him up against the wall. "And now Bill Amery has been shot and you're due in court as an accessory to the crime."

Jason swallowed visibly. "I didn't know it would happen, honestly. I was just trying to explain how I knew about—" he squirmed and forced himself to meet Rex's stare "—our dad."

Rex gripped his lapels tighter still, annoyed at the reference to their blood bond. "What the hell has any of this got to do with your case?"

Jason shook his head. "This isn't meant to be an excuse. I'm just trying to explain why I was at the house." He held up his hands. "Please, I really just wanted to see him again. Let me explain."

Rex loosened his grip a tad. "You better speak fast. I've got a restraining order to file and it has your name on it."

Again, Jason held up a hand. He looked afraid, as if daunted by what the order would mean. "I talked about it, big mistake. I told Mum and Charles about seeing Dad and the house and stuff and Charles got this crazy idea in his head. He wanted to go see the manor, too. I had no idea—"

"Yeah, right."

"No, really, I had no idea they'd do what they did."

"Tell me this, who set the trap on the stairs for Carmen?" Rex had already figured it'd been Charles in the tube station in London. His build matched the assailant's. The obvious candidate for the dangerous trap in the manor was Jason himself.

Jason's eyes closed momentarily. When he opened them he shook his head. "Had to be Mum. I never would've let her wander around the place if I'd known, but I guess I talked too much about Carmen's habits, too, and the day it happened…Mrs. Amery was out shopping and Mum had been up there in the afternoon…visiting me." There was a pleading look in his eyes. "I can scarcely believe it myself."

Anger barreled through Rex and he released Jason, throwing him back against the wall, where he slumped. "Save your performance for the judge."

Jason shuffled upright. "It's not a performance."

Rex was about to turn away.

"I'm ashamed of what they did, really, and if I could go back…"

Rex scrutinized him. Was he telling the truth? Had they taken advantage of his innocent enthusiasm to get close to his father again? For some reason, Rex wanted to believe it. Cursing silently, he realized that version of events would be easier for him to accept than if both of his half brothers turned out to be vindictive criminals out for revenge.

Bottom line, it wasn't his job to decide. "If it's the truth, then keep your head down and stay out of trouble—and that means stay away from Carmen Shelby, above all—then you'll get to say your piece in court."

Jason nodded. "I will. You have my word."

Rex turned away quickly and strode toward his car, straightening his jacket collar as he did so. But he was irked by some odd notion clinging to his back as he went. Compassion, he guessed, compassion for the lad's predicament if he was indeed telling the truth about his innocence. They might well have used him—and ruined his life in the process.

"Rex," Jason called out behind him, "thank you for hearing me out."

Goddamn it. Rex didn't have to glance back to feel the genuine gratitude there in the younger man's voice. That's when he saw his own error. He'd somehow spoken to Jason as an older brother might, advising him to stay out of trouble, which was the last thing Rex had intended to do.

CHAPTER TWENTY-SIX

Carmen knew the note on her desk was from Rex the moment she saw it. Curiosity swamped her, despite her best intentions to ignore any such maneuver on his part. Then it occurred to her he might have delivered it himself. Her body grew warm and responsive at the suggestion of his presence nearby, possibly only minutes earlier.

Unable to resist, she picked up the envelope. On the front, her name was handwritten in anonymous capitals. She turned it over and felt the thickness. It was sealed and contained only one sheet of paper.

No pages of long heartfelt messages, then.

No, it wasn't Rex's style. Rex would be cleverer. He'd go for a devastating hit, holding her attention with a carefully crafted erotic suggestion, a command that would floor her, bringing her to her knees with yearning for his mastery. The very thought of it turned her on.

Resistance was futile. The call he had on her was too strong.

Be sensible. By the look of the envelope, it was an invitation card. Some fancy racing industry event or something he was trying to impress her with. Big deal. She was a grown woman, a businesswoman who managed a successful national retail chain. This shouldn't be hard to deal with. Ripping the envelope open, she slipped out the piece of paper inside.

The simple statement written on it was nothing she expected.

The police have reopened their investigation into your mother's car crash. It's important you know why.
Rex

Carmen's mind reeled, her heart aching. She'd never believed her mother's car crash was accidental, and she'd told Rex as much. She never expected him to act on it, though. The simple note was an olive branch of some magnitude. The implications quickened her thoughts and made her mouth go dry. Rex had listened to her and acted on it. She couldn't take the risk of spending time with him again, and yet through this grand gesture—

this effort to allay her fears and suspicions about the past—it was exactly what he was asking her to do.

She glanced at the clock. She had a meeting to attend. Grabbing her notes, she prepared to make her way to the boardroom. That's when her phone rang. Glancing down at it, she saw it was Rex calling. When she considered ignoring it guilt stole into her heart. He'd gone to some lengths on her behalf.

Thank him for the information. It was common courtesy, nothing more, and it would stop him calling if she handled it right. Establish a barrier, then thank him. She reached for the phone. "Which part of 'time out' didn't you understand, Rex?"

"Four days seems more than adequate, to me."

"And I don't get a say in how long it should be?"

"Of course you do. Look, Carmen, whatever went down before, there are still things we need to sort out, things that bind us together."

Frustrating, but it was true. "The house."

"And other things." His tone said it all. Intimate, deep and resonant, his words stimulated every sense, every nerve ending.

She closed her eyes.

That was fatal. When he spoke again his voice locked her to him, daring her to deny him.

"I won't lie. I want to see you again, more than I've ever wanted anything in my entire life." His voice was hoarse. "I miss you."

When he said that, she experienced an ache so deep it was painful. A meeting could never remain neutral. "Please, don't do this—"

"I know," he interrupted, his tone soothing. "I'm sorry. It's just…hearing your voice." He paused. "What I meant to say was, did you receive my note?"

She glanced down at the message he'd sent, focusing on that. "I did. Thank you for letting me know. No doubt the police will be in touch with me if there is anything new to discuss."

"I'm sure they will be."

When he paused again, the tension ratcheted. Rex was so able to express his will and his desires in the tone of his voice that Carmen instantly felt on edge, waiting for another drop in his tone, the alteration to suggestion, command and intimacy that made her malleable, feminine and without doubt. Emotion knotted in her chest.

"I want to make this right for you, Carmen."

When he said her name, her legs felt unsteady.

"I've got a private investigator looking into it as well. I mean to discover the truth."

"I have no doubt you will. When you set your mind on something you usually succeed." The comment was out before she thought through the implications.

"Usually? Except when it comes to you, is that what you're saying?"

Had he set his mind on her? Well, yes, he'd trapped her in an arrangement which had sexually compromised her, preying on long-withheld desires, but she'd wanted it, too. The important thing—her anchor on reality—was she knew it was a temporary thing and she never forgot that. Rex was a player and she wasn't. Simple.

She took a deep breath. "Except when it comes to me, yes."

Silence.

Why did she feel the need to fill the silence? "I do appreciate your efforts."

"There's been too much...wrong. Around us." He was choosing his words carefully. "I want to concentrate on what was right between us. I need to sort the rest of the mess out, and I will. We need closure on the past."

Carmen tried not to think about the hidden meaning there. The thing right between them was their sexuality. By some weird alignment of the stars they keyed into each other's deepest desires. Everything else was wrong. Wasn't it? Suddenly Carmen wasn't sure. It was the eternal draw between them. It defied logic, causing her to question everything.

"My private investigator has some questions. I've jotted them down. Meet me for dinner tonight and we can work through them."

There it was—the alluring command. Carmen braced herself to deny him. "I can meet with your investigator myself."

"I'd rather I handled it. I know you. He doesn't."

Someone anonymous would be so much easier than a man who knew how to play her. She gave a dismissive laugh.

"Carmen, give me some credit here. I believe I can be more sensitive about this than a stranger."

That really didn't help. The image of Rex being sensitive reminded her of their previous intimacy. Images invaded her mind, images she'd tried to obscure: the sight of him going down on her while he had her bound and helpless, the feeling of him covering her eyes, blindfolding her in order to lead her to a new level of understanding about her sexuality. She couldn't afford to let him get close to her again. "Is it really necessary?"

"Yes." Tension was heavy in that one word. "Carmen, I'm not expecting anything other than what's necessary. A public place, a few questions to expedite the investigation."

The fact she didn't trust him to stick to it was a secondary issue. Most of all she didn't trust herself. She wanted him too much.

When she didn't answer, he continued. "There's something else, but I'd rather not discuss it over the phone."

Something else? Yes, of course there was. "If you don't tell me what this something else is," she responded, keeping her tone businesslike, "I don't see any need for a meeting."

He gave a low, throaty laugh. "It's good to hear you in such fine form."

Carmen sighed into the phone. "I'm already late for an appointment, spit it out."

"It's Jason, the one who was working up at the house. He's out on bail. Olivia and the other son are being held in custody until the trial."

It wasn't what she'd expected, and it took a moment for her to absorb the information. "Well, none of them are going to stay locked up forever."

"I want to put a restraining order on him. I don't want him coming anywhere near you."

"I'm sure that's not necessary."

"I'm not taking any risks. I want you to be safe, always."

The tone of his voice made her skin prickle, the genuine concern for her well-being undermining her resolve to resist him.

"I've taken advice, but you need to be involved to action the paperwork. Meet me this evening and I'll explain." Before she mustered a response, his persuasive words continued. "I won't overstep your current boundaries. Not unless you indicate it's what you want." He paused. "I promise."

She willed herself to keep a grip on reality. Instead, she felt it spinning away. "Your promise better be sound," she responded, her voice scarcely above a whisper.

For a moment he didn't respond, and when he did victory echoed through his words. "Meet me at eight. Raphael's in Mayfair. I've reserved a table."

He'd already reserved a table? Carmen didn't trust herself to respond.

Instead, she cut the connection and left for her meeting. As she strode down the corridor, she shook her head, annoyed with herself. She'd given him the tiniest of openings and he'd played her, well and truly. *I hate you, Rex Carruthers.*

Nevertheless, anticipation began to bubble inside her.

CHAPTER TWENTY-SEVEN

Rex glanced at his watch. In four hours, he would be meeting Carmen. It felt good, although he had a lot of work to do in order to prove himself to her. Right now, however, he was seeing another woman, and he was pretty sure Carmen wouldn't approve if she knew.

But it had to be done.

A buzzer sounded and a door at the far end of the visiting room opened. The women prisoners filed into the room. Rex watched with interest. Instead of uniforms they were wearing their own clothes, except each wore a blue bib marking them out as what they were. It wasn't what he expected, but he'd never visited a prison before. He'd envisaged being behind a Perspex screen. Instead, he'd been ushered to a numbered seat facing another, with just a low table in between. The women fanned out across the room as they caught sight of their visitors.

Olivia Fordyce was one of the last to emerge. She peered across the room, narrowing her eyes. Was she reluctant to see him? Rex didn't think so, because as soon as he'd asked for permission to visit she'd immediately granted it for the following day.

When she spotted him, she smirked.

Rex meshed his fingers together and rested his elbows on his knees as he watched her approach, forcing down his anger.

"Rex," she said smoothly as she took her seat opposite him, "how lovely of you to come and visit me."

"You think so?"

She gave a sardonic laugh. "I don't suppose you're here to forge a deep friendship with me, but you remind me of your father…how could I resist your request?"

Every word grated on him. "I'll be brief. I doubt I can stomach your company for long."

"But you want to talk about what happened…to understand." The condescension in her tone riled him.

"Not at all. You already said enough last week. I don't need to hear any more about that particular event." It was the truth. He was far more interested in what had gone on before then, and his P.I. had uncovered something about Sylvia Shelby's death that hadn't been revealed before.

Olivia's eyebrows lifted. "Go on."

The fact she was treating it like an audience with the queen irked Rex to no end. Her refined lady act didn't fool him. The woman had a heart of ice and a wicked, vengeful nature. "Sylvia Shelby's death. My suspicion is you were involved."

Something flickered in her eyes, and then she laughed.

"I see you do know something about it."

"Of course I knew about it. Sylvia Shelby was the reason your father stopped seeing me. I celebrated when I read about her tragic death in the papers."

She really was vile, Rex decided. He cut to the chase. "There was a witness that day, the woman who called the police to report Sylvia's accident. I have a private investigator tracking her down. He's already uncovered the fact your son, Charles, was seeing the woman at the time, which doesn't look good now, does it?" He paused but she didn't react. "As you're probably aware, she emigrated to Australia, but my investigator has contacts there and it's only a matter of time until we find her. If you or your sons were involved in Sylvia's accident, I *will* find out."

She gave a slow smile. "Even if there was something to tell, why on earth would I tell you?"

The truth was written all over her—she knew exactly what he was talking about. Rex gestured about the walls of the prison. "This can't be easy. Wouldn't you rather be at home in your apartment?"

She shrugged and for a moment Rex thought she really didn't care. "I'm willing to do you a deal," he continued. "If you tell me everything you know, I'll back up Jason's story about him not being involved."

She shook her head. "No deal. I intend to take all the blame myself."

Rex was sure Charles had little chance of escaping conviction, but he thought she might bite if he covered Jason's back. "You're enjoying prison that much?"

"Say whatever you want. It's meaningless." She gestured fluidly with her hands. "You think you know all about me. You don't. I'm already a condemned woman. I've got nothing left to lose because I have cancer and I'm going to die soon, anyway."

Rex was shocked, but the pieces fell into place.

"My sons have a life to lead," she continued. "I'll make sure they're both cleared."

Rex's frustration grew.

"I'm going to die inside a year. Frankly," she added icily, "you were well provided for by your father, and you can bloody well bugger off if you think I'm going to assist you in any way."

Rex bit back his annoyance, but this wasn't his only option. "Fine. If you don't want to make amends for your actions, so be it. Take it to your grave." He rose to his feet. "The police have reopened the case. The new evidence means we won't need your help to know what happened."

He began to turn away, then he paused. "It's ironic, though, isn't it? Because the charge will be added to your list, and yet your cruel actions against Sylvia Shelby made not a jot of difference. Even with her out of the picture, my father would rather be alone than with you."

She narrowed her eyes, but he saw the pure venom reflected there.

He'd finally touched a nerve. Good.

With that, Rex turned his back on her and left.

CHAPTER TWENTY-EIGHT

Rex's mood remained dark until the moment he saw Carmen entering the restaurant that evening. He watched as the *maître d'* approached her. She spoke briefly and the man smiled and offered to direct her. When she returned the man's smile, the sight of it made Rex grateful to be alive.

Rising from his seat, he watched as she approached. She wore a sleek red sheath of a dress and matching high heels. When she met his gaze, he was sure. Passion flared in her eyes. She blinked and it was gone, but not before Rex absorbed it. They were meant to be together. It was his firm belief. It was also the only thing sustaining him since she'd walked away the week before.

"Rex." She nodded and took up the seat opposite him.

"I'm glad you came." He battled his desire to touch and claim her, attempting to be cautious when he really wanted to push things forward to a solid relationship as soon as possible.

"You didn't give me a lot of choice."

She was nervous, he could tell, but those sidelong glances she gave him proved one thing—this was an exercise in resistance for them both, and it was hard, because the simmering erotic tension between them was as evident as ever. It was his job to keep the situation on the middle ground, for the time being at least. He wanted her to relax. "I hope I wasn't too demanding."

She arched her eyebrows at him.

He shrugged. "I'm trying to be straight with you."

"You can stop giving me the sexy eyes. I didn't come here to flirt with you, as hard as that may be for you to accept."

Sexy eyes? "I was just looking." It was the truth, but there was a spark he couldn't ignore. "You could've arrived wearing a nun's habit and I'd still admire you. That's never going to change."

Her gaze dropped. "Well, don't expect me to do more than exchange pleasantries." She rearranged her cutlery as she spoke, shifting it from side to side before returning it to its place. "I came here for one thing, the information you said you had about the investigation into my mother's death."

The waiter approached. Rex accepted the menu and encouraged her to look at hers.

"Given the difficult nature of this meeting," she said after a few moments faking interest, "my appetite is nonexistent."

"In that case, I'll order you something light." He shut the menu and gestured at the waiter, encouraging him to step forward. "I'll take a steak, rare, with the usual sides, and for the lady—" he glanced over at her "—a Greek salad, heavy on the olives, light on the feta."

Her eyes widened.

Rex restrained a smile. It always surprised her when he remembered details about her and what she liked. It's why he couldn't resist doing it.

"Thank you, sir. Anything from the bar?"

"Your best medium white wine for the lady—make sure it's well chilled, with a sparkling mineral water on the side. And I'll have a Scotch on the rocks."

When the waiter retreated, Carmen observed him warily.

"Why so mistrustful, Carmen? We know each other well now, do we not?"

"You need to ask? You lied to me and kept me in the dark. I can't trust a man who keeps secrets."

"Okay. Maybe it was the wrong way to handle it, but I was trying to protect you. It's too late to alter that now. No more secrets." Even as he said it he was certain Carmen wouldn't approve of him meeting Olivia, but he wanted to present a result, not narrate his frustration. Before he'd thought of a way around it, she spoke.

"So, you really think a restraining order is necessary with Jason?"

He rested back in his chair. "Probably not, but I can't be sure. He approached me after the hearing. He was in a state. He does seem to be aware his life has been completely derailed by his mother's actions."

She nodded. "I found it hard to believe. I mean, I don't know him well, but I talked to him a few times when we were up there."

He could tell she instantly regretted referring to their time at the manor, albeit inadvertently. To keep things neutral, he told her about the hearing, and then brought the subject around to her mother's car crash and the renewed investigation.

"I wonder if they'll find out what happened," she said, and she was deep in thought. When the waiter brought the drinks, she immediately reached for her wine. "If the truth is she made an error in judgment, so be it. At least I'll finally know."

It was so important to her. "Oh, there's more to it. I'm sure you were right."

She stared at him for the longest moment, and it was a combination of relief and hope that he saw.

"There was a witness, did you know?"

"Yes. I don't recall her name, but she was walking nearby and heard the crash. She was at the scene within moments and called the police."

"The police records state she said there wasn't anyone else around. No other vehicles or pedestrians. The road conditions were a bit misty when she got there."

"It wasn't misty when I got there."

"You were at the house?"

"Yes."

"The police say they had no reason to doubt the witness, but my private investigator has discovered she was seeing Olivia Fordyce's eldest son at the time."

Carmen was about to pick up her wineglass again, but froze. "Seriously?"

He nodded. "I'm working on getting to the truth of it."

"You really meant it," she murmured. "You really want to find out."

"Of course I meant it. I want you to have the answers you need, and if they're painful, I want to help you get through it."

"Thank you for trying."

"I don't want your thanks."

Carmen inhaled audibly. Wariness shone in her eyes.

Rex hated to see it there, but they had to get past this to find their way back to when it had been good. "I want something else—your trust."

Their food arrived.

Once the waiter had gone Carmen picked up her fork and stabbed vaguely at her salad. "I can give you my thanks, and I can give you Burlington Manor, but that's all I'm offering in return for your help this time around."

"This time around?" Rex smiled. "So you thought you knew what I was going to say next. The same deal as before—is that what you thought? Four weekends with you all to myself?" He allowed his gaze to drift over her, remembering again how good it had been. "And in return you got my half of Burlington Manor. You thought it was a good deal at the time, I seem to recall."

"It was a deal based on old desires, as you pointed out at the time," she said sarcastically. "Well, we already had plenty of time to 'burn it out,' don't you think?" Her eyes looked molten, her cheekbones slashed with red.

REX

The atmosphere was thick with erotic tension. For Rex it only proved they were meant to be together. "I don't think we'll ever burn out, but I'd happily die trying."

"Stop right there, please." Her eyes blazed. "You got me here on the vague promise of information. It was a trick. We both know you have a knack for this...with me. Don't abuse it."

It was a warning, but Rex experienced it as a red flag in all the wrong ways. It only served to show how aware she was—how aware they both were—of the tug of desire between them. It hadn't gone away; it never would. The more she denied it, the more Rex knew it wasn't something either of them could walk away from. He reached for his drink. He didn't want to charge at her red flag, but God knows he wanted her. More than anything else in his life. She'd drawn a line, and now she was teetering on it. One sign, if she even gave him one sign, he would take her in hand. It was within his grasp, and he would edge her over that line of hers very soon.

"A knack? No 'knack' would make you give yourself to a man, not if you didn't want to."

Her hand trembled and she put down her fork. "Okay, so I wanted you. I've said it out loud. Happy now?"

"Only if it stays that way."

She shook her head, slumped back in her seat. "I can't...I mean, I know we need to be in touch, to sort out ownership of the manor—"

"And the rest."

"Yes, but we don't have to..." She stared at him, blinked, like a rabbit in the headlights.

This was it, time to show his hand. "Carmen, we can't be alone and not be intimate. Sitting here is an exercise in restraint for me. I want to hold you. I want to love you...and I know you want to be loved. Is it so wrong?"

She stared at him, and for a moment he thought he saw the whole of the world spinning in her eyes. "No. In itself it's not wrong...exactly. I should be able to do this." She lifted one shoulder and her eyes glistened. "I'm an adult and a businesswoman and having an affair shouldn't be such a big deal...but..."

The edge loomed close. Rex had to take the risk; he had to edge it forward. "What are you afraid of?"

"It's so intense, when I'm with you, and I'm afraid of how I'll feel when it's over—"

"What if it never was over?"

She faltered, but ignored his comment. "I'm afraid of what it'd do to me, what it *has* done to me…and yet I do want to know. Human nature, whatever. I do want to experience it again. You." Her eyes darkened and she swallowed.

Never had she looked more sensual.

Their eyes locked.

"But it's a big risk," she added. "Too big."

He felt her indecision and pounced on it. "I don't agree."

Her lips parted and she took a deep breath. Rex saw desire in her eyes and silently willed her to say it, to give them a proper chance.

Before she had time to speak they were interrupted.

"Rex, how lovely to see you."

It took a moment before he could even bring himself to drag his attention away from Carmen. When he did, he realized it was his ex, Kelly, who was speaking. She was blinged to the rafters and stood alongside their table with three friends in tow. "I heard about your dad. I'm so sorry."

Rex acknowledged her with a nod.

"Is this Carmen?" Kelly smiled at Carmen, who had reacted to the interruption by putting her napkin back on the table, as if making ready to leave.

"Yes, I'm Carmen." She gave a forced smile, then threw an accusing look Rex's way.

He hadn't responded to the interruption, that's why.

Before he had a chance, Kelly continued. "I thought so. As soon as I saw you I thought you must be Rex's sister. I read about you in the obituary and I looked you up. It's lovely to meet you. I'm a good friend of your brother's."

Carmen stared at Rex.

He knew what that look meant—it was never going to go away, the brother/sister thing. "I'm sorry, Kelly," he said, "it's not a good time. We're right in the middle of something."

"Of course. I'm sure you have a lot of family stuff to deal with at the moment. I'll leave you to it." Kelly touched him on the shoulder and smiled before she moved on. "We must catch up though, soon."

Rex frowned. Nate had said something about Kelly wanting to get back together. It seemed ludicrous to Rex because he was sitting opposite the only woman he would ever love. How did everyone in the world not know already? Frustration bit into him, hard. They'd been so close to a breakthrough.

Carmen bent to pick up her bag where she'd put it under the table, her actions jerky and hurried. "I knew this was a mistake."

"Carmen? People will make that error, and she obviously read the obituary wrong, but once we announce we're in a proper committed relationship they'll all know the truth of what we are to each other." He blurted it out in response to her imminent departure, but as soon as he did he realized he'd gone from teasing it out of her to a full-on demand, and for all the wrong reasons.

"You're crazy," she muttered, but the look in her eyes was confused and emotional. She was pulling away, guarding herself again.

Even before she rose to her feet, Rex knew he had some major backpedaling to do. "Wait, please, I apologize for the interruption—it was unfortunate." He gestured at the waiter. "I'll see you home."

"No, you won't." The defensive look in her eyes was reflected in the way she held her shoulders, as if she was ready to bolt.

"I'll see you to the taxi rank." He rose to his feet and held her gaze.

"It's not necessary."

"It'll be busy, you'll have to queue. I'm not letting you wait alone."

She shook her head, but then she paused.

They'd come so close.

Rex went after her.

He wasn't about to let it end now.

CHAPTER TWENTY-NINE

The street outside Raphael's was busy with traffic. It had started raining and Carmen pulled her jacket tighter as she weaved through the people on the pavement, headed to the taxi rank on the corner of the street.

"Carmen, wait up." Rex's arm encircled her waist as he ran alongside her.

For a moment she thought she might be able to slip away, and he would get snagged waiting to settle the bill. She didn't want him to see how upset she was. Pausing, she attempted to pull free. "I'm going home."

"A moment?" He soothed her with his hands on her shoulders.

How she wanted to slide into his arms. She ached for him. It was worse than ever, a gnawing ache in her chest that would only be filled by him. It was as if seeing his ex made her realize she was lost to him, even though the encounter made her feel foolish and transparent.

She met his gaze.

"You said you wanted more," he reminded her.

"I also said it'd be wrong for me."

"It won't be wrong, not for either of us."

He seemed so sure, and the way he looked, rain streaming down on him while he steadfastly ignored it, melted her to the core. She swayed unsteadily. "I can't go there again."

It felt like a lie. It was a lie. What she needed was to be in his arms. Heat built fast at her center and every part of her yearned for him.

"Give us a chance." He stroked his hands down her arms to her wrists.

His dark good looks mesmerized her, his intense, determined personality evident in his actions, his appearance and his posture. The scent of his cologne made her want to move close to him, but she was too vulnerable. "Let me go."

"I'm taking you home. That much is set in stone." He flicked back the damp hair on his forehead. "But be warned. I want more. I want you to give me a chance. Things happened too fast last time, things that'd been on hold for too long. It unraveled when we were under pressure. I'm willing to work at it."

His words were sincere, and the way he held her…it all served to undermine the fact she was losing the final shreds of resistance she clung to.

"I want you, Carmen," he added.

There it was: *he* wanted, *he* got. Frustration gripped her. "You don't know me. Not really."

"I want to know all there is, but I believe I already know you better than you think I do."

She looked at him, wary, afraid. If she opened up, it would be too hard. He'd be gone soon, anyway. That's what he was like, and she'd be alone, exposed and vulnerable. She had to keep it buried.

His hand locked on her wrist.

When she shook her head and turned her face away, he tugged on her wrist and reeled her into his arms.

He silenced her with a kiss. Possessive arms held her to him and his mouth crushed hers. Stunned and winded, she resisted, fighting him, but the more she levered against him with her hands on the wall of his chest, the more tightly he held her, and then she was swamped with it—recognition, desire and need. It was so easy for him, to click his fingers and women came running.

"I want you," he repeated, his voice hoarse when she pulled back, "and as hard as this situation is, I like the fact I couldn't bear you walking out of there without me."

She went to respond, but couldn't muster the words when she saw the emotion whirling in his eyes.

"Damn it, I like that I hurt like hell when you're not around." His voice was hoarse with emotion, and getting louder. "And I like the way I'm ready to do everything and anything it takes to be with you. You challenge me, and that's a good thing, but it's so much more. It was always there and I see it now. I see why it was always there."

She blinked rain from her eyes. It was surreal, seeing him this way.

He thumped one fist against his chest. "I like this, Carmen. I want this—" he gestured around them "—to be here standing on the pavement in the cold driving rain laying myself on the line for you. I like what you do to me."

"But I don't like what you do to me."

His jaw turned to granite and his eyes blazed at her. "Why not?"

"Because…" She hunted for the words, and as she did her feelings bottled, then frothed and exploded out in a rush. "Because I lose myself when I'm with you and I need to stay in charge or I'll let people down. That's the way it is. It's like a mountain I've had to climb on my own and I'm there now, I'm on top of it, but I can't cope when you unravel me. You're my undoing and I can't risk it."

He moved in and cupped her face in his hands. "Okay, slowly. I need to know about all of this."

Shit. Why did I even say that? Her stomach knotted, her backbone dissolving as vulnerability disarmed her. "Forget I said anything."

He was silent while he considered her.

Adrift on a tide of unleashed emotions, desperation gripped her.

"If something's stopping us from being together I want to know about it."

"For crying out loud, Rex," she blurted, finding her mast and strapping herself to it again, "you aren't ever going to truly be 'together' with someone, not for any length of time. It's not in your nature."

He shook his head, as if astonished. "I disagree. I do want that, and it's you I want to be with. For a very long time. I love you, Carmen."

Her stomach flipped, her chests tightened. "Please don't say that," she whispered, "not if you don't really mean it."

"But I do mean it."

She turned her face away, wrapping in on herself.

He stroked her arm. She shivered, her senses tormented by his proximity, his tender words.

"Why don't you start by telling me what were you thinking back there, before Kelly arrived."

She shook her head.

"I need to know."

She was about to deny him verbally, then his hand snaked around the back of her neck. "Don't do this to me, please."

He stroked her chin with his thumb and her head instinctively dipped back, absorbing the comfort he offered her—a seductive tactic he used while he probed deeper. She felt as she did when he was sexually demanding, but here on the edge of the pavement she wanted to get into a taxi and he'd taken over.

"I'm here, holding you. I want it all, Carmen, tell me."

What she wanted to feel was denial, but it was hope overwhelming her. *Hope is futile.* She stared at him, hating him for what she felt. *I love you, and I hate that.* The need to let him know how much she hurt because of him reared its head, and she let rip. "I wanted to say, yes! I think of being with you often. All the time. Fool that I am."

His attention sharpened. "And then you were upset. I saw how upset you were. I want to know why."

"Because I was right back there, goddamn you! I was giving in to my emotions, wanting anything you offered…like I was a lovesick teenager all over again." Blood rushed in her ears. There wasn't any switching it off though, not now. "Then your gorgeous girlfriend walks in—"

"Ex."

"Whatever! I was right back there with women waltzing in when we felt so right together, and you went off with them instead of me."

Rex's expression broke, his frown lifting. "We were so right together." He nodded. "I agree. The rest is just hurdles. Together we can get past them. Say it again, we were so right."

No. But she couldn't help herself. The genie was well and truly out of the bottle. "Oh, bloody hell! You knew how much I wanted you!" She trembled all over. Her legs had turned to water. "You filled my every thought, you still do! My body was on fire for you." The words tumbled out in a confused torrent, her emotions spilling over like hot lava. "For crying out loud, I was madly in love with you Rex."

He tossed his damp hair back and closed on her mouth. "Madly in love with me?"

He breathed the words against her lips.

She squirmed and shook her head. Hearing him repeat her words left her feeling exposed and raw.

He laughed softly. "I'm not going to ask you to repeat it because you'll give me a load of bullshit excuses. What's important here is we're meant to love one another. On that we're agreed"

We were meant to love one another. The words echoed around her mind.

Had he really just said that, and was it true? Reason deserted her. Then it was back with startling clarity, as if a curtain had dropped. She stared at him, and saw a man speaking honestly—a man who had forced her to speak honestly, too.

Mercifully he didn't make her repeat it. Instead he put a finger to her lips and nodded, and then he looked away at the roadside and signaled. "Here we go."

A London black cab pulled alongside them. He opened the back door and helped her in. For a moment she thought he was going to close the door, to let her go home alone like she'd requested—demanded—minutes before, and she felt a desperate sense of loss.

He spoke to the cabby, then climbed in after her, and the relief she felt was instant and obvious. There was no denying it. It made her heart ache, painfully so, but there was elation, too. She reached out for him.

He held her tight against his chest.

Under her hand his heart beat fast and hard, and she felt his will and his fierce desire, so strong and sure—his yin to her yang—and she melted. She lowered her head, looking at him from under her lashes, eager to feel the intensity of his sexual domination again.

"I'm scared."

"Don't be." He stroked her hair, untangling it with his fingers. "I asked for your trust earlier today. You give yourself to me so totally when we're intimate. I want the same level of trust in every aspect of our lives. I know I have to earn it, and I have some making up to do." He lifted her hand to his lips, and kissed it. "Will you give me a chance?"

He held her gaze, and as he did images flashed through her mind, images of them locked together in passion, images of her crawling to him, confessing her darkest desires. Her heart hammered in her chest. She couldn't deny it anymore. She nodded.

While his mouth claimed hers she pushed her fingers into his hair, her desire rising to meet his. His hands on her were possessive, giving their shared kisses the deepest intimacy. Even after their kiss broke, she clung to him, her cheek against his chest where she could feel his heart beating.

She stared with unseeing eyes at the lights zigzagging through the damp streets as the cab sped across the city. Rex kept his hand locked around her wrist, holding her, anchoring her. Time blurred. All she could think about was his hand holding her. Oddly the action made her feel as if she were flying, as if freedom was there, under his hand. It was exactly how she experienced him, though. As a lover he'd unleashed some part of her previously untapped. It was little wonder she couldn't refuse another taste of his sweet medicine.

When the taxi drew to a halt and they emerged, she saw he hadn't taken her home.

"My place," he explained as the taxi drove away.

"Oh." Why did that make her nervous? He'd taken her to his home, somewhere she'd never been before.

He took her hand and led her to the door.

I'm in his private space, she thought when he ushered her inside.

It was a massive glass fronted apartment complex overlooking the River Thames. All security conscious, gleaming stainless steel elevators and stark white corridors. It seemed like a lonely place to Carmen, but only because her ideal home was so very different.

Rex urged her inside and turned on a lamp. In the half-light she scoped a sparsely furnished bachelor pad, long low leather sofas and not a lot else. The floor to ceiling glass windows at the far side revealed a breathtaking view of the city.

Clinging close to the door, she watched as he did a quick circuit of the room, dropping his keys in a dish on a shelf as he passed. He shrugged off his jacket, resting it over the back of the sofa, and then turned back to look at her.

Tension built fast, as if the dimly lit room magnified it. *We're alone, and I've agreed to this, to whatever he wants of me.*

When he ran his fingers along the back of the sofa, she almost felt as if he touched her instead. His gaze covered her possessively. "Come here."

His request triggered her reaction—a racing pulse, an inability to do anything other than step closer. "Take off your jacket."

She did so, leaning forward to rest it over the back of the sofa, next to his. She thought he was going to tell her to strip, as he had done before, but he went back to the shelves where he'd left his keys.

"I brought you a little something I thought you might like." He lifted an object and held it up.

Carmen took one look at the sparkling cuffs in his hand and gave a soft laugh. It sounded nervous, because the implications made her that way. "You were so sure of my capitulation?"

His mouth lifted at one corner. "I'm a man who likes to be prepared for every eventuality."

He closed on her, and held the cuffs aloft in front of her as he observed her reaction, his stance at once powerful and so easily attuned to the suggestive object.

The sight of the cuffs made her weak at the knees. Her mind flooded with thoughts of being bound and at his mercy while she observed the way they glinted in the light from the lamp.

"You like?"

"Maybe."

He stroked her wrist. "I'd happily keep you locked up around the clock, but I know it's only part of what you are. It's an important part, though, and I want to honor it, to show you what it means to me when you give yourself into my hands so totally."

Carmen wavered in his grasp, feeling both light-headed and restless. His natural air of command was pure seduction under normal circumstances. The added intensity of the conviction he'd offered overwhelmed her.

He stepped closer still, resting his hand on her waist, and the gem-studded cuffs rested heavily against her hip bone. The weight of it against her felt like a warning and a promise all wrapped up in one. "No objections?"

She shook her head. The pounding pulse in her core wouldn't allow her to pretend otherwise.

"I thought not." His insinuating tone ran fire along her nerve endings. "Too tempting a toy for you, my precious."

This was when he was fatal to be around, because he was so sure and that broke her apart.

"Offer me your hands, and in doing so accept this is more than a game. This represents so much more to me. It's a deep bond, and I want you to acknowledge that, too."

Tremulous, aware of the immensity of what was passing between them, Carmen put out her arms.

He closed the cuffs around one wrist.

"And I intend to show you how well I know you." With his hand splaying the free cuff open, as if readying it, he led her down the hall and into the bedroom.

She caught sight of black covers on a ridiculously wide bed. It had a black wrought iron headboard that coiled and leapt from the top of the bed, casting shadows on the wall beyond it. While she tried to get the measure of her surroundings, he quickly stripped her and carried her to the bed.

Maneuvering her arms above her head he clicked the second cuff closed.

When she tugged, she realized he'd tethered her to the headboard. Moaning and writhing, she tugged again, caught on a razor wire between the promise of pleasure and fear of losing herself to him totally.

"You like the cuffs, I can tell."

"I'm not sure," she whispered.

"The best part of having you this way is I get to adore you without you arguing with me. Being tied up seems to demand all your attention."

It was true, she was speechless. But it was partly because she was watching as he pulled his shirt free from his trousers, and she was mesmerized by the sight of him getting naked. His chest was hard and strong and chiseled, his shoulders muscular and gleaming. When he shucked off his pants and jockey shorts, his abs flexed enticingly. His cock stood out, half-risen and rising still, long and lovely and eager. The look of it made her even wetter.

"It's you. You demand all of my attention," she retorted, "not a good thing for a woman."

"Too late for doubts now. You agreed."

She eyed him dubiously. "The doubts linger."

"In that case I'll have to find a way to distract you." He climbed over her, and dipped his head to kiss her cleavage while he molded her breasts in his hands. His lips were hot on her skin and he mouthed her flesh hungrily, making her shiver with arousal.

Distract her he did. She arched up to him on the bed when he toyed with one nipple, outlining the stiff peak with his tongue before grazing it with his teeth. The action tugged at her core. Her sex throbbed in response, her anticipation for him building. When his fingers trailed along the insides of her thighs, she moaned aloud.

He lifted his head and studied her while he stroked his fingers into the groove of her sex. She jerked her wrists, but it only made her hotter still, the confinement emphasizing their connection and how easily he won her.

"Rex," she murmured, attempting to stay still. Part of her wanted to plunge down on his hand, rock her hips and beg him for more, but there was part of her that recognized the deliciousness of restraint. He was taking his time with her, and the pleasure/pain of the anticipation was a heady drug.

He smiled as he moved one finger inside her. "You do realize I intend to keep you this way all night?"

Before she had a chance to say anything, he ducked down between her thighs to lap her clit, nursing it in his mouth. Pangs of pleasure shot from the swollen nub, his ministrations overwhelming her senses. Her orgasm built fast, swelling as it did on a tide of unruly emotions.

He drew her first climax that way. Then he was over her, driven and passionate, filling her while he arched over her to kiss her lips, her face, her eyelids.

She wanted his thrusts, but he stayed still.

Lifting up on his arms, he stared down at her. "Carmen Shelby, I love you, I always have."

Writhing, she burned up. Her flesh tightened around his cock, her core pounding.

"Tell me you accept that," he commanded.

"Rex, please." Tugging her cuffs, desperate for release, the swell in her chest grew painful. Fear rattled at the door of her heart. She shook her head.

He shifted, closed one hand around the base of her throat. The look in his eyes was desperate. His cock was rigid inside her, the muscles in his neck standing out as he held back.

Pressing his lips together tightly, he pulled back, then rode her deep.

A garbled cry escaped her when he pressed at her center. Her senses swam. Tears dampened her cheeks.

"Tell me you know it."

Her body caved. A second orgasm rocked her, her body exploding with loops of pleasure. "Yes! I know it! I know!"

Only then did he allow himself to move, and he stroked her damp skin as he pressed on. Their naked bodies shunted together, frantic in their physical reunion. When he came, he gathered her limp body in his arms, holding her tightly, whispering her name.

It was the early hours of morning when Rex finally freed her.

"This is why you brought me here," she said, nodding at the cuffs as he unlocked them, "because you had these stashed."

In the lamplight his features looked chiseled, his handsome mouth full and passionate as he smiled at her accusation. "That's not the only reason. I did like having you cuffed, though. It meant you couldn't try to make a break for the hills when I told you how I felt."

She took a deep breath. "Some things you said really surprised me."

"But you still don't trust me?" He stretched out on his side next to her.

Instinctively she touched his chest. "I do, it's just that I've had to be completely self-reliant."

"The mountain?"

She nodded. "I can't seem to let that go. It makes me afraid of investing in other things I might never fully understand."

"By things you mean people?"

"Maybe."

"There hasn't been a man who you could rely on?" It was tentatively asked.

"There hasn't really been a man at all." Sheepishly she got the confession out. "A couple of brief encounters at university, nothing significant. Please don't tease me."

He studied her at length before he replied. "I'd do anything to make you feel secure."

Her eyes closed while she imagined it. When she opened them, he was still studying her.

"I know I went about this the wrong way. I should've told you I never stopped thinking about you."

"I thought you only wanted me because—"

He silenced her with a finger on her lips. "I've been cutting myself up inside because I handled it wrong, I knew it a week ago. Now I'm fighting for my second chance."

There was humility in him. It drew on her. It also intrigued her when he'd declared love, but hadn't demanded it in return.

"But you know that, so tell me this…why are you here? Be honest."

"Because I can't resist you." It was so simple she wanted to laugh.

"You want to resist?"

"Sometimes, but it doesn't seem to work. I'm here, agreeing to your demands."

He didn't answer; instead, he stroked her hair. It soothed her, and when she allowed herself to peek up at his face he looked so serious she wondered if she'd hurt him, and immediately wanted to take back the words. She didn't have the chance.

"I want you to go to the manor for a couple of days, alone. Like you always wanted."

Carmen couldn't help it, she laughed aloud. "Now, when I'm willing to give us a go, you send me there on my own?"

God, he looked so handsome, so devastatingly sexy, when his eyes twinkled and the corners of his mouth lifted.

The laughter made her feel light and free, and she sighed, letting more of the weight she'd carried drift.

"I want you to enjoy the place without me pressuring you, but believe me, I'll be joining you. The most important thing I've learned this past week is I can't be without you long." His eyes burned into her. "I've got some business in London and then I have a meeting with a potential partner on Saturday. He's based near Oxford. I'll come straight home from there and we can spend Saturday evening together."

"Home?" She smiled, unable to withhold her reaction.

"Our home."

Pleasure burned in her chest, and she had to move on quickly to avoid getting tearful and silly again. "So, Saturday evening, and what about the rest of the weekend?"

"If you insist."

"Me!" She laughed. "You're the one outlining the agenda, as usual."

"I know how much you love the place."

"So did our parents."

"There's no reason why we can't make it work."

"You believe that?"

He nodded.

"Then we'll give it a go."

"Music to my ears, my little bird."

She drew back, curious. "Bird?"

"Uh-huh. Hard to lure and keep, so enticing, so magical. I've always wanted to hold you like this." He was silent a moment, just staring into her eyes. "Promise me you won't throw this away without giving us time."

Carmen swallowed, touched by the depth of emotion she saw in his expression. Moving her hand to his jaw, she chaffed it. "I promise."

CHAPTER THIRTY

Friday was looking hellishly busy for Rex, but he was fueled by a zest for life he'd never experienced before. Carmen had left for the manor the evening before, and he'd worked into the night. Timing was tight, though, and he needed everything to go smoothly.

Fate didn't seem to want to play along.

"I'm sorry, Rex, but some guy wants to see you."

Rex looked up from his computer and studied Ayo's face.

"Didn't want to give his name, but he's being really insistent and he refuses to leave until he speaks to you."

Out of all the team, Ayo was the best at fending off curious neighbors and tenacious journalists. Rex usually heard about unwanted visitors after the event. Not this time. "Describe him."

"White guy, scrawny, wearing a hoodie and a beanie hat." Ayo looked disapproving. When he wasn't wearing his overalls, Ayo was the personification of dapper.

"Longish hair?"

"From what I could see of it, yup."

Rex already knew who it was when the visitor appeared in the doorway. Jerry was there, telling the young man to back off. Rex rose from his desk and stared across the room at his half brother Jason. He was about to pick up the phone and call the police when he saw the pleading look in the young man's eyes. For a moment he was reminded of his father's portrait. That threw him. "Let him in."

Reluctantly Rex's employees stood back, but when they departed they left the door open. That suited Rex. He could kick Jason out if necessary.

"Thank you."

Rex clenched his jaw before he brought himself to reply. "Believe me, I might still change my mind. I thought I'd made it clear last time. Just because we share some DNA doesn't mean I can overlook what you did."

Jason paled. Staggering to a nearby chair, he slumped into it. "I know."

Warily Rex returned to his seat, staring across the desk at the man who was both assailant and half brother.

Jason sighed and looked down at his feet.

The tension Rex felt eased marginally. "Go on."

"I had no bad feeling toward anyone, but it's my fault."

Rex cocked his head. "Why?"

"She'd finally given up on him. Mum. When dad didn't return to her, after the death of his second wife, she realized it was over. Then I couldn't help talking about him. She got angry and she remembered." Resting his elbows on his knees he put his forehead to his fisted hands.

The strange action disturbed Rex. But if his tale was true, it made sense that he'd feel bad. However, the whole thing could be a clever ruse, a plea to sanction his cause in court. "You're the only one who's been bailed, so you're the only one who can come to me and attempt to redeem your image before the court case."

Jason hung his head. "That's not what I'm trying to do."

The penitent look was too much for Rex to stomach. He rose to his feet. "Enough. I think you should leave."

Jason's head shot up. There was a desperate look in his eyes.

"Nothing changes the fact you put Carmen's life in danger. I'll see you in court."

Jason rose to his feet, shaking his head as he did so. "You don't understand."

"Leave."

"But I came here to confess."

Rex frowned.

"It was me. I think I killed him…I killed our dad."

Rex's blood rushed in his ears.

Jason swayed, snatched at the desk edge.

Rex circuited the desk and forced the younger man to face him. "What the hell do you mean?"

"I spoke to him, and I think he recognized me. He was so shocked, he backed away from me." Jason gulped. He shook his head, as if he had to remember it. "They found him dead in his bed the next morning. Heart attack. It was my fault. I should never have reached out to him."

Stunned, Rex stared at the man, trying to take in what he was saying.

His mind worked furiously. Even if it were true, it wasn't Jason's fault his father had reacted badly. Ironically the new information lessened the loathing Rex felt for his half brother. The young man was heavy with guilt, and this confession would do him no good. What it did reveal was the rest of his tale was sound. If he believed he was guilty of attempted murder, why would he add it to his list of potential charges in court? This was a genuine burden for him.

Jason was shaking.

Rex eased him toward the chair he'd been sitting on. When he slumped down, Rex leaned up against the desk with his arms folded across his chest. He gave the lad a while, and when he seemed suitably recovered Rex asked a question. "Does your mother know how you feel? That you feel responsible?"

Jason looked confused by the question, then shook his head. "You're the first person I've told. I wasn't going to tell anyone, but it's been eating away at me." He gave Rex a furtive glance, as if to gauge his mood.

Rex assessed him silently for some time. "You want my opinion?"

Jason shrugged. "I guess so."

"The old man's time was up. I was told there wasn't a post-mortem because he'd been advised he needed a heart bypass operation. He'd ignored the advice. Whether or not he recognized you is irrelevant. If I were in your position, I'd be more worried about the court case and being locked up like your brother and your mother. You assisted an attempted murder."

"I didn't know what they intended, not until that day, and by the time I did it was too late."

The cracks were showing. "Was it?"

Jason did everything to avoid eye contact for several moments but, with effort, forced himself to look up.

"It's never too late to step in. You could have called the police."

"I tried to talk them out of it." Jason buckled, and buried his face in his hands. He gulped air convulsively as he sobbed.

It was pitiful to watch, and whatever happened in court, Rex knew this young man would forever carry the burdens of what he might have done, and what he didn't do. He glanced at his watch. Jason wasn't in any shape to be put out on the street.

"Take your time, when you're ready you can leave." With that he stepped away. He had to pick up some stuff for a team meet later in the day.

As he made his way out, he urged Ayo to keep an eye on the visitor, just in case. Though Rex doubted Jason had it in him to do any damage. Despite his best efforts, he felt sympathy for the lad. And it only served to show how much their father had impacted both of their lives. Was there any end to the shadows he'd left behind?

Yes, Rex vowed. *Yes, I'll make it so.*

When Carmen awoke in her old bedroom in Burlington Manor on Friday morning she felt at home, and happy. Rex was close in her thoughts. That was to be expected. What was amazing was how elated the very thought of him made her feel. *Am I being a fool?*

Never had she felt so good, so right. She'd even driven to the manor the evening before, the first time since she'd moved away. That in itself was liberating. The new level of understanding and intimacy with Rex was altering her state of mind, opening a world of possibilities. She'd been a little afraid, because of what had gone on there in the past, but when she entered the house, sunlight filled the hallways and the hope she carried in her heart was reflected in every surface there.

While she drank her morning coffee, she wandered from room to room, simply reveling in all she loved about Burlington. The connection was deeper still, after the previous weekends she'd spent there with Rex. In fact, there was only one thing missing, Rex himself.

Had he done this on purpose, to show her she would miss him? She wouldn't put it past him. He'd been here alone without her the weekend before and he'd probably been bored. He was giving her a taste of it.

How she ever thought it would be the same without him was beyond her, though. He was a big part of her connection to the place, she had to face it, and as much as she wanted to believe his promises, she had to be cautious about the future. It might fall apart. If it did, leaving the manor forever would break her heart, yet at the same time she really couldn't imagine being there without him, the master of the house.

The master of my heart.

The unbidden thought both amused and unnerved her. It was the truth. He was the master of both her and the estate, but there was a strong possibility she could end up living here alone, single, and with only her memories of their time together to keep her warm on a cold night.

Acknowledging her potential fate, she tried to focus on the things she wanted to do that day. It was important to try working long distance. It wasn't something she'd ever done, outside of minor meetings online with her mother while she was studying for her degree in business management.

With Leanne's help she moved some things around in the old library and set up her laptop on the desk. Then she checked in with Estelle via her webcam.

"Good morning!" Estelle waved. "Those distribution quotes you requested came in so they should be in your mailbox."

Carmen waved back. "I see them. I'll prioritize that and get back to you soon."

"This is almost as good as having you next door," Estelle said.

Carmen nodded. "It is the twenty-first-century way. I do believe I could manage it if necessary."

"Hey, you can leave the cam on all day if you need to, and we can conference call with other staff when necessary, too."

"Are you trying to keep me out of the office?"

"Not at all. I'm making sure you get settled in so I can visit soon."

"If a permanent arrangement comes to pass, you're still first on the list." Estelle grinned.

"I'll check in with you later." Carmen waved before closing the connection.

Once she got into her work, the time flew and she only noticed it was lunchtime because her stomach growled.

Making her way to the kitchens, she wondered how Rex was doing that day. Then she heard someone humming. Pushing the door open, she stepped into the kitchen expecting to find Mrs. Summerfield at work. However, it wasn't Mrs. Summerfield who was humming to herself.

"Well, hello," Amanda drawled from her seat. She was wearing riding gear and she had her booted feet up on the table. By the looks of it she'd helped herself to one of the freshly baked scones cooling on a wire tray by the cooker.

It was weird seeing her that way, because it took Carmen back to when they were teenagers and Amanda would let herself in the back door. Neither of them thought anything of it then, but things were different now. Carmen immediately felt territorial. "I suppose you came to see Rex. Well, he's not here."

"Shame," Amanda said, lowering her feet to the floor. "Sexy Rexy is always such a pleasure to be around."

She had a damn cheek, Carmen thought, annoyed at the way the situation made her feel. "Did you intend to make a fool of yourself all over again?"

Amanda laughed. "My, my, you're touchy."

"Are you surprised, after Rex had to provide you an escort home last time you were here?"

"Actually, I've seen Rex since then. I called by last weekend when he was here…alone." She widened her eyes suggestively. "We had a nice chat about him…and me…and you."

Carmen's stomach tightened. "If your intention is to upset me, don't bother wasting your time. Any friendship we had was completely dashed by your behavior here at the housewarming. I don't care anymore."

"Oh, Carmen, I'm winding you up!"

Carmen blinked back her surprise.

"I knew Rex wouldn't be here so you don't need to worry. I'm here because he told me I should apologize to you…and I suppose he's right, so here I am." She folded her arms loosely. "I'm sorry."

"I can see how hard that was for you." Carmen laughed.

"Yeah, well, between him and Nate putting the spotlight on me and laying down laws, I'm feeling pretty sheepish here, so go easy on me."

"I make no promises, but I'll try." Was Amanda actually trying to be friends again?

"Thank you. Things haven't been easy. You can imagine what people say, married and divorced from the local vicar inside a year."

"Yes, I can imagine." Carmen bit her lip. "It's going to take you a long time to live that one down. You really didn't need to add to your colorful reputation by going after Rex and bad-mouthing me at the party."

Amanda groaned. "Look, I had no idea you two had rekindled your old flame."

"That probably wouldn't have stopped you," Carmen retorted.

"Probably not, but can you blame me? Rex is the sexiest thing to hit this place and far beyond for a long time. Hell, the next best thing was the local vicar and next to Rex he looks positively anemic. You're always going to have women looking at Rex and wanting him, so you better get used to it."

Get used to it? Carmen puzzled over that.

"Congratulations," Amanda continued. "He's a gorgeous man, and from what he said last weekend, he's totally committed to making it work with you, long term."

He'd decided back then, right after she'd walked out on him? Carmen was touched.

Amanda stood up. "Oh, my, the look on your face is priceless! I'll put the kettle on. You need a cuppa."

Carmen wasn't going to argue on that point. She pulled out a chair and sat down, trying to work out what had surprised her most—the message, or the messenger.

"This must be an important meeting," Lance said. "Normally you'd have us drinking beer out of paper cups."

REX

Rex smiled as he set out the glass flutes he'd purchased on his way to work that morning. "Slipstream is going places. We can't drink out of paper cups now." He popped the cork on the champagne bottle and filled the glasses as the small team took up their seats in the kitchen area. It's where they held their group meetings because Rex wanted them to be as comfortable and relaxed with one another as possible.

When they chinked glasses, he nodded. "First, I want to thank you for the hard work you've been putting in over the past few weeks. I believe it'll be worthwhile for all of us, but I appreciated it, especially when my time has been divided with personal stuff." He sipped the champagne, then set the flute down. "I've got something else I want to run by you guys. At this stage it's only an idea and your feedback's very important to me, so don't worry if you don't like the sound of it. Just say so."

All three of them looked concerned, as if they expected not to like it.

"As you're aware, I've been dealing with my father's estate in Oxfordshire. When we were at Rashid's place his setup stimulated an idea. I was intending to sell out my share of my father's estate, but the situation has changed…hopefully. I see potential there, in the way that Nikhil Rashid has developed his business outside the city. Now, this is just a crazy idea, nothing's set in stone, so just hear me out.

"The estate has disused stables that could be used as workshop space. It would be way bigger than this." He gestured around the unit. "We'd also have space for our own track to test things out."

"Cool," murmured Ayo.

Jerry frowned. "You're telling us you're going to move the company?"

"No, I'm asking for your take on an idea that's very fluid at the moment, and I'm also aware that you've got families and commitments here in London. If it was something we thought we could run with, I wouldn't just be expecting you to rebuild from scratch. You've put your heart and soul into this business just as much as I have. I'd be offering a complete package, including accommodation for your families and a new lifestyle. It's something I know you'll have to discuss with your families, but there are cottages at Burlington Manor undergoing renovation soon."

That part had been Carmen's plan. He paused as he wondered—and not for the first time—how she would react to the suggestion they be for his guys and their families, rather than holiday lets. He couldn't think too deeply right now. He had his goal, and soon enough he'd be discussing it with her in the same way he was putting out feelers with his men now.

"I'm not asking you to say anything right now. I know you need to go away and think about it and discuss it with the people it will affect. However, if you could give me an initial response after you talk to your families I can either look into it as an option this weekend when I'm up there, or I can let the plan go. Trust me when I say I mean it—if it's not the right thing for you guys, it's not the right thing for me."

Rex looked from one to the other of them, assessing their thoughtful expressions. If it wasn't the way to go he would commute to Carmen and the manor at the weekends as he had been doing. "On that note, we'll close up early today so you guys can go and give it some thought. But please let me know as soon as you decide. I've got another bottle for us to get through first, so let's cheer the merger. I take the signed contracts to Rashid tomorrow and we're in business!"

When the men made their way out later on, Lance lingered. "My Amy would bite your arm off for this if you make this offer for real. She's always dreamed of a life in the country."

"And you?"

Lance nodded. "I'm all for it. I hope you can make it happen."

"Go talk to Amy. Be absolutely sure about it."

It's what he needed to do, too. Talk to Carmen about all of this. The task seemed immense, complicated as it was by history and the games he'd played in recent weeks, before he'd realized what he really wanted. The basic premise was simple enough. He wanted them to be together. That meant he had to exorcise the ghosts of the past, as well as make a working future viable. No matter how simply he spelled it out for himself, Rex knew he was still on fragile ground with Carmen.

CHAPTER THIRTY-ONE

On Friday evening Carmen stood in the center of the music room and stared up at the elaborate ceiling. The room had been closed up for a couple of years and she'd asked Leanne to open the shutters and take down the dust sheets earlier in the day. Carmen planned to spend the evening making notes on restoration needed.

The room maintained many of its original features and was the most obviously Georgian in the house. The walls were covered in red damask and the white marble fireplace was large and beautifully carved. At the center of the ceiling, the molded plasterwork depicted a muse playing a lyre. Around the coving, a musical score had been inscribed into the plasterwork. The piano was a genuine eighteenth-century piece, but hadn't been used for some years. Carmen made a mental note to have someone come up from London to tune and service it.

She was on her knees, examining the upholstery on the chairs, when Leanne entered. "You have a visitor."

"Really? Who is it?"

Leanne rounded her eyes. "Didn't give her name, but I think I've seen her in magazines."

Carmen leaned forward and saw Kelly Brown standing there in the hallway. Within an internal groan, she rose to her feet. When Leanne looked at her quizzically, she put the girl out of her misery. "Rex's supermodel ex," she murmured as she walked by.

As she approached, she noticed Kelly was assessing the place with a half smile and a possessive look in her eyes. "Kelly, isn't it?"

"Yes," Kelly replied as she turned to face Carmen, and flicked her long hair back over her shoulder. "Oh, it's you." She spoke with obvious disappointment.

"You were expecting Rex." Carmen felt quite composed. Amanda's comments earlier that day had hit home.

"I thought I'd stop by to see if he needed any help with anything."

Carmen smiled. "We don't need any help, but thanks for offering."

Kelly pursed her lips, making no attempt to hide her dissatisfaction. "So, is he here?"

"No, but I'll tell him you came by."

Kelly looked really put out.

She didn't have a clue, Carmen decided. When she looked back on it, she recalled that Rex had given his ex no signs of encouragement the night at Raphael's. In fact, he'd been quite distant with her, yet here she was. "Look, you've obviously come up here with good intentions." Debatable, but Carmen felt generous. Besides, as Amanda had so rightly pointed out, she was going to have to get used to women wanting him. "I should probably inform you Rex is seeing someone else now."

"Oh, right." Kelly cursed and grimaced. "Who is the bitch?"

Nice. How different she was when Rex wasn't around. "The bitch is me," Carmen said calmly, and laughed. "Don't look so shocked. I'm not his sister. That was an error on your part."

Finally it seemed to dawn on the woman she'd walked into their home on a misguided mission. Her perfect porcelain skin colored dramatically on the cheekbones. "Well, this is awkward."

"No, of course it isn't. You didn't know. Can I offer you a drink before you leave?"

Kelly shook her head and reached into her shoulder bag. She pulled out a set of car keys. "No, thanks. I'll get on my way."

Carmen followed her to the door and watched as she climbed into a two-seater sports car and shot off down the drive at breakneck speed.

She smiled. *I've grown up,* she realized. *I really can fight for my man.*

It was late, but Rex had one last thing to set in motion before he could leave the office. He picked up the phone and rang the family's solicitor.

It was time to play his trump card.

"Chris, I'm sorry to disturb you after hours, but there's something I want you to do for me. It involves drawing up a contract."

"Name it. I know you've been through a lot recently. I read about Olivia Fordyce's handiwork up at the manor."

"I'm sure you did."

"I met her once, years ago," Chris said rather awkwardly, "and I thought she was trouble then. Told your father as much. I'm sorry it's affected you and Carmen...your dad would be sorry, too."

Rex couldn't answer directly because the comment made him want to demand why Chris hadn't mentioned Olivia before, but he was first and foremost a professional solicitor. That came before being a friend to the family. "The shadows are long in our family, or so it seems. But I think I've found a way to deal with her, above and beyond what's in line for her courtesy of the Crown Courts."

"What have you got in mind?"

"I believe she was involved in Sylvia Shelby's death. I've visited her in prison and she didn't deny it, but she won't give me a confession. I need the confession for Carmen's peace of mind and I think I've got a bargaining chip that could work."

"How can I help?"

"I need you to draw up a contract you can take to her acting solicitor. In exchange for her full story about the circumstances surrounding Sylvia Shelby's death, I'll give Jason Fordyce part of the estate my father left me."

"Goddamn it, Rex, are you sure?"

"She won't budge." Rex summarized the situation with Olivia's health and her lack of concern about her own destiny. "She knows I've got a private investigator tracking down the so-called witness, who at the time was seeing Olivia's eldest son."

Chris inhaled sharply. "That's pretty damning in itself."

"It is, but even if we get a statement I've got to offer Olivia something substantial to admit it, something that represents the recognition she wanted for her sons. Charles, well, I've got nothing but disgust for him. He's her willing henchman. But I believe Jason was largely innocent of her real intentions. I'm thinking if we offer Jason the property in the Channel Islands, part of Dad's estate, it gives him a chance for a new life…somewhere else."

"I catch your drift."

"How soon can you do it?"

"I can have the paperwork drawn up within the hour, then it'll just be a matter of getting in touch with her solicitor in the morning. No saying how long Olivia will sit on it, but we'll make it sound as tempting as possible."

"Do you think her solicitor will be comfortable presenting her with this option?"

"It'll result in another charge against her, but in my professional opinion, if she reveals her involvement in Sylvia Shelby's death, a confession would be better in the long run. If the link between her son and the witness is likely to be mentioned and a witness statement is also a possibility, then I'll make sure the solicitor takes it into account."

"Thank you. Keep me informed."

When he put down the phone, he prayed it would work.

While he'd been on the landline, three text messages had appeared on his mobile phone. He could see they were from his staff, the team of three that made up the rest of Slipstream. Their reactions were important. He opened Lance's first.

You better make this happen. Amy has already told the kids. We're both delighted about what this might mean for their future. If it goes ahead, count us in.

Rex smiled and nodded. The scheme felt ambitious, and he wasn't entirely sure of it, but there was a feel-good factor about that response the made him believe that anything was possible. The second message that had come in was from Ayo.

I'm not sure. Sounds good but I got my people here. I'll check it out, but I need to be sure it's right for me.

Ayo was the one with the happening London life, the single man in the city. Rex understood he didn't want to commit as yet. If it came to fruition and Ayo didn't want to make the move, Rex vowed he would find a good opportunity for him elsewhere. The final message was from Jerry.

The wife is in tears! Look what you've done to me, Rex. She says it's the next best thing to winning the lottery. I guess this means it's a yes. ;)

Would Carmen feel the same way about his proposal? He hoped so. She'd said she wanted the place to be alive with people again, and other than holiday lets, she had no specific plans of her own, unless that had changed. He took a few moments to compose himself before he picked up the phone and rang Carmen.

"I hope you're pleased with yourself, Mr. Playboy Stud," she said as she answered.

"Are you being cryptic?"

"Not in the least. I've been fending off women left right and center here today."

"Women?"

"First of all Amanda turned up."

"I hope she apologized."

"Yes, as a matter of fact, she did. We had a good talk." Carmen paused for a moment before continuing. "Then your supermodel girlfriend turned up."

"Kelly? What the hell was she doing at Burlington?"

"Looking for you. She seemed to think you were worth another go."

"I hope you explained I was otherwise committed."

"I did. I figured that even if this setup turned out to be a temporary whim on your behalf—"

"It's not."

"—well, I figured she was intruding on my time and space with you and I fought my corner."

Rex could hear the teasing tone in her voice. Less than a week ago, she took flight at the very prospect of another woman turning up. Not anymore. "I'm glad you sent her on her way."

"I'm glad you're glad." She laughed and the sound of it was too good. Things couldn't be turned back the other way, not now, surely? "I'll show you how glad when I get there tomorrow."

"When can we expect you?"

"Sometime in the afternoon. I need to go over some paperwork with my new business partner."

"The partnership is going ahead?"

"Yes, and I've got some other ideas I'd like to run by you—business—if you're interested?"

"I thought you'd never ask," she replied.

It felt like a huge step forward, and she was taking it with him.

Rex closed his eyes, grateful for the hope that gave him. The next day, he would lay out his proposals for her—all of them.

CHAPTER THIRTY-TWO

Saturday dragged for Carmen because she was counting the minutes, waiting for Rex to arrive. Waiting for her man to come home. That's what it felt like, although it made her nervous to even think it. Being in the manor wasn't enough. Rex had to be there, too. She tried not to dwell on what it might mean for her long-term happiness and concentrated on thinking about what he'd said, the way he'd ask for a second chance.

In the morning, she visited with Bill Amery at their cottage. He was in good spirits, and itching to get back out on the grounds. A friend from the village called in, too, and Carmen noticed Bill's version of events the week before became more dramatic with each retelling. His spirit certainly hadn't been diminished by the drama and injury, quite the contrary. She was glad.

At three o' clock Rex sent her a text saying he was on his way. Butterflies fluttered in her stomach, and it took her back to her teenage years when she'd been waiting for him to come home from university. For a moment, the intervening years vanished. She ran upstairs to check her appearance and then lingered at the viewing window on the upstairs landing, peering down at the driveway expectantly.

I can't have him finding me this way, she thought. She stayed there, though, right until she saw his car on the drive, then she ran down the stairs and opened the door to greet him.

When he emerged from the Maserati she wondered if she'd dreamed this handsome, sexy man had told her he loved her. Unable to hold back, she darted out to hug him.

"Mmm, that feels good," he said.

Pleased, she reached up and kissed him.

"So did you like being here on your own without me?" His eyes twinkled.

He was teasing her, because she'd thrown herself into his arms. "I'm not answering. I might incriminate myself."

"It's only fair. I didn't like being here without you."

"So you wanted me to know how that felt."

"Yes."

"You're shameless." She reached up and ran her fingers through his hair. "Have you eaten? Can I make you something?"

"I'd like to go for a stroll around the grounds. I understand it's something you always do when you return to Burlington Manor." There was mischief in his eyes. He took the lead, first ushering her with his arm around her waist. When they walked along the gravel path at the rear of the building, he held her hand, meshing his fingers with hers. The simple act made her feel light-headed. He'd never held her hand like that before. Walking alongside him with their fingers clasped together felt deeply significant.

"I've done a lot of thinking about this place, about ways to make it work. Your fault." He smiled her way. "You got me thinking with your proposals for renovating the stables and cottages."

Carmen peered at him. "Why, Rex Carruthers, I do believe the shadow of mortmain has finally gone from your eyes."

"Ah, well, that's your fault, too. Although I'm not entirely sure that you'll like my proposal, but it is negotiable."

"Okay."

"Some of the things you said really stuck with me. You want to see the place alive with people. I liked your proposal for the holiday lets, but that'd be transient."

"You've got a better idea?"

"Maybe. I was thinking of something more permanent."

Permanent? "Go on, I'm fascinated."

She was, although it was making her nervous because he was talking about his plans for Burlington. The familiar fretful feeling came upon her as she realized what that might mean for her—saying goodbye to the manor.

"I currently rent premises for Slipstream in South London, at a hefty cost to the business. We don't really need to be based there, other than my team live there. It occurred to me the disused stables could be used for the workshop and offices, and the old cottages restored for accommodation for the team."

Carmen was shocked. If Rex was making plans on his own, was he already thinking past their time together? She clung to her role as a businesswoman and tried to address the proposal without letting her emotions get involved, difficult though it was.

However, when she looked out across the land where he was gesturing, she could picture it all. The businesswoman in her recognized it as an amazing idea. When she saw the light in his eyes as he talked about a mini racetrack, she knew what it meant—he was glad to have found a way to work with the responsibility he'd walked away from so many years before. She was proud of him, but she barely had a hold on her emotions. When she forced herself to respond, she could hear the tremble in her own voice. "It's an amazing plan. It would bring new life and that'd be so positive for the estate."

"I'm glad you think so."

She saw relief in his eyes. He'd been worried about her reaction.

He studied her quietly for a moment, then squeezed her hand and they continued on their circuit around the house. "I tentatively proposed it to my team. I was dubious at first because the two lead engineers both have young families. I asked them to discuss it with their wives and they're both keen. They see it as a positive move."

Her stomach knotted. "It's a done deal, then?"

"Not at all. It depends on you."

"Because you want to buy me out?"

"No. I'm suggesting you be part of it."

She stopped dead in her tracks, confused. "You want me to support your business being run from here?"

"That'd be nice." He smiled.

How could he be so relaxed with this when her emotions were all over the place?

"I was hoping for more though." His expression grew serious. "Carmen, I want you to be my wife."

She stared at him, astonished.

Rex laughed softly and took both her hands in his. "Carmen Shelby, will you marry me?"

She opened her mouth, but she was too stunned to speak.

"Hold that thought," he said, and pulled his phone from his pocket. It was vibrating. He looked at the screen. "I need to answer this, it could be important."

Carmen watched, bewildered by the turn of events as he took the call. She turned her face to the breeze coming up from the river, and tried to breathe evenly. When he ended his call, he looked concerned.

"Chris Montague, he had news for us."

She tried to focus.

"Olivia Fordyce is currently giving a new statement to the police. It's about your mother's car crash."

Carmen covered her mouth with her hand.

Rex nodded. "She was behind it. We'll know the full story soon, but for now…it's enough."

"I always thought there was more to it...."

"You were right. I went to see her in prison, and it was obvious."

"You did that..." Finally she had the truth about her mother's death. It was upsetting, but it was a relief, too. "Rex, hold me," she begged.

"Always."

She clung to him, her face against his chest. She wept silently for her mum, the innocent victim, and emotion poured out of her.

He held her tightly to him all the while. "Come on, let's go inside," he encouraged eventually.

She wiped her face. "How did you get her to confess?"

"I offered her a deal, a new life for Jason in the Channel Islands, the property Dad left me there."

"You did all that for me?"

"I told you, I love you. I'd give up everything I owned for you to be happy. I'd even give up Burlington Manor to make that happen."

She shook her head and wiped her face with her hands. "You will not, ever!"

"Does that mean we're going to share the playground, after all?"

She smiled, but lowered her eyelids. "Oh, you've got me all emotional and I can't think straight."

"Trying hard to think of an excuse, huh?" He raised his eyebrows and gave her a chastising stare.

"Rex!"

Their conversation was interrupted a second time by the sound of a car pulling into the driveway.

"Ah, we have a visitor." He didn't seem surprised.

"Is this another one of your women on the prowl?" Carmen asked when she caught sight of a blonde woman in the back seat of Andy Redmond's taxi.

Rex glanced over. "Actually, yes, it is."

When she looked at him for more of an explanation, he grinned at her.

Bemused, Carmen followed his gaze. "I don't think I can deal with any more surprises today," she murmured to herself.

A glamorous woman emerged from the car, and Rex strode over and embraced her.

"I'm so glad you could make the journey," Rex said as he led the visitor over to Carmen.

"Well, I had to." The woman beamed at Carmen and then glanced up at the house. "Swore I'd never come back here, but I had to meet my son's fiancée, didn't I?"

"Fiancée?" Carmen repeated, staring at Rex in astonishment.

"Oh, dear, have I jumped the gun?" She stepped forward and grasped Carmen's hands. "Ignore me, darling. It's lovely to meet you at last. Now whatever you do don't call me Mum, it's Bea."

Carmen mustered herself, and welcomed Rex's mother, instantly fascinated by her.

"You were so sure I'd accept?" she asked Rex later when the three of them made their way inside.

"I was sure of me, the rest I could only hope for."

That held great weight for Carmen and she nodded. "I've always loved you. You know that. But this is all a bit hard to take in."

His eyes twinkled with pleasure. "Take your time."

Bea wandered across the tiled entryway. "Never thought I'd stand here again. I vowed I wouldn't. But my God, it's a beautiful house." She looked over her shoulder at them. "I always liked the place, deep down. I can admit that since your father isn't here to hear me." She chuckled and continued her exploration.

"Burlington Manor draws everyone back to it," Carmen said.

Rex shook his head. "You brought me back here."

When she looked into his eyes she saw how much he loved her. "And you really think we can make it a happy place again?"

"If you marry me, yes, without a doubt."

"Blackmail!"

Beyond them a squeal erupted, followed by another.

Carmen turned and saw Bea and Mrs. Amery embracing each other, both talking rapidly in excited voices and hugging several times over.

"There's your proof…happy times ahead." When he caught sight of her staring at Mrs. Amery, agog, he laughed. "They were close."

"You're not kidding. I've never seen Mrs. Amery so animated."

"You haven't answered my question."

She shot him a look. "You already decided I was your fiancée, according to our visitor."

"Planning ahead."

"Just as well I'm playing along."

"Is that a yes?"

Her heart brimmed. "I suppose it is."

He wrapped his arm around her shoulders. "In that case, we have the perfect ingredients to make sure Burlington Manor is always a happy place.

You as its mistress, and the estate put to good use. Maybe children would help, too. What do you think?"

She gaped at him. "You're rushing ahead. I've only just agreed to marry you."

He shrugged. "I'll give you some time to think about it. No running off and changing your mind, though." He leaned in and whispered. "I've bought some new bondage toys that'll keep you tied up for a while."

"Rex Carruthers, you're shameless."

"When it comes to you, yes, yes I am."

If you enjoyed Rex and Carmen's story, please consider leaving a rating or review.

Thank you!

ABOUT THE AUTHOR

Saskia Walker is a USA Today Bestseller and award-winning author. Her short stories and novellas have appeared in over one hundred international anthologies including BEST WOMEN'S EROTICA, THE MAMMOTH BOOK OF BEST NEW EROTICA, SECRETS, and WICKED WORDS. Her erotica has also been featured in several international magazines including COSMO, PENTHOUSE, BUST, and SCARLET. After writing shorts for several years Saskia moved into novel-length projects.

Fascinated with seduction, Saskia loves to explore how and why we get from saying "hello" to sharing our most intimate selves in moments of extreme passion. Her novels DOUBLE DARE and RAMPANT both won Passionate Plume awards and her writing has twice been nominated for a RT Book Reviews Reviewers' Choice Award. She has lots more stories in the pipeline! Saskia lives in the north of England on the edge of the Yorkshire moors, with her real life hero, Mark, and a house full of felines.

Why not visit Saskia's website where you can sign up for her newsletter

to keep in touch.

www.saskiawalker.com

If you enjoyed **REX** you might enjoy:

DOUBLE DARE

A truth or dare game.
A mutual desire for erotic discovery.

Investment broker Abigail Douglas has got it all, but Abby—the woman—
longs for a secret affair, a playmate who knows nothing about her high-
powered business world, and Zac Bordino might just be the man. He's
mysterious and sexy—just right for Abby's walk on the wild side—but very
soon she finds that she wants more, and his mysterious, evasive nature makes
her curious. Is there more to this sexy, entrepreneurial club owner than meets
the eye? And why does she suddenly feel as if her every move is being
watched?

Zac Bordino is perplexed when he realizes that the woman managing his
business investments is the same woman he's having an affair with. She's
pretending to be a little nobody out for a good time, and because she's a red
hot number he plays along, cautiously observing her to get to the truth. From
high-powered offices in London to pulse-pounding nightclubs in Paris, they
find an insatiably perfect match in business and in pleasure. But when Zac
begins to fall for Abby, he has to decide whether to reveal the secret link
between them, or try to win her heart first.

SWEET-TALKING THE OPPOSITION

Step aboard the River Queen for a red-hot love affair.

London-based journalist, Eliza Jameson, is on an idyllic assignment on a
luxurious European river cruise when she finds the perfect distraction on
board — old flame, Marcus Weston. But Eliza came dangerously close to
falling for Marcus last time around, and in order to protect her heart she
decides to play him at his own game, take control and call the shots. Little
does she know, Marcus has his own agenda.

Marcus Weston is a man used to getting his own way. The archetypal adventurer, he has no plans to settle down. But Marcus has been thinking about rival journalist Eliza Jameson ever since they had a fiery liaison at a conference in Zürich, and now here she is on board the same river cruiser. He simply can't resist. When things get complicated Marcus realizes he's going to have to win Eliza, and it's going to take a lot more than some clever sweet-talking to overcome her stubborn opposition. In the ensuing battle, who will end up on top?

www.saskiawalker.com

REX

Printed in Great Britain
by Amazon